Praise for Jenelle Hovde

In *No Stone Unturned*, Jenelle Hovde has written a sweeping Regency romance filled with heart and history. Fans of Mimi Matthews and Julie Klassen will find much to love in this tale which melds the atmospheric intrigue of Jane Eyre with the rugged beauty of Poldark. Against the backdrop of the rural English countryside, Hovde's characters unearth not only ancient Roman mosaics but also deep, hidden truths about themselves. I thoroughly enjoyed the novel for its intelligent characters and fresh take on a turbulent Regency romance.

ELIZABETH CAMDEN, RITA award–winning author

As fresh and lovely as its cover. . . . A feast of romance and suspense unfolds against the picturesque backdrop of West Sussex, a world inhabited with richly detailed characters you'll want to befriend. Jenelle Hovde makes an unforgettable debut!

LAURA FRANTZ, Christy Award–winning author of *The Indigo Heiress*

What a delightful story, filled with the intrigue and wit of *Bridgerton* and the deep emotional connection of *Downton Abbey*. If you love Regency romance with subtle but fascinating historical nuggets and novels that lead you to gently measure your heart, *No Stone Unturned* should be on your TBR list now!

MESU ANDREWS, Christy Award–winning author of *Isaiah's Daughter*

I was utterly enchanted by this story! The unconventional heroine and the broken hero were a perfect pairing in this novel of ancient ruins and noble families. Mystery, romance, and history come together beautifully in this heartfelt, endearing novel. Readers will be eager for Hovde's next book!

> **JOANNA DAVIDSON POLITANO,** award-winning author of *The Curious Inheritance of Blakely House* and other novels

As someone with an endless fascination for archaeology and old homes, I was captivated by the charming yet dangerous estate of Hawthorn Abbey. *No Stone Unturned* is a mysterious treasure hunt with a dashing hero and an undaunted heroine, both determined to save the British manor in their own way. If you enjoy reading Jane Austen, you'll love Jenelle Hovde's Regency romance.

> **MELANIE DOBSON,** award-winning author of *The Wings of Poppy Pendleton* and *The Curator's Daughter*

What could be better than a feisty heroine and a broodingly handsome hero? A story full of intrigue set against the windswept English countryside, that's what. Author Janelle Hovde has crafted a Regency tale that's as emotionally stirring as it is delightfully engaging. With every turn of the page, expect suspense, snappy dialogue, and heart-melting moments that linger long after the last chapter. This one is going on my keeper shelf!

> **MICHELLE GRIEP,** Christy Award–winning author of *Of Gold and Shadows*

I loved the mix of history, romance, archaeology, and faith in this adventurous and delightful Regency tale. Bridget's determination to uncover Roman ruins and her search for recognition and love will inspire readers and take them on an exciting and surprising journey. Those who enjoy novels by Julie Klassen, Roseanna M. White, and Carolyn Miller will be delighted to find a new author who brings the era and English setting to life. Well written and highly recommended!

CARRIE TURANSKY, award-winning author of *A Token of Love* and *The Legacy of Longdale Manor*

What a delightful, heart-wrenching, edge-of-your-seat ride! This story is a must-read for fans of Julie Klassen, Michelle Griep, or Erica Vetsch. Jenelle Hovde is one to watch!

SHANNON MCNEAR, 2014 RITA award finalist, 2021 SELAH winner, and author of the Daughters of the Lost Colony series

NO STONE UNTURNED

JENELLE HOVDE

No Stone Unturned

Tyndale House Publishers
Carol Stream, Illinois

Visit Tyndale online at tyndale.com.

Visit Jenelle Hovde's website at jenellehovdeauthor.com.

Tyndale and Tyndale's quill logo are registered trademarks of Tyndale House Ministries.

No Stone Unturned

Copyright © 2025 by Jenelle Hovde. All rights reserved.

Unless otherwise noted, the cover and interior images are the property of their respective copyright holders from Shutterstock, and all rights are reserved. Girl © Abigail Miles/Arcangel.com; flying paper © klyakson; country manor © Naffarts; male horse rider © Tony Marturano; old paper © Ecco; map © Jenelle Hovde and used with permission.

Author photo by Johnny Gonzalez, copyright © 2024. All rights reserved.

Cover designed by Sarah Susan Richardson

Published in association with the literary agency of The Steve Laube Agency.

Matthew 6:19-21 in the author's note is taken from the Holy Bible, *New International Version,*® *NIV.*® Copyright © 1973, 1978, 1984, 2011 by Biblica, Inc.® Used by permission. All rights reserved worldwide.

All other Scripture quotations are taken from the *Holy Bible*, King James Version.

No Stone Unturned is a work of fiction. Where real people, events, establishments, organizations, or locales appear, they are used fictitiously. All other elements of the novel are drawn from the author's imagination.

The URLs in this book were verified prior to publication. The publisher is not responsible for content in the links, links that have expired, or websites that have changed ownership after that time.

For information about special discounts for bulk purchases, please contact Tyndale House Publishers at csresponse@tyndale.com, or call 1-855-277-9400.

Library of Congress Cataloging-in-Publication Data

A catalog record for this book is available from the Library of Congress.

ISBN 979-8-4005-0287-3 (HC)

ISBN 979-8-4005-0288-0 (SC)

Printed in the United States of America

31	30	29	28	27	26	25
7	6	5	4	3	2	1

For Karen Kelly

1

> The gods favor the bold.
> **OVID**

> Lay not up for yourselves treasures upon earth, where moth and rust doth corrupt, and where thieves break through and steal.
> **MATTHEW 6:19**

BRAMNOR, WEST SUSSEX
MARCH 1811

On a Wednesday afternoon in the village of Bramnor, one does not expect much excitement beyond sugared gingerbread and tea. I had settled into a quiet afternoon, absorbed in the latest copy of *Archaeologia* when the steady clip-clop of hooves interrupted my thoughts. Molly answered the door swiftly, and moments later, muted voices reached me from the hallway.

A startled cry was followed by heels clattering against the floor as Molly ran past the drawing room and rattled the door handle to Father's study. My obsession with antiquities lay waiting on the desk as I strained to hear.

"Sir! Sir! A message about Daniel," Molly's strident voice echoed throughout the parsonage.

The mention of my missing brother brought a fire to my veins. For the past eight months, we had searched high and low for him, his last letter sent from Portsmouth instead of the London address. I rushed to the study at the back of the parsonage overlooking a small garden where Father claimed he needed perfect quiet and peace to finish his sermons.

By the time I reached the door, it was locked. He always locked the door when drafting a sermon, or whenever he felt morose.

"Let me in, Father. I must know what has happened," I demanded after I jiggled the handle. Molly, her brown hair hidden beneath her cap and her eyes wide, backed away to return to her work. "I heard you received a letter."

No answer.

I rapped until my knuckles hurt. "Father! Please."

Finally, he opened the door, his thin features wan and the wire-rimmed spectacles slipping down his long nose. His hair, a white halo, appeared mussed and his cravat lopsided. He thrust the letter into my hands where a bold scrawl from our barrister made me flinch.

"There is nothing, Bridget. Nothing to tell us of my son."

I regret to inform you that Daniel remains missing.

My heart plummeted at the matter-of-fact language. My younger brother, at one and twenty, had been pressed by the Royal Navy. We had not received a single communication during the past eight months. Was he lost at sea? Dead in battle with Napoleon's fleets? Or . . . had he stirred up trouble at another gaming hell while on liberty from his duties? I scarcely knew what to think. Two years prior, he had been forced by Father to study at seminary in Cambridge. A futile task for the wildest member of the Littleton family.

"I need a moment alone, Bridget. This is but another dead end and I haven't the heart for much more disappointment." How weary, nay—how broken—Father sounded as he pushed up his spectacles. His eyes welled and tears spilled down his cheeks.

The letter in my hand brought a heaviness to my chest, but I was not so willing to cave in to defeat. "Send for a Bow Street runner instead of a barrister. You cannot abandon him so readily, can you?"

Father sucked in a loud breath at my suggestion. "I daresay I have drained all available funds in our search for him. We have employed so many men in London and I have no more money beyond providing for our necessities. My son is beyond my reach and has been for several years. He repeatedly refused my counsel and is now in some predicament of his own making. Until he repents of his errors, there is nothing else I can do but pray and wait for his return. You cannot save him either, my girl. I must instead focus on my parishioners and finish my sermon. Any day the new viscount will arrive to take over his estate, and he will expect to see his vicar at work. I cannot let my duties slide."

Your duty is also to your family, I wanted to protest. Not to the new viscount. Not to the parishioners who clamored for his attention.

But I didn't say anything, crumpling the note in my palm as Father motioned for me to exit his sanctuary. He shut the door with a decided click. And locked it again, creating a solid barrier between us as he often did when grieving.

Numb, I backed away even though I craved some comfort, some assurance that all would be well. After retreating to the drawing room, I sank into my chair and reached for the antiquities journal. Daniel and I used to pore over them in the evenings. Somehow, it made me feel closer to him since he had taught me the joy of the ancient world, adding to my education in ways that a girl's finishing school never could.

Molly cast me a sympathetic glance as she hurried past to the kitchen to prepare afternoon tea. I had no appetite for treacle or any other sweets.

Reading the fine print of the journal proved futile with my vision now blurred with tears. At four and twenty years of age and most certainly on the shelf, I felt very alone and useless within the stuffy parsonage.

After Mother's death from scarlet fever eight years ago, I had raised my brother as my own. I'd promised her I would look after him.

And I had failed. Terribly.

Blinking furiously, I resigned myself to further silence with only our housekeeper, Mrs. Herriot, and Molly to keep me company. A curious section of the journal published by the Society of Antiquaries drew my attention as I dashed at my eyes with the back of my hand.

A Call for Learned Submissions

The Society of Antiquaries of London cordially invites all enthusiasts of antiquity to submit their research, observations, and discoveries concerning the ancient history, monuments, and artifacts of Britain and other lands. A grand prize of £50 will be awarded . . .

When I was five and ten, I had found Roman coins near the now-deceased viscount's estate, only two miles north of the parsonage. On many occasions, I accompanied my father to visit the former lord, who had passed away two months ago. Despite being a melancholic man, he had chuckled at my obsession with historical discoveries, patting my arm in dismissal as if I were his basset hound.

My collection of coins remained tucked within a handkerchief in my dresser, much like my dreams shelved for another day.

Daniel had suggested that I write to the Society of Antiquaries and the Dilettanti in hopes of stirring their excitement regarding the find. The society never bothered to answer, and the secretary of the Dilettanti sent a clipped reply, admonishing me to confine my activities to embroidery.

I pushed aside the paper just as Mrs. Herriot, dressed in severe black with her white frilly cap, entered the drawing room with Molly following behind carrying a tray of tea.

"Good heavens!" She stopped abruptly. "Is that Miss Perry *running* down the path toward us?"

I perked at the mention of my dearest friend, who was the same age as Daniel. Rising from my seat, I glanced out the window and knew something must be amiss. When she burst into the drawing room moments later, her chest heaving, she pushed back her straw bonnet and loose gold curls, so different from my red frizz, tumbled onto her shoulders. With her gray gown splattered at the hem and her slippers covered in dirt, she held up a hand to stop Mrs. Herriot from inviting her for tea.

"Oh, Bridget, do call for the vicar. Father has found a demon in his field!"

"A demon?" I repeated slowly while Mrs. Herriot snorted.

Abigail nodded, her cheeks flushed pink. "Yes, and Papa is quite beside himself. He swears it is a terrible omen, especially since—since the last harvest . . ."

She faltered but I knew what she meant. The previous harvest proved miserable for the entire valley, and as a result of mounting debts, Abigail and her father might have no choice but to leave for the factories in the coming year, like so many other families who had abandoned the valley.

"I daresay the vicar won't want to be disturbed." Mrs. Herriot sniffed as she poured the tea. Ever a stickler for propriety, she guarded my father's study hours well.

My friend cast me a stricken look, silently begging for my intervention. Ever since her mother passed three years ago from childbirth complications, Abigail ran the Perry household by herself as the only child. Just as I did with my absent-minded father, too immersed in his theological studies to pay much attention to me. We were more like sisters, doing everything we could together.

"Tell me more," I demanded.

"Horns, Bridget," she hissed in a loud whisper. "I saw them myself." She pointed in the direction of the Perry farm, a short walk from the parsonage. "Devil horns protruding from the fairest face you can imagine!"

Goose pimples flared across my skin at my friend's declaration. "I daresay I need a change of scenery and Father remains indisposed. Let me gather my shawl and we shall battle this monster together." I took my friend's hand when she frowned and gave it a squeeze.

She exhaled as I drew her away from the drawing room. "I'm ever so grateful, Bridget. I can't imagine what Papa will do. He's been so worried, stewing over his finances and the farm. Now this . . ."

I blew out a long breath, eager to escape the confines of the parsonage and head outside into nature, away from the weight of my family's concerns.

I would rather confront a demon in the field than the frustration roiling within me at my father's distance and my brother's disappearance.

Mr. Lewis Perry, in his excitement, quite forgot himself, and his muddy boots encroached on the hem of my oatmeal-hued muslin gown while Abigail and I knelt on the damp ground.

With trembling fingers, I brushed away the crumbling dirt his plow had shaken loose and inspected the hole at the edge of the field next to Hawthorn Abbey.

Sheep bleated far off, their soon-to-be-shorn wool dotting the emerald-green landscape, and in front of me, rows of apple trees formed straight lines leading off to the moss-covered abbey in the distance.

"Look at the tiles, Bridget. So many broken ones. Do you think there are more? Who is he?" Abigail's curiosity was stronger than her father's nerves.

I took out my long-handled art brush and swept away the dirt. A roguish face emerged, the tiles of his ivy-crowned head cracked, yet still visible. Faded tones of red, gold, and green peeked through the grime. The workmanship was undeniable, the tiny tesserae fitted together with care.

Abigail leaned closer, studying the mosaic in silence while her father muttered a quiet prayer.

"Bacchus," I proclaimed.

"Eh?" Mr. Perry squinted as he bent lower to study the mosaic partially hidden within the ground.

"Bacchus. The god of drink and desire and . . ." I pressed my lips together. Most people wouldn't consider Bacchus appropriate knowledge for a young lady. No need to scandalize Mr. Perry any further, especially as I was the vicar's daughter. Abigail winked at me, her rosy mouth turning into a saucy curve.

I crouched lower, my heart racing as I stared at the mosaic. Something more lay here—just beneath the surface. The tiles were worn and cracked, but the way they stretched beyond the dirt hinted at a design far grander than the small patch Mr. Perry had uncovered. A larger piece of the past, waiting to be unearthed. I could scarcely believe my eyes. Daniel and I had always assumed more artifacts lay within the Bramnor vicinity after I had discovered the Roman coins on the very edge of Hawthorn land.

The advertisement in my latest antiquities journal came to mind, along with the call for submissions of research. Fifty pounds would prove more than enough since most Bow Street runners collected a guinea a day.

I cleared my throat, tucking away painful thoughts of Daniel, who would have so enjoyed this cheeky fellow's grin. "It's a Roman god, Mr. Perry, and your field sits upon the ruins of something large, I suspect. An ancient villa, perhaps part of an atrium or another grand room."

Mr. Perry shifted nervously, muttering something under his breath. "First the crops, now this . . . It's those curses again, I swear it. That estate of Hawthorn's has always brought bad luck to Bramnor."

I glanced at Abigail, raising an eyebrow. "Curses?" I asked lightly, trying to keep the mood from turning too ominous. Father had alluded to the former lord's melancholic spirit and penchant for liquor, but as a vicar, Father also never broke a confidence. And I had never cared for gossip.

Mr. Perry waved his hand dismissively. "Oh, the old tales, Miss Littleton. Nothing good comes from this estate, and with the old lord's passing and this ghoul on my land? How can I remain on my farm when I can scarcely earn enough to put food on the table?"

I shook my head, refusing to be swayed by superstitions surrounding the reclusive old Lord Hawthorn. "It's history. Not a curse. And this find might bring you much-needed funds since it's on your land."

Mr. Perry spat on the ground. "Nay. What man alive has time for such fancies? I've got a daughter's dowry to manage. I must plant the field, not dig up this cursed tile or . . . atroo? Aloo?" He coughed into his fist, his weathered cheeks blooming red.

"Atrium," I supplied as I brushed my gloves to remove some of the dirt. "It was the middle room in a grand mansion with an inner pool to collect water. Only a wealthy Roman would have had access to such a floor. If you excavate properly, you might uncover a statue or pottery you can sell to a museum or private collection. The highest circles collect Roman and Grecian art."

"Oh, do listen, Papa. An atrium sounds delightful!" Abigail exclaimed as she gestured to the tiles. Her blue eyes glowed.

"Bah!" Mr. Perry nudged at the dirt with the patched heel of his leather boot.

Bacchus continued to leer at us with a knowing grin. I couldn't let him hide any longer. Not while I devoured every book I could find regarding Greek and Roman history, thanks to Daniel's encouragement. For as long as I could remember, I'd dreamed of uncovering artifacts.

I turned to Mr. Perry. "Allow me to excavate. I promise to include you in the accolades. I simply want the opportunity to document and catalog the mosaic and submit my findings to *Archeologia*. They are offering fifty pounds to the best discovery. And whatever I find will belong to you. Bacchus, demon or not, might prove priceless."

"You need the money?" He frowned.

I nodded, ashamed to admit it, but tithes had been meager in recent years due to the financial strain in Bramnor. "I must resume searching for Daniel, and we have exhausted our savings."

Abigail crossed her arms as she cast a pointed stare at her father. "We must help the good vicar and his daughter. Besides, think of the fame when the papers declare you found lost treasure! Consider our family and how we might benefit. Why, we might even travel to Bath, and I—" She bit her lip to stop her words, but I knew what she'd almost said. For the past several months she had spoken of almost nothing but her desire for a season—a proper season, with balls and gowns and maybe a dance or two with a broad-shouldered soldier. Or maybe even a squire. Half of the unmarried local farmers, of which there weren't many, fluttered around her as helpless as flies drawn to a picnic lunch.

Mr. Perry lifted his leg as if to kick aside the soon-to-be mud. I wasn't certain if he intended to further uncover Bacchus or destroy him.

"No!" I placed a warning hand on his arm, stopping him mid-step. "This is an endeavor for a careful scholar, for a . . ." *A man,* my mind immediately supplied. I shook my head as soon as the thought took form. No, I couldn't let such a discovery go unattended.

Tomorrow I would bring a sketchbook and copy the Roman god at my feet and draft a series of notes for a paper. But would the societies reject me as before?

How unfair that the word *dilettare*, which meant "to take delight in," could only apply to men and not to me. Father liked to remind me that I, as a vicar's daughter, however admirable that might be, had no place pestering men who insisted on studying pagan artifacts. But I was determined to try again and make the antiquity societies take notice.

I turned to Mr. Perry, resolve flaring in my chest. "What you need, Mr. Perry, is a lady of quality and intellect. Look no further," I declared. "Abigail and I shall handle your monster for you, but not with your boot or shovel."

Before Mr. Perry could respond, the sound of hooves pounding against the dirt interrupted us. Abigail stiffened beside me, her hand clutching her bonnet as we all turned toward the pitted main road.

Emerging from the thick brush, a thin, gangly figure on horseback approached. His face was lined with age, a hooked nose casting a shadow over his pinched expression. The horse trotted toward us, stopping a few feet away with a snort.

Mr. Spencer, the steward of Hawthorn Abbey.

His sharp eyes darted between us and the excavation site at the very edge of Mr. Perry's field, where the land sloped toward the abbey, no more than a quarter of a mile away.

Mr. Spencer pushed up the brim of his hat. "Pushing into

Hawthorn boundaries, again, aren't we? Don't you dare be digging posts to fence in your sheep, man. I won't allow it."

"This is my land, you toothless gaffer," Mr. Perry snarled as he placed his hands on his hips. "You are wrong on the boundary lines and you have no proof. Show me the papers that say I'm in the wrong."

An old feud simmered between Hawthorn Abbey's steward and Mr. Perry. The former lord, too lost in his cups, had neglected his affairs, and Mr. Perry, unable to read, lacked the proof to settle his claims. An uneasy peace persisted, stirred only by the steward's overzealousness.

Mr. Spencer narrowed his eyes as he shifted his weight on the horse. "The new Lord Hawthorn is on his way, and this land dispute will be settled soon enough."

My heart gave a small jolt. Father had mentioned the new lord's arrival in passing, but it had seemed a distant, almost trivial matter—until now. The idea of someone new, with fresh authority and a claim to these contested lands, suddenly felt more real, more urgent.

Mr. Perry's face drained of color. "The new lord?"

"Aye," Mr. Spencer confirmed. "Soon. And I'll warn you—the new viscount won't take kindly to any digging or trespassing. Best you pack up and head back home before you find yourselves in more trouble than you bargained for."

Instead of retreating, I straightened my back, determination swelling in my chest. "Thank you for the warning, Mr. Spencer. But the former lord never took action on those threats. Why would the new lord prove any different?"

Mr. Spencer's thin lips curled into a tight smile. "We'll see, Miss Littleton. We'll see."

With that, he tugged on the reins, turning his horse with a sharp jerk before riding off, leaving us standing in the field.

I exchanged a glance with Abigail, her face pale. But I felt something else stirring within me—something far more powerful than the fear of curses or lords. It was the pull of discovery, the thrill of history waiting to be unearthed.

Beside me, Mr. Perry scowled. "I won't be told what to do on my own property."

I turned back to the mosaic. Bacchus stared up at me from the ground, his smirk daring me to continue, just like Daniel's wink when he was about to embark on something rebellious.

The land had been waiting for centuries to give up its secrets, and I intended to uncover every last one. My brother would want me to. Whatever the new lord might say or do, neither I nor the Perry family had felt hope for a long while.

I would not abandon it so lightly.

2
Bridget

> She walks in beauty, like the night of cloudless
> climes and starry skies; and all that's best of dark
> and bright meet in her aspect and her eyes.
> **LORD BRYON**

A week had passed since my first encounter with Bacchus, although I returned to the site repeatedly to work to uncover the full mosaic. Upon learning of the possibility of riches and robbers, Mr. Perry and Abigail had vowed to keep the mosaic a secret. Mr. Perry had also secured a canvas to cover the site and protect it from the spring rain.

As usual, Father had kept to his study, his door mostly locked as he lost himself in the tomes scattered across his desk, leaving me much to my devices and to my fretting over my brother's plight. I was accustomed to managing on my own. Instead of further indulging in fear, I marched to the Perry field with renewed vigor, preferring the bright afternoon sunshine to the musty parlor.

Together, Abigail and I knelt in the field, cleaning the six-by-six section we had unearthed with the aid of damp cloths. We worked in tandem, our movements careful as we wiped away the layers of earth that had hidden the ancient art for centuries. The stones gleamed with myriad colors—ochre, cerulean blue, and a startling crimson. The painstaking care required meant our progress was slow, and I doubted we would clear much more of the original floor today.

"I can't quite decide if I should fear him or like him," Abigail muttered as she shifted on the canvas intended to keep our gowns dry.

We paused and stared at Bacchus.

"Isn't it fascinating that vice often carries a pleasant facade?" I murmured.

I didn't catch a glimpse of her expression, but I heard her soft intake of breath. "Aye. I confess this Bacchus reminds me of your brother with those curls. That impish grin . . ." She no longer met my curious gaze. Her neck flushed as she picked up one of my paintbrushes to study the bristles, running a thumb against the tapered edge.

I inhaled the fragrant air as I considered her statement while rummaging in my satchel for a charcoal stick to sketch Bacchus. For years I had suspected she carried a tendre for my brother, although her affection was not quite as loyal as my own.

Daniel would have related to this cheeky god. Especially with his proclivity to drink wine and cavort with friends. Pressing my lips together, familiar emotions surged—ire, shame, regret, and the disappointment of not being able to save him despite my efforts.

She brushed the dirt from her hands. "What a pity he remains missing."

An understatement if ever there was one. Men who frequented taverns often found themselves with a king's coin slipped into their drink—a shilling, marking them for service in His Majesty's Navy. Sipping from that fateful cup meant conscription, sometimes before the poor soul realized what had happened. A life-or-death consequence that few could escape.

"Until I publish my findings and receive a fee, I don't know what else to do to earn enough to continue searching," I finally admitted after a long pause.

"Marry?" She arched a brow at me, but the former amused smile had softened to something akin to pity. "You might find a reasonable man who would be more than happy to assist you. Surely you could wed a curate or a vicar or a farmer in the area."

I was considered a spinster, even labeled a bluestocking with an absent-minded father who couldn't tie his own cravat without help each morning. Most of the men in the village regarded me with amused tolerance as the vicar's daughter. The only man—a curate, no less—to ask for my hand had been a man far past his prime with a set of wooden teeth, and a waistcoat straining at the buttons.

Besides, the men in my life had failed me far too often for me to rely on anyone beyond myself.

"I shall leave marriage to you," I said. "Surely you must be fighting off the offers of half a dozen or so men by now."

Instead of looking pleased, she released a heavy sigh. "None of them are suitable . . . except perhaps the inn owner, Mr. Barron."

"Mr. Barron?" I cried out, picturing the man with a loud voice who put on foppish airs as if he were a fine gentleman. At least he retained most of his hair, even if the auburn hue unfortunately matched mine. Jim Barron ran two inns along with a tavern, the Jolly Wench, infamous for its overcooked mutton and blackened, greasy biscuits with the only redeeming quality being ale so sharp and strong, it left a man with fire in his belly. "Nay, promise me you won't consider him."

She shrugged a slim shoulder. "He's well-off, Bridget. What can I say? At least I'd live in comfort. Better that than being a governess." A sparkle appeared in her eyes. "If the children misbehaved, at least you could punish them with endless history lectures and writing out the Greek alphabet. I, on the other hand . . ."

A worse fate I could not imagine for her, other than Mr. Barron, especially if saddled with an imperious master who forbade me from being wholly accepted by the family or the servants. What could be lonelier than living in some forgotten wing, only to be taken out when needed? Never fully belonging or having a voice of my own?

I hit her lightly on the shoulder with my fist even though her teasing chafed. "I save those lectures for *you*, you ungrateful miss who calls herself a friend."

"We've been friends for many years now," she said quietly once our laughter subsided. "This mosaic could change our situations. It is a miracle."

I winced. Did I believe in miracles anymore? I dare not admit such a traitorous thought, even if we shared much of childhood grievances and delights with each other.

Abigail leaned closer to study my work. A stray blonde curl grazed her rosy cheek. "I should think those scholars will finally recognize your accomplishments."

"I hope so." Her praise warmed me as I placed my notes, along with the sketch of Bacchus into the leather satchel. The hour was late, the sun melting into the horizon, bathing the fields and grass in gold. We both rose and shook out our wrinkled gowns. I waved goodbye to Abigail after refusing an escort home. I wanted to reflect on what I might write to the Dilettanti and the Antiquarians, and I could hardly compose a letter with Abigail chattering or probing into my family affairs. I loved her dearly, but I needed a moment of quiet to compose my thoughts.

Surely we would uncover more ruins. The Romans had pushed back the Iceni tribes and conquered the land with brute force, taming it with bathhouses, amphitheaters, straight roads, and, of course, villas like the one I believed resided beneath Mr. Perry's land.

As I glanced around the countryside at the gentle, verdant slopes of the valley, I could almost imagine myself transported back to ancient times as the lady of the villa. My hair would fall free with a ribbon wrapped around the crown of my head. My dress would be a simple tunic covered with a stola pinned at the shoulders. I would wear dangling silver earrings and cover my bare feet in soft leather sandals instead of itchy cotton stockings and snug slippers.

I tugged at my bonnet to loosen the tight strings. If only I could feel as free as I imagined the lady of the villa might live. Moving the leather satchel under one arm distracted me from the sound of thunder in the distance.

By the time I turned to greet the rushing menace, a stranger on horseback barreled down the road heading straight toward me. Clods of dirt shot from beneath the pounding hooves. For a moment I thought I stared at a Roman conqueror with a sword slapping at his side.

Twilight bathed the road in shades of muted gray and purple, with shadows hiding its poor condition. The man's great coat billowed like raven wings, and his head was bent low. As he raced past the fields, flocks of birds scurried into the air, squawking their outrage.

I jumped out of the way as the fearsome horse thundered past and splattered mud against my gown, allowing me a glimpse of the man's stern face with a harsh mouth pulled into a thin line.

Would he see the holes in the road ahead? Or would he break that poor beast's legs?

My bonnet, freed from the knot that had secured it under my chin, slipped from my numb fingers and tumbled down my back as I hurried southward, away from Hawthorn Abbey. In my shock, I dropped the satchel, causing brushes and papers to scatter over the damp ground.

Crying out, I reached for the drawing first, only for a rebellious breeze to snatch it out of my grasp. I chased after it, my bonnet bouncing behind me as I ran toward the village and my father's parsonage.

"You there, miss!" I glanced back to see the horse jerk to a halt.

I gaped for a moment, mesmerized by the height and breadth of that massive beast pawing at the ground. For once, I wished I had taken Miss Perry's offer to escort me home. Good heavens, what a sight I must present! Nothing could disguise the state of my attire, not even the falling twilight. I wanted nothing more than to avoid the imposing man on the road and recapture my sketch of Bacchus before slinking back to the parsonage.

"Can you speak?" The man's voice, deep and velvet, carried an edge I didn't care for.

I swallowed hard, forcing my beating pulse to slow. The paper rolled out of my reach, fluttered in the breeze, and became trapped among the grass.

"I assure you, I can speak quite well."

He drew closer, giving me ample opportunity to study him. Towering over me on a horse the color of midnight, the man assessed my bedraggled form from head to toe. His gaze dropped to the ground where my unfortunate picture lay. When he raised his head, his eyes narrowed.

"Your paper?"

"Yes, it is. I believe your horse is about to crush my drawing. Would you be so kind to remove yourself so I may retrieve it?"

I met his bold gaze with one of my own. His clothes, though marred with mud, were serviceable rather than stylish, from the Hessian boots to the buckskin breeches clinging to his legs. A simple knotted cravat and fitted coat hinted at something finer, and his clean-shaven jaw, though as dimpled as the satyr's, clenched and unclenched.

Flinty eyes, almost black within the gathering darkness, stared at me. He was younger than I first surmised, and upon closer inspection, I recognized the military cut of the coat. Pain stabbed in my chest when I noticed the brass buttons. But this man was nothing like Daniel with his round cheeks and gap-toothed grin.

Without a word, the stranger dismounted. He snatched up the damp sketch of Bacchus and limped toward me. Of course, as fate would have it, the soggy paper chose that moment to unfurl into its full glory, providing a glimpse of the smirking god. The stranger glanced at it, one black eyebrow arching in question.

"Interesting. An acquaintance of yours?"

"That is not your concern," I responded coolly, my frustration at odds with his limp. Had he sustained a recent injury? The frostiness of his tone drowned out any sense of pity.

Clearing his throat, the man offered me the paper, and I was careful not to wrinkle it as I took it.

I did not care to explain the drawing or the mosaic within the field. Nor could I help noticing how his greatcoat emphasized the stranger's broad shoulders. He appeared equally intimidating on the ground without the benefit of his mount. A gentleman, perhaps—judging from the cut of his clothes—but not a dandy.

He tilted his head, indicating the lane ahead. "How much farther on this cursed road until I reach Hawthorn Abbey?"

"You have less than a mile to traverse, sir. There are holes ahead and should your horse stumble into one—" I let my warning slide into the space between us. The horse snorted as if in agreement. Curiosity made me want to ask who the man was and why he felt the need to travel so recklessly. Instead, I bit the inside of my cheek.

"Is nothing tended here in this godforsaken place?" His icy gaze dropped to my stained gown, his censure clear, as if the careless state of my dress extended to the state of the roads.

I flinched at his disdain despite my best effort to appear calm. "The farmers of Bramnor work hard and contribute their share to the turnpike trust." Unfortunately, with the rising costs of farming, the fund reserved for roads and bridges had shrunk in recent years.

"Clearly their efforts are not enough."

Ire bubbled up at his caustic response. "It is also the responsibility of the lord to tend to his community's needs. And since Lord Hawthorn passed away two and a half months ago, we have yet to meet his heir. One can only hope he will be an improvement, though I don't hold to it considering previous experience with the Hawthorn family."

A harsh laugh—a bark, really—exploded from the stranger. He tipped his beaver hat up to better view my face. "Your opinion is duly noted. Pray, just who might you be, other than a woodland sprite sent to misguide my way?"

I wasn't in the habit of handing out my name to strangers, and I had no intention of doing so this evening. "I must bid you good evening if you are to arrive at Hawthorn Abbey at a decent hour." I edged closer to the field. He was boorish and demanding—all qualities I disliked in a man.

"The hour certainly isn't decent for a miss to walk the roads alone." The stranger pursed his lips as he mounted his horse. With a grimace, he settled into the saddle. Once astride, he pulled on the reins and turned his horse as if to accompany me. Was he concerned as a gentleman or curious in a predatory sort of way?

"It's not a long walk. My father waits for me." With my art trapped beneath my left arm, I retrieved my bonnet. Unfortunately, my hair, though still pinned, remained uncovered, with loose strands playing about my face.

"Your father! What kind of man lets his daughter roam the countryside alone at night?" His faint mockery made me bristle.

I tugged the bonnet onto my head with a violence that surprised me. How could I hide my identity? He would soon know my name if he spent any time in Bramnor.

"Good night, sir," I replied firmly as I resumed my walk home. A few of my brushes lay hidden within the long grass, but I would rather suffer three enormous bottles of cod-liver oil than scrounge on the ground for my precious tools in front of him. I would return to search for the lost brushes tomorrow morning.

He didn't follow, and before long, I heard the rhythmic pounding of hooves once more before they faded into the distance. My pulse, however, didn't slow with his disappearance. Instead, it raced through my veins until my heart rattled.

I was sick with dread that I had just met the new Lord of Hawthorn Abbey.

3

> If you really want to escape the things that harass you,
> what you're needing is not to be in a different
> place but to be a different person.
> **LUCIUS ANNAEUS SENECA,** *LETTERS FROM A STOIC*

The abbey loomed ahead, its aged stone walls smothered with overgrown vines, and as inhospitable and isolated as I remembered from childhood. The entire estate appeared lost within the middle of the countryside now swathed in the deepening twilight.

Despite the dull ache in my calf, courtesy of a bullet from the Battle of Bussaco, I swung off my horse, repulsed by the profusion of weeds clinging to my boots. Chickweed in full bloom and grass, as thick as could be, brushed against my legs.

One step forward and my leg buckled, the pain stabbing and sharp. Was it only six months ago that I could force my body to do whatever I willed?

As if to comfort me, Chaucer snickered and bumped against my arm with his nose.

The ride had proven more treacherous than I'd expected. The young woman had warned me well, and I'd adjusted my pace accordingly. My rush seemed all for naught as I studied my surroundings.

Everything about Hawthorn Abbey felt untamed and forlorn, from the moss-covered stones dotting the walls of the once magnificent hall to the boarded windows beneath a slate roof. Even the young woman I met had a wildness to her, her pert nose smudged with mud and her dirty gown fading in the twilight. Nothing seemed manageable about her, including the red hair frizzing about a small face and pointed chin.

A waif or spirit come to waylay my journey. If this was my reintroduction to Bramnor Valley, I groaned to think of what I might encounter next. How she had clutched that expensive paper to her breast, her white face indignant. I sensed her fear of Chaucer when she kept a careful distance while eyeing the horse. A misplaced fear, of course. There was no gentler creature than Chaucer, even if he was bred for war.

I rubbed my neck. After such a long journey, I felt disoriented and exhausted, and anger flared again. Anger that the military had forced me to leave my regiment. I had a title I cared nothing for, with a property in near ruin, according to my barrister, and the frantic letter from the local vicar begging my return. I could not evade returning to the home I despised with all my being and ignore the diminishing rents forever, especially when my barrister informed me of the estate possibly returning to the Crown if I walked away from my inheritance.

And now, thanks to my barrister's ill-timed meddling, I was to anticipate a visit from an auditor, a Mr. Edmund Talbot, with the understanding that I had to prove the estate's worth or risk losing everything. The clock started ticking the moment I set foot on this cursed land. My barrister's warning echoed through my head.

It's you, my good viscount, and you alone who must shoulder the burden of the family estate. No one else remains to carry the Hawthorn title. The powers that be will absorb the land and all it entails and give it to another family. Is this how the Hawthorn name shall end? Will the tenants be left to the devices of an unfeeling lord who spends his days cavorting in London and Bath? A shame, since Hawthorns have held this land for well over three centuries. What else will you do now that the military has closed its doors to your service?

I nearly told him to let it burn. But I had nothing else of worth to claim these days, other than the sale of my military commission and this estate. No future waited. I couldn't even join the Bow Street runners, an investigative service, thanks to my injury.

Nor could I ignore the letter from Vicar Littleton begging me to tend to the needs of the impoverished families.

The throbbing ache in my leg reminded me to rest, a new reality I abhorred. Rest brought a host of memories I had no desire to recall. I gathered the reins in my left hand and guided Chaucer to the back of the building, where I hoped to find the stable in decent shape.

The abbey was unlit and quiet. The chirps of crickets and the scuttling of an unknown creature through dead brambles were all that greeted me behind the house. After spending my days with other military men, crowded into cramped quarters with the continual hum of voices for company, the silence felt oppressive.

Gritting my teeth, I limped past a decayed garden surrounding a dry fountain toward the stable.

The image of the woman from the road flashed again in my mind. And that of her art. She spoke with cultured tones, an odd mixture of reserved and saucy replies, but then again, her appearance . . . Well, I couldn't quite decide what her appearance reminded me of, exactly.

What in the world had I gotten myself into? I was not a superstitious man, but I couldn't suppress a chuckle mixed with a shudder.

"Who is there? I see you!" A thin, reedy voice called out from behind the extensive stable with a thatch roof in better repair than the dovecote and coach house.

"Captain Rafe Hawthorn," I said. My new title of viscount felt too surreal to use after thirteen years in the military.

A wizened man, wiping his hands with a filthy cloth, ducked out from behind a low lintel. His eyes widened when he took in me and Chaucer. A hurried bow followed after he tossed the cloth onto a nearby barrel, not even caring when it slid off the rim and into the long grass.

"My lord! Welcome! Forgive me. I didn't realize you would come today. We've been in a state of preparations following the former viscount's passing. God rest his soul." He hastily added the blessing as he smoothed the remaining strands of hair over his balding head. "You remember me, eh? Of course, you were nothing more than a wee lad at the time. I'm Mr. Whittle. Frank Whittle. I tend to the grounds of Hawthorn Abbey."

"I remember," I said after a pause.

"My wife now manages the household, and our daughter, Lucy, serves as a maid." When I offered no further pleasantries, he jammed a filthy hand into his waistcoat, stained the color of molding butter, a putrid mix of green and yellow. A pair of large breeches, the color of rust, hung on his thin frame.

I sighed. "Are there no other servants left?"

"Other than the steward, Mr. Spencer, no. Only us, my lord." Mr. Whittle shook his head. "The previous viscount hired the tenants as need be for the orchards, but he didn't entertain company in the later years. Didn't care for people much, especially when he fell into one of his spells."

I froze at such blatant impropriety while Mr. Whittle had the grace to flush. With a hand still jammed into his waistcoat, he rocked on his heels as if he might bolt.

"Forgive me, my lord. My wife oft complains of my tongue flapping in the breeze. But it's best you know the history of this place."

Dare I admit I knew more than most might realize, considering my long absence? My dismay must have shown, for Mr. Whittle, perhaps eager to distract from his blunder, pointed to a path winding around the stable.

"One thing is for certain: no one loved the orchards more than your uncle. Do you recall how we had row upon row of the finest apples a man ever did taste?"

"Ashmead's Kernels, perfect for cider," I murmured, my attention redirected to the orchard beyond the abbey.

Mr. Whittle flashed me an approving smile. "Indeed. You ran among the trees often enough to take what you could. Why, I remember you climbing one tree with bare feet, no less. Best climber in all of Bramnor, I always said."

I did not return his smile as I stared at the trees. I couldn't. My throat tightened as my mind drew shadowy pictures of the orchard and abbey from before. Perhaps I could stay long enough to hire additional staff and then find a place to live elsewhere. Anywhere but the abbey.

Mr. Whittle watched me for a moment, as if expecting an answer.

"I shall visit the orchards first thing in the morning," I finally said as I offered him the reins.

Mr. Whittle blinked at me, uncomprehending.

"Have you worked with horses, Mr. Whittle? Or must I hire a stable master?"

The groundskeeper swallowed hard, his Adam's apple bobbing. Finally, he took the reins. "No, no. It's just the size of this creature.

I shall take care of him while you . . . er, inspect the house. His name, sir?"

"Chaucer. After the poet, of course."

A twinkle entered Mr. Whittle's eyes. "An appropriate name, if you don't mind me saying so. Imagine the adventures this horse has encountered."

I was loath to leave Chaucer in the hands of Mr. Whittle. He felt a stranger to me, even if he presumed to know me so well. Any protests died on my lips when my leg threatened to buckle yet again. To my relief, Mr. Whittle gently led my able companion into the stable. He called over his shoulder, "I'll find fresh water and oats right away."

A single light appeared within the diamond panes of a window next to a door leading to the kitchen. The main entrance back around in the front boasted massive double doors covered with iron scrollwork and faced west. I was too tired to insist on formality. The tiny pinprick of light piercing the growing gloom descending upon the house and gardens beckoned with the offer of comfort.

The heavy oak door creaked as I pushed on it and entered the kitchen. While the outside of Hawthorn manor repelled, the kitchen appeared clean with a swept flagstone floor and a large wooden table pushed against a cracked, plastered wall yellowed with age.

A plump lady with gray curls peeking beneath a white cap bent over a stone fireplace, lighting shaved kindling with a matchstick. She jumped when the door shut behind me, then tossed the smoking stick into the fireplace and straightened.

"Goodness, what a fright you've given me, young sir!"

"My apologies. I am Captain Rafe Hawthorn, and I've just arrived . . ." *Home.* The word stuck in my throat, stubbornly resisting any effort to utter it.

She gasped before curtsying, her mobcap sliding askew. "It's you! The little master returned home at last."

The little master. I tried not to flinch at the title, especially since I was no longer a lad of six years. Instead, I felt weathered at one and thirty.

Without noticing my discomfort, she prattled on while fluttering her hands as if nervous. "We weren't sure when to expect you, my lord. You'll meet my daughter before long, I'm certain. She's somewhere about the abbey at this late hour."

"Of course, Mrs. Whittle."

Her gaze brightened at the use of her name. With a quick tug, the housekeeper fixed her drooping cap, the action familiar, again reminding me of the woodland sprite I had met earlier. "Shall I have my daughter prepare your rooms and light a fire? Spring brings such a damp chill, doesn't it? Would you like a cup of tea? I haven't much food on hand, but I have some meat pie from earlier." The dubious rise of her voice made me question how much earlier she had served the pie.

I nodded regardless, my stomach threatening to rumble. "Thank you, Mrs. Whittle. Your offer will have to suffice."

She winced slightly, her hands fluttering nervously as she smoothed her apron.

"Follow me, and I will show you to the drawing room. The green room, your uncle called it. When you are ready on the morrow, my husband will take you to meet the tenants. They've been so eager to have a lord oversee the estate again."

"I'm an early riser." I pulled off my great cloak and handed it to Mrs. Whittle. Unlike her husband, who seemed unused to service, she immediately took the heavy woolen garment, the brass buttons gleaming within the meager firelight. "I remember my way, thank you. I would appreciate tea as soon as possible."

She nodded, biting her lip until the skin pinched gray beneath crooked teeth. "It's good to have you home, sir. It's been so long since we laid eyes on you. Why, it seems like yesterday you were sneaking ginger biscuits when you thought I wasn't looking. And now you've grown into a fine man."

She edged around the table and raised her hand as if to touch me, and then, perhaps thinking the better of it, let her arm fall to her side. A sheen filled her eyes.

"Thank you." My throat tightened at the emotion playing across her face. I'd hidden beneath that very table, clasping my quivering knees to my chest while my father bellowed my name as he marched through the abbey. Yes, I remembered her too. Standing like a sentinel with her mixing spoon in one hand and a bowl in the other, hiding me from view while I cowered beneath the table.

"Is there anything else I can do for you, sir?"

I shook my head. A few lit candles waited on the table, and I snatched one. Without further preamble, I headed down the hall, driven by the fierceness of my desire to be alone. The musty hall, covered with the same flagstones as the kitchen floor, stretched into darkness. Wood paneling, so deep a hue as to appear nearly black, lined either wall.

A prison.

I shut my eyes tightly against the invasive memory threatening to latch sharp tentacles into my mind.

"Not today," I whispered to myself. *Not today.*

Despite my resolve, another old image resurfaced, one of Mrs. Whittle holding open the door as my mother brushed past into the deep night with her long hair streaming behind her. My mother always wore her hair up in elaborate styles with ribbons. But the night we left the abbey had been one of strange events and dressing quickly. With a smile that didn't quite reach her eyes, Mrs.

Whittle had gestured to the waiting carriage in the circle drive when I balked at leaving.

Hop in. Quick! It's just a game of hide-and-seek. Shh. No crying, wee lad. You cannot properly hide if the entire abbey hears you at this late hour. What a lark this will be.

The thud of my boots echoed in the silence as I headed down the hall I had escaped as a child. Pots banged from the kitchen, setting my nerves further on edge.

Doors lined the left and right, but one remained partially open. Raising my candle, I examined the room, noting the green walls, leaded windows, and an unlit fireplace with a heavy oak mantel. Above the mantel, a white-haired man with curls framing flaccid cheeks sneered at me with disapproval from a grim portrait. A basset hound at his feet gazed upward in adoration. A recent portrait of the viscount, although the navy coat, waistcoat with dangling pocket watch, and tights were from another time. I knew him immediately. The former Lord Hawthorn, my namesake. A man I never cared for, nor attempted to write during my military service.

My father's brother.

I scowled back at the likeness. Rumors swirled about the Hawthorn men, and possibly many of the tales were true. How could I forget my mother's fear or the purple bruise marring her left eye as we escaped while both men spent a night out carousing? Eventually my uncle tired of my father's antics and mounting debts and barred him from entering the abbey. The last I'd heard, my father was stabbed in a shady inn. Long, long ago, as Mrs. Whittle had noted.

Hadn't my father and uncle abandoned my mother and me, refusing aid and comfort? Well, here I stood, though not of my choice. A paltry victory.

After setting the candle on the nearest table, I sank into a chair next to the barren fireplace. A groan escaped me as I stretched out the injured leg. Alone at last, I could at least privately massage the once-torn flesh. The frayed fabric covering the chair smelled of dust and old sweat, and the limp cushions sagged beneath my weight. But I was too tired to care.

My uncle's small-set eyes glittered from above the fireplace, as if in silent mockery. A faint whisper curled inside me, much like the smoke drifting above the sputtering candle.

You failed your men at Bussaco. What will be different this time?

Battle images flashed through my mind, alongside the accusatory voice. Despite the scent of moldering books, I could still smell the black powder from the cannons. I could still see the men of my regiment, including my friend and lieutenant, falling helpless to the ground. We had won but at what cost? Men who had relied on me only to be let down by my hesitancy during the heat of the battle. That guilt would forever cling to me.

I clenched my fists before slowly releasing my fingers and the pent-up tension with them, built up over many months, perhaps even years. Regret and bitterness seemed to taint the abbey, claiming that it had no future and no hope. I would not succumb to such a bleak fate, even if it had claimed my father and my uncle.

My mother, if she were still alive, would remind me that good people yet remained within this valley. How could I abandon them, especially after Mrs. Whittle had done her best to watch over me as a lad? Who knew if a new lord would keep the Whittles hired? And what would happen to the families who tended my uncle's estate? No child should be forced from a home and driven into an insecure future as I had been.

No, I must remake Hawthorn Abbey into something worthy of pride. Duty demanded it. I couldn't fail those who depended on me—not again. Nothing hollowed out a man more than failure.

If I could no longer serve my regiment with this blasted injury, then I would carve out another future—a better one for myself and my tenants. The land would find rebirth through the revitalization of the orchard, its once-thriving trees bearing fruit again. The apples could be sold at market, bringing much-needed income to the estate and ensuring the tenants had work to sustain their families. With careful management, the estate could return to its former glory. Once the land was secure and the Crown's representative satisfied, I would purchase another home far from Bramnor, hopefully within a year or two. One with far fewer ghosts.

4

Bridget

> The oldest, shortest words—yes and no—
> are those which require the most thought.
> **PYTHAGORAS**

Father liked to remind me of Elijah's flight from Queen Jezebel whenever my spirits were low. Then he'd say, *A nap, a spot of tea, and a couple biscuits, and soon enough you'll see that the Lord Almighty will set things right again.*

I found the advice helpful on most occasions, particularly the part about devouring treacle tarts or shortbread. That evening after encountering the new viscount, however, I found nothing in common with the prophet who subsisted on morsels from ravens.

Night had fallen when I pushed on the weathered door to the parsonage and removed my filthy slippers to tend to later. I untied my apron and braced myself for yet another lecture. Yet as I crossed into the hall, and the housekeeper, Mrs. Herriot, heard my loud sneeze, I found myself led upstairs as she muttered her sympathy.

She handed me a handkerchief. "Poor thing, you look as though you took a nasty tumble. How wan your skin is. Tell me you have not taken a chill from all your gallivanting about the countryside."

I sneezed again and dabbed at my eyes. "It's been quite an evening. I just encountered the new lord on the road leading to the abbey, and of course, I managed to bungle the whole affair."

"You met the new lord? Dressed like this?" Mrs. Herriot reared back, gesturing to yet another ruined gown. "Oh, my child. Molly will be scrubbing this for hours."

I sighed on behalf of my maid. Mrs. Herriot and I had an unusual relationship, tolerating each other, pushing each other, and occasionally finding a truce. A friend of my mother's, Mrs. Herriot had been forced to find employment after her husband's death. When my mother passed eight years ago, Mrs. Herriot was the closest thing I had to female guidance other than an aloof aunt on my father's side, who refused to take me as a companion because of my eccentric tendencies. Not that I was complaining.

I had always spoken my mind with Mrs. Herriot. We had an understanding—I preferred scholarship over society.

"I don't mind a ruined gown. I can use it solely for excavation. If only I could find a pair of buckskin trousers. And boots! A far more sensible ensemble, to my way of thinking."

"Never let me hear the words *buckskin trousers* out of your mouth again," she hissed, all maternal affection scattered to the breeze.

I stifled a groan as I allowed her to help me shrug out of the damp gown. My best tools remained scattered across the grass, and I had been bound by far too much pride to retrieve them in front of the viscount. Tomorrow morning, I would reclaim them.

She clucked her dismay. "Let us hope you will make a better impression in the days to come. I don't need to remind you that a vicar relies on the favor of his superior."

I could not hide my grimace. "A challenging command, Mrs. Herriot. I always disliked the Hawthorn men."

"Why?" she probed. "Are we not to love our neighbors as ourselves?"

Patting my hair, I considered my answer. "Because Father spent his days at the abbey over the past six years, running to soothe each nervous ailment the old viscount had. Growing up, Daniel needed a father." I turned to her, my ire rising. "I needed him too, especially after Mama died. Do we, his flesh and blood, matter so little? Or must precedence be extended only to his flock?"

Mrs. Herriot pursed her lips. "A reverend often serves at the expense of his family. It's a holy sacrifice."

Was it such a noble sacrifice? Perhaps my brother would have had a stalwart presence to guide him, had Father been around more often instead of leaving me to raise Daniel. Perhaps I wouldn't have had to coddle Father, taking on tasks such as organizing the parish charity work and visiting the sick in his stead, while ensuring the household ran smoothly.

Did that make me selfish? Maybe. Judging from Mrs. Herriot's narrowed gaze, I could only surmise the chiding thoughts running through her mind. My brother was lost to me. And I had sat by my mother's sickbed, caring for her alone.

Father had given his all to Viscount Hawthorn in the name of divine love. And the rest of us had no say in the matter.

Mrs. Herriot's gaze softened. "I never cared much for those Hawthorn men either, truth be told. Too much wine addled their faculties." She sniffed as she reached out with a smoking taper to light our tallow candles. "You poor lamb. Imagine being run down by a horse. How utterly terrifying, especially considering that mishap you had riding all those years ago. What kind of gentleman does not escort a woman home at such a late hour?"

"I do believe one without manners," I answered without hesitation, although a warning voice in my mind soon followed—a pox upon my pesky conscience—and reminded me that I had soundly rejected him when he pointed out the same.

"A shame. Rather brutish manners for a man of the titled gentry. I suppose that hard nature comes from the military. How they beat those poor men into submission . . ." She placed the candle on the wardrobe and left me to my turbulent thoughts, mumbling about how it was a mercy I didn't twist my ankle on the road and that she would bring something hot for me to drink.

By late evening, following yet another supper alone, I resolved to write several additional letters on behalf of my missing brother. Again to the Secretary of the Admiralty, the Bow Street runners, and a few barristers of my father's acquaintance.

A shudder rippled through me as I considered Mrs. Herriot's offhanded remark about the military.

A flash of lightning stabbed outside the window near my desk in the parlor. How did my free-spirited brother fare within the cruel and rigid confines of the Royal Navy? Men were lashed without mercy for the smallest infractions and imprisoned for insubordination.

Daniel had fled the rules of this parsonage and a strained relationship with Father. Part of me always felt responsible for the break between them. I fingered my quill while eyeing the storm outside the ripple-paned window as I thought of Daniel. The fire's glow reminded me of that day shortly after Mother's death, when everything began to fracture.

Daniel had promised Abigail a thrilling sight tucked away near Hawthorn Abbey. Of course, I knew what it was, but Abigail, with her blue eyes glowing, eagerly agreed to his offer.

"You'll close your eyes, won't you? And you'll promise not to tell a soul about what you see? It'll be our little secret." He loomed over my friend, tugging at his messy cravat—so like Father's. I resisted the urge to fix it, suppressing my frustration that he might spoil the adventures we'd once shared, just the two of us. Those outings had taken us into the fresh air, away from the prying eyes of the village women eager to guide me after Mother passed.

Abigail glanced at me with her eyes wide, but Daniel's narrowed gaze forbade me from hinting at my dismay. I sighed, realizing I was sorely outnumbered since the formidable Mrs. Herriot had left the parsonage on errands and could not provide a suitable escort. Who knew where Father was during the early afternoon?

With nary a breeze to cool us, our drawing room sweltered and a fine sheen had collected on my forehead. Even Abigail fanned herself, her cheeks unnaturally flushed.

Or was Daniel the cause of her heightened color? I'd seen the sly glances she cast toward him when she thought no one was looking. Leaving her alone with my brother was unthinkable, and my attempts to coax them into taking Father's chaise for a country drive were futile.

I soon found myself perched precariously on a skittish mare, while my brother took Father's horse and Abigail rode her father's. How I wished for the tamer workhorse instead of the one beneath me—Betsy, as she was called.

Once I was astride, Betsy pawed at the ground with her ears flat back when I tried to nudge her with my heels.

"Stop sitting so stiff," my brother scolded me, even if his tone was softened with matching dimples on his cheeks. "See, you must hold the reins loosely, Bridget." He had been tasked by Father to teach me to ride before winter coated the valley in ice and snow.

I preferred to walk, finding exercise freeing for my soul. I tried to obey his advice, but the bumpy ride with me hitting the saddle in all the wrong spots promised sore muscles and earned a giggle from Abigail.

Daniel led us to the edge of Hawthorn Abbey where he jumped down with careless grace, then snatched the reins to guide his horse next to the stone wall. As he did so, Abigail dismounted, her feet landing softly on the ground. I followed suit, fumbling with the reins as I slid down from the saddle, grateful when my feet finally touched solid ground.

"Bridget and I sneak out whenever we have the opportunity," he confided as he maneuvered his horse to walk beside Abigail, leaving me to follow behind.

"I wondered why the two of you disappeared Friday afternoons," she said, sounding rather put out. "It's rude, Mr. Littleton, not to include me in your nefarious plans, especially when sneaking onto Hawthorn land."

He winked at her while leaning closer than propriety demanded. "Mrs. Dray insists she'll teach Bridget the art of embroidery and my poor sister cannot take another session of the cackling hens. Of course, I cannot stand the sermonizing Mrs. Dray offers. Eh gad, but she can put me to sleep while extorting the virtues of Proverbs. She knows the entire book from memory and is determined I shall memorize it too!"

Abigail laughed while I frowned. Mrs. Dray, ever intent on extolling propriety, was no favorite of mine, but Daniel's mocking tone made me cringe. I had no wish to cast in a poor light all the parish ladies who visited us. A dull ache filled my chest at the thought of my kind mother and her whispered admonishments to guide my mischievous brother.

Daniel, despite his angelic looks and charm, was proving to be more of a handful than I ever could have anticipated. He pointed to the ground where I had found a small cache of Roman coins only a week prior in my effort to escape the stuffy parsonage.

Holding my breath, I watched him fish through his pocket for one of the coins before showing it to Abigail—a coin the rascal had surely pilfered from my dresser.

"See what my clever sister discovered? A silver denarius." He puffed out his chest, appearing smug.

With a laugh, he ducked Abigail's outstretched hand as she tried to take it. Raising both palms, equally empty, he proved himself ever the tease.

"Up to your usual tricks, Mr. Littleton. I am not impressed with silly games." Abigail pouted as she folded her arms across her chest.

With an elaborate bow, he straightened and reached for my friend's ear, where a fat curl dangled. "Why, what is this I see?"

A tarnished coin appeared pinched between his fingers.

Abigail wrinkled her nose with distaste as she plucked it from his hand. "A rusted, useless thing." She tossed it back to him, snickering when he swiped only to miss it.

"Give it back or you shall owe me a kiss." He puckered his lips.

"Daniel, do behave!" I cried, much to his laughter.

Why had he ruined our secret without a second thought? Yes, I was pleased that he gave me credit for the find, but I wanted this hunt for antiquities to be for us—to draw us closer together. He beamed at me.

"No one is as clever as Bridget. My sister is top of the tree and can outwit any scholar."

"On that, we can agree, Mr. Littleton," my friend said.

Their compliment warmed my heart, but as much as I enjoyed Abigail's company, I cherished quiet moments in the rolling hills, where I could escape my grief and think. Mama had loved wandering through nature, gathering herbs for her remedies. She preferred the sunshine to the drawing room and taught me all she knew about healing. I felt closest to her on these grassy paths.

Weeks earlier, while walking by the Hawthorn wall, I stumbled upon a hidden Roman coin. Clutching it in my scratched hands eased my broken heart. I showed it to Daniel later, coaxing him from his sullen mood into the sunshine, where I hoped we'd both find healing. We escaped the tomb-like parsonage whenever we could, finding freedom and dreams in the fields. Daniel shared his lessons on Greek and Roman history, opening a new world that helped me mend. We talked of Mama, of missing her garden and wildflowers. Exploring the outdoors was my way of remembering her.

Now on my knees, I frantically searched for that denarius.

How often had she told the parable of the lost coin? My throat ached at the loss of her lessons—so different from those of the brusque village women or our housekeeper.

"Bridget, surely you will ruin your gown!" Abigail called out with concern.

"That was a Roman coin," I sputtered as my fingers combed through the short grass and the wind tore my bonnet from my head. "Not a ball to be flung about."

"Don't mind my sister. She has an obsession with all things ancient."

So intent on finding the coin, I scarcely heard what else Daniel said. Then a crack of thunder resounded, followed by Abigail's shriek.

"It's going to rain and I can't ruin my bonnet!" my friend cried. "Do hurry, Bridget."

"One moment," I murmured as I willed the Roman coin to show itself yet again.

At last, I found it and was about to cry out with triumph when the sound died before it left my lips. Daniel and Abigail had mounted their horses and now raced across the sloping countryside. Above, clouds the color of a bruise roiled in the sky, and I rushed to Betsy, determined to catch them both.

Yet, as soon as I mounted, a jolt of lightning stabbed the ground as if Zeus himself had flung a bolt from Olympus. The horse jerked the reins out of my hand and galloped full speed ahead, leaving me to cling helplessly to the pommel.

No one heard my cry as Betsy swerved into the thicket. I slipped and fell, landing hard on the ground. My shriek resounded alongside the thunder.

Pain radiated from my ankle, pinning me to the ground when I tried to move. Had I broken a bone? Fearing the worst, I waited for my brother's return, but the minutes stretched into something far more terrifying until I grew dizzy with panic while the sky decided to unleash her full fury. Rain mingled with my salty tears.

I waited for Daniel. I waited for Abigail. The once-lost coin warmed within the palm of my hand. Would anyone search for me? Would anyone in my family notice I was missing? I had no answers as I fingered a relic that had remained hidden and forgotten for centuries. Struggling to breathe, I forced myself to calm and focus on the coin. There was comfort in its round, solid shape. Buried for so long, it now saw the light of day. As I rubbed away the grime, revealing its rusted surface, I doubted its worth but found it no less precious.

A faint whisper drifted through my mind, altogether mocking. *If only I held meaning to those who loved me.*

The twilight deepened as I huddled near the roadside, more and more convinced that I would spend the evening a shivering mess. When I lay down as a wave of nausea roiled within my belly, the road shook with a rhythm. Father's black chaise rattled down the road, and I cried out, relieved when he stopped with Abigail sitting beside him. He enveloped me in a rare hug, pulling back only when I moaned and gestured to my ankle.

"I fear it is broken," Father murmured as he gingerly probed my foot with careful fingers. "We spied your horse bolting past the parsonage."

"Bridget, forgive me. Daniel swore you would follow in your own time. I never thought . . ." Abigail wrung her hands and suddenly she could no longer meet my gaze. How long had they ridden together, alone?

Another dark figure on horseback swiftly dismounted beside Father's carriage. My brother stalked through the foliage, his mouth pressed into a grim line when he spied us.

"Oh, Bridget . . ." A low moan escaped him as he rammed fingers through his hair. "This is all my fault. I should have waited for you."

"Indeed, it is your fault, you foolish, foolish boy. Why did you not stay by your sister's side?" Father's voice shook, which was a good sign of the wrath to come. "I can trust you to do nothing right, it would appear." He would have said far more but for Abigail's inarticulate cry. Daniel shrank into himself, his expression turning as bleak as the sky above.

I tried to reassure them both that I would be fine—as I often did—but I remembered nothing more after Father reached for me again. Not when my vision faded to black.

The storm hammered the parlor window as I sat at my desk, the quill resting idle in my hand. The inkpot waited, but my thoughts circled around Daniel—how much more could I have done? The questions lingered like shadows, never answered but always there, a quiet reminder of the choices that led us here.

Promise me you'll look after him, Bridget.

Abigail and Daniel had been extra attentive after my accident, and the terror of the memory faded—though I swore I'd never ride again. Months had passed with my leg propped on a stool as summer gave way to fall. As expected, the village women fussed over me like I was their own, murmuring about the poor motherless children.

Father had saved his harshest words for Daniel until they were behind the locked door of the parsonage office, but I heard enough to feel ill. *Honor. Propriety. Scandal. Marriage. Riding alone with an unaccompanied woman.* Daniel's voice rose, hot with anger, and Father's followed, until their words struck like blows. *Debauched. Rebellious. How could he lead his flock if his own children disobeyed?* I'd cowered on the settee, wishing I could escape. Why did Father twist every conflict into a betrayal of his ministry? Couldn't he see that Daniel grieved in his own way?

Afterward, Daniel withdrew, and Father buried himself in work, leaving tension to simmer. I tried to mend the rift, but the harder I worked, the more tangled things became, until our family felt like a knot impossible to unravel.

But despite it all, Daniel had always been the one to encourage my spirit. Before leaving for seminary, he had scoffed. *Why can't a woman publish her work? Make those stuffy old chaps recognize you, Bridget. You were never meant to be a caged thing.*

His challenge had warmed me . . . and yet his last comment chilled me simultaneously.

The front door clicked softly, arresting my attention from gathering wool. I laid down the quill just as Father tiptoed down the hall, appearing wanner than he had in some time. He did not pause to see me in the shadows with only the candlelight to illuminate my desk. A sigh escaped him as he shrugged out of his coat. Something like a muttered prayer.

Swallowing my disappointment, I let him shuffle past without calling his name. He was weary of conversation, no doubt, from visiting the parishioners. Earlier this week, he had repaired Mrs.

Eacher's thatched roof. Then he stayed by the bedside of an ill Mr. Claven, who lay near death's door.

Fever had taken hold of the village again as spring thawed.

I would not worry him with my mounting concerns over my brother. Instead, I resolved to do something about it myself. Taking the jar of ink and a quill, I set out to finish my stack of letters in the hopes of finding Daniel, starting with the Secretary of the Admiralty.

5

Rafe

Men think highly of those who rise rapidly in the world; whereas nothing rises quicker than dust, straw, and feathers.
LORD BYRON

Morning pierced the slit between the faded velvet curtains, a blade of light cutting through the gloom after the storm. I blinked, still bleary from dreams of rearing horses and the screams of men in battle. A groan escaped me. My first day at Hawthorn Abbey.

For a moment, I lay still, the lumpy bed foreign after nights spent within dubious inns. My uncle's room, once elegant, was now dust-covered and threadbare. The Jacobean chair by the fireplace seemed to hold the weight of his lonely nights.

I flung aside the covers, keeping my gaze averted from the glass decanters pushed against the desk—a reminder of the Hawthorn vices that had plagued the family for generations. Did no one clean my uncle's room?

Correction, my room.

The thought of ownership brought no comfort as I took in the decay—cobwebs draped across the vaulted ceiling and heavy beams, wood panels buckling beneath their walnut stain. Pain flared in my calf as I swung out of bed. I paused, rubbing the ache, and a knock sounded at the door, followed by Whittle's overly cheerful voice.

"Begging your pardon, my lord, but would you like breakfast in your room or the solar?"

My stomach rumbled in answer.

"Solar," I grunted. The flesh surrounding the scar tissue of the bullet wound throbbed as my feet met the cold floor.

"Very good, sir. Shall I attend to you in any other way?"

"No, thank you, Whittle." I rose, leaning against the bedpost. Blasted injury. I had pushed myself during the journey to arrive as soon as possible and now suffered the consequences. I gritted my teeth. Work remained. And work had always proved an efficient distraction from the turbulent thoughts within my head. Or any discomfort in my body.

Dressing proved agonizing, but I managed well enough on my own, at least until I reached for my boots, thankfully cleaned of the splattered mud the night before. Jamming my swollen leg into the confines of the leather boot brought out a low moan.

By the time I descended the stairs and entered the solar, a simple breakfast waited—sausages, eggs, and tea—while the fire crackled in the hearth. Mr. Whittle's daughter, Lucy, entered the solar with a fresh pot of tea, her wide smile in place. Her golden hair was carefully curled today, but the image of the red-haired sprite from the day before lingered in my mind. Lucy curtsied, teapot in hand. I raised my hand, declining more tea.

"My thanks to the cook, but I am quite finished," I said, hoping to ease the look of dismay from her face.

"'Tis no trouble at all," she gushed as she clutched the pot.

I rose from my chair in haste to escape and hissed as a stab of pain spiked once again through my leg.

"My lord, your leg. Would you like one of my herbal remedies? Old lady Gains swears by my remedies, she does! Says there's nothing better than my devil's dung." She blushed as soon as the words escaped her. "Pardon my language and all."

I had no desire to try her sulfurous devil's dung. "I'll manage. Thank you."

"Sir, if I may . . ."

I halted.

She gripped the teapot. "Begging your pardon, but did you hear the strange sounds in the hall last night?"

"No." Other than my nightmares, which I had no intention of ever admitting. "What sounds, exactly?"

Her cheeks lost some of their rosy hue. "I swore I heard someone creeping past the servant quarters. Feet shuffling and the squeak of a floorboard. I shook so much, I got up and locked the door to my room."

"Perhaps it was your parents."

She shook her head with surprising vigor. "Nay, they both deny it. No one sleeps harder than my father. I believe we've got a ghost or two haunting the halls. The sounds started several weeks before you arrived. I fear they're a bad sign of what's to come."

"Miss Whittle," I gentled my voice, wishing to set at ease the daughter of the woman who had offered a quaking boy similar comfort. "I shall investigate the abbey today, and if I find anything ominous, rest assured, I will not let it stay."

Her wobbling smile brought one of my own. Before the conversation could turn to spirits, I hobbled back to my chamber as quickly as I could, where the desk awaited—still cluttered with decanters half filled with the brandy my uncle had favored.

I rummaged through disorganized papers and odds and ends in hopes of finding something to satisfy Mr. Talbot's demand to rectify the estate's finances. At last, I stumbled upon some records and several small leather-bound books. After flipping open the cover of the first, I suspected I viewed my uncle's handwriting.

1798

My brother begged me to leave for London and abandon this godforsaken land. Our mutual friend, Cunnington, assures me that the list of Covent Garden ladies contains plenty of pocket Venuses to try. The gents are itching to see the lasses and judge for themselves which one is the prettiest. After Randall has sampled what he may, he claims he shall find the nearest club and enjoy a good bet, though I daresay we seem to have the most terminable luck of late. I suspect I won't be welcome at the faro table much longer.

I slammed the diary shut. Here lay my family's disgrace—gaming hells and Covent Garden trysts. My father and uncle, so alike in temperament and vice, had lived unchecked. While my father had married, my uncle remained alone, too stubborn to settle down. No one and nothing had curbed their selfish inclinations. Nothing of value remained to be read within this diary.

Had my pious mother not taken me far from the abbey, I might have followed the same path with such men as my guides. I remembered her agony in trying to cling to respectability, even in genteel poverty. Ignoring the diary, I reached for a linen-covered book.

A cruel voice—or a memory of it—whispered in my mind, raising the hackles along my neck.

Are you sure Rafe is even my son?

I shook my head to clear my thoughts and opened the book.

The estate records, though less sensational, still brought a staggering blow to my chest. The entries, like the crumpled papers stuffed into drawers, detailed a series of income reports and mounting debts, all jumbled together. It was only in the final years that I noticed any attempts at remedy, marked by my uncle's scribbled notes proposing the purchase of a cider press and a plan to reinvigorate the valley's cider trade. But those efforts had come too late.

An hour had passed while I performed a series of rough calculations. With an audit in only four months, how could I demonstrate any progress? If I could not make a go of it, the Crown would absorb the estate and give it to another lord. I would be like any soldier cast off from duty with not a coin in my pocket.

At last, I shoved the records away, mulling over what my barrister and Mr. Whittle had shared. As I descended the once-grand staircase lined with paintings, the gilt frames swathed in dust, I calculated the value of each item. Why not sell the art?

At the foot of the stairs, I pushed open the large entrance doors and stepped into the outdoors. The air was thick with the scent of overgrown vegetation. Stone pathways led to alcoves where monks might have sought solitude for prayer and reflection. Such irony, considering the sins of the Hawthorn men.

My uncle had left most of the buildings untouched, with no changes since the Elizabethan exterior was added to the abbey. A slow walk, hampered by my leg, brought me to a brewery with a freshly thatched roof—the only recent repair. Inside, however, all progress had halted with the old man's death.

Beyond the brewery, a few moldering workshops stood forgotten. Finally, I returned to the once-majestic stables and barns near the courtyard. The damp smell of earth and the rustle of leaves filled the air as Mr. Whittle stepped out with another man, both striding toward me with urgency.

Bits of hay covered Mr. Whittle's pants and boots. Apparently, the staff shared duties at the abbey, ranging from cook to maid, to butler and stable hand.

"My lord, may I introduce your steward, Mr. Spencer. He has a concern, if you'll give him but a moment."

Mr. Spencer was a small man with a long nose and hunched posture. He eyed me with as much curiosity as I eyed him.

The steward finally bowed. "Forgive me for intruding at such an hour, but I've encroachers on our property, and the matter cannot wait."

"Tell them to leave," I replied curtly.

"They won't, my lord. Stubborn chits claim they have the right to *your* field."

Within moments, I had mounted Chaucer and was delighted to have my faithful companion with me again. The other men found two workhorses in the stables, where they had been left with some old harnesses and equipment. After quickly saddling them, they joined me.

I followed Mr. Spencer's lead as he guided us away from the courtyard heading west, past the neat rows of trees. The apple orchard promised a fall harvest, and the two hundred sheep would provide wool come May.

Mr. Whittle noticed my interest in the orchard. He drew up his horse beside mine, his cheeks nearly as rosy as his daughter's. "Those trees will produce fruit soon enough come fall and bring a fair price. All that you view to the northeast belongs to you."

My moment of triumph was soon ruined when Mr. Spencer swore loudly and nudged his horse away from mine. "Blasted neighbors. See how boldly they've stepped onto our land again?"

I shielded a hand over my eyes, straining to see. Two slender forms appeared in the field next to the apple trees. One figure stood, while the other kneeled on the ground.

"Who borders our land?"

The steward scowled. "Mr. Perry. He's a stubborn sort. Wouldn't sell to the former lord, but somehow he refuses to budge even when crops disappoint." Then he added, "Some of the newer farmers in the vicinity have been pushing their luck, moving their fences bit by bit. They assume our neglected fields are fair game."

It was my turn to frown. "Neglected or not, this is Hawthorn land."

"I've confronted a few of them, my lord, made it clear where our boundaries lie. But these are stubborn folk, and words may not be enough. I shouted at one. The vicar's daughter. She waved her pencils and papers at me, claiming she had important things to do."

I blew out an exasperated breath, following his finger to where he pointed. "We can't let others encroach."

A feeling of certainty crept through me the longer I stared at the two figures. That woodland sprite with her nose pointed to the sky, answering me with such disdain, had found her way onto my property.

"Have no fear, Mr. Spencer. I will sort the issue within the hour. Surely, two women can't keep you from your duties."

How she had chided me the evening before. Clearly, she had no regard for my family, not that I did either. Why then, should her opinion nettle me?

Their behavior was strange for two women, particularly a vicar's daughter. My pulse thrummed at the idea of encountering her again. A foolish response, really.

All the same, I leaned into Chaucer and let him fly.

6

Bridget

> They say that knowledge is power—I used to think so, but I know now they meant money.
> **LORD BYRON**

The next morning, Abigail and I walked across the damp grass toward the dig site. As we approached the covered area, something caught my eye—small sections of freshly turned earth. Mr. Perry had clearly been at it again, though I tried to push aside the irritation that prickled at me. We had more important matters to attend to, such as making the mosaic the talk of London after I submitted my research to the Society of Antiquaries and the Dilettanti.

A realist, my friend didn't share my confidence that we would avoid Mr. Spencer's determination to fight the land border issue.

Abigail propped her fists on her hips as she stared at the abbey across the fields. "That's if the new viscount doesn't take Mr. Spencer's advice. I visited with Lucy early this morning at the abbey after dropping off a basket of eggs since her hens refuse to lay. Apparently he's been in a foul mood since his arrival. She complained that he's making them air out the unused wings of the abbey."

I had kept my disastrous encounter with Lord Hawthorn hushed, not daring to relive it aloud. But no one could deny the state of the abbey. "She shouldn't complain," I said, forcing a smile. "The abbey needs a good airing out."

"It does. The Hawthorns have been a taint on our valley for many years. Brutes, the lot of them. Papa says the younger brother, the new lord's father, often whipped his horse. He could hear the whinnies clear across the fields on a frosty morning. Only a cruel man hurts his animals."

I winced, remembering how the young lord barreled down the road, headed straight for me. Peerage didn't ensure that a man had honor. Or wisdom.

She continued, despite my silence. "I asked Lucy if he is anything like his father and uncle, but she's too enamored with him to say anything bad."

I kept my features neutral. Father always said a closed mouth caught nary a fly.

Abigail eyed me. "She swears she heard a floorboard creak in one of the cloister cells one afternoon when she was alone at the abbey. And then, one night, she heard sounds in the attic."

I huffed as I folded my arms across my chest. "No doubt there is a bat caught in the eaves."

Abigail chuckled. "I should have thought you of all people would enjoy a good gothic tale."

"I enjoy a lurid tale or two, but rarely does life match the adventures caught within the pages of a book. It is far too complicated to end up wrapped in neat endings." I must have sounded bitter, considering how Abigail arched her eyebrows at my declaration. She waited, as if to hear an explanation for my mood, but I wasn't about to describe why my leanings drifted away from the tenets of faith I once held dearly.

Abigail leaned closer to me, almost conspiratorial in her manner. "Will the vicar meet the new lord today? I should like to know both your opinions on the man."

I fidgeted with the frayed ribbon of my bonnet. "I doubt anything could keep Father from meeting his patron. I suppose time will tell if the viscount is a decent sort."

"Ah, of course." Abigail shot me a sly look. "Why speak ill of the hand that feeds you?"

Yes, vicars needed the support of their benefactors, but I disliked her comment immensely for it sounded mercenary.

"Do you think we'll find any more Roman coins like you and Daniel did?" Abigail sounded wistful. "It feels so much quieter without him pestering us. If only I had known the value of those denarii." Then, softer, under her breath. "It's a pity he never found something worthwhile to keep him tethered to Bramnor. But your brother was always a free spirit. Not wanting marriage, I suppose."

The raw ache in her voice brought a swell of sympathy. "At least we have this dig."

She huffed a laugh, blinking rapidly, perhaps to hide the tears sheening in her eyes.

"And we have an upcoming dance this May, where you will no doubt charm all the eligible young men," I added.

The May Day gathering, with dancing around the maypole, enticed many a village lass to wear her best. I suspected Abigail planned to flirt with as many eligible young men as possible.

A sigh escaped her. "I haven't anything to wear. Nor the money to purchase a new gown."

"I'm happy to lend you a dress and ribbons," I hastened to say. I needed Abigail's favor to continue excavating her father's field.

She immediately perked up. "Would you? I'd be forever grateful."

I had more than enough dresses, borrowing what I needed from my mother's trunk. Mrs. Herriot proved a genius at thread and needle and enjoyed altering older gowns into beautiful creations I had no use for.

I started to fold back the canvas that was stretched over the site and pinned with heavy stakes to protect the priceless mosaic from ruin. After it was situated out of our way, I surveyed the field. To my dismay, there were even more new holes than I first realized. Mr. Perry had taken it upon himself to do extra treasure hunting without my guidance.

Abigail winced when she caught my surprised expression. "Don't blame Papa for his zeal. It is likely that he came at dawn to dig by himself."

I mustered my firm voice. "Your father's zeal is commendable, but you must inform him that he'll damage the mosaics or shatter an ancient pot. Patience is a virtue. Such carelessness has ruined many a dig. I've heard horrible tales of men destroying statues with a shovel."

Thankfully, Mr. Perry hadn't disturbed the area around Bacchus. The mosaic appeared relatively untouched. However, at the next freshly dug hole, I sank to my knees, suddenly weak. Beneath the scattered mud were flashes of black and crimson.

While my irritation was still hot with Mr. Perry boldly seeking artifacts on his own—after all, it was his land—I couldn't stifle the excitement rippling through my veins. He had dug deeper into the earth, and whatever was buried here was a good two feet lower than the other one.

The pit was modest, roughly five feet long and three feet wide, with the earth dug down to about two feet, revealing just a corner of the tiles lined with intricate patterns.

I looked over my shoulder at the canvas. "Go back to Bacchus," I choked as I gestured to the tarp. "Count your steps carefully and come back to me."

Abigail frowned, but she did as she was bid, wisps of her blonde hair escaping from a loose chignon. By the time she reached me, we had both counted eighty-three steps.

"This is no ordinary floor," I gasped as I braced myself with my knuckles while tipping forward. "It sits significantly lower than our friend Bacchus. It might even be within a shallow pool. If so, we may uncover a villa encompassing much of your father's field. A palace, if you will."

"A pool?" Abigail knelt beside me to peer into the new hole. "How grand. It's as lovely as a ballroom floor."

My heart sang and all former anxieties were forgotten as I stepped into the space. In my eagerness, I had forgotten my trowel.

"Is it made of jewels?"

"No, it's natural stone, pottery, brick, and tile. Sometimes the Romans used limestone or chalk for soft colors. Purbeck marble for blue and gray, and sandstone for reds and yellows."

I paused, my excitement mounting as my fingers traced the new scrolling pattern. "I've even heard of gold being used."

"La! Gold! We truly found gold at last!" she cried while clapping loudly until the sound echoed across the field.

I imagined Mr. Perry digging faster at the news and flinging shovels of mud. I could not deny the thrill of such a find—not if Father needed money to hire another Bow Street runner to locate Daniel—but caution must be observed.

"I doubt you'll want to claw out that muck with your fingernails." Abigail chuckled as she handed me the trowel. The brush followed, much to my gratitude, then a soft cloth.

"No, indeed," I murmured. Brushing away the mud left only streaks, yet the face of a beautiful woman soon materialized with each brushstroke and a final rub of the cloth. Instead of Bacchus, Medusa's cold eyes and snarling lips stared back at me.

Abigail leaned forward for a better look. "A monster?"

"Medusa, I believe. I've always pitied her. She became an object of men's disdain and cruelty."

Abigail wrinkled her nose as she stared at the Gorgon. "Do I detect a new lecture about to commence?"

Already warming to the subject, a wry chuckle broke free as I fumbled for my satchel and the sketchbook within so I could draw the writhing snakes sprouting from the outraged Gorgon.

"Come now, Abigail. Her story is worth studying since it involves the deepest of betrayals."

A loud groan escaped my friend, but to her credit, she remained by my side with a tolerant twinkle in her eyes.

"Do tell since you will never let me rest until I hear the end of it."

"Medusa served faithfully in the temple of Minerva the goddess of . . . chastity."

Abigail's neck turned a rosy hue at my explanation. I decided to spare my delicate friend the more sordid details. "In that temple, Medusa, who happened to be the most beautiful woman with curling blonde hair—"

"You lie," Abigail interjected as she tugged on a springy curl escaping from her bonnet. Unlike my uncouth locks, which could only be termed a *fright wig* or *frizzled*, her hair matched the perfection of Greek tales.

"Nay, Ovid tells the story quite distinctly. She had blonde hair not unlike yours, although her looks could hardly compare to yours. Unfortunately, one of the gods desired her beauty for himself."

"A male god cursed her?"

I regarded the mosaic, thinking of Neptune's treachery with the beautiful maiden within Minerva's temple. The tale was full of twisted motives and misplaced vengeance.

"Actually, it was Minerva who cursed Medusa with snakes for hair and eyes that turned people to stone when they met her gaze.

Minerva also later sent a favorite hero, Perseus, to behead Medusa. He had no qualms using her asp-covered head as a weapon to quell monsters and men alike." Poor Medusa, ruined and abandoned by the ones she had worshiped. Used and destroyed by her fellow man who ought to have been her hero, instead of her conqueror.

My friend curled her upper lip, not so dissimilar from Medusa's disdainful expression. "Why would a goddess not protect her own?"

A fair question. I had asked it of God when He took Mama away from me during that season we dubbed the Scarlet Spring when so many succumbed to sickness. He had not heard my cries for her when her fingers slipped from my grasp as she breathed her last. Nor had He saved my wayward brother.

Did God even exist in the shadows of so much pain and loss? Was He just as much a myth as my Greek and Roman legends? I didn't know if I could trust a heavenly Father when my earthly father remained so distant.

Such traitorous, rebellious thoughts clogged my soul. Before I could answer Abigail's question, a pounding shook the ground, scattering debris upon the mosaic. I leaped to my full height. Mr. Perry had dug deep enough into the ground that I stood lower than Abigail, but I saw enough to make my blood run cold.

"La! We have company!" Abigail struggled to stand, her slipper catching the edge of her gown.

The large black horse, the one I'd dreaded seeing again, galloped across the fields toward us. I spied the new lord astride, with two other men struggling to keep up.

Although my mind demanded that I should do something . . . *Move* . . . I stood pinned to the spot, helpless as those massive hooves pounded closer and closer.

7

Bridget

> Life is very short and anxious for those who forget the
> past, neglect the present, and fear the future.
> **SENECA**

The viscount halted in front of us, his expression fierce in the sunlight. No, I had not imagined the flash from that narrowed gaze the night before. In fact, I felt the full force of it. Ice mingled with heat.

Despite my resolve to appear fully in control, I shivered beneath that stare.

He glared at me and then at Abigail. "My steward told me I had trespassers in my fields. I scarcely believed my ears, yet here I find two recalcitrants digging holes on *my* property."

The Good Lord gave me a tongue, and I found it just in time. "We're not trespassing. This is Mr. Perry's land."

His eyes widened at my confident answer. Mouth pressed into a line, he swung himself off the horse, but as soon as his boots touched the ground, his left leg buckled. He grabbed the saddle and averted his face. I recognized pain in his face.

"Sir, are you all right?" I called out as I attempted to climb out of the pit to assist him. The wet soil would have none of it, squelching its loud protest, and my soggy leather slippers, better suited to a drawing room, provided no grip. To my chagrin, I stepped on the hem of my dress and staggered forward with my arms flailing in the most undignified way as I fell and Abigail squeaked.

When I tried again to climb out, my feet sank farther into the mud left uncleared. I stumbled and lost my footing. With a clenched jaw, Lord Hawthorn approached me and held out an ungloved hand, for which I stared at him rather stupidly.

"Take it," he ordered. "Or you and I shall be forced to continue our conversation under the present circumstances."

Well, I did not like the idea of him towering over me so much that he blocked out the sun. Of course, he would loom over me regardless, but it was rather difficult to answer a man with confidence while stuck in a hole. And I couldn't climb out without pulling up my gown by a fistful and raising my legs to be viewed. I wouldn't have minded with only Abigail present, but with three men goggling, I had no intention of providing further entertainment.

I blew out an exasperated breath, and after a long pause, wrapped my fingers around his. His hand felt warm as he pulled me from the pit with one strong motion, plunking my slight frame onto the ground beside him.

My mouth suddenly dried. He was strong. Very strong. Yet I could have sworn his skin blanched even with the action.

"I don't believe we have been properly introduced," he said, slightly winded as he released his grip. He brushed his fingers free of the dirt I hadn't even noticed on my appendages. "I am Lord Hawthorn."

"Miss Littleton," I muttered, choking on the following "pleased to meet you" bit.

By then, the other two men had dismounted and joined Lord Hawthorn. I recognized Mr. Whittle immediately, but I had scarcely encountered the other man, with his brown felt hat pulled low over his eyes. I surmised he was the steward, since I had seen him before on the former lord's lands. A Mr. Spencer, if I remembered correctly.

"My lord," Abigail hurried to my side, linking her arm through mine and speaking before I could. "Forgive Miss Littleton and myself. We've been uncovering an—an—agri—an alium?" She shot me a desperate glance, her frown deepening as she struggled with the pronunciation, clearly hoping for my help.

"An atrium, a room used to greet guests, with a pool often in the middle to collect rainwater," I supplied as I wiped my hands on my apron, leaving muddy streaks and drawing the lord's attention again. What lay behind that flickering gaze? Dismissal?

With my stained apron and soggy attire, I was not at my best. "Lord Hawthorn, this is Miss Perry, the daughter of the farmer who owns this field. To echo her, we have discovered something marvelous that will be of significant benefit to your lordship."

The men said not a word, each one staring at me as if snakes or horns sprouted from my head.

I cleared my throat. "It's an ancient Roman mosaic, installed in the floor of a villa, I suspect, though I'm uncertain of the year it was built. Enough time would have had to pass for the Romans to conquer the Iceni tribes and domesticate the valley. However, I think we can estimate a fairly accurate date if we discover pottery or some other household artifact."

Lord Hawthorn's black eyebrows could not have climbed any higher. Without another word, he angled himself at the edge of the hole to better view the newest mosaic. The other men peered at it and exclaimed their surprise.

Mr. Whittle pushed his hat back. "Zounds! Why are there snakes on her head?"

"It's Medusa," Abigail said in a smug tone, raising her chin.

Mr. Whittle blinked at her, then at me. "Medusa?"

"In other words, a troublesome woman, Mr. Whittle." The new lord slanted me a wry look before turning his attention to the other men to explain the mosaic. "A very troublesome woman, should you cross her path, who will turn your heart into stone."

I inhaled sharply. He reminded me of the letter hiding in my desk from the Society of Dilettanti. Full of condescending assurance. But at least he knew something of Roman mythology.

Regardless, I kept my voice light. "Lord Hawthorn, may we continue excavating? I believe we are standing on top of the vast grounds of a palace likely extending into your property. The findings ought to be published in antiquity journals across Europe. In fact, I suspect the Romans quarried the stones used to build your abbey."

I braced myself for an immediate dismissal, but he unfolded those massive arms and stepped closer until I caught a whiff of sandalwood and leather. "If you are asking me permission for access to my property, how large are you assuming the site to be?"

Expecting dismissal, my jaw dropped at his question. "Some Roman villas were as vast as forty thousand square feet, like Sicily's Villa Romana del Casale, known for its elaborate mosaics. And Nero's Golden House, while once covering about three hundred acres in grounds, enclosed a substantial space with its sprawling, frescoed rooms. To think that Mr. Perry stumbled across this with his plow"—I brushed aside an annoying strand of hair determined to blow across my mouth, which drew the lordship's flinty inspection to that area, making me almost lose my train of thought—"it's a-a rare gift for our valley. Did you know that the artists Raphael and Michelangelo crawled underground in the shafts in Rome to study Nero's palace? Their discoveries changed the world of antiquity.

"I believe Mr. Perry's find will do the same. But to ensure that, we need to buy a wagon, horses, and perhaps hire a night guard. Treasure seekers swarmed Fishbourne six years ago after a similar discovery. If we continue the dig, the rewards could be astounding. Bramnor might even host tours, allowing the public to view the mosaics. It would be a tragedy to keep such a prestigious find hidden. We have so much to uncover about the Romans. Who knows what secrets we'll discover?"

I stopped to catch my breath, and a muscle in Lord Hawthorn's jaw jumped. Was that a spark of interest in his eyes?

"How long to complete such a dig?"

An intelligent question, and one that encouraged me considerably.

"It's hard to ascertain. One year. Three years. Perhaps more. It all depends on what we unearth. Of course, there might be nothing more than a few mosaics on Mr. Perry's land."

He shoved a hand through his midnight hair, which remained shorn as befitting a military man. "Miss Littleton, as intriguing as your proposal sounds, I have other plans for my estate. Plans that will bring a reliable income to the valley."

A vein throbbed in my temple. Surely, I could somehow save this unraveling situation.

"Aye, the Good Lord made these fields to be planted and this grass above for sheep," Mr. Whittle interjected as he jammed his thick hands into his coat pockets and rocked on his heels. "And for orchards and rye. Not for jabbing around in the dirt for a bit of tile. Don't you be pestering his lordship with such fangled notions, miss. The lordship has only just returned, and he's got more than enough to deal with at the moment."

"Your lordship." I drew out the title as carefully as I could. "My proposal will bring excellent income for all involved. I only need permission to explore further. With the right benefactor to fund the project, and I'm certain you are the—"

"No."

His blunt answer sliced me to the quick.

"No?"

Instead of answering, he turned and motioned for the men to return with him. "Check the borders of the property, Mr. Spencer, and be certain that we possess this section. Otherwise, we are finished here."

Mr. Spencer's mouth curved in the most unpleasant manner. "Miss Perry, you run along and tell your father to keep to his side. I've warned your family before, and we'll not do it again. Not unless you want the full force of the law pressing down on you."

Abigail cried out, but desperation propelled me forward to follow the new viscount. I had no trouble keeping up with his uneven stride as he reached the great onyx horse, who waited patiently. I withheld a shiver as I approached. I'd hated horses since that awful accident with my brother.

As Lord Hawthorn swung himself into the saddle, whatever pity I might have felt for his injury dissipated at the coldness in his manner.

"Please, sir, imagine the accolades and national interest you would achieve!"

He leaned over, his saddle creaking, affording me a view of his eyes. Not the hue of ebony as I had assumed last twilight, but polished mahogany gleaming in the sunlight, and just as hard. Each word was enunciated with exaggerated care.

"Miss Littleton, I do not want acclaim. Nor do I want my land crawling with greedy men. I want to—how is it you so delicately put it?—be an improvement and tend to my community's needs. I suggest you stay on your side of the fence from hence forth."

With that curt answer, he bent low and muttered a curse, then urged his horse to gallop. Speechless, I could only gape at his flight and flair for dramatics.

"A vicar's daughter ought to be visiting the sick." Mr. Whittle shook his head, tsk-tsking and drawing my attention away from the lord. "She ought to be in service to her community, not running around chasing after buried rubble and childish notions." He grabbed his reins and tried to place his foot in the stirrup, albeit far less gracefully than his lord had done only moments before. The bay horse edged forward, leaving him to hop with it. He finally swung himself onto the saddle with a loud plunk as Mr. Spencer followed suit on the other horse.

Mr. Whittle tipped his hat, his mouth curved into an amused line. "Many plans are in play, miss. Oh yes, you'll see soon enough. Our viscount will be the one to make things right again within our valley. Don't be pestering for money or wagons and taking men from their work because of foolish dreams. It won't do. Not at all."

I threw up my hands in disgust as they left. Instead of impressing the viscount, I had further bungled my case.

Abigail chewed her bottom lip, her arms folded across her middle, appearing like a chastened child. "That went rather . . ."

"Abysmally," I supplied as I descended once more into the pit to retrieve my tools. I slid them into my pocket and motioned for her to assist me.

"Er, yes." She eyed me with dismay, then held out one calloused hand and then the other, and with the most unladylike grunt, pulled me up onto the level ground. To assist her, I jammed my foot into the soaked dirt and heaved myself out, a disheveled, sweating mess, revealing plenty of ankle and ruining my stockings.

Meanwhile, my heart sank. I had utterly failed in my quest.

I might have bluestocking tendencies, but even I knew a lady had only one opportunity to impress, whether on the ballroom floor or amid a farmer's mucky field. As Abigail and I gathered our tools, frustration welled inside me. We had no choice but to stop for now—at least until we heard back from the Society of Antiquaries. Then, perhaps, we'd have the ammunition to defy Lord Hawthorn.

8

Bridget

> For many men, the acquisition of wealth does not
> end their troubles, it only changes them.
> **SENECA**

The next morning, I dressed with extra care in case I encountered anyone of interest during my errands in town. Mrs. Herriot always reminded me of the power of a woman's attire *to cut a dash*. Today, I willingly took her advice. I needed all the ammunition I could gather. A pale-blue muslin dress with a delicate lace fichu and a sapphire pelisse trimmed in velvet suited the cool spring weather. My poke bonnet, topped with monstrous ostrich feathers, completed the ensemble.

A silly amount of effort for one man, my mind chided without pity as I set out for town.

Despite my best efforts, I briefly pivoted from the path leading to Bramnor to stare in the direction of Hawthorn Abbey and that singular man. During my walk, I recalled Lord Hawthorn's curt response to my pleas. Not even walking past the charming fifteenth-century houses, nor the whitewashed cottages with thatched roofs and ivy creeping up the side, could improve my mood.

I pushed open the door to the apothecary and was greeted by the tinkling of a brass bell hanging overhead. A young man measured out a vial of clear liquid while a plump woman in a gray pelisse and matching bonnet waited near the counter. I recognized Jonathan Cording, the apothecary's youngest son, who was about my age.

He smiled when he saw me, and the woman glanced over her shoulder, her gaze distracted. Mrs. Whittle, the housekeeper of Hawthorn Abbey. Beside her stood a thin man with a beaver hat and reddish hair curled and plastered against his shiny forehead in the latest style. His emerald waistcoat gleamed in the sunlight as he fidgeted with a silver watch fob, his gaze fixed on Mrs. Whittle.

Jim Barron, innkeeper and owner of the Jolly Wench and the man Abigail entertained thoughts of marrying. I swallowed my amusement at his attempt to appear a Corinthian. The man leaned forward as if an intimate friend to the housekeeper.

"Oh, Mrs. Whittle!" Mr. Barron gushed, nearly knocking over a jar of herbal remedies as he gestured broadly. "Fancy meeting you here! I was just admiring the new confectionery. Have you tried the peppermint creams? They're positively delightful!"

Mrs. Whittle's eyes widened. "Peppermint creams? No, I—"

"You must try them, Mrs. Whittle!" He leaned in slightly, lowering his voice as if sharing a grand secret. "I hear they're good for digestion and sweeten one's breath. Perhaps your husband would enjoy them?"

"Er . . . I suppose, but I'm here on other matters, Mr. Barron." She frowned.

He gestured to the row of glass jars. "I'm also here for some tonic. A chill in the air has given me the sniffles. But what brings you to the apothecary? Not any trouble at the abbey, I hope?"

Mrs. Whittle's plump face reddened as she cast a quick glance at the counter. "I . . . I've come on behalf of Lord Hawthorn. Nothing to concern yourself with, Mr. Barron."

"Oh, but I do concern myself! It's in my nature, you know." He chuckled, fingering his lace cuffs. "We all must look after one another in these parts. And after all, I hear the new lord is quite the war hero. Injured according to the rumors, yes? Surely a man like that doesn't need laudanum?" He gestured to a glass vial on the counter.

I despised laudanum. It dulled the senses and proved nearly impossible to quit. I had seen the results too many times among the villagers. My mother had refused it even when dying of scarlet fever, preferring her own blend of herbs to manage the pain.

Was the laudanum for the viscount?

Mrs. Whittle drew back. "Lord Hawthorn's affairs are his own, Mr. Barron."

"Ah, yes, yes. Of course," he soothed. "But if there's anything the good Lord Hawthorn needs to soothe his suffering—brandy perhaps, or some company during those long nights—I'd be more than happy to oblige. Nothing does the soul and body so much good as excellent company."

Moving past the shelves lined with tinctures and powders, I waited my turn while pretending to study the vast array of medicinal supplies. Of course, Mr. Barron would find a way to ingratiate himself with the new lord. If only I could witness the viscount's expression when he encountered Bramnor's premier dandy.

"I also have the marshmallow root you ordered. You can't be too careful these days. The Aster family remains under quarantine for fever," Mr. Cording informed Mrs. Whittle.

Tension coiled in my belly at the proclamation. Fever again? Was it the dreaded scarlet fever that had stolen so much from me? It would take Father away on his many errands of mercy. I swallowed a sigh, resolved to spend more evenings alone at the dinner table.

Mr. Cording lowered his voice, unable to hide his stutter. "Is the new lord t-truly a hero from B-B-Bussaco? I've heard so many different tales, I cannot make out what is true and what is fable. I heard he was shot in the leg."

Her hands fluttered to her fichu, but her expression brightened immediately. I held my breath as I slipped farther into the cool interior, my ears finely attuned to hear anything of interest.

"Yes, he's a hero. Noted by Wellington himself, though he rarely speaks of what happened."

Mr. Barron tsk-tsked. "It's a shame how the viscount was injured."

"It's only temporary, the lord insists. Isn't his return a blessing, gentlemen? Lord Hawthorn has many plans for the old abbey. Why, imagine the apples and cider business booming once again and the—"

"Cider. How exciting," Mr. Barron interrupted, his eyes flashing. "Why, my customers would beg for more, if it is as good as the old days."

"Indeed!" Mrs. Whittle's smile stretched wider. She leaned in close, her dingy bonnet shielding her face. "I'm not one to share the viscount's plans, but I believe he's hoping to brew once he receives a new cider press. If you know of anyone needing work, send them to my husband."

"Such good news." Mr. Barron nodded firmly. "Let us hope a turn of fortunes will chase the old spirits out of the abbey once and for all, and may the new lord sleep peacefully without nightmares or haunting spirits."

"Mr. Barron!" Mrs. Whittle sounded horrified as she stretched to her full height. "How can you make such a salacious claim?"

By then, I had crept forward on my kid slippers without realizing how far I had traversed.

He chuckled. "Dear lady, your lovely daughter crossed my path early this morning during one of my country walks, and she happened to mention that the new lord cried out around midnight, as regular as clockwork. Something bloodcurdling. Of course, I detest gossip, but one does care about the state of the Hawthorn family, considering the old lord's peculiar nature. And, of course, I share this as a friend. Perhaps you could have a word with her about trusting whom she speaks with, eh? It's she who is convinced that ghosts have returned to the abbey to haunt it."

Mrs. Whittle sputtered again, clearly speechless at the accusation of impropriety leveled at her daughter.

Mr. Cording planted both palms on the counter. "We all know that madness and death cling to that abbey. Didn't the Hawthorn brothers quarrel, with one later dying in an inn? Convenient, if you ask me. I've always said secrets lie buried on those grounds. And the old lord wasn't right in his mind, no matter what the good vicar says. *He* murdered his brother, aye? How many other bodies lie buried on his land since the law cannot touch a viscount?"

"Mr. Cording, I'll take some chamomile tea if you have a moment," I spoke up to spare Mrs. Whittle from answering. How unfortunate that the truth was so often mingled with lies within this superstitious village. I doubted the old viscount had killed his brother. He had more than enough sins to blacken his soul without that extra embellishment. I had no patience for slander.

Mrs. Whittle snatched her supplies from the counter. "I really must be off. Oh, Miss Littleton! I hope I'll see you and the good vicar at the abbey soon for a visit."

I smiled, although it felt a mask. I planned to see the parishioners, not the lord. Although . . . the idea of poking him further, especially after his command, might prove somewhat entertaining.

"Please, Mrs. Whittle," Mr. Cording called out as she began to leave. "I must insist on payment. I'll take no more credit until Hawthorn Abbey settles its debts."

Now mottled red, Mrs. Whittle returned to the counter and paid for her items, then bustled out the door with only a harried nod in my direction.

"Miss Littleton, I haven't seen you in ages." Mr. Cording's blond hair fell over his brow in tight curls, no less tame than my own, though he tried to smooth them as I approached the counter.

I opened my beaded reticule and pushed across several shillings while doing my best to ignore Mr. Barron's intense stare.

"I've been rather busy of late."

"Miss Littleton found something in Mr. Perry's field," Mr. Cording said as he pivoted to retrieve two glass jars from a pristine shelf. I watched him scoop the fine brown tea leaves and slide them into the smaller tin.

"Ah." Mr. Barron sidled up closer to me until his sleeve brushed mine, much to my ire. "Mr. Perry mentioned something about an old Roman site when he stopped by the inn. I should like to see what you've uncovered." His gaze flicked over me, and he added with a chuckle, "Can't say I've ever seen a lady do a man's work, digging up dirt."

His eagerness was palpable, and I couldn't help but groan inwardly at the thought of Mr. Barron trying to impress Abigail with his newfound interest in antiquities. Worse still, he had encroached on my personal space in a manner that most gentlemen would avoid.

"We've found lovely patterns made of tile from an old settlement worthy of a museum." I forced a smile while I opened my reticule to deposit the tin of tea inside. "You do visit museums, don't you, Mr. Barron, Mr. Cording? I would think any educated gentleman would have a healthy interest in history."

Mr. Cording and Mr. Barron both gaped, but I plunked the coins on the counter and turned on my heel and reached the door as quickly as I could before anything else popped out of my mouth that I would later regret.

Outside the apothecary, the morning sun shone bright in my eyes, momentarily blinding me despite my poke bonnet. A form brushed against me, stopping me in my tracks.

"Miss Littleton, I have offended you. I must beg your forgiveness." A contrite Mr. Barron stood before me with hat doffed.

My heart softened a smidgen. "No matter, Mr. Barron. All is forgiven."

"If you need any assistance, you'll ask for my help? I do count the vicar as a friend. And hopefully Lord Hawthorn one day soon as well."

I tensed at the thought of the prickly lord. "It may not hold interest to you unless you admire old pottery and fragments of an ancient floor." Caution made me color the find in the blandest of hues.

His brow furrowed. "If I may be so bold, there have been unsavory types wandering these parts—men with no work heading to London. One can't be too careful. Mr. Perry might find himself in need of a guard or two to watch over things and assist with the excavation. And of course, I'd be more than happy to lend a hand."

I paused at the image of Abigail and me mostly alone within the field, with nary a person close by to hear us scream. A shudder rippled from one shoulder to the other, but I kept my voice firm. "I may not be able to dig much longer. In fact, there seems to be some misunderstanding that a portion of Mr. Perry's field might belong to the Hawthorn estate. I don't believe it to be true, of course. Mr. Perry's family has owned that farm for the past seventy-three years."

Mr. Barron's expression changed, the left side of his mouth tilting in a rueful smile. "How unfortunate. My recommendation is to involve the magistrate at once and assess the boundary lines. I believe the former Lord Hawthorn had a tendency of taking what didn't belong to him. I hate to speak ill of the dead, but I would defend Mr. Perry's right to use his land as he sees fit."

"Thank you, Mr. Barron. Excellent advice."

He preened before stopping on the road cutting through the heart of Bramnor. "You will extend my offer of assistance to Miss Perry as well?"

A grin broke free at his enthusiasm. His reason for asking about the dig must be motivated by my friend. I liked him a little better for wishing to impress her, even if I found his taste in fashion to be that of a coxcomb.

I nodded and bid him good day, then hurried on my way, pondering all the gossip I had heard—the laudanum and the ghosts and the interest in the dig. The more people who learned of the discoveries in the Perry field, the more muddied the situation became.

I blew out a long breath to steady my nerves as I considered my next visit. Mrs. Eacher's cottage was on Lord Hawthorn's land. At least today I was prepared with my new bonnet.

But surely I wouldn't run into the peevish lord again. That would be far too much for the Fates to spin.

9

Bridget

> Leisure without books is death,
> and burial of a man alive.
> **SENECA**

My visits with Mrs. Eacher were always enjoyable. I could usually be myself around her and never perceived judgment reflected from her filmy eyes. She peered into the hearts of men and women better than most, yet rarely said a word of condemnation, instead plying them with tea while offering a seat by her fire.

We were both satisfied with the developments of our shared story, *The Mysteries of Udolpho*. I tucked the book into my satchel after closing the door behind me, torn about leaving the safety of my friend's cozy cottage to head home. I had stayed longer than planned, discussing my brother. When Mrs. Eacher asked me to lead in prayer, I muttered rote phrases, but when her blue-veined hand clasped mine, a tear slipped free.

Bridget . . . my sweet Bridget, your heavenly Father sees your concerns. Surely you can take these burdens to Him and trust His provision. She could not see the emotions no doubt twisting my features as I muttered that it was late and I must be on my way. I, however, saw the flash of disappointment play across her face.

Time wasn't a luxury I had. And I was tired of discussing my pressing concerns with a mute God.

As I walked away, a harsh wind picked up, matching my mood, tempered with the tangy sweet scent of coming rain. The long grass brushed against my skirt as the storm gathered. I took the quickest route through Lord Hawthorn's estate, doubting he'd see me in such foul weather. Surely he hunkered within that great dining room with the deer head frozen on the wall as he sipped claret or port or whatever it was he preferred.

Chagrined that I would think of him at all, I defiantly marched across the winding trail beaten into the grass, past the fields and the apple trees offering a boundary line.

Thunder cracked above my head, and I jumped, already nervous of the incoming storm. If I hated horses, I hated storms just as much.

I hastened along the path, and the moment I reached the farthest edge of Mr. Perry's field, the heavens broke loose, roaring with fury and sending sheets of rain that formed pools in the indentations of the field. Already my best slippers were soaked and likely ruined. My embroidered blue hem was splattered with mud, and the once jaunty ostrich feathers on my bonnet drooped forward in defeat. I would never hear the end of ruining my best outfit. Vanity of vanities, to wear my prettiest gown in the rare happenstance that I might encounter Lord Hawthorn. How foolish to think I could ever come close to a diamond of the first water and impress anyone at all. What I needed was a pair of sensible boots and more dresses the color of mud.

Then another fear—beyond destroying fashion and dealing with the formidable Mrs. Herriot—took hold, forcing me to lift my skirts and dart across the mucky field. The mosaics! Surely the rain would ruin the progress Abigail and I had made in uncovering them. I had persuaded Mr. Perry to cover each section with canvas and dipped into my meager funds to purchase the supplies.

As I reached the dig site, my lungs straining for air, I spied a large puddle forming in the center of the canvas covering the Medusa mosaic. Worse, one of the stakes securing the canvas appeared loose, promising an imminent waterfall when its hold released. Then the pool would indeed fulfill its original purpose.

I pulled on the stake, ignoring my white gloves now streaked with filth. Grunting, I tried to stomp on it to sink it farther into the ground and stretch the canvas tighter, but the weight of the water puddling in the middle proved too much for me.

"Miss Littleton! Is that you?" a deep male voice shouted across the field. I groaned, then slipped and fell in an undignified heap of lace-trimmed skirts.

A black shape trotted across the field until I found myself staring through the downpour at the colossal horse and its owner.

Lord Hawthorn scowled beneath the dripping wide brim of his felt hat as he surveyed me, then the site. Another coat, this one in gray, made him appear more farmer than lord, although no less intimidating sitting astride his obsidian beast.

"Lord Hawthorn, what a delightful evening for a walk," I shouted over the rain from my muddy seat.

I kept my tone fearless although embarrassment coursed through me as he continued to study me. Embarrassment turned to alarm when the canvas sagged farther, pouring water on the mosaic and filling the ancient pool with a gush.

"Medusa will be ruined!' I cried, struggling to rise and secure the loosened stake, though it was hopeless.

Suddenly, I was aware of a great form looming over me, a hand reaching over mine and tugging on the stake with a strength I could not match. Without a word, he shoved it into the ground, although I feared that the damage had already been done.

He glanced down at me, his gaze tightening when I ignored the hand he held out to assist me. Unfortunately, my limp feathers chose that particular moment to flop back over my face after I tried to brush them out of the way. At the very least, I managed to rise on my own, flinging the mud from my hands. Even though I pivoted away from him, a speck or two must have landed on his coat.

"Miss Littleton, we must stop meeting under such circumstances."

"I find nothing more invigorating than being outside in nature."

"No drawing room or gentler pursuits for you."

I huffed loudly, forcing the ostrich feathers to puff away. "No, Lord Hawthorn. But it would appear we both prefer the great outdoors to musty interiors."

He nodded once. "True enough. This wicked storm caught Chaucer and me on our way home from visiting tenants, but I've encountered worse on the battlefield. Although, I doubt either of us should linger. There isn't much more you or I can do to secure the canvas. It won't protect your pool, not without additional center stakes to prop up the weight."

I felt ever more the fool for not having consideredsuch a factor.

"But I can't abandon her to the elements," I sputtered as I gestured to the sagging tarp. The wind turned cold and stinging, and despite my best effort, I started to shiver in my drenched gown, plastered to my form. Rain dripped down my back, but I was loath to leave the site until I could assess the extent of the damage.

"I suspect Medusa will survive a bit of rain," he said. "She has endured far greater trials. You, on the other hand . . . Forgive my bluntness, but I thought we had come to an understanding that you would leave my field alone."

"Mr. Perry's field, sir. And as my memory serves, I agreed to no such terms. When the magistrate assures me otherwise, I will continue on as Mr. Perry's guest in the manner I see fit."

To my surprise, his lips quirked ever so slightly.

"And that will include wandering the fields alone again, I see."

"If you must know, I visited a blind widow on your property and was caught by the storm on my way home. I often help my father with his pastoral visits."

The rain poured even harder, blurring the man before me. I glanced at the horse, nervous that it might bolt or worse, but it appeared steadier than I was at the moment. Perhaps it was used to hardship, like its grim owner.

"Widow?" He frowned as he stepped closer to me. "One of my tenants?"

I frowned as well. "Surely you plan to visit all the tenants, including my father, the vicar, who enjoyed the patronage of your uncle."

His jaw clenched. "I have been making my rounds. The Hawthorn holdings are rather vast and spread out in distance, but I have not had the pleasure of meeting this widow. In fact, I'm just returning from the Dillon cottage. What is her name?"

As for my father, the viscount made no mention. Had I ruined the relationship between them with my singular pursuit of antiquities?

"Mrs. Eacher," I responded more curtly than I ought thanks to Lord Hawthorn's blunt manner, but I felt protective of my friend, and I hoped she would not be the last on his list. Many would consider her a burden.

He sucked in a sharp breath through his teeth, as if the name were personal to him.

"You know her?" I demanded as I brushed aside the ridiculous dripping ostrich feather a third time.

He nodded, flicking raindrops from his hat in my direction. "I often stopped to see her when I was a child. She is blind, you say?"

"For the past ten years, her vision has faded until she can only discern a piercing of light through the shadows. I read to her whenever I am free. I do hope your ban of me will not include calling on the parishioners. My father spends a great deal of his day fulfilling the needs of your people."

I wanted to further prod the viscount on whether he had met my father or not, but a sizzling bolt struck a nearby tree, far too close, and the resulting boom made the horse flick its ears backward.

Lord Hawthorn glanced over his shoulder then back at me. "Come, Miss Littleton. We cannot dicker over fields and land boundaries within this sodden field. I suspect neither of us will survive the exchange if we linger."

"I'm but a few miles to home," I said quickly, my pulse racing at the thought of riding with him.

He shook his head. "I cannot let you walk home in such inclement weather. Allow me to give you a ride."

"A highly improper suggestion, sir. I know my way. I've traversed these hills alone for years."

"Propriety be hanged in this moment since neither of us cares for it. Clearly your adventurous spirit doesn't balk at the idea of wandering at night, but mine does." He reached for the reins of his horse. "Who knows what would befall you? You are soaked through as if you swam in a lake. Meanwhile, several tenants of mine are stricken with fever. What kind of gentleman would I be if I let you walk in the elements when I have a perfectly good horse?"

More lightning flashed white against the blackening sky, highlighting the sharp planes of the man before me. Sobered by the mention of illness once again sweeping through the valley, I considered his admonishment while fidgeting with the satchel slung over my shoulder, which by now, must be quite sodden. I feared the condition of my precious book.

But to ride a horse... and with *him*, no less.

"Please, Miss Littleton, a truce. At least allow me to escort you home," he gentled his voice. "Shall I put you on Chaucer and lead you home?"

I eyed the large animal beside the viscount and stepped backward. It snickered and tossed its head as if to protest at such an indignity. I couldn't deny that a walk would take far too long in this weather.

Lord Hawthorn eyed me as if to pierce my thoughts. "Chaucer is a gentle soul at heart. He won't hurt you. Nor will I."

"Chaucer, after the poet," I murmured. "That is an adventurer's name."

"He loved chivalry, truth, and honor," Lord Hawthorn replied, *"freedom..."*

"And courtesy," I added, recognizing the familiar words about the knight in *The Canterbury Tales*.

The viscount nodded with another barest hint of a smile. I found I almost liked it, despite my better judgment. How would a smile in full bloom change his stern features?

A sigh escaped me. "For the sake of my book, which is in danger of becoming waterlogged, and the glaring fact that Mrs. Eacher will never forgive me if I do not finish the ending, I accept your offer."

He swung up on the horse, more limber than the first day I had seen him. Then he reached out and pulled me up to sit in front of him in one easy swoop that managed to knock the air out of my lungs.

The arm that held me felt as strong as an iron gladius. I had never ridden so close to someone, not where I could feel each breath he inhaled and smell the sandalwood clinging to his damp skin. Again, the gossip I had overheard in the apothecary swirled within my mind. Lord Hawthorn's father had been murdered and the surviving uncle deemed a rakehell.

Despite my boldness at accepting a ride, a tremor rippled through me. I did not know this man and I was certain to hear of my indiscretion as soon as I arrived. My only consolation was that, as usual, Father would not be home, and hopefully Mrs. Herriot remained occupied with her embroidery.

"Does this mean we are not at war, Miss Littleton?" The viscount's warm breath brushed against the back of my neck as he guided Chaucer away from Medusa's pool. My skin turned to gooseflesh in response.

"War? Whatever do you mean? Unless you wish to unfairly advance on Mr. Perry's land, then yes, I shall raise the banner and do what I must to preserve the mosaics. They belong in a museum."

A low chuckle rumbled behind me, but I dared not pivot to see his expression, for I would be far too close to those mahogany eyes likely glittering with amusement at my expense. Instead, I clenched my teeth, weary of being dismissed for my notions.

"You are singularly determined to uncover the past. Why?" he asked after a pause.

I swallowed hard as I tugged at my blue pelisse, yet any semblance of modesty was proving harder and harder to attain with the thin fabric clinging to my legs as if I were Aphrodite rising from the sea. Why had I agreed to this ride? Surely, I could have bought another copy of my book on the next visit to London.

I had planned to make my defense of the dig within the safety of a parlor over tea and shortbread, not riding horseback during a storm with the brooding lord pressed against my back and his left arm about my waist. How uncomfortable, especially now that the rain had lessened somewhat, dripping down my nose and that horrid feather that refused to stay in place.

Yet, his question dug into the quiet corners of my heart, unearthing a strange rush of emotions.

"I believe the past should be studied so we can avoid the same errors today," I began. A rote, comfortable answer. Then, I added softly, "But the study of antiquities is more than a lesson. A story waits to be uncovered. I brush against lives spent in tragedy and loss and beauty and joy. Someone laid the mosaics of that pool with the greatest of care. A woman likely trailed her fingers in it on a hot summer day while dreaming of her future. Children laughed and played near it. When I discover something lost, no longer seen and without use, it brings a sense of . . ." *Wonder. Wholeness. Purpose.* "They are not forgotten. They are no longer unseen or uncared for," I finished, albeit lamely.

Clutching the pommel, I halted lest I share more than I had intended. The man behind me made no reply, but he shifted ever so slightly, brushing unintentionally against me as we trotted toward the parsonage. My pulse stuttered in response.

"You are quite the romantic, Miss Littleton. No wonder you wander the countryside like a woodland sprite in search of her fairy glen. How fortunate I am to have found you on such a dismal evening before your gossamer wings took ruin."

His remark pricked more than it ought to. I ought to be used to being either ignored or forgotten while being left to my own devices. I was certainly used to being dismissed as fanciful. Did he mean the comparison to a woodland sprite as an insult, or had he only meant to clumsily flatter me?

"You have quite a remarkable history at Hawthorn Abbey." I tried to change the subject and take the focus off myself, but as soon as the words left my mouth, I knew I had made a mistake. Immediately, the arms about me tensed.

"That is to say, the abbey must hold fascinating stories reaching back to the monks who lived there. And then, before the abbey, the Saxons . . ." I hurried to add.

"Yes, a long history," he finally agreed, his voice rough.

"Have you studied the history of your home?" I finally relented to my insatiable curiosity as he led Chaucer down a flooded path.

A puff of air, as if he sighed, brushed the back of my neck where a stray curl or two lay plastered against my skin.

"I have always thought the past was better left buried. Some things are not meant to be known."

I wanted to ask more, but from the rigidness in his arms and the weariness in his voice, the topic remained forbidden, as if carefully secured within a locked box.

"I see the parsonage ahead," he said.

In the distance, golden lights spilled from the multipaned windows set within the thick whitewashed walls, illuminating a stone path lined with wildflowers. Along with my father's parked chaise.

Oh dear. Considering the previous exchange, I had made no effort to include myself in calling on Lord Hawthorn, preferring to leave the duty to my father. Had he called in my absence?

Lord Hawthorn secured his grip on my waist and for one startled moment, I turned and glanced at him, helpless to resist. Water droplets sluiced down his cheek and dripped off his chin. But his eyes . . . A long moment stretched between us until he deposited me on a muddy stretch of grass.

"Thank you," I said, feeling disoriented. "For the ride."

The front door to the parsonage flung open, and there stood my father, his eyes bright and owlish from behind his round glasses and his cravat mussed as always. I could only imagine the questions swarming within his mind.

"Lord Hawthorn, a pleasure." Father sounded strained as he stood in the doorway instead of Molly, our maid, or Mrs. Herriot. Unconventional to say the least, but I was not one to judge considering the state of my arrival. "You have brought my daughter safely home. Please, come in from this horrid storm and let me properly thank you."

Lord Hawthorn made no move to dismount. Instead, he gathered the reins. "Perhaps another day, vicar. I found your daughter on Hawthorn land. Miss Littleton has been most persistent in her efforts to uncover unusual antiquities."

"Lord Hawthorn—" I began, fully intending to defend Mr. Perry's right to his property, but the viscount held up a hand, which only made my ire boil hotter. I was no minion of the Navy or military to be ordered about.

"Good evening to you both." Lord Hawthorn tilted his head in Father's direction, cutting my protest.

"I called upon you earlier, but you were not home. I should like to meet with you at your earliest convenience." Father shot me a warning look to hold my tongue.

Lord Hawthorn edged his massive horse back onto the beaten path. "I've been rather busy of late meeting the tenants, some who are ill."

"I would be happy to go with you and provide any assistance you might need," Father offered as he stepped beyond the door and into the rain. A wounded look flashed across his face and, judging from his tone, he had been surprised at the rebuff of his services.

"Soon," the viscount said through gritted teeth as he swung his horse around. Chaucer snorted and I ducked out of the way, but not before the viscount smiled grimly at me. "Now that ride on Chaucer was nothing to fear, Miss Littleton, was it?"

I did not reply, far too aware of the tension sizzling between the lord and his vicar and me. Nor could I dismiss the fact that I had indeed accepted a ride with a man, unchaperoned.

After the sound of galloping faded, Father eyed my disheveled state. For a long moment, he said nothing, just stared.

10

Bridget

> What profit hath a man of all his labour
> which he taketh under the sun?
>
> **ECCLESIASTES 1:3**

As the sun sank into the horizon after I was sufficiently dried and had endured a lecture from Father on propriety with men, I sat at my desk with a quill in hand. The Dilettanti letter lay open to my right, the creases still crisp despite the years passed. I could scarcely bring myself to reread the derisive words from Mr. Thomas Beaumont's secretary. The words remained branded in my mind. Yet I glanced at the paper again, the elegant slope of the handwriting impeccable.

I scratched out several letters, dissatisfied with each attempt at a second plea for publication. Balled papers filled the bin beside my desk. Frustrated, I twiddled the feathered pen between my fingers while rereading my latest effort.

Too desperate. Too strongly worded and certain to be rejected. Too weak. Finally, I kept to the simplest approach.

I have found what I believe to be a mosaic in a sizable Roman villa, perhaps third century...

I also drafted a letter to the more formal Society of Antiquaries, located at Somerset House within the apartments courtesy of King George III, but I dared not hope for an answer from them, especially after their prior silence years ago. I suspected they would throw out my letter upon receipt when they discovered a simple country miss was the author. Regardless, I addressed it, referencing the latest journal of *Archeologia*, even if my knees shook when I signed my name. One missive for the young bucks who loved adventure and one for the white-haired scholars who hid in their libraries. Perhaps I might even stimulate a competition between the two groups.

As I held a cylinder of crimson wax over my candle, my mind wandered.

I had wrongly assumed the younger Lord Hawthorn would want prestige, to be known as a gentleman with a vast collection of ancient art, just like the aristocratic dilettanti who gallivanted across Europe and the Middle East, hunting for treasure. Their reputation for scholarly pursuit had led to the sponsorship of many unusual antiquarian expeditions and the documentation of newly rediscovered classical sites.

Truly, the process felt no different from a debutante seeking entrance at the Almack's Assembly Rooms, where a group of snobbish women, known as the "Lady Patronesses," issued invitations and determined who might attend the events. I had not a single chance in all the world of entering Almack's. No doubt, I fooled myself into thinking I could entice or impress either the Dilettanti or the Society of Antiquaries.

I had hoped to publish my findings and earn that fifty pounds so tantalizingly offered by *Archeologia*. I nudged aside the nearest letter with the cooling wax seal and removed my art journal from beneath a stack of history books. After flipping open the pages, I thumbed past several notes regarding the dig, along with illustrations, until I reached a clean sheet. I grabbed a piece of charcoal and began scratching out an image.

Instead of sheep munching grass, or pillared ruins, or even a dominus, a man's face started to take shape, followed by a hint of a shadow along a firm jaw.

Lord Hawthorn.

I put my charcoal stick down. Why had I ever thought to tempt him with fame? His derision scalded me. He was a private man, it seemed. Ambitious, too, and not afraid of trade, unlike his fellow lords. A smudge of charcoal, and I darkened the new lord's eyebrows into something nefarious. He looked devilishly handsome now. A proper rake, with a contemptuous curl to his lips.

If I could convince either society to take interest in the history of Bramnor, perhaps then Lord Hawthorn might be more receptive to my cause.

I had nothing to lose in trying again with my letters.

No, not true.

I had *everything* to lose.

11

Rafe

> That's one of the greatest curses ever inflicted
> on the human race, memory.
> **OVID**

The mist enveloped me once again, swirling with tendrils as if it were a living thing. And with it came the ghosts.

I shook my head to clear the visions, yet I remained pinned on the mountain. I could not escape, helpless to see events play out once more.

'Tis only a dream, I warned myself. *Wake up, you fool.* Sometimes the plea worked and I would wake up, drenched in sweat, my leg aching. Other times . . .

The fog lifted as the morning sun cleaved the ridge, revealing the shadowy shapes of the advancing enemy. The French. So many of them. Though I braced for battle, I couldn't prevent a shudder.

"Fire!" I at last screamed. Dimly I heard Lewis's shouts to do the same.

Guns blasted, the smoke acrid, stinging my nostrils. The twelve cannons belched flames and fumes even as the French scurried to change from the formation of a column into a line.

I was not a coward. I wouldn't tolerate defeat.

Yet even as the French fell, bile crawled at the back of my throat at the sight of so much blood and destruction. But orders were orders. I yelled again, the battle cry scarcely recognizable. Lewis charged alongside me, faithful as ever. Lewis, my dear friend, whom I'd sworn to his pregnant wife, Mildred, I would protect with my life. Lewis, who died in these dreams.

I collapsed, a bullet ripping into my lower calf and hobbling me when I reached for the man who had been like a brother. But his eyes were glazed and unseeing, his throat a mangled mess. I had indeed failed him. How could I forgive myself when I lived, alone in the world, while he died with a family left behind?

I cried his name again, and rough hands shook me.

"Blast it, I cannot wake him!"

I jerked awake to Mr. Whittle's concerned face.

"Forgive me, my lord," he said, gripping the bedpost. "You were hollering, and my wife bid me check on you."

A breath escaped me as I sat up, the sheets and coverlet a tangled mess about my legs. I no longer stood on the ridge. Instead, the four stalwart posts of the bed surrounded me, reminding me that it was my third day in Bramnor.

Plunging a hand through my hair, I tried to even my breathing and my racing pulse. "I'm all right. In the future, please inform your wife that there's nothing to be alarmed about. It would be better to let me be."

He took an enormous step away from the bed. "Of course, my lord. Perhaps my daughter's tales of spirits have us all spooked. Might I commend you on a wicked hook? You nearly took out my jaw."

A red welt appeared on the left side of his stubbled chin. He rubbed the spot with a rueful smile.

"Ah," I said, at a loss for words as embarrassment heated my skin. "It's my turn to apologize." The dream had haunted my steps all the way to Bramnor. I had alarmed plenty of innkeepers at the midnight hour.

"I've met men from battle who've gone through similar. War is an ugly affair. It never leaves you." He offered an awkward bow. "Breakfast awaits at your leisure."

I nodded, still too caught up in the nightmare. That morning, September 27, 1810, would forever remain branded in my mind. Although I had received an honorable discharge and sold my commission, I couldn't shake my grief. Or my dereliction to keep those I cared about safe.

My friends were few, and those who stayed with me, I kept for life.

I had no one to rely on. No one at all, save an overfamiliar groundskeeper and his odd family.

I shrugged into clean britches and a coat from the warped wardrobe, thinking of my mother's reliance on God during the hardest seasons. How had she retained hope in the midst of so much suffering? The more I spent time within the abbey, a place of so much sorrow, the more I thought of her. Resolve filled me not to let my father's legacy taint me any further than it had.

When I reached the solar, the tantalizing scent of sausage links, tea, and porridge greeted me. Mr. Whittle interrupted my moment of respite just as I settled and started to eat.

"Pardon the interruption, my lord. A Mr. Talbot is here to see you."

Appetite now fled, I left my breakfast unfinished. When I entered the green room, Mr. Talbot stood by the window, his black coat impeccable despite the morning's mist. His sharp gaze shifted toward me as I approached, the weight of his presence already filling the room.

"Mr. Talbot." A tightness clung to my voice. I already had a sinking feeling as to why he had come. "I was not expecting your visit so soon."

Talbot wasted no time on pleasantries. "My lord, the Crown demands immediate action. As you are aware, your uncle's passing has left matters of your estate in a precarious condition, including unpaid taxes. The Office of Woods and Forest has taken a keen interest in seeing if you can restore Hawthorn Abbey to its former standing—and if it will be profitable enough to sustain its people."

I groaned inwardly. *Unpaid taxes?* "I fear that you will find my uncle's records in disarray. Please, I have only just arrived. At least allow me a year to prove that Hawthorn estate will turn a profit."

He inclined his head, something akin to understanding flickering in his eyes. "Last year, I stood in this very spot, hearing the same assurances from your uncle and I looked the other way. Alas, my position will be in danger if I do not act. The Crown is weary of excuses, and I fear the pressure to act has only intensified. You have four months to present a clear plan not only to revive this estate, but to bring in enough coin to support the village. The road leading to the estate, for example—it's in disrepair. The tenants have lodged complaints, and I've experienced it firsthand, rattling in a carriage. You'll need to begin rebuilding it at once, or I'm afraid I will be forced to recommend that the Crown absorb your estate immediately."

I ground my teeth at the threat but kept my composure. Anger boiled within me at the assumption that I would prove no better than my uncle. "The road? I can scarcely afford such a construction if taxes are owed."

"A full reconstruction, my lord," Talbot urged. "It would serve not only your tenants but the estate itself. Particularly if you intend to expand the cider business as your uncle promised me—ease of transport will be key. This road is a vital link to the village and beyond."

"And if I fail to meet these expectations?"

Talbot's lips pursed. "Then the Crown will likely decide the estate should transfer to other hands—ones more capable of handling its affairs. Truly, I am sorry to deliver such ill news."

Before I could respond, the door flung open with a loud thud, and Whittle rushed in yet again, his eyes bulging with alarm. "Begging your pardon, my lord, but it's urgent. The sheep—most of the flock—are running loose through the valley! The tenants are in an uproar."

"What?" I cried. The estate was already teetering, and now this.

Talbot raised an eyebrow, his demeanor steady despite the sudden chaos. "Perhaps you should attend to your sheep, Lord Hawthorn. Rest assured, we will continue our discussion later."

I grimaced as I followed Mr. Whittle into the sunshine, where men waited in the courtyard, twisting their felt hats within filthy hands. I had not yet had the pleasure of greeting these tenants. As I walked toward them, I could feel Mr. Talbot's eyes trailing me, no doubt assessing every movement, ready to report each issue back to the Crown.

The oldest man inclined his head, coughing into his fist. "I'm Hinsley, and this be Mr. Malcolm, Mr. Cobb, and Mr. Dixon. We woke up to see your sheep out in Mr. Malcolm's pasture. My sons are rounding them up as we speak. When I rode past the Hawthorn bush, I noticed someone had cut the hedge and dug a hole directly beneath where the bush was. Big enough for my sheepdog to fit through."

Hawthorn, just like my namesake, created a tall barrier of sharp thorns to keep the sheep from escaping and prevented predators from entering the pastures.

From behind me, Mr. Talbot cleared his throat, a small noise that grated on my nerves. I knew what he was thinking—another sign of disarray on the estate.

My blood boiled at the impudence of someone intentionally cutting the hedge to let my sheep out. I couldn't afford another setback. Not with Talbot witnessing my latest debacle.

"Thank you for alerting me, gentlemen," I said, meeting each of their eyes. "I'll see to it immediately. And rest assured, the person responsible for this will be found and dealt with."

I turned on my heel, determination fueling each step as I headed toward the stables. This wasn't just an act of mischief—it was a challenge, and I wasn't about to let it go unanswered. At the stables, I called for Chaucer, my trusted stallion, and wasted no time saddling him. As I mounted, the cool air of the morning hit my face, sharpening my focus.

I rode alongside Mr. Whittle, while the other men followed on foot. To my annoyance, Mr. Talbot had also insisted on mounting one of the horses and trailed behind with a measured pace, as if content to observe rather than offer any real assistance.

Mr. Whittle and I reached the area first, where the remains of an ancient stone wall ended next to a hedge of hawthorn. I dismounted, the representative of the Crown doing the same behind me.

I peered at the upturned dirt. The hole mirrored the ones in Perry's field, and the hawthorn branches lay strewn, leaving a gap in the hedge. My gaze fixed upon the shredded section of the once formidable hedge.

Balling my fists, I forced a calmness into my voice. "Who would dare to do such a thing? And why?"

The groundskeeper shook his head. "I cannot say for certain, but we'll not let whoever it is succeed again. With your permission, I'll fill in the gap with stones after we secure the sheep."

I nodded, my resolve hardening as I struggled to count the white bodies making their grand escape. "See to it, Mr. Whittle. And hurry! The sheep are still fleeing." My groundskeeper didn't need to be told twice. He ran to his horse, and soon galloped over the field.

Mr. Talbot stood beside me, peering down at the damage. "You've certainly inherited quite a few challenges, my lord. A mismanaged estate, dissatisfied tenants, and now this." He gestured to the hedge. "And yet, you seem to think you can turn the ship around in a matter of months."

"I'm well aware of my responsibilities," I ground out. "I don't need reminders."

His smile thinned. "As I mentioned earlier, the Crown will not look kindly on delays. This sabotage could be seen as a reflection of the estate's lack of order. *Your* lack of order. Don't make me regret my decision to allow a small measure of leniency."

By then the other tenants had joined us, their expressions curious as they studied Mr. Talbot. I turned to them. "Mr. Hinsley, run ahead for the local constable. Someone will have to answer for this breach." Mr. Hinsley nodded and left while his companion, Mr. Dixon, sprinted toward the flock to assist Mr. Whittle. He shouted and waved his arms to steer the sheep back toward the pasture.

Mr. Cobb sniffed loudly as he folded his arms across his chest. "Will ye be collectin' rents right o'way? It's been a tryin' year with poor crops, and most of us don't see how we can keep going."

I mulled over the ill-timed question. I needed the goodwill of Bramnor's residents, but I disliked how his shifty gaze slid to Mr.

Talbot as if gauging how much pressure he could insert on me. Had he been the one to complain to the Office of Field and Stream?

"I'll give you an extra month to come up with rent." The words came out so certain, yet I recoiled all the same. How could I promise such a boon?

From the corner of my eye, I saw Talbot's brow arch ever so slightly, though he said nothing.

Mr. Malcolm whistled low at my answer. Yes, I had debts to pay. Salaries to catch up. I also awaited my barrister's reply regarding the abbey's art and sculptures collecting dust. Who needed it more? The shadowed halls or the men who couldn't put food in their bellies?

Mr. Malcolm's eyes glowed. "Well now, you've most certainly made my missus happy, milord. She'll be most relieved. You'd make the former lord right proud."

That shocked me speechless for a moment as the men turned and left me with Mr. Talbot next to the gutted hedge.

"Choose your next actions wisely, my lord, for my patience grows weary from years of Hawthorn excuses. You have four months to impress me," Mr. Talbot said, his voice echoing loudly. "Not a single day more. For both our sakes."

When a sweating Mr. Whittle returned to the abbey later that afternoon, I pulled him into my study. "Mr. Malcolm implied that my uncle offered a boon to his renters. That does not sound like my uncle at all. I do not remember him or my father indulging in mercy."

My groundskeeper nodded, but his face had taken on a sickly hue as if troubled by the conversation. Was he that loyal to my uncle to be offended by my remark?

"The former lord wasn't the man you remember, my lord. Near the end, he changed. Offered rent relief for two months during a drought, and the tenants haven't forgotten."

I shook my head, unwilling to change the picture within my mind.

"He wasn't always easy to understand. There are some who suffer from a deep melancholy—a darkness of spirit, you see. And he was often lost in his cups and more and more forgetful as the years passed. But in the end, he turned toward God," Whittle added quietly. "Lucy found his Bible the other day in the library. Perhaps you would care to see it. A gift from the vicar."

His words followed me to the library, where a worn Bible rested on the desk. Opening it, I found a yellowed letter from Vicar Littleton, dated 1798.

> *The Most Honorable Lord Hawthorn,*
> *I have pondered our last conversation. You will forgive my frankness, my lordship. I believe the best course of action is to seek forgiveness. All may seem lost, but may I remind you of Romans 8:28. And we know that all things work together for good to them that love God, to them who are the called according to his purpose. I will speak further on the subject when we visit again. Take courage. Do what must be done.*
>
> *Yours faithfully,*
> *Vicar John Littleton*

That year had proven a pivotal one. I had enlisted in the military a month before my mother passed of consumption. I wondered what penance my uncle desired? Part of me wanted to toss the letter into the fireplace to wither into ash. Instead, I placed it back where I found it.

It had only been a few days since I'd arrived at Hawthorn Abbey, but the weight of my family's past still bore down on me. I did not know from whom my uncle needed to beg forgiveness. He had never spoken to my mother in the years that followed our escape from Hawthorn Abbey. Nor to me during my years of military service. If he had attempted to do so, any pleas would have fallen on deaf ears.

I could never forgive the Hawthorn men, especially my father, even if their tainted blood ran through my veins. And I wasn't certain I wanted to meet the vicar who encouraged such foolish ideas. Nor was I certain I wanted to encounter his daughter for a third round of sparring, no matter how appealing those wide green eyes appeared.

Yet . . . I couldn't deny my growing curiosity. I was the viscount of Hawthorn Abbey, and to refuse going to church would hardly improve my standing with the villagers. I had questions. Many questions for the vicar and possibly his daughter.

Reluctantly, I resolved to attend the following day.

12

Bridget

> We should be rigorous in judging ourselves
> and gracious in judging others.
> JOHN WESLEY

The Parish Church of the Holy Cross, with its small belfry and trim graveyard, appeared serene on a Sunday morning. Yet I felt only turmoil as I entered the church, which smelled of linseed oil.

Not even my freshly pressed gown and matching green hat could lift my spirits as Mrs. Herriot and I took our usual spot. I felt the eyes of the women and men, most whom I had known for the past twelve years since our family first moved to Bramnor. Despite the rumors of fever, the church appeared unusually packed.

Father would be so pleased. I hoped no one else would fall ill.

Dust motes danced in the beams of sunlight cascading onto the polished pews. Father had spent a good deal of the previous day ordering a complete cleaning of the church to impress the new viscount, just in case Lord Hawthorn made an appearance. I wanted to inform Father that such efforts would be wasted, but there I sat, dressed in my second-best attire, with my second-best gloves, and holding a new reticule embroidered with white flowers. My maid had attempted to tame my frizz into something pretty, with manageable curls carefully arranged on my forehead, until I bid her stop with the fussing.

Regardless of my appearance, my chest fluttered from nerves.

Several women bent their heads together, their whispers carrying over the pews.

"Roaming the fields at night."

"Shocking for a lady! Can no one rein her in?"

"Chattering magpies. For shame, in a church no less," Mrs. Herriot muttered as I turned my attention to my reticule, refusing to strain my burning ears. Perhaps I could encourage Father to preach a sermon about the dangers of such prattle. Then again, I was used to being the subject of gossip.

Dressed in a pristine cassock over his newest suit, my father cleared his throat while raising both palms over the congregation, which barely ceased its babble. Instead, the whispers increased in loudness, hissing and echoing across the cavernous sanctuary.

I shot him a glance, arching my eyebrow, but Father appeared transfixed, his startled gaze directed to the church entrance. Gasps resounded. Someone coughed loudly.

I shifted in my seat, my bonnet blocking my view of the entrance.

As I angled myself better, a man walked in late, his large form drawing attention. Our gazes locked briefly before he headed toward the raised lordship seat, positioned near the front of the left side, just before the chancel.

A tingle rippled through me. I felt frozen as I watched him stalk down the aisle.

His boots echoed hollow, if uneven. Despite his war injury, all I could remember was the strength of his arm as he pulled me out of the pit, and the way his arm curved about me during the ride in the storm. From my position sitting on the bench, I had an ample view of the proud tilt of his head as he walked past. He did not bother to look at me again.

I had hurt him when he pulled me out of the hole the other day at the field. Yet he had barely uttered a murmur, even though his skin blanched when he set me on firm ground. He certainly knew how to inflict damage with his curt dismissal. No, I couldn't pity him. He had proven to be unbendable. Boorish. Without another look at the church members, he sat on his family's bench, his expression as hard as marble.

"Welcome, Lord Hawthorn. We are delighted to have you with us this morning." My father offered a warm smile before stepping into the pulpit to expand upon Ecclesiastes.

Vanity of vanities; all is vanity.

What profit hath a man of all his labour which he taketh under the sun? One generation passeth away, and another generation cometh: but the earth abideth for ever.

My mind scarcely took in anything of value. I knew Father reserved one of his best sermons for this Sunday, yet his words scarcely registered through my tumbling thoughts. Instead, my feelings battled for control as I surreptitiously studied the new lord through lowered lashes.

Before long, we sang the last hymn, our voices high and out of tune, and then Father offered a closing benediction. I wondered if and how I should approach Lord Hawthorn again regarding the mosaics. I needed to know what secrets lay beneath the soil on Mr. Perry's farm. Somehow, I suspected Lord Hawthorn would accuse me of vanity.

I do not want acclaim. He had all but ground out the statement before fleeing on his beast.

As if he sensed the weight of my stare, his eyes flared open, and he angled his head to catch me in the act. I ducked my head to study the beads trimming my reticule, waiting until Father finished his prayer with a resounding, "Amen."

The parishioners left the sanctuary, all except the viscount, who glowered from his bench.

Was he wishing to speak with Father? Dread shuddered through me. I hoped the two of them would at least come to a reasonable understanding regarding Mr. Perry's land. Father couldn't undertake finding a new vicarage or a lowly curate position at his age.

I slipped to the back of the church, hoping for another chance to speak with the viscount, but he marched past me. Again, he refused to glance in my direction, his desire to escape evident by the stomp of his boots.

"Lord Hawthorn," I said, my voice louder than I intended and holding a decided note of challenge to his bad manners. "A good day to you."

He pivoted, his boots squeaking on the polished floor.

"Miss Littleton, isn't it? My apologies. I scarcely recognized you." His flinty gaze moved from my face to the plumy white ostrich feathers surely dancing from my bonnet, courtesy of the breeze rippling in from the open doors. He seemed to catch the error of his blunt speech at the last moment and added in a low voice, "A lovely change."

The inclination to behave for the sake of my father dissipated like dandelion puff in the breeze. I arched an eyebrow at the viscount's offhand comment and uttered in an equally clipped tone, "Come now. There's no need for such flattery. I am still the same, whether on the field or in the church."

The muscle in his jaw jumped, and I felt as if I had piqued him.

"I scarcely know what I'll encounter. A fairy or a sprite, an antiquarian knee-deep in research, or . . . perhaps a sheep herder."

My mouth dropped open in the most undignified manner. "I beg your pardon?"

He leaned forward, that tantalizing scent of leather and sandalwood teasing my nose again. His hard gaze pinned me to the floor. "Miss Littleton, you wouldn't happen to know who dug holes on my property or let my sheep loose?"

Shock filled me, though I did like his use of *antiquarian*.

"I confess you have me at a loss, my lord. Neither I nor the Perry family would ever consider trespassing on *your* land, even for research purposes. Although, if you allowed it, I should like to see that hole."

A dry chuckle escaped him. "I bet you would. You'll find naught but stones. There is nothing of value hidden on my land. Although, you did warn me about the greed of others and the swarm of treasure hunters soon to devour us. Have a care, Miss Littleton. I intend to plant more trees for my orchard and lay the foundation for a service road to cut from the orchard to the brewery. Do not stand in the way of true progress."

My nostrils surely flared at the thinly veiled insult while my heart dropped at the breadth of his plans.

"I hope, Lord Hawthorn, you won't forbid my father and me from our ministering visits. I have dear friends who happen to be tenants of yours. Mrs. Eacher is one of them."

His hard expression morphed into a smirk. "Ah yes. Your afternoons of reading gothic novels. I confess I've never met a vicar's daughter who enjoyed such fiction."

Heat bloomed across my cheeks. "My father and I have worked hard to cultivate our relationships in Bramnor." Then I added, as if stabbing him with a pin. "Might I add how good it is to see you at church. My father has so looked forward to having you join our humble congregation. Will you be joining us next Sunday?"

He offered the barest nod. "I shall. Your father preached an excellent sermon."

Apparently, he had manners, even if dusty. Too late, I remembered

Father's warning not to cause offense. Struggling to retrieve my tattered manners, I plastered a bright smile on my face.

"And how do you find Hawthorn Abbey and the surrounding estate so far, despite your adventure of missing sheep?"

"It will be to my liking soon enough." He narrowed his eyes as he regarded me. "Perhaps we shall encounter each other again, out in the field."

"Mr. Perry's field," I corrected firmly. "I look forward to the magistrate's assistance in this affair."

"Rest assured, I have already sent out inquires," Lord Hawthorn replied in a frosty tone.

As we stood in the center aisle, regarding each other warily, I had the impression of two fencers parrying gently and tapping the foils for weakness before lunging for the kill.

I wanted to return to the subject of the dig, to press him further, but something in his hard gaze told me this wasn't the moment. Better to retreat and save my strength for another day.

With a sharp nod, as if reaching the same conclusion, he turned away, his attention already shifting from our skirmish to the larger battlefield of church society. My breath caught as he approached my father, the two exchanging a few terse words. I remained rooted to the spot, watching as the villagers quickly closed in around him, drawn like moths to a flame. His rigid posture and clenched jaw betrayed his discomfort, but he stood his ground, engaging with the fawning parishioners with a politeness that appeared to be more duty than desire.

Out of the corner of my eye, I saw Mrs. Eleanor Hawkins and her husband, one of the landed gentry, approach Lord Hawthorn. Both smiling wide enough to cause cheek spasms. I slipped away, leaving him to the delight of the other parishioners.

Another man paused at the nave, hovering at the back of the crowd before lunging forward to the small group clustered around the new viscount. Mr. Barron, of all people, dressed in a navy coat of fine wool and a flamboyant gold waistcoat. I paused to observe as he bowed, snapping his heels together after pushing through a cluster of tittering misses, all daughters of the Hawkinses, to make himself visible. Only my friends, the Perry family, ducked out of the church, leaving before I could speak with them.

Mr. Barron waved his hands. "My good viscount, how fortunate we are to have you within our humble valley. I extend a warm welcome to you."

The viscount appeared stunned at the forwardness of Mr. Barron while I grinned. Good. Perhaps listening to Mr. Barron prattle was all the vengeance I needed. Snippets of the one-sided conversation drifted through the stuffy air. *Cider. Sales. Would you be so good as to provide barrels to several inns?*

All too soon, Lord Hawthorn's icy mask thawed. Such magic Mr. Barron wove with his words, and how different the two men appeared from each other, even if they stood at the same height. The paunchy redhead with a tendency to balding, dramatically gesturing next to the stoic, dark-haired statue . . .

No. I would not indulge in such unscientific observations, especially if they related to a breadth of shoulders and flinty gaze that chafed me. Instead, I halted beside Father.

"Did I hear correctly? You've finally obtained a parish call with our new lord?"

Father appeared bemused as he clutched his book of sermons close to his chest. "I have." He glanced my way. "Your dig is the talk of the town, and Lord Hawthorn has questions about the area. Perhaps I can help settle the boundary lines."

So the viscount had not told my father about the missing sheep, nor the ridiculous thought that I might be behind the trouble.

"Are you saying there are no reliable land records in the care of Lord Hawthorn?" I demanded.

Father placed a hand on my arm, drawing my attention back to him. "Shh, Bridget. Lower your voice. Be at peace. I will get to the bottom of the issue."

His assurance brought no relief. Instead, I felt only further dread. What questions did the viscount have? Would he and Mr. Perry continue to quarrel over the land rights? I dearly hoped the magistrate in Chichester maintained rigorous records. No one could fault either man for making an error regarding the Perry farm. Yet the viscount's demeanor had suggested anything but a pleasant visit over tea.

13

Bridget

> Opinions are made to be changed—
> or how is truth to be got at?
> **LORD BYRON**

By Monday afternoon, after reading *The Mysteries of Udolpho* to Mrs. Eacher, my spirits had risen. Nothing lifted me more than good company and a thrilling book.

Mrs. Eacher smirked after I finished a particularly thrilling chapter.

"Upon my word, Miss Littleton, is this Udolpho considered proper fiction?"

"No, it's not," I whispered, peeking over the edge of the leather-bound volume. "Most think it shocking. Scandalous, even."

With her cataract-clouded eyes, she could barely see, but she heard well enough. We sat by the fire, enjoying thick-sliced bread and sharp cheese. I had offered to leave her a basket of supplies, but she refused the tinctures, claiming that my visits were all she needed.

"Well, carry on then," she said with a laugh, motioning for me to continue. "I hope Emily finds the courage to do something bold. These characters are so helpless. Can't she at least bash a villain over the head with a vase?"

"A brilliant suggestion, Mrs. Eacher, and quite bloodthirsty."

Before I could resume, a knock at the door interrupted us. I expected Mrs. Dixon, but to my surprise, Lord Hawthorn stood there, filling the doorway.

"L-Lord Hawthorn," I stammered, clutching the book.

"I've come to call on Mrs. Eacher," he said after a pause. "And to see if she needs anything."

"Lord Hawthorn! Do come in." Mrs. Eacher sounded as eager as a young girl as he stepped inside and I closed the door. "I daresay it has been years since I saw you last. At least I could see in those days. Come! Have a seat by my fire and join Miss Littleton and me. She reads to me every week, and we've recently discovered *The Mysteries of Udolpho*."

"I fear I cannot stay long, not when I've planned to visit each tenant this week." He shot me an unreadable glance as he obeyed and sat opposite Mrs. Eacher. "I'm glad you have found stimulating company. I, too, am quite intrigued by Miss Littleton's taste in art and literature, especially since she is a vicar's daughter."

Like a chastened child, I found another chair to sit on, feeling ever so foolish about the gothic fiction I clutched to my chest.

Mrs. Eacher laughed. "Miss Littleton brings a great deal of excitement with each visit. I don't know what I would do without her assistance."

"You cannot see anything," he stated lowly as he studied the older woman. A frown passed over his features.

She shook her head. "Not for many years, although I remember *you*, the little master and your lovely mother, Lady Hawthorn. She often came to visit me in those early days. How I missed her after she left. Do you remember sitting in this cottage? I gave you biscuits and you would eat them ever so politely, careful not to drop crumbs on the floor. These days, I rely on the kindness of Miss Littleton, and of course, your other tenants, the Dixons, who help me clean the cottage and bring me what I need."

I was hard-pressed to envision the grim man in front of me as a young boy brushing crumbs from his chin. As I studied him, a curious change came over the viscount at the mention of his mother. His hands resting on his knees suddenly tightened into fists. When he caught my probing gaze, he relaxed his fingers, forcing them to straighten.

"If you need anything, you will let me know. Repairs to the cottage. Anything at all."

She beamed and leaned forward as if sharing secrets with a confidant. "I only request novels. Gothic in particular. Ah, I remember Lady Hawthorn describing the magnificent library in the abbey. It's the only way I can truly see these days."

"Gothic fiction? I prefer Shakespeare," he said, much to my surprise.

"The bard has plenty of drama." I couldn't resist prodding, curious that a man of the military would have a taste for literature. "*This above all: to thine own self be true, and it must follow, as the night the day, thou canst not then be false to any man.*"

"*Hamlet,*" he said. "Surely you can't deny the beauty of the bard's words, Miss Littleton? Shakespeare offers a far meatier read—complete with poetry while examining man's nature—than your lurid tales."

"I think *The Mysteries of Udolpho* is just as compelling. And far more entertaining. You might try it and see for yourself, if you care to peruse my novel." I held up my beloved volume in my eagerness to challenge him. "I've read enough Shakespeare to last a lifetime."

He almost smiled, turning his attention to Mrs. Eacher.

"An interesting trade of books. In the meanwhile, consider the library at Hawthorn at your disposal."

The visit ended as abruptly as it began with him standing. He nearly reached the low ceiling. Mrs. Eacher begged him to return and asked if I would send him home with the bread I had brought, in memory of the boy who visited with his delightful mother.

He halted at the door, silent for a long moment before accepting Mrs. Eacher's humble gift. I slipped a crusty loaf into a clean handkerchief and walked outside the cottage into the cool spring air. He mounted his horse, Chaucer. The wandering medieval poet.

"Thank you for visiting my friend and taking her gift," I said as I handed him the wrapped loaf.

He took it, the frown still captured between his brows. "She has enough food to eat?"

I pressed my lips together, not wanting to diminish her effort at welcoming the new viscount.

"Then I shall see that a basket is dropped at her door tomorrow," he said thickly.

"Very kind of you. I know the tenants will greatly appreciate any gesture on your part. They've struggled so these past years."

"I remember a certain miss informing me that the previous lord had not done much to help them."

I straightened, refusing to lie or back down, regardless of that disastrous first meeting on the road, and then in the rain. I wrapped my arms about my middle.

"Yes, the tenants need a viscount who will watch over them and care for them."

He blew out a harsh breath. "Unfortunately, the Hawthorn estate lives up to its name. Full of prickly thorns meant to keep others out. I was always under the impression that my uncle proved no different. However, some of the tenants have shared that he changed in his last years. What do you know of a person's ability to change, Miss Littleton, speaking as a vicar's daughter, of course? If you know history and literature, I am certain to be astounded by your grasp of theology."

I suddenly wanted to flee. Literature and history were fine topics for discussion. But to delve into my faith? Or lack of it? A flare of panic rendered me mute.

Father believed a person could change with repentance. It was my experience that far too many would rather pretend than embrace genuine change, including my brother.

"Perhaps if one is honest about his faults and tries harder, he may achieve success." My readings of the enlightenment suggested that all man needed was reason and scientific discovery. Yet the answer rang false this evening, and the viscount pursed his lips as if tasting something sour.

"Fair enough. But do you believe that God can change a man?" he asked, his gaze penetrating mine.

Did I believe God could change a hardened heart? I no longer knew, especially after my brother's problems. I had witnessed far too much hypocrisy to believe much of anything—a price I paid as the vicar's daughter. But I could hardly share such scandalous thoughts.

"I've seen too much of habit and human nature, my lord, to believe a man, or a woman, can so easily find redemption," I finally replied.

"And if so, who can change?"

His lips quirked with wry amusement . . . and something else, very much akin to sadness when I did not answer his question right away.

"Why Miss Littleton, I do believe you are a cynic."

"Does that surprise you, Lord Hawthorn, especially as a man who has fought battle after battle and witnessed the bleakest side of humanity?"

Impolite conversation, no doubt, but my guard had slipped, and though I tried to parry words with him, he didn't return the attack. Not right away, at least.

Something flickered in his eyes. "And you, as a vicar's daughter, has her fair share of scars, I believe."

I did not expect him to read me so well. A vicar's daughter was to be all sweetness and sunshine. All hope and reassurances that pain was temporary and fleeting, and joy waited in the morning.

My voice cracked as I fidgeted with the edge of my sleeve. "Yes, well, we are not all hardened warriors."

"No," he agreed, "we are not."

He rode away, leaving me to wonder at such a statement. When I returned to the cottage, Mrs. Eacher pointed to the stove.

"Would you be a dear and pour another cup of tea, Miss Littleton?"

I tore my gaze from the door, bemused by a man who would visit a blind woman and offer her assistance then grant access to his library. A man who named his horse after the father of English poetry. And a man who wondered about redemption and asked a jaded vicar's daughter about her thoughts on theology.

"Poor lad," Mrs. Eacher murmured when I handed her a cup of tea. "I daresay coming home must be a painful thing, considering how his father often frightened Lady Hawthorn and Rafe so . . ." She caught herself before revealing any more and took a long sip, her blank gaze drifting to the door. "Sometimes life proves far stranger than our novels, Miss Littleton."

When I asked her to tell me more, she refused to elaborate.

14

Rafe

> Do all the good you can, by all the means you can, in all the ways you can, in all the places you can, at all the times you can, to all the people you can, as long as ever you can.
> **JOHN WESLEY**

As soon as I swung my feet off the bed and touched the floor, the room spun. Last night, I dreamt of the abbey collapsing, my father watching from the shadows, his raspy voice mocking me. Even in dreams, he held power over me.

But he was dead. And I was no longer a child.

I stumbled against the armoire and rubbed my throat, which burned like fire. Worse, my temples throbbed as if I had taken a beating during the night. So much for exhausting myself with tenant visits and work to guarantee a dreamless sleep.

Today was Tuesday. I expected a call from the vicar considering our last conversation on Sunday at church. Would his daughter come as well? Part of me hoped she would, and another part of me desired privacy to grill the vicar who'd considered my uncle a friend. One could hardly have a frank discussion regarding the men in my family with a vicar's daughter listening in.

All the same, as I pictured her, an unbidden smile crossed my lips. Her desire for benefiting the valley echoed my own. A pity we were at odds for how to go about it. I pushed aside the image of her saucy expression at church, along with her indignation over my hints as to who might have cut into my hawthorn hedge and released my sheep.

Despite Constable Wickham's visit, an inept man by all appearances, Mr. Whittle and Mr. Spencer and I had no further information or answers about the sabotage. Only Lucy offered solutions. Ghosts.

I'm telling you, my lord, I heard a sound late afternoon on Sunday in the west wing. A door closed suddenly, but when I entered the guest bedroom, no one was there. I waited several minutes. I swear I heard breathing. It must be the old viscount come to pay a visit. I can feel his eyes watching me from the portrait in the library.

It was pointless to argue with her. I, too, felt my uncle's presence, albeit in a more solid way. This morning, as I opened my armoire and pushed aside a cloak, my fingers brushed against the back until I touched something cold.

I pulled it out, not at all surprised to see a silver flask still sloshing with drink. I uncorked it and poured the amber liquid into the banked fireplace. My uncle had not changed, no matter what the tenants or Mr. Whittle claimed. The flask had likely kept him company until his last breath.

I dressed quickly as rain pelted the windows. Outside, the wind moaned through the cracks and flashes of lighting sparking on the horizon. It sounded like a cry or an eerie weeping, reminding me of that fateful night before my mother and I escaped the abbey.

She had smiled wanly during a similar gale. "It's only rain, my brave little man. Go to sleep." When she had drawn the covers over my shoulders, I spied red welts on both her wrists.

The vision receded, but my breathing quickened. The flask, propped up where all could see it, glimmered in the morning light, catching my uncle's elegant initials etched into the silver.

Should I trust the vicar who had chosen friendship with my uncle, and perhaps even my father?

Vicar Littleton, damp from the rain, bowed when he entered the solar, alone. I quelled the strange flutter of disappointment, realizing few ladies would want to travel in such inclement weather. Yet I had foolishly hoped she might come. At least it meant my battle with Miss Littleton over the fields would be halted until the rain ended.

He stood dripping water and dabbing at his cheeks with a handkerchief. Quite a determined man to come in this storm. "My lord, you are a busy man and I will make my visit short. Mr. Whittle informed me that you are not feeling well this afternoon."

I nodded. "My apologies for not having greeted you sooner. As for illness, it is nothing."

"From your injury in battle?"

"That is nothing more than an irksome bullet from the Battle of Bussaco," I replied. I hated being considered an invalid. The surgeon had done what he could to remove the shrapnel, but he could never fully repair the damage in my leg. At the moment all I felt was fire in my throat. I pulled on my cravat, struggling to breathe. Had I caught a chill from my tenants?

"No apologies needed. Bussaco, you say? When the Duke of Wellington duped *l'Enfant chéri de la Victoire*, one of Napoleon's greatest generals? I should like to hear your account."

"I don't care to remember," I said, immediately regretting my harsh tone. I hastened to add, "I lost a dear friend that day."

After motioning for him to join me in front of the fireplace, I sat, my body taut, as I rested my fist on my knee.

He followed my example. "Not an easy loss, I'm certain. You have my sympathies. How do you like our valley so far?"

"I certainly have plenty to occupy me."

He smiled. "A new lord must attend to his duties, of which you have many indeed. You have only newly arrived and have done splendidly based on what I've heard from your people."

I wasn't used to hearing praise. To my surprise, his warm words settled into me like a healing balm. "Much work remains. If it wasn't raining, I would be in the fields instead of lounging by a fire like a man of leisure."

"Nay, rest will do you much good. The Sabbath was created for our benefit." Reverend Littleton frowned as he studied me.

"If you don't mind me saying so, my lord, you do appear paler than when I saw you last. If you are agreeable to the notion, my daughter has some skill with tinctures and teas. Perhaps at my next visit, I'll bring a remedy." The vicar's words carried a quiet concern that seemed to burrow deeper beneath my defenses.

"If it isn't devil's dung, then I accept," I replied.

The vicar chuckled as he leaned back in his chair. "Lucy Whittle's remedy. Oh yes. I've smelled it from afar."

Sweat beaded on my forehead, and I resisted the urge to cough as a rough tickle lingered in the back of my throat. The growing discomfort mirrored the tension I felt, pushing me to cut through the pleasantries. I appreciated bluntness and decided to offer the same to my guest.

"Vicar, when I brought your daughter home during that storm, and forgive me for doing so but I had no luxury for propriety in such weather, you mentioned there were matters we needed to discuss. One of them has unfortunately grown more pressing. Mr. Perry and I are at odds over the boundary of our properties. I had no choice but to ask Miss Littleton to cease digging on what I believe is my estate, particularly after someone tampered with my hedges and let my sheep loose."

"She has not trespassed, I assure you. Nor would she or Mr. Perry release your sheep." The vicar's bushy eyebrows rose. "However, Mr. Perry has asked me to inquire after the records as soon as the magistrate releases them, which is one of my reasons for calling today. Your neighbor struggles to read and I have promised to intervene. I believe you will find Mr. Perry to be well in his rights. Have you found your uncle's property deeds?"

Ire bubbled up within me. I had found no such documentation within my uncle's records. It was possible I would later find them stuffed into some obscure cupboard.

"Not all of them. And I've been told that the magistrate has taken a trip to Bath to settle a family affair for the next two weeks. Until then, I have no choice but to hunt for papers hidden in the oddest of places."

The vicar sighed. "Lord Hawthorn's mind turned for the worst in his last years. He couldn't remember where he placed his inkpot or his watch most days. At first, I assumed it melancholia. But then I realized more was afoot."

This was also news to me. I had not considered that my uncle might have suffered memory loss.

I fingered my aching throat. "I must speak frankly. I've heard that you had an affable relationship with my uncle."

"I counted him as a friend," the vicar answered. "He carried many burdens to the end, one of which included restoring his holdings."

I thought of the half-filled flask in the armoire, clear evidence of a man still chained to his weakness. "I fear the estate has been neglected far too long."

"No doubt you have a challenge on your hands, but in time, with wise decisions, the Hawthorn holdings will flourish again. The crops failed thanks to blight a few years prior, and the expenditures grew. Many good men and women left Bramnor for the factories."

Lucy entered the room with a steaming pot of tea and two teacups. She poured the fragrant brew and curtsied, leaving us alone with little fuss. The tea, mixed with honey, soothed my throat, if only for a moment. More troublesome was another flush of heat rippling through me as my vision wavered. Still, I continued.

"I have seen nothing of my uncle's wisdom."

The vicar frowned at my caustic bluntness, but again, he did not disagree. "No, I suspect not. At least not until the last few years of his life. The former lord battled his demons to the end."

"If demons include drink, then I'm well aware of the obstacles."

The vicar picked up his gold-rimmed teacup. "His greatest battle. It worsened, from what I understand, after your father's death."

My uncle had likely been too drunk to care, but I kept that thought to myself, changing the subject to more hopeful topics.

"Unfortunately, both men left me with no choice but to do what I must to protect Hawthorn Abbey. I'm determined to rebuild the orchard and sell cider. I may even sell the art, books, and silver within the abbey since I have no use for any of it. I've written to my barrister to inquire about buyers. Discreetly, of course."

A pained look crossed the vicar's face before he took a sip of tea.

Perhaps it was the fever heating within me, but my tongue seemed strangely loosened while my head felt like it had its own rebellious drummer, each beat sending shock waves through my thoughts.

I set down my teacup and rubbed my temples. "I was surprised to hear that you were friends with my uncle. I did not have any semblance of a relationship with him over the years."

"You received no letters?" The vicar's frown deepened. He set his cup on the saucer. "Not even one?"

I shook my head and immediately regretted the action as it reverberated through me. "Nothing in all my years living with my mother. We stayed in a cottage, provided by her relatives at Portsmouth."

The vicar shook his head. "Most unfortunate."

"Did you know my father?" I demanded.

"He died before I moved to Bramnor." A careful answer to my way of thinking.

"Then you've surely heard the gossip by now. Both men were brutes. When my mother took me from the abbey, it was to save her life. Not a single soul intervened to help her."

"I am truly sorry. No woman should endure such terror. Nor any child."

To my surprise, the vicar made no excuses for the men in my family. Instead, he regarded me with sympathy.

"My mother was a brave soul. Despite her meekness of spirit, she had the courage to leave this forsaken home. Her faith never wavered no matter her circumstances." My fingers flexed over my knee. No longer did I know what hurt more . . . the battle wound or the fever rising or the pain of remembering my past.

"Your mother's faith is a gift," the vicar said quietly.

Yes, it was. If darkness chased my heels, something else lingered too. The longer I spent in the abbey, the more I remembered her lessons and example, but I did not welcome his intrusion into my interrogation. I wanted to know *why* he had remained by my uncle's side. If my uncle promised money or influence, surely the vicar would have seen through such blatant lies.

"So you see, I cannot fathom why any man would want to be friends with my uncle or my father. My earliest recollections are of my father accusing my mother of being unfaithful, even though I believe such an accusation could only be the lie of a crazed man. I do not know who is my father. My uncle or . . ."

Pressing a fist against my mouth, I curbed myself at the last moment, ashamed to have shared so much. I was not myself. Nor had I ever divulged so much with anyone other than Lewis.

A wave of dizziness swept over me, scorching my skin even further. The room wavered before my eyes. I was aware of a rustle as I tipped forward, caught by the edge of the table, and rattling the teacups. The vicar reached my side, his hand on my arm.

"My lord—"

I licked my lips, trying to answer to assure him not to worry, but my vision faded to black.

15

Bridget

> Nothing happens to anybody which he
> is not fitted by nature to bear.
> **MARCUS AURELIUS**

Hawthorn Abbey appeared almost romantic in the evening with ivy covering the stones. My pulse thrummed despite the peaceful setting spread before me. The sunset revealed signs of new activity along the estate. A line of stakes marked the beginnings of a road cutting through the fields, portions of the ground freshly turned and awaiting the first stones. My pulse quickened at the sight—evidence of the viscount's determination to bring change, even in his weakened state.

I dreaded this visit, especially when Father returned to the parsonage appearing distressed, demanding I procure Mother's time-tested tinctures and return with him to tend to the feverish viscount, now rendered immobile with the same fever sweeping the valley.

Considering our last encounter at church, would he even welcome my presence?

Father cast me a worried glance as we approached the main entrance, dripping with Hedera leaves.

"I didn't want to say anything in front of Molly or Mrs. Herriot, but I am deeply concerned for our viscount. He's young and quite determined to prove himself."

"As he should," I answered drily.

"Even to the point of selling the tapestries, paintings, and silver. He even threatened to sell the library."

My steps faltered. I had delighted in that library, especially when the former Lord Hawthorn had allowed my father and me use of it. It saved me an extra trip to the lending libraries in Chichester and had been the one saving grace of the former lord. How desperate the viscount must be to part with his family's items. A measure of pity wormed its way into my heart. A very small measure.

"I cannot imagine being in worse straits than to be forced to sell books." The thought set a dull ache within my chest. There was nothing I loved more than tomes with yellowed pages and the scent of leather. Daniel's books had saved me, allowing me the freedom to travel the world from the comfort of our drawing room.

Father sighed as he lengthened his stride, clearly in a hurry. "Nor I. It's a shame to see a viscount reduced to such circumstances. However, his military bearing and his upbringing seem to have prepared him for hardship. He is unconventional, to say the least. He refuses to let his tenants suffer."

One could hardly discount the idea of a viscount caring for his tenants.

"He has endured a great deal, in this abbey and abroad. I cannot share everything I heard. A clergy man's privilege. Some wounds fester within the soul long after the body regains strength, and our viscount is a man in desperate need of healing."

I mulled over Father's pause. "Were you able to settle the dispute between Mr. Perry and the viscount?"

My father shook his head. "I fear I will need to pay a visit to the magistrate. Lord Hawthorn has already made inquiries but the magistrate is in Bath. This matter with Mr. Perry and the estate boundary must be settled, and the sooner the better. We must pray for peace between our neighbors."

What good had prayer done for Daniel or my mother?

The abbey, usually quiet, seemed even more so this evening, even after Father's smart rap. The door creaked open and Mr. Whittle greeted us, his ready smile most welcome. He wore tight black breeches and a livery jacket far too small, a relic of the past. "Vicar. Miss Littleton. Do come in."

I took in the dim hall, noting that the black-and-white tiles appeared remarkably clean. And the magnificent hall table flanked by two heavy chairs also seemed freshly dusted. Above the table, a large painting of a fox hunt commanded attention, now hung straight after years of dangling crooked.

"Is Lord Hawthorn better?" My father dropped his voice to a discreet level.

"Somewhat. The physician, who came over an hour ago, said the lord has the same sickness as the tenants, along with a sore leg. It's not good, Vicar. Not good at all. I don't know what that physician did, but our viscount cursed something fierce." Mr. Whittle glanced at me as if remembering a lady was present. "Lord Hawthorn awaits you in the green room. He's in a fine temper this evening."

Oh dear, that did not sound promising at all.

Following Mr. Whittle's quick steps, I nibbled my lip as I considered how the meeting might proceed. Within my reticule, I carried an assortment of herbal remedies. Would the lord be receptive to my medicinal advice, considering his past demeanor?

My pulse flickered when Mr. Whittle pushed open another door.

"I said no disturbances, Whittle!"

I couldn't see into the room, only the back of Mr. Whittle's too tight coat. His shoulders raised as if he heaved a great sigh.

"Vicar Littleton and his daughter, Miss Littleton."

Something else was said . . . too low to make out, but I braced myself all the same.

The green room lived up to its name with walls the color of faded emerald finally subdued by years of sun streaming through the immense windows. My gaze fastened on the man reclining on the arm of a sofa, his leg propped up by a stool, his feet encased in tasseled velvet slippers instead of his usual boots. He looked like a king of the orient about to hold court, if not for his loosened cravat and mussed hair.

If I had expected a weak invalid, I would have been disappointed. Yet I could not dismiss the paleness of his skin, nor the sheen gathered along his brow. He gazed at us through hooded eyes, but I was no shrinking flower who wilted under the blistering sun. Instead, I offered him my brightest smile.

He gestured to the chairs closest to him. "Vicar Littleton, Miss Littleton, a pleasure to see you. I must warn you, I might be yet contagious."

A pleasure to see me? I had my doubts. Father did as he was bid, and I followed suit and perched on a chair facing the sofa.

Father cleared his throat. "I hope you are feeling better, my lord. You saw Dr. Smithy?"

Lord Hawthorn shifted on the sofa, moving his arm slowly as if it pained him. "He left an hour ago after draining me until I finally bid him to stop."

"A barbaric practice," I said, easily imagining the tools used for scarification, where a syringe and a spring-loaded lancet or glass cup created a vacuum and drained the poor victim's life away.

Father placed a warning hand on my arm, squeezing lightly.

"You don't approve of bloodletting?" Lord Hawthorn glanced at me with something akin to curiosity.

"No, I do not," I said firmly. "If God created it to flow through us, why must we abandon it so readily?"

Lord Hawthorn's mouth tilted slightly. "At last, Miss Littleton, the two of us have something else we can agree upon, other than exploring the great outdoors during rainstorms. I was a fool to let him try."

I dared not glance at my father, but I heard his gentle cough all the same, as if he feared I might needlessly descend into a lecture regarding the history of bloodletting, reaching all the way to Hippocrates and the famed Greek physician Galen.

I found myself cheered we might find common ground after all.

Father was quick to add, "My daughter brought a collection of herbs and tinctures. Hopefully, you will find your strength bolstered again, my lord. I have found the remedies in the valley, grown by several of the local women, to be most remarkable in their healing properties, and far less invasive."

On that cue, I reached into my reticule and pulled out the vials, then rose to take them to him.

"You will forgive me that I cannot stand," Lord Hawthorn said gruffly while eyeing me with some curiosity. "It appears I've overextended the use of my leg from visiting each tenant."

"Such formality. There is no need," I replied, but I was pleased he had continued to make the effort to meet each of the men and women renting his land. His mouth lifted ever so lightly again and, miracle upon miracles, a dimple carved into one cheek. He had the ability to truly smile after all.

The first vial contained a tincture of sage, fennel, and basil, mingled with plenty of garlic to ward off ill humors. When I handed it to him, my fingers grazed his, sending a surprising jolt rippling through me. His eyes widened as if he felt it too, but he took the vial without a word and uncorked it, his nose wrinkling.

"Miss Littleton, am I to believe that I will remain completely unharmed after imbibing such a concoction?" A sparkle in his eyes countered the gruff words. This close to him, I noticed a series of scars on his fingers and knuckles, with faint white lines tracing a path up his wrist.

"You've been a hardened soldier, sir. I believe you will be up to the challenge. You'll find this tin less odious." I handed him the second tin, a balm of peppermint and rosemary to rub on his leg. Instead of risking touching him again, I set it on the small marble-top table beside the sofa, ever aware of how his gaze followed me.

"And perhaps a forced rest will do you good," I added before returning to my chair. "Especially considering all the projects you have planned, including the new road running past the orchards."

"A capital effort. How goes the building, Lord Hawthorn?" My father interjected with a forced pleasantness as he shifted in his seat.

"Slow but certain since we've only just begun," the viscount answered as he set the balm next to the other vial. I wondered if he would even make use of the gifts.

"I do hope you'll skirt Mr. Perry's land," I added after a moment's hesitation. "He is quite invested in the mosaics at this point. To halt the dig now, especially with so much at stake, would prove disastrous for his finances."

Any hint of his former dry humor fled when the viscount swung his attention back to me. "Miss Littleton, was this the purpose of your visit? To charm me with pleasantries and put a stop to my efforts with a service road for my orchards? To encroach on my property?"

"Well, no . . . not entirely, as long as we can continue our dig," I faltered, heat climbing my cheeks at his accusation. Perhaps I seemed a tad presumptuous. "Mr. Perry's concerns have weighed on me. It's a matter of his livelihood, after all. He needs income or he shall be forced to abandon his family farm."

Lord Hawthorn appeared duly chastened. "My apologies. You've come on an errand of mercy, and I have forgotten my manners with such talk."

"It's the least I could do," I said briskly, although I clasped my hands tightly before I betrayed my discomfort.

Father held up a hand. "No apologies necessary. You are not yourself, and I daresay pain or illness will test any man's patience."

Lord Hawthorn's wry smile returned. "I am grateful for your visit," he said. "To be honest, I've found myself ill-prepared for such involvement in my affairs."

I arched a quizzical eyebrow. "What surprises you, Lord Hawthorn? That the people of Bramnor care for one another? That they take a vested interest in each other's lives? We are not London, sir. You cannot wander the streets in anonymity here. True, village living may prove irksome. The butcher knows exactly what the baker is up to. We are simple folk and wish to benefit equally. All we want is a decent living and a solid roof over our heads."

"But you aspire to so much more," he challenged, folding his arms across his chest as if bracing himself for a pretty speech.

"I know we disagree about the dig, and I apologize if I was too forthright. But I believe we both want the same thing—a prosperous future for this valley. I've heard glowing reports from your tenants—how you allow delayed payment of rent for those struggling. Already, they speak of the fine new lord who will improve their lot in life. I want the same. I want the men and women in this valley to thrive. Surely an investment in the dig will prove beneficial to all involved."

I couldn't bring up my need to hunt for Daniel. Not with Father present. I couldn't discuss the fifty pounds offered by the Society of Antiquaries. But my reserve melted as I thought of the others who would benefit from the mosaics.

The viscount grew still. I continued, "I realize accolades hold no appeal for you, but perhaps a visitor's center for tourism and education might? Think of the people who would pay to see such a sight if you cared to invest."

He blew out a measured breath. "I don't care for the financial risk to myself involved, especially when indulging romantic fancies of lost civilizations. What if we dig and find nothing but rubble? I can hardly afford to put money into such speculation." He tapped his fingers on the carved armrests. "As I said before, I have always thought the past was better left buried."

"Yet you live in an abbey surely haunted with the memory of ghosts," I teased lightly. "Have you encountered a lonely monk wandering the halls yet? Or perhaps the lady of the house with a starched ruff topping her Elizabethan dress?"

His nostrils flared, despite my teasing tone. "The dead ought to be left alone. Any dig I allowed on my land would ruin the property forever. Wouldn't crops of apples and a cider business prove less risky if you want what is best for the families of Bramnor?"

"No. Crops fall prey to storm and blight," I answered. "The history of the mosaics and their owner would attract visitors year after year. Does that not intrigue you?"

"Not in the slightest. I don't want to know the secrets of history. I assure you, if the man was a landowner, and perhaps one who knew how fickle the Roman emperors could be, he lived a life driven by . . ." The viscount didn't finish his statement. His eyes darkened.

Frustration simmered within me, but I couldn't let it show. We needed those mosaics uncovered to the fullest extent, for the Perrys' sake and ours. "We can't know what his life was driven by if we do not excavate thoroughly."

Lord Hawthorn's lips thinned. "I've come to realize that you, Miss Littleton, are not above sharing your opinions. Let us see what the magistrate says regarding the property lines, and then we will be free to go our separate ways and do as we determine best."

Father touched my arm again, his warning more urgent. "My lord, I've been meaning to ask you about your thoughts on Wellington's recent advance. What do you think of the current situation?"

The conversation blurred as it drifted to different topics. I sensed the visit coming to a close, despite my father's efforts. Romantic fancies, indeed.

16

Bridget

> Everything comes gradually and at its appointed hour.
> OVID

I exhaled with relief as Father and I left the abbey. Lord Hawthorn had cooled, but I failed to persuade him about the excavation, which left me all the more unsettled.

To my surprise, Mr. Cobb stepped out of the shadows of the stable just as we were about to depart. My unease grew as he approached us.

"Mr. Cobb, what are you doing at the abbey at so late an hour?" Father asked.

"I've been doing some work for the viscount, although he's as close-fisted as they come. But I've been meaning to speak with you, Vicar, about the dig at Perry's," Mr. Cobb replied, his gaze shifting between us. With long hair the color of straw falling over his brow, small-set eyes, and a long nose, he reminded me of a rodent.

Father waved a dismissive hand in my direction. "Then you must speak with my daughter about the matter."

Mr. Cobb tipped forward so close I inched backward. "How much will you or Mr. Perry pay me to work those fields?"

"I fear not much, if anything," I answered bluntly. "Although we hope for more income should an antiquities society take interest."

Mr. Cobb glowered as he shoved his filthy hands into his coat pockets.

"You'll not tempt me or anyone else with that fare," he said as he pulled his felt hat over his narrowed eyes. He spat on the ground just as the chaise pulled forward.

We rattled down the rutted road filled with puddles from the rain. A sigh escaped Father. "I fear our conversation offended Lord Hawthorn."

Our conversation? More likely mine, but Father was altogether gracious.

When we arrived home, Mrs. Herriot greeted us in the parlor, waving a missive with a crimson seal. "A courier brought a letter for you all the way from London!"

"When did it arrive?" I cried as I removed my bonnet.

She beamed, still holding the letter pinched between her forefinger and thumb. "Shortly after you left."

A letter sent by courier suggested urgency. I didn't recognize the seal, but the Roman column in the center made my heart beat faster. Had the Society of Dilettanti or the Society of Antiquaries relented at long last? I opened it and was immediately greeted with a Latin phrase.

Publicae causa, studio rerum antiquorum.

I gulped and my hands trembled.

"What is it?" Mrs. Herriot cried while Father peered over my shoulder.

"For the sake of the commonwealth, with zeal for ancient things," I translated slowly.

"Don't keep us waiting!" she cried, wringing her hands. I obliged her, reading it out loud.

"My dearest Miss Littleton, I trust this letter finds you in the best of health and spirits. I am writing to you on behalf of the esteemed Society of Antiquaries of London, an association dedicated to the preservation and study of our nation's rich history and cultural heritage. Word has reached our esteemed society of your remarkable discoveries and scholarly pursuits in the realm of antiquities. The account of your diligent efforts, particularly in uncovering mosaics of historical significance in the village of Bramnor, has captured our collective imagination. We are eager to discuss these findings further and intend to visit Bramnor near the end of April to explore the site firsthand. We hope this timing is convenient and look forward to meeting with you and your esteemed colleagues."

I gasped, reading the name of Mr. Archibald Harrington, the Society's secretary.

Father squeezed my shoulder. "Well done, Bridget."

I closed my eyes, hardly believing it. The Society of Antiquaries, with their prestige, seemed certain to dismiss me for lacking formal education. I had believed that the Dilettanti, with their free-spirited noblemen, would support passion and talent over credentials. But the Society of Antiquaries surprised me, willing to recognize my work.

"They are coming for a visit!" I exclaimed. "Father, they received a royal charter from King George! The king follows them with great interest."

Mrs. Herriot clapped her hands, her cheeks flushed. "Imagine the Society of Antiquaries in the vicar's parsonage!"

My father cleared his throat, his gaze as misty as my own. "Remarkable news. I shall have to prepare a special set of sermons for the occasion, should Mr. Harrington's stay extend to a Sunday. Shall I title it The Miracles of Prayer?"

I had not prayed for this blessing, too intent on drafting letters and preparing my excavation notes. Had God intervened regardless of my lack of belief?

Father's innocent question would chafe at me in the days to come.

Late the next morning, I ran to the Perrys' cottage, lungs burning from the effort. Breathless, I knocked on the door.

Once within the warm cottage, I brought out the letter, allowing them to hold it, to finger the portion of the wax seal now severed in half as it clung to the paper. Abigail exclaimed over the seal before enveloping me in a tight hug.

"You're marvelous!" she exclaimed, her eyes sparkling as she pressed a kiss against my cheek. "You did it, Bridget!"

After finishing a light lunch, Mr. Perry had planned to return to his field, where he had been planting crops in a different section to avoid the contested area. However, the sight of the letter made him pause.

"This turns the whole game around," he mused, holding the letter carefully. "Do you think this society will pay me for the use of the farm? If they're serious, I might earn enough regardless of our crops."

I nodded, still out of breath. "I hope so." Never before had I held so much expectation that my plan might actually work. My only regret was that Daniel wasn't present to share in our triumph.

Show them, Bridget, what you can do. You were never meant to be a caged thing.

"We will be the talk of the town!" Abigail motioned for her father to return the letter to me. He did, albeit reluctantly.

"It's a marked change in fortune," I said, pleased with their enthusiasm but mindful of the need for discretion. "But we must keep this quiet for now. We don't want to draw attention until everything is secured."

Mr. Perry nodded in agreement, and I felt a surge of relief. The thought of furthering my studies and finally being taken seriously in academic circles was almost too wonderful to imagine.

"If that is true, then I wonder at the footprints around our cottage?" Mr. Perry asked. "They appeared a few days ago. I woke up to the sight. Thought I heard rustling outside the cottage late at night, but I dismissed it as only the wind."

Abigail rummaged through a basket and pulled out a shirt. She ducked her head and began stitching a tear with her thread and needle.

"You always hear things during the midnight hour, Papa. I investigated the fields after your fuss and there was nothing missing."

My skin prickled at the idea of someone creeping around the Perry cottage.

"Might have been a farmer," Mr. Perry said, although he didn't sound convinced. "Rupert Miller often wants to borrow something or other when I'm not home. Remember when he tried to take my ax without telling me, Abigail?"

When I turned to see Abigail's reaction, her attention seemed pinned to the square window where she sat next to the small table, another pair of shirts waiting to be mended.

"Yes," she said faintly, before turning to offer me a tepid smile. "Perhaps it was old Rupert, after all."

Mr. Perry had provided a perfectly reasonable explanation, but the thought lingered in my mind. The villagers' interest in our affairs had been growing. Only yesterday, Mrs. Herriot mentioned that two women stopped her in the village, asking if the rumors about our excavation were true. And then there was Lord Hawthorn's fury over his sheep.

"Mr. Barron offered his services, should we need them," I added, though with some hesitation, for I feared he might prove more flash than substance.

Abigail flushed prettily before she pivoted to the cupboard to retrieve two teacups. "When did you speak with him?"

"At the apothecary the other day, just before the rains ruined our dig. Now that things are drying out, we can resume as soon as the boundary lines are reestablished."

Even the viscount's tenants, especially Mr. Cobb, had been asking questions about the excavation, his probing persistent and unsettling. The last thing we needed was word spreading and treasure hunters descending on our valley.

Mr. Perry snatched his pipe from the table and stuffed it into his coat pocket. "I didn't tell you, but Mr. Spencer said the lord might be willing to buy my entire farm."

"Did he?" I asked. If Lord Hawthorn intended to expand the orchards, that could put an end to our excavation altogether. It wasn't just about the boundary lines anymore—he might try to halt our work entirely, claiming the entire stretch of land for his own use.

He chuckled without humor. "I told him my price would be too high."

Relief washed over me. "Father reached out to the magistrate, but it seems the man has traveled to Bath on family business."

Mr. Perry's grin faded. "I can't wait much longer, whether we dig for mosaics or plant the field. The growing season is slipping away, and I can't afford to miss it. But I won't give up my land without a fight. I'll not stand for what's rightfully mine to be stolen."

A similar anger flared within me. I wouldn't let the viscount outmaneuver us. The memory of him lounging on that sofa, listening to my plans for the valley, stung more than I cared to admit. I gnawed the inside of my cheek, chastened by how easily I'd shared our plans with the viscount.

"I confess I am surprised to hear of such an offer. When I visited Lord Hawthorn earlier, he did not mention it."

Abigail sighed as she reached for the steaming teapot. "Men are such troublesome creatures." Her tone held an edge as she poured me a cup of tea. As I took the cup, she hesitated, glancing at me with a mix of curiosity and concern. "I heard you took herbs to the viscount yesterday?"

I froze, surprised. "How did you hear about that?"

"Lucy mentioned it when she stopped by earlier this morning to see if I had anything to help her poor hens start laying again. I didn't realize you'd gone back to the abbey so soon."

I nodded, trying to hide my unease. "Yes. It was an errand of mercy, just as Father and I would offer any sick parishioner. But it didn't change his mind." Had my actions the appearance of something more like a tendre?

"I say we dig, and dig tomorrow," Abigail replied evenly. "We shouldn't hold back and wait for the magistrate's decision."

"It would be best to wait for the law to be on your father's side," I advised.

She huffed. "Remember your loyalties, Bridget. As your closest friend, I must advise you that we've come too far now to stop. Never forget who the Hawthorns truly are. Such men do not change."

Father would disagree with that sentiment, but my brother's disappearance had left a void that I couldn't ignore, and every delay in the excavation felt like another step away from finding him—or at least understanding what happened to him.

I reached for a biscuit, but the taste barely registered. Daniel believed Bramnor's secrets held the key to something greater if I had but the courage to look, and I needed to prove him right.

Lord Hawthorn had once teased me about the war between us ending. Perhaps he had spoken too soon.

17

Rafe

> Time discovers the truth.
> **SENECA**

Two and a half weeks had passed since my fever, and each day my strength returned with Miss Littleton's remedy. The vicar's visits were comforting, but I missed her razor wit. The abbey felt strangely dull without her, and I often watched her and Miss Perry digging next door—a quiet race unfolding between us.

Her determination mirrored my own. I didn't mind her father's report of their progress: a four-by-ten-foot section of mosaic—Venus and her cupids, the goddess of love, he said with a twinkle in his eyes.

But my attention needed to return to the estate. The road skirting the orchard had become my focus. Progress was slow, but necessary to secure Mr. Talbot's approval. His suggestion to angle the service road through the mosaic field nagged at me, though ownership remained disputed.

How I needed more coin! I had written to my barrister, requesting the discreet sale of the abbey's finest pieces. His delayed response was another frustration. Later that morning, after checking on the men's progress, I returned to the study, seeking any records or receipts that might prove my uncle had tried to redeem the estate. Mr. Talbot's accusation of missing taxes loomed over me like a shadow. Reluctantly, I opened my uncle's diary again, hoping to find something of value to prove the Crown representative might be wrong.

Flipping through the familiar pages, I stopped short—a page had been ripped out. A chill ran through me. My heart raced as I turned to the next entry:

I never want to see his miserable face again. I will never forgive him. I wish he was dead.

Had my uncle killed my father? The rumors had haunted me for years, but seeing his words in ink . . . I couldn't bring myself to read further. The past seemed determined to haunt me.

Before I could close the book, shouts echoed from outside. I stood quickly, my leg protesting the sudden movement, but I ignored it and hurried outside. The men had gathered near the road where the orchard began, their brows furrowed.

"My lord," Mr. Whittle began, "we've struck something near the old orchard. It appears Mr. Perry isn't the only one blessed with ancient ruins. I say it isn't right to dig up those demons. Best leave them in the soil and cover it all up for decency's sake."

Dismay filled me as I followed my groundskeeper outside to the orchard. All the men, seven including Mr. Spencer and the Dixon boys, gathered around me, their eyes wide with terror. As we approached the far end of the orchard skirting my property, where the old lane leading from the abbey now took a turn to the right, a mound of dirt waited.

"What did you find?" I asked Mr. Spencer.

My steward pointed to a mound of dirt near several apple saplings waiting to be planted. "We saw men hacking at each other with swords, blood everywhere. These ancients fought like brutes. But there's more—you'd better come see for yourself."

"Land's cursed," one of the Dixon boys whispered to his younger brother. "Mr. Cobb says ghosts haunt Hawthorn Abbey, howling their outrage, and this proves it. Miss Whittle says she's heard things in the abbey going bump at night too."

The only one howling happened to be me, a curse of war and nightmares, but I had no intention of sharing that tidbit. No doubt most of them had heard about it already.

"Aye, wicked, wicked things have happened here," Mr. Hinsley muttered.

"There are no ghosts," I corrected them, irritated that my tenants would spread vile slander. "Men either go to heaven or to hell. There is no in-between."

A barely contained shudder passed through me as I recalled my uncle's journal entry.

You must forgive those who hurt you. My mother's voice drifted to me on the edge of the wind rustling through orchard branches. She had raised me to forgo bitterness, to let go of the past. I had not been allowed to ask questions, yet how could I forget the night we bundled into the carriage and fled? The longer I stayed within the abbey, the more those memories poured into me until I felt like a cracked vessel about to burst. No wonder I wanted to spend each waking hour out in nature.

When I reached the spot where mounds of dirt lay, my breath caught in my chest. Another mosaic appeared in the ground showing two armed men with chests and legs bare clashing in an eternal battle. I had read enough about the gladiatorial combats of ancient Rome during my military years to recognize the net and trident entangled with the short sword of the other opponent. Both men wore heavy helmets with enormous plumes. Tiles painted the color of rust indicated a fight to the death.

"Looks like the animal fights at the Bear Garden in Southwark where a man can pay to watch a bull maul a pair of dogs." My steward snickered.

I glanced at him, curious if he had pursued such entertainment. He shrugged, neither confirming nor denying it. Rubbing my chin, I studied the mosaic. Miss Littleton would not likely shy from the gladiators, unlike some of the men clustered around me. My gaze rose to the nearby Perry field where two canvases lay over the ground like bandages hiding gaping wounds.

Had I been too hasty, too harsh, in refusing her request? Her desire to help others mirrored my own, as she'd said.

"My lord, please, we found something else." Mr. Spencer sounded strained as he removed his hat. "You must follow me immediately."

Now thoroughly curious and alarmed, I hurried as fast as I could, my leg far less painful these days, thanks to Miss Littleton's medicinal herbs. Mr. Spencer motioned me forward, pointing to another mound where a fragile sapling, the roots still wrapped in burlap, lay discarded on the ground.

"Our shovels hit something and when we scraped aside the dirt, we saw a pile of bones. At first we thought it was nothing more than roots . . ." The oldest Dixon boy stopped and backed away. His younger brother stood behind him, eyes large and round.

Within the dirt, a tiny skeleton lay in a contorted mess as if discarded. I was not a squeamish man, but the sight of an innocent child buried and now uprooted within the orchard I had run barefoot through as a boy made me ill. I sucked in a noisy, horrified breath, unfortunately drawing the attention of the surrounding men from their talk of evil spirits and wicked men.

The men surrounding me grew silent as the wind whistled through the orchard trees.

A place intended for growth and life, now tainted with death. Who was this poor babe?

"Satan's work," a man mumbled from behind me while I groaned inside.

No matter what I did, I could not escape the secrets and the curses of the Hawthorn legacy.

18

Bridget

> The thorns which I have reap'd are of the tree
> I planted; they have torn me, and I bleed.
> I should have known what fruit would spring from such a seed.
> **LORD BYRON**

"Bridget, they've found a child's bones at Hawthorn Abbey." Father's voice broke as his hand trembled on my shoulder.

I had just placed my sketchbook on the desk, where I planned to write about my latest findings regarding the Venus mosaics, when a frantic knock at the front door had interrupted my documentation.

"What?" I cried as I swiveled in my chair. "What do you mean?"

"Yes, the tenants found a skeleton this morning while planting trees in the orchard."

The hair on my neck rose as I pushed aside my notes. My mind filled with lurid possibilities, none fit for polite company."

"A murder? Or a sickly child, buried due to tragic circumstances?"

Father shook his head. "Mr. Dixon came to the parsonage a moment ago, begging for us to go to the abbey. He claims they discovered the remains close to a gladiatorial mosaic. I plan to offer what guidance I can, at least until the constable arrives."

Father continued babbling while my mind whirled, struggling to latch on to the tumbling words. A dead child? Gladiator mosaics?

He did not protest when I grabbed my satchel of utensils to join him.

I stepped out of the chaise, my wide-brimmed straw hat shielding me from the sun just as Mrs. Whittle hurried out of the abbey entrance, wringing her hands.

"Oh, Miss Littleton, such dreadful news! Who would have thought, an innocent child found within our orchards?"

I offered some consolation but needed to see the site before the men caused more damage.

"I won't sleep a wink tonight," she bemoaned as she clutched my arm, preventing me from leaving. "And the Dixon boys won't stop with their tales of ghosts wandering through the abbey. Did I tell you my Lucy hears the strangest things in the afternoon and at night? And I don't need to tell you how the lord cries out so in his sleep. Like a wounded lamb."

My heart clenched with pity for the viscount, no matter how loudly Abigail's words of caution echoed in my mind.

"He has nightmares?" I asked in a low voice while glancing around to make sure we were alone, aside from my father, who secured the chaise. It would be a shame if anyone overheard Mrs. Whittle. I suspected the Dixon boys would gladly spread idle tales, and nothing thrilled quite like those of nighttime sounds echoing through the cloistered halls.

The older woman's plump hand fluttered to her throat. "Yes.

My husband says it's on account of the war, but the lord keeps it all tightly bottled within until the midnight hour."

Placing what I hoped was a comforting hand on hers, I offered her a sympathetic smile. "He needs a touch of compassion, Mrs. Whittle. Those nightmares will eventually fade."

I refrained from adding that Lucy needed a cat to keep her company and to chase away the scuttling.

Father waited at the edge of the courtyard, shooting me a meaningful look to hurry, and I rushed to follow him. Past the stable with the slate roof, I spied a group of men clustered together when we rounded the bend. My pulse sped even though I sternly bade it to slow.

Lord Hawthorn's form towered over the others. He folded his arms across his chest, the forearms bare with sleeves rolled high enough to reveal a sprinkling of black hair. Clad in linen trousers, minus the country felt hat the other men sported, with only a black waistcoat, he seemed no different from the other farmers pressed close to him. I found I rather liked his rugged appearance. Far less formal than the military man with his uptight bearing.

One man jabbed a pointed finger toward the orchard. Voices raised, fearful or angry, I could not tell, but I had the distinct impression of a storm about to break.

"This is a grim business." Father lent me his arm as we approached the group. Nerves sparked to life as I considered the scene.

Lord Hawthorn lifted his head, his gaze colliding with mine. Dare I admit I saw relief, yet he was too far for me to make such a presumption. After seeing us, he walked in our direction. I couldn't deny the rebellious spark of pleasure at witnessing his improved health since my last visit.

He spoke first. "Vicar, Miss Littleton. Thank you for coming so soon."

"I hope you don't mind my intrusion," I said. "Father told me your men uncovered something, and I would like to see—to see . . ." I faltered, uncertain how to proceed when describing such a find. "If you are willing, I want to examine what you found."

"Have you discovered anything about the child?" Father spoke boldly.

The lord shook his head, his lips pressed into a thin line. "Nothing so far. I have the constable hopefully arriving soon," he warned me. "I want nothing disturbed further until he's cleared the area of any foul play."

"Constable Wickham? Goodness. He's hardly the brightest . . ." I caught myself just before saying something I would truly regret. "Carry on, Lord Hawthorn. Perhaps Father and I can be of some assistance in the meantime."

"It is not a pretty sight." He studied me, as if expecting me to swoon, then nodded as if assured I wouldn't. I trailed him through the orchard, noticing a slight shudder in his shoulders. Even a hardened military man could blanch.

At last, the old orchard ended and we came upon row after row of new saplings spread to the edge of the western stone wall. I must have exclaimed my dismay, since he halted mid-step and pivoted until he faced me.

"I've ordered a cider press," Lord Hawthorn explained to my father while observing me. Almost defensively, to my way of thinking. "I intend to expand the orchards as much as possible."

My heart clenched. "All the way to Mr. Perry's land?"

He inhaled sharply. "I have asked the men to leave the edge of the orchard alone until the magistrate determines where my land ends and Mr. Perry's begins. I'll curve the service road to the west. You should have more than enough room to excavate until the property lines are settled."

My jaw must have dropped in the most undignified manner since Father touched my elbow. What had prompted his decision? I would have said so much more, but I stopped at the edge of the orchard, next to the tender saplings planted this morning, where my gaze finally dropped to a small pitiful mound in the dirt.

"The Dixon boys stumbled across the child there while planting the new trees." He scowled, gesturing to the site where additional saplings lay discarded on the ground, ready to be planted.

I knelt beside the grave, reaching for the bones before pulling my hand back.

"Poor child. I wonder at your sad story. I'm not an expert on bones." I turned to Father. "Based on the size of the skeleton, how old do you think this child might have been at death? I think only two years at the most."

He stroked his chin, leaning over my shoulder. "I agree."

I frowned as I removed a long-handled artist's brush from my bag and nudged aside one bone. The passing years had stripped away all sense of identity.

"But the exact age, or date of death, might be harder to determine."

"Why do you say so?" Lord Hawthorn demanded, his voice rough.

With my brush, I gently nudged aside the ancient earth, flicking away the remaining debris. A gasp escaped me as I studied a slender shape emerging with each brushstroke. The form of a miniature woman, jointed and yellowed.

"Miss Littleton, please—" Now he sounded anguished. "I promised the constable that nothing would be unduly disturbed."

I raised my head. "I suspect this grave has existed for centuries. I can't help but wonder if there is a connection to our Roman villa?"

"A Roman child?" Lord Hawthorn blew out a long breath while palming the back of his neck. He visibly relaxed with my proclamation, his relief palatable. Had he worried that the grave might implicate further secrets hidden by the Hawthorn family?

I nodded. "And buried with a doll, I think."

"A doll?"

By then, the tenants had gathered around us, forming a tight circle as they jostled for a better view, their boots nearly stepping on my gown as I knelt. Lord Hawthorn pulled one man away who dared to tip too close in order to see better.

I pointed to it. "An ivory doll with jointed limbs. Her hair looks Roman in style, carved into rolls with a ribbon holding her curls in place."

Father placed his hand on my shoulder, squeezing gently. "It could be more recent."

"Yes. Even the Saxons buried trinkets with their loved ones, but not with dolls with Roman-era hairstyles," I agreed readily. "Now, if it was a Roman family, that is interesting. Children needed no funeral rites since they were considered pure of spirit. Their deaths polluted none and hence they could not haunt the family. The smallest were buried *under the eaves* of the family home, otherwise known as *suggrundarium*. According to the Romans, children only gained full humanity by degrees, with careful teaching and discipline. Yet someone loved this little one enough to ensure a proper burial, which is unusual."

My emotions must have played across my face, since Lord Hawthorn's gaze softened a touch. My throat clogged at the idea of a mother forced to bury her beloved child. After all, I had buried someone I loved and the pain of it lingered still, ebbing and flowing with the seasons.

I forced myself to speak. "Do I understand, Lord Hawthorn, that you also have another mosaic?"

"Gladiators," Lord Hawthorn answered readily as he reached for my hand to assist me. He wore no glove. After a moment's hesitation, I took his hand. His warm fingers engulfed mine, lifting me to my feet. The touch was all too brief. Flustered, I allowed him to guide me to the recently discovered mosaic.

A gasp escaped from my lips when I saw the image of two men locked in immortal combat. "You have a *retiarius*, the fish man, tussling with a *secutor* and his sword. We know what vices the owner preferred, don't we? Is it possible he hosted gladiatorial matches here? Did he dabble in buying and selling gladiators? Or was he but a simple landowner, following the latest decorating trends?"

Father winced, drawing back from the sight. "*There is no new thing under the sun.* Sin has always been, and always will continue."

With a sigh, I retraced my steps to the grave to gather my satchel from the ground. "There is nothing so reliable as the blackness of souls."

"And nothing so reliable as God's grace to redeem us from that darkness," Father replied gently.

I paused at his quiet admission, something in his tone striking a chord I hadn't expected. Could I have misjudged him all this time? I had always assumed his sternness had driven Daniel away, that his countless hours spent with the old viscount were neglectful of us. But hearing him now, I wondered—had he been longing for Daniel's return too? Had I been mistaken in thinking he cared more for duty than for his own children?

It was safer to change the subject. I moved closer to Lord Hawthorn. "May I take the ivory doll? It could help date the villa."

I expected a firm no. Instead, he exhaled slowly.

"After the constable views the site," came the careful answer.

A breath escaped from my own parted mouth as I stared at Lord Hawthorn to see if I had lost my senses. "I beg your pardon, did I hear you correctly?"

"The doll is yours. As long as . . ." He paused when the murmuring of other men rose, including one sullen man, Mr. Cobb, who was whispering about ghosts and curses and Hawthorn Abbey.

"It's yours to study," Lord Hawthorn said more firmly. He moved closer as well to peer at the crumbled earth and in doing so, his sleeve brushed against the sleeves of my pelisse. I could scarcely believe his acquiescence.

"Thank you," I said as emotion clogged my throat. *"Thank you."*

Something tightened in my chest at the hint of vulnerability in his eyes—or perhaps it was my imagination.

I glanced at the doll, itching to examine it more closely, but restrained myself, remembering his words. The constable needed to see it first. Instead, I carefully tucked the clean handkerchief back into my satchel, waiting for the moment when I could properly gather it safely and bring it home.

"Of course, I shall have to ask the Society of Antiquaries what their thoughts are on the subject and have them confirm the find," I added absently as I stared at the doll as if I could coax answers from it.

The viscount's softened expression dissipated just as quickly as it appeared. "They will insist on trampling on my lands. It's one thing if you study the grounds, but a society will require far greater involvement."

I held his gaze, hoping he would understand my position. "I've written to them about the finds so far. I believe this will intrigue them further when they come to visit. I wrote the Dilettanti as well. All I need is one society to respond to my letter."

A muscle ticked within his jaw as he glanced again at the grave site. "I do not want *any* society rummaging through my orchard."

"You may want to rethink that sentiment when Constable Wickham arrives. At least you can tell him you've done all you can to find out the age of the child. But I beg you, don't let him take anything. Antiquarian experts must first examine the site."

Lord Hawthorn plunged a hand through his hair until the ends stuck up in whorls. "I have a road to finish and trees to plant. None of them can wait or I'll lose my investment."

Father lightly touched my arm, signaling for me to cease before I created further trouble, but I nudged his hand aside, determined to speak my piece.

"My lord, I have no intention of causing you further trouble. Please believe me; I want to help you as much as possible. Let us put the rumors of spirits to rest." I meant it, especially considering how he had treated Mrs. Eacher and the tenants, along with assuring me he would leave the edge of Mr. Perry's field alone.

Abigail cautioned me about him, but the more I saw, the harder it was to view him as an adversary.

And if his actions continued to surprise me, my declaration certainly had the same effect. His mouth parted before one of the tenants called to him, drawing the viscount's attention from me while leaving me to wonder at what he might have said.

19

Bridget

> For in much wisdom is much grief: and he that
> increaseth knowledge increaseth sorrow.
>
> **ECCLESIASTES 1:18**

The constable, as expected, had yet to arrive. His absence had not gone unnoticed, but with the day drawing to a close, Father and Lord Hawthorn were among the last to leave the mosaic site, their low voices carrying the weight of the day's discoveries.

As they finally joined the rest of us in the abbey courtyard, the men began packing up their tools, resigned to resume the investigation in the morning. Most of the tenants dispersed and left the abbey grounds, though a few lingered behind, including Mr. Whittle and the Dixon boys.

While we waited for Father and Lord Hawthorn to finish their conversation, an argument broke out among the men who remained, their voices rising as dusk settled over the courtyard.

"Can we find a buyer for the mosaic?" Mr. Whittle asked. "Someone might pay a pretty sum for it. If Mr. Perry can do it, why not you, my lord?"

"What about the bones? Why not sell them? Or advertise them as a roadside attraction, eh? With ghost stories to boot," one of the Dixon boys suggested.

At that, I cringed, although museums did much the same, displaying Egyptian scarabs and sarcophagi for anyone to see.

"No." Lord Hawthorn's deep voice rose over the others clamoring with suggestions. "In fact, I want you all to plant west from the site." Then he added in a clipped tone, "And keep away from Perry's property as much as possible."

"An excellent decision, my lord," my father said. "I don't relish disturbing graves either."

"It would hardly be decent otherwise," Lord Hawthorn noted. "We'll wait for the proper authorities to assess the remains. You and your daughter are welcome to return for further study."

He glanced my way, almost as if he had intended for me to overhear his offer. My cheeks heated to be caught studying him in so open a manner. In the evening light, with the sun touching the newly trimmed hedge and turning a profusion of flowers to gold, something shifted within me. He was not at all what I had expected in a lord. He actually listened to his tenants, allowing them to give advice, and responding in turn when questioned, giving careful reasons for his decisions.

I assumed Father and I would soon leave in the chaise, but Lord Hawthorn left his workers, his uneven stride eating up the distance in the courtyard.

"Thank you, Miss Littleton, for your assistance. Where did you gain such knowledge of Rome?"

I shrugged one shoulder to hide how much the compliment affected me. "Bramnor offers so little that I had no choice but to turn to history books and journals to escape the confines of village life."

His lips quirked. "Yes, your nose in a book, getting a regular dose of isolated castles and blackhearted villains."

"I do not read only about women trapped in castles, Lord Hawthorn. You might enjoy Samuel Squire's dissertation on the antiquities of the Anglo-Saxon government."

"Doubtful," he replied with a smirk. "But I am impressed, Miss Littleton. And I do not impress easily."

I didn't share that my brother had often written to the librarians on my behalf, requesting certain classical volumes. All that changed when he squandered Father's money at the gambling hells in London instead of attending seminary. Now, in his painful absence, I latched on to the things that made me feel alive.

"You may have nipped a clandestine rumor of the Hawthorn family before it started and I am truly grateful." His voice thickened as he rested a bronzed hand against the chaise.

Whether he liked it or not, rumors would continue to haunt him.

"I must warn you, sir, the story of a grave will still spread, unfortunately. We can only turn the light to it and expose the truth for what it really is."

His jaw clenched, a tiny muscle jumping once again. "The truth? It may cause more pain than it's worth."

He was no longer speaking about the mosaics and the grave site.

"Leave no stone unturned," I answered firmly. "How can we learn or grow if we do not understand the past? How can we heal if we do not fully examine what happened to us?"

He folded his arms across his chest. "I know how poorly you think of my family's name."

My cheeks heated. "I spoke hot, rash words that evening we

first met, my lord. Words from an impetuous woman fretting over a damaged sketch. I am sorry for any offense I caused."

"But you spoke the truth. In my experience, neither my father nor my uncle cared much about anyone else's needs," he said in a low voice. "Unlike your family. You might be the most outspoken woman I've ever met. One with a stinging quip and a healing balm. I am indebted to you in more ways than one. You seem to work enchantments, even with your tinctures, bringing healing wherever you go, whether with Mrs. Eacher or . . . myself."

"It is my pleasure." I could not hide my smile, relieved that he had not chosen to take offense at that first meeting or my suggestion to bring in the societies. "And, speaking truthfully, you will find a ready friend in my father, as he was to your uncle. He cared deeply for the former viscount."

Lord Hawthorn looked over his shoulder to where my father stood speaking with the tenants. Had I overstepped my bounds by saying that a viscount and a vicar could find friendship? I bit the inside of my cheek, ruing my frank speech. I had lived in the countryside for too long, far away from the well-ordered rules of the ton. My manners must seem rustic.

The viscount turned to me. "And you, Miss Littleton, may I also consider you a friend? I find them a precious commodity." His voice had dropped to a husky note.

The words were innocent, but the way he said them, it was almost as if . . .

My breath caught as his gaze held mine.

"Yes, I should like to think we could be friends."

His mouth tilted in a full smile. And it was quite a pleasant thing, completely transforming his face. His admission settled within me, stirring sympathy as he left me to join the tenants.

A man could have everything and still be very much alone.

Later, within the comfort of the drawing room, I removed the doll from my satchel and gently laid her on the desk just as Mrs. Herriot brought the requested bowl of warm water and a soft cloth.

"La!" She curled her upper lip as she leaned over my shoulder to see better. "A naked woman."

I skimmed a gloved finger against the smooth ivory stained from centuries of earth. "Once clothed, Mrs. Herriot. But you see if your clothes will last over a thousand years."

She did not appreciate my flippant answer, yet she remained by my side as I dipped a scrap of fabric into the bowl. I recognized the scrap of cloth as having been snipped from one of my brother's shirts.

Daniel. The fine weave brought a host of memories of him. Better days. Awful days, especially when I tried to raise him just as I had promised Mother.

How I loved him, even if I wanted to throttle sense into him. If only he knew how his absence, his weakness of character, continued to hurt Father. And hurt me in equal measure.

Why couldn't we recover from my mother's death? Why did Father bury himself in work, and Daniel turn to vice? Was this how we managed without her?

"I do hope you didn't bring an idol into the parsonage," Mrs. Herriot told me as she leaned even closer, smelling of lemon oil. "This obsession of yours won't garner the respect of the rectorship."

"On the contrary, I've met many a curate or rector who appreciates history, especially since that era connects to our Lord and the early church. And this isn't an idol. It's a child's toy, created to be as lifelike as possible."

Each stroke of the cloth revealed a yellowed hue of ivory. And joints for the slender legs to bend and the elbows to swing.

"At any rate, that ugly thing seems scratched."

My pulse sped as I cleaned the ivory, coaxing two symbols to emerge on the back of the doll. An inarticulate sound escaped me as I stared at the antiquity, scarcely believing my eyes.

Not scratches, but rather letters of the Greek alphabet. A faint line curled to make a *P* and a crooked *x*.

Frustrated with my lack of conversation, she abandoned me to my pursuits, which truthfully, were as intense as Father's obsessions.

The markings on the doll were of a Christian nature. Stunned, I turned the doll over, searching for a name or anything else, and finding nothing of further interest.

I had discovered a humble Christian symbol near one of the most majestic homes paying homage to Bacchus and Medusa.

If the Almighty had a message for me, I scarcely knew what to think.

***

The sound of a man weeping, from my father's study no less, slowed my descent on the staircase as morning light poured through the window above the entry door. I had planned to leave for the Perry field after breakfast. Straining to hear better, I could not discern if other voices accompanied the weeping. At last, I tiptoed down the hall to my father's study.

Familiar scents greeted me as I slipped inside. Leather, ink, and the faint whisper of chamomile tea. Father's shoulders heaved with one long shuddering breath as he removed a handkerchief to wipe his face. His glasses sat on the desk alongside a letter.

"What is the matter?" I asked, my heart clenching at this new display of grief.

He pivoted, his eyes reddened. "I have just received word that the authorities have placed your brother under arrest in a hulk outside Portsmouth."

"A hulk? A floating prison?" Shock rippled through me. I was not prone to hysterics or smelling salts, but suddenly my stays pinched in the most uncomfortable manner as I struggled to breathe.

"The charge?"

"Riot and striking an officer," Father said, his voice thick with shame. "He incited the men—he was at the center of it. And now they're going to court-martial him."

"But the conditions—" I protested, trying to steady my shaking hands. "He was compelled against his will to join!"

Father shot me a disapproving look as he tucked a sodden handkerchief into his coat pocket. "Conditions or not, Bridget, Daniel has disgraced this family. Striking an officer in the middle of a riot? He is fortunate they haven't hung him already. The Royal Navy presses men from all over the country, forcing each area to meet their quota. You think Daniel is the first to disagree with his superiors? He should have followed orders and learned something of discipline."

My heart sank. I picked up the letter from the desk, its formal tone making the cold reality clear.

"Can we hire a lawyer? Plead his case?"

"With what funds?" Father said, sinking into his chair. "Who would extend us a line of credit after this? We're ruined, Bridget. Completely ruined."

I turned away, desperate for air. The society's fifty pounds felt so far away, so out of reach, yet it was my only hope. Father didn't know about my plans—the idea of telling him now felt laughable. How could I secure Daniel's defense when I had nothing to offer but a dream of publication?

I did the only thing I could. I walked out and shut the door, letting the barrier fall between us. After I gained control of my breathing, I escaped the parsonage with my book and tools in my satchel.

When I reached Abigail's cottage, the curtains were drawn. After rapping on the door, I found myself face-to-face with my dear friend. Desperate for comfort and companionship, I gestured to my trusty satchel loaded with supplies.

"Care to join me for an hour?"

"La, how I wish I could," she exclaimed. Her cheeks seemed unnaturally pink, and she refused me entrance into the house I considered as familiar as my own home. "I'm feeling a might peckish of late with a sore throat." As if to reinforce her point, she fingered her throat, where I noticed her fichu sat somewhat astray to reveal a flushed collarbone. A bright smile bloomed on her face, though it didn't quite reach her eyes. "I shall rest today, if you don't mind."

"Shall I bring a poultice or herbs for you?"

She shook her head gently. "Nay, I wouldn't want to cause any further trouble. I heard you've visited the viscount, so you must be running low on supplies. But if you happen upon anything interesting in Papa's field, you'll let me know?"

The door slammed shut just as I murmured an agreement, too shocked to argue. From the deepest part of the main room, I heard a loud sneeze. Someone was with Abigail, but I couldn't quite place who it might be. Perhaps it was Mr. Perry, although I hadn't noticed him being ill earlier. Abigail had always been private, but her guardedness felt new, making me wonder if I had upset her.

I whirled and marched to the field. Heavy in spirit, I crouched down at the villa floor, willing the earth to bring some distraction to the hollowness threatening to consume me. I pulled out my notebook and pencils and sketched a magnificent border with entwined loops to accompany my latest notes regarding the dig. With the endless sky stretched above, I had never felt more alone. More than once, the charcoal broke within my pinched grip.

Daniel . . . Father . . .

My mind drifted to the child's bones. It was far easier to focus on the burial spot and the doll than to examine my family. Such a loving action to honor and cherish a beloved daughter, to place her in the prettiest spot of the valley where the butterflies danced among the wildflowers. Before I realized it, a tear splattered against my sketchbook as a writhing Medusa took shape with each stroke, her fierce stare forcing me to examine my own heart. A heart slowly freezing to stone.

Unable to stand Medusa's gaze much longer, I fled to the only other place where I might find safety.

My dear friend greeted me at the door of her cottage. Her filmy eyes never wavered in staring at me, and a girlish smile brightened her face when she heard my voice.

We sat by the cozy fireplace. I arranged my skirts and opened the book, flipping the pages to our last spot.

"As the carriage-wheels rolled heavily under the portcullis, Emily's heart sunk, and she seemed, as if she was going into her prison; the gloomy court, into which she passed, served to confirm the idea, and her imagination, ever awake to circumstance, suggested even more terrors, than her reason could justify . . ."

"Bridget, stop."

I halted at the gentle command.

"Something is wrong," Mrs. Eacher said. "What is it?"

Closing the book with a decided thud, I debated sharing everything since I was so used to being dismissed. She patiently waited for my answer as the fire crackled and popped beneath the fireplace mantel. Before long, I found myself spilling the entire sordid story regarding my brother, including the promise I made to my mother on her deathbed. I even shared that fateful accident years ago when Abigail and Daniel left me behind.

"I've completely failed," I told her. "I cannot get through to Daniel, nor can I ensure Abigail's future, nor even my own. I cannot see God's hand working in these circumstances. He remains ever remote from me."

A heavy sigh escaped her as she leaned forward, reaching with tentative hands to clasp my own.

"You know the answer, Bridget, but I sense it isn't enough for you. You no longer trust God to work in your life. Your relationship with your father has colored your relationship with your heavenly Father. Don't misunderstand me. This village loves the vicar for all he has done, but he never should have sacrificed you and Daniel on the altar of service. We all grieve in different ways. Your father chose to do it alone, distracting that pain with duty."

"Mrs. Eacher . . ." I breathed, feeling terribly guilty about casting any shame or blame on his shoulders. Father also sounded remarkably similar to me.

"As much as you seek purpose and recognition, have you considered what truly matters? What good is acclaim if it cannot save your brother? You are chasing after things that may never bring you the peace you long for. God's path offers clarity and assurance—will you let it guide you to what you truly seek?"

I pulled free of her loose grip, my mouth suddenly dry. Her challenge hurt, but I couldn't deny the truth of it. "I must go."

"Before you leave," Mrs. Eacher interrupted me, "is it true that they found a child buried on Lord Hawthorn's land?"

Grateful she couldn't see my facial expression, especially when she'd surprised me with such a direct question, I answered, "Yes, they uncovered a child, a daughter buried with an ivory doll. She died far before the Hawthorns ever took possession of the land. How did you learn of the news?"

She tugged her shawl tighter across her frail shoulders. "Mr. Cobb, one of the tenants, heard the tale. He says the child was likely murdered."

"I went to see the grave for myself. I suspect he heard snippets and stretched the tale for entertainment."

"He holds no regard for the new lord, and makes no bones about sharing his feelings," Mrs. Eacher answered. "I remember the Hawthorn brothers. Of course, I was younger then with decent eyesight. Handsome, both of them. Turning the head of each lass in Bramnor. Their father had a reputation for his abject cruelty, and they grew to become just like him."

"What do you recall of the family?" I asked. I didn't want to indulge in gossip, but I wanted to understand the viscount better. My father would likely tell me to manage my own affairs, as he usually hinted whenever I probed too deeply into the lives of the parishioners.

"Lady Hawthorn was more a prisoner than a beloved wife. You and I may enjoy our gothic tales, but to see such wicked events unfold within this sleepy community . . ." Mrs. Eacher paused, her sightless eyes drifting to the window.

"Is there any truth to the tales?" I probed.

"Truth often exceeds fiction. Anne Hawthorn had no title, but her family engaged in trade and had money. She must have witnessed unfathomable things within that abbey since her husband, Randall, chased after farmer's wives and female servants alike. She fled when Rafe was only six years of age. It was not long after her departure that her husband's murder made the papers all across England resulting in a scandal that shocked the country. The circumstances surrounding his death were murky, with whispers that the viscount himself had a hand in his brother's demise, all for the sake of Anne. Following the scandal, the viscount withdrew completely from society, becoming a pariah in nearly every circle." Mrs. Eacher shook her head.

"Then something happened in the old viscount, and no doubt on account of your father's influence. When the former lord learned of my husband's sudden passing, he asked what I needed. The costs of the funeral overwhelmed me, and he promised to pay for my expenses and never raise my rent, a boon that the current viscount has promised to extend. I can't ever forget such kindness."

Lord Hawthorn's question circled in my mind. *Do you believe that God can change a man?* I shifted again in my chair, uncomfortable. I had hoped that good common sense and logic would change Daniel. Not faith, nor God.

She paused for a long moment before resuming her story. "Lady Anne's faith was a testament in the darkest of hours. I'll never forget how she shared with me in this cottage her plans to leave. We all wanted to protect her and young Rafe. When I asked her what I could do to help, she asked for prayer. She told me that no matter what happened, she would trust God to watch over her son and her."

I swallowed past the lump in my throat. Mrs. Eacher, of course, had eschewed subtlety with her lesson, but I understood perfectly. Would I release my brother into God's care at long last?

A ragged sigh escaped at the same time a flood of compassion for Lord Hawthorn filled me. No wonder he had paled at the idea of others crawling over his property, scrutinizing his family's torrid past. No wonder he felt tremendously alone—an emotion I was well acquainted with.

20

Bridget

The necessity of circumstances proves friends and detects enemies.
EPICTETUS

Three days later, I visited Abigail at her cottage to ask after her health and to see if I could persuade her to accompany me to view Lord Hawthorn's mosaics. I dreaded offending her, but I could hardly go alone.

To my shock, and with hardly any persuasion, she changed her morning dress and joined me, her attitude a far cry from what it was on my previous visit. In fact, she seemed in such good spirits, I could only wonder at her change of heart regarding a visit to Lord Hawthorn.

When I asked her, she merely winked. "Perhaps I need to keep an eye on the competition. Let us see how impressive Lord Hawthorn's mosaics really are. You don't think he'll open a tourist center, do you? Papa wondered if we could charge per guest next year."

"A wonderful plan." I nodded. "The mosaics could bring a steady income for years."

She brightened considerably at my agreement, and I was glad to have my friend back. However, I noticed she carried no extra handkerchiefs within her reticule. Nor did she appear to suffer from a fever. A swift recovery by all appearances, but I was relieved for it.

I longed to share the latest news regarding my brother and to find assurance that my trials would resolve in the end, but Abigail filled the silent spaces of our walk with constant chatter regarding the town, Mr. Cording's failing attempt to court her, and the other young men who begged her to save a dance for them at the upcoming May festival.

I stifled my own thoughts, my nods perfunctory.

"Your attention is drifting like a dandelion puff, Bridget. Did you hear a word I said?" Abigail demanded as she pushed back the brim of her straw hat to view me better.

"Plenty of men wish to dance with you. Yes, I heard you, and I heartily agree that you should set your sights on none of them. Let them play the role of the noble knight and woo you so thoroughly you'll have no regrets if you do marry this year."

She laughed, the sound bright and tinkling. "How romantic you sound."

Romance was the furthest thing from my mind, even if a certain man had accused me of such fancies.

Ahead, the great stone abbey waited against a brilliant blue sky—a sky far too cheerful for ghosts and family curses. I found my steps quickening, forcing Abigail to keep pace with me. I knocked the door rapper, but no one came to greet us for several minutes.

At last, just as Abigail and I were about to turn for home, the grand door opened. Mr. Whittle admitted us into the hall, his expression harried.

"Forgive my delay," Mr. Whittle whispered, ushering us inside as he shut the door. His worn livery jacket pinched at the seams. "The viscount is meeting with the constable."

Mr. Whittle might hold the title for the most inappropriate butler in all of England, but I could not fault his concern for Lord Hawthorn.

"We've come to examine the gladiator mosaics in further detail. Lord Hawthorn invited me to do so," I replied.

Mr. Whittle nodded, already distracted. Voices rose within the drawing room to the left of the spacious hall.

I recognized Constable Wickham's nasal tone. "Are you quite certain it's from the Roman era? Sounds rather convenient, don't you think? A man buries an unwanted child out in the trees."

"Are you suggesting foul play on my land?" Lord Hawthorn's voice deepened.

"You must admit the finding is most unusual," the constable retorted.

Abigail grasped my arm and shook it, her eyes wide as we waited in the quiet hall, forced to eavesdrop. Mr. Whittle, poor man, cleared his throat.

My thoughts, however, remained with the viscount. How easily I could imagine his eyes flashing with anger at the constable's insinuations.

"Allow me to speak with Constable Wickham," I urged Mr. Whittle while gesturing to the closed door of the drawing room. "We can put this investigation to rest."

A moment later, Mr. Whittle announced me into the drawing room. Both men glanced at me with surprise.

"Forgive my intrusion, Lord Hawthorn, but you offered me the opportunity to look over the Roman child and the gladiator mosaics."

Constable Wickham scowled while Lord Hawthorn inhaled deeply, his nostrils flaring. The high color in his cheeks receded when he nodded.

"Of course. Constable Wickham was just leaving."

The constable, a small man with greasy blond hair and a shabby coat, stretched to his full height. "Let us not be too hasty. I must take the body with me and make a full report to the magistrate."

Lord Hawthorn's jaw jumped—a reaction I was beginning to recognize.

"There is no need for such action," I said quickly. "You will rob the British Museum of one of the greatest findings in our country's history. Why, I found an ancient figurine buried with the child. A doll with Greek inscriptions, no less. I assure you, the Society of Antiquaries will want to see the evidence for themselves first. They have the patronage of the king."

Constable Wickham gaped, his eyes bulging.

"The king," I repeated slowly for his benefit.

The constable, now flustered, hastened to assure me that he would not incur the wrath of His Majesty. I hid my smile, but Lord Hawthorn was not so discreet. His cheek dimpled when he locked gazes with me. Amusement chased away the ire in his eyes.

As the thoroughly chastened constable left, Lord Hawthorn tilted close to me, his warm breath tickling my ear. "You are indeed a force to be reckoned with."

This time, I could not hide my smile.

21

Rafe

> Be thou the rainbow in the storms of life.
> The evening beam that smiles the clouds away,
> and tints tomorrow with prophetic ray.
> **LORD BYRON**

As I led Miss Littleton and Miss Perry to the gladiator mosaic, my spirits lifted. Unaware of my attention, Miss Littleton knelt with a brass magnifying glass to study the artifact while Miss Perry wandered through the orchard. Whenever I tried to engage Miss Perry, her gaze slid away, likely resenting that the border dispute remained unresolved despite our efforts.

Miss Littleton retrieved her sketchbook, briefly revealing several Roman-era drawings as she flipped through the pages. Finally, she turned it to show me a portrait—a haughty profile of a man that bore an uncanny resemblance to my uncle.

She pointed to the page smudged with charcoal. "This is how I imagine the owner of the villa might have appeared. Was he a government official, or a military general, or perhaps a wealthy farmer? Perhaps he was not so unlike you, my lord, wanting to take care of his people and the land."

I sat beside her, studying her sketchbook in the dappled sunlight while Miss Perry wandered off, leaving me alone with Miss Littleton.

She leaned closer, just enough that I caught the faint scent of lilac water. I pointed to another picture of a Roman woman. A beautiful woman, but she didn't compare to the sprite by my side, with her flaming hair glowing in the sunlight. Bridget. My pulse sped to a traitorous beat.

Miss Littleton, I corrected mentally.

Her expression changed to something wistful. "Somehow, I can't help but imagine that the owner of this villa built a magnificent home, a place of belonging, for his family, far away from Rome. Oh, don't look at me in that distracting manner. I know you think I nurse my whims, but isn't it lovelier to imagine that a happy family lived here among the hills?"

A bluestocking enamored with a love story.

It wasn't the curve of Miss Littleton's cheek, nor the sparkle in those green eyes that made me study her. It was her outspoken passion for something most would dismiss.

She was altogether appealing. A dangerous situation.

I hadn't given much thought to love. Not with a disappointing estate forcing me into trade. The ton would never consent to let their daughters marry someone such as me. Nor would many applaud a viscount courting his vicar's daughter.

Despite my best efforts, I sounded more tender than I intended. "You dream of fairy tales, Miss Littleton. Charming enough but hardly evident in real life. However, when you speak in such a manner, I almost believe that they are possible. I find myself wanting to hope that happy stories exist."

Her smile disappeared, and with it, the tiny dimple in her

creamy skin. Something flashed within her eyes that I couldn't discern. I hoped it wasn't pity.

I studied the charcoal lines, so much so that the glass tile almost sparkled on the paper. I swallowed against the dryness in my mouth and changed the subject before I revealed too much, including my fascination with her.

"I'm far more interested in your skill, which goes beyond the average school miss. I've never seen such talent, except in museums."

In fact, I wanted nothing more than to flip the pages and study what else might have poured forth from her soul and learn about the spirited woman beside me.

"The path to becoming a scholar with academic publications is not an easy one," she said quietly. "At least, not for a woman. Although I welcome such compliments, I have faced more rejections than I care to count. If I could publish a paper on the mosaics, along with illustrations, for the people who cannot afford to escape their small world, then I would count myself blessed."

"You are ambitious, to say the least, but I admire you all the more for it. I hope you never lose such a free spirit." I could have said more, reminding her that such a quest might prove heartbreaking in the end, yet I couldn't form the words and add to further rejection. Had no one believed in her?

Further intrigued with her desire for such recognition, I turned the page, finding more sketches of the ruins and elegant tiled swirls of the mosaics. Then the hillside just beyond the lane leading toward Bramnor, sprouting of wildflowers, the pastel colors from pencils, with sheep munching grass at sunset. Portraits of the villagers came next, the lines bold as she captured the Dixon lads and Mrs. Eacher, portraying them within a noble light. My admiration grew for the woman by my side. She was much like her father, wanting the best for the valley and her friends the Perry family.

I looked up to see if Miss Perry had returned. She had not, her carelessness at leaving us alone in stark contrast to Miss Littleton's care. I was about to recommend that Miss Littleton and I return to the abbey for propriety's sake when the wind pushed another page into view.

I lifted that page, pinched between my fingers, yet mesmerized by the peaceful countryside when I heard a horrified gasp. I looked up to see her wide-eyed gaze as she snatched the book out of my hands.

But not before I caught sight of longish black hair and a man's face. The book snapped shut before I could discern more, and for once, Miss Littleton fidgeted with her lace fichu as if she couldn't quite get enough air into her lungs while clinging to the book with her other arm.

She kept her voice light, though I thought I caught a touch of breathlessness. "That will be all for now, I believe. You will excuse me, my lord, but I must return to check on my father. I don't think we need to burden you any longer. I'm sure your day must be filled with—"

"I may not see the rest of your work?" I interjected though good manners forbade me from doing so.

Her cheeks flushed and she held the sketchbook tighter to her chest. "I doubt you'd be interested in foolish sketches."

I couldn't resist poking a little, perhaps enjoying her blush more than I ought to. It appeared Miss Littleton could be flustered after all.

"Are not your drawings to be displayed? So many ladies desire to showcase their embroidery and piano skills to the world."

"Some of us are more modest, and these sketches are of a personal nature," she responded tartly despite the high color suffusing her. If possible, she turned a shade pinker.

I wondered what personal art would keep her so tight-lipped, and why she shut the book so quickly and seemed to guard it with her life. Mysterious dark-haired man included.

Raising a hand, I hid a smile. "Keep your secrets, Miss Littleton. I won't pry any further. Not unless it involves my land. Then I shall demand complete transparency."

She exhaled as she slid the sketchbook into her satchel, along with the magnifying glass. I found myself reluctant to let her go just yet.

"Would you be interested in sketching a Ming vase?" I asked her on a whim, secretly hoping she would agree.

She still had a pencil tucked behind one ear, and several damp curls clung to her neck and forehead. "I'd be delighted. I've long admired that vase in the library. Do you want a catalog of art items?"

"Yes. I plan to sell what I can," I admitted. Would she think less of me because of my financial straits? I could think of no better way to advertise the vases and tapestries. "I have an interested buyer whom I'd like to persuade to come to the abbey to see the antiques for himself."

"I shall do my best," she said after a pause. Then she fixed me with a firm look. "After I finish working with the Perrys."

I couldn't resist smiling again. If she illustrated the vase, a spectacular piece of white porcelain laced with deep blue, I was certain I could sell it. And I would see her again.

"You won't sell the books, will you?" Her eyes turned pleading. Darker in hue.

My throat tightened. "No. I will not." *For you, I'll keep every single tome.*

Relief warmed those mesmerizing eyes. She rose, brushing the dirt from her gown. I rose too, albeit far less gracefully.

"You have my gratitude, Lord Hawthorn. A library is a treasure beyond compare." Her voice wavered just as Miss Perry returned from her walk among the trees. A careless friend, to my thinking, and one who should not have abandoned another young woman so readily.

I walked with them to the courtyard, not unaware of the curious look Miss Perry shot me as she slipped her hand through her friend's arm.

"Come when you are able. I will have Mrs. Whittle show you the vases to sketch in your free moments," I offered both of them.

A startled sound echoed from the stables—a yelp from Mr. Whittle and a subsequent whinny. Had one of the horses nipped him? They seemed on edge as of late, including Chaucer.

"Tarnation!" Mr. Whittle cried from the stable. "Who left the stalls open? The horses have escaped!"

"Good day, ladies," I said over my shoulder as I darted toward the stables.

I glanced back to see Miss Perry poke her friend in the ribs. Her voice carried across the courtyard.

"Perhaps you'll find a dance for yourself during May Day."

The idea of spinning on a dance floor with Miss Littleton proved to be far more appealing than I would have first assumed. But she refused to answer her friend, leaving me to wonder what exactly Miss Littleton thought of me.

As April wore on, it brought more rain clouds. The tangy scent of rain filled the air, perfect for the newly planted crops and rows of apple saplings along the rock fence. The orchard would nearly double in size this year, with a harvest ripening in four years. The longer I spent outdoors, the more my thoughts of returning to London faded.

An unusual humidity hung in a sickly haze over the valley. Despite the beauty, the more I tried to fix the estate, the more events occurred to thwart me. Mr. Whittle had spent a good portion of the day rounding up the horses that got loose from the barn. Even stranger, after an inquiry on timing, Stewart's Cider Press company sent a curt letter noting they had never received my order for a cider press. I replied to them, asking for a press as soon as possible.

Mr. Spencer and Mr. Whittle both decried any role in the barn or press.

Irritations, each situation.

Then, past midnight one night, I perked at a shuffling sound . . . like that of slippered feet sliding across the floor. I had already spent the evening tossing and turning as I calculated the expenses accrued from the purchase of the new saplings and the wages of the men hired to build the service road. Who knew when Mr. Talbot would return. I suspected he wanted to keep me on edge. Just as I decided I was on the cusp of doom, awaiting one small misstep to tumble, a whisper raised the hair on my arms.

Outside my bedroom door, the steps slowed. Stopped.

I threw off my coverlet and tiptoed across the floorboards to reach for my pistol. An ancient abbey, however, amplified sounds, including the click when I drew back the hammer. Skin prickling, I waited one moment and then flung open the door to peer into a pitch-black hall. Not even a glimmer of moonlight pierced the thick gloom.

The only sound I heard then was my own rapid breathing.

No spectral vision appeared as I crept along the corridor gripping my pistol. I returned to my room to fumble for the tinderbox. With practiced ease, I struck the steel against the flint, a shower of sparks leaping onto the tinder. I blew gently, coaxing the glow into a flame. Once it caught, I lit the candle, the room filling with a reassuring light.

No spirits lurked within the halls, nor intruders. When I spoke to Mr. Whittle about the affair in the morning, he merely shrugged.

"I heard nothing, sir. Nothing at all. Of course, my wife swears that I snore."

Without answers or much sleep, I refused to give in to Lucy's maudlin fears. Still, fear crept in. I wasn't a gambling man, but had I pushed fate too far to save the Hawthorn heritage and my tenants? Lewis's face and that of his widow haunted me. What if I could no longer send her funds? So many relied on me, and I felt as useless as my namesake. Surely, I was just tired and imagining things.

By late morning, I resolved to banish any idea of ghosts with work. Inside the stifling brewery, I mopped my brow as the youngest Dixon boy scampered up the walls with the help of a ladder and painted the overhead beams with white limestone, transforming the dingy space. How he could sit there, swinging his legs on such a beam while whistling a ditty and not keel over, was beyond me.

So engrossed I was debating with Mr. Spencer the best position for the cider press, I didn't see the new arrival until the other men stilled.

Miss Littleton waited at the entrance, her green gaze lifted to the ceiling where the Dixon boy tipped forward with his brush, daring as he dragged it across the ceiling.

"Good heavens, he's going to fall," she cried.

"No, he'd be suited for climbing the mast while a ship slices through rough water. It takes a lad or a man with balance," I reassured her.

As if to prove the point, the Dixon boy stretched even farther on the beam, winking at Miss Littleton and causing a splatter of white paint to hit the floor. "See, Miss Littleton, it's not that frightening being up so high. If only you could try it yourself."

"Careful, man," I called out. "Or you'll be painting us too."

She self-consciously touched her bonnet. "No, thank you. I like my feet firmly on the ground."

"Or deep in the mud," I teased her.

Her smile lit her face, bringing twin dimples on each side. "Ha, very true, sir. I'll take the trenches over the sea any day." Then her gaze sobered, as if a cloud passed over it.

I held out an arm for her to take, the action natural, and after a pause, she slipped her arm through mine as we hurried to the abbey where Mrs. Whittle awaited. Yet my pulse sped at the thought of being alone with Miss Littleton. The gentle pressure of her fingers on my arm lingered even when she removed her hand.

A spot of rain splashed against my cheek. Above, dark clouds roiled, stirred like a bubbling caldron. I didn't like the look of the storm.

She didn't seem to notice, her expression troubled. "You are a military man. Perhaps you can answer a question."

Bracing myself, I led her into the abbey's main entrance, away from the sound of the hammers.

"If the navy presses a young man, and he . . ." She paused.

I froze. Was there another suitor? Why had I so foolishly assumed she was unattached?

She halted, swallowing visibly. "And the navy arrested him for rebellion. Will he face a court martial, or . . . far worse?"

"It would depend on the circumstance," I said carefully. "When was your friend taken?"

Her brow furrowed. "Men stole my brother, Daniel, during a trip to London with two friends, and now he resides within a hulk. Please, I share this news in confidence. Precious few know about his predicament."

Sweet relief and sharp regret filled me at the admission. She was not spoken for. But her grief over her brother concerned me. Prime Minister William Pitt required each county to provide a quota of men willing or unwilling. London alone was required to round up nearly six thousand men. Her trust touched me since she had shared something so carefully hidden.

She sighed. "Daniel is too much like Father and me. Stubborn. Opinionated. And not at all impressed with the rules. I have shocked you, I see, especially considering a military man as yourself."

A man not at all impressed with the rules. A grim prognosis for anyone trapped within the Royal Navy. I sensed there was much more to the story than I had been told, especially considering our conversation when I had asked if she believed a man could change.

I had wondered then at her hesitancy.

The sudden sheen in her eyes made me want to erase her sorrow. "You have not shocked me."

"Then, I fear I must tell you more. You will learn of it regardless. A riot occurred."

I studied her closely. "Your brother acted as leader?"

Her silence stretched, heavy with uncertainty. "I don't know. I only know he's in grave danger. Can we even rescue him? Or is all hope lost?"

She had trusted me with a painful secret. I did not take that action lightly. And she had come asking for my advice.

"I cannot tell a lie, Miss Littleton. The situation is grave. Would you like me to make a request on your behalf? Of course, I can't promise anything will result from my efforts, but I will do my best to assist your brother. If possible."

"Would you?" In her excitement, she placed her free hand on my arm only to snatch it back to her chest. "Lord Hawthorn, I—"

I found myself caught in those green eyes. Warmth thawed any lingering reserve I had held as a protective shield.

Thunder cracked right above the abbey, followed by a flash of lightning sizzling outside the window. She jumped at the sound, and the sketchbook once trapped beneath her arm tumbled to the floor. It fell open with a flutter of pages.

22

Bridget

> The great art of life is sensation,
> to feel that we exist, even in pain.
> **LORD BYRON**

Lord Hawthorn stooped to pick up my sketchbook just as another crack of thunder boomed. In my clumsiness I had dropped the book, and my secret art lay bare. He stared at the page, his brows slanting downward. I realized, too late, the cause of his silence—he held my sketch of him. My breath froze.

"Is this how you see me?" he demanded in a strangled tone.

I tried not to flinch, my gaze no longer able to bear his. "In the beginning. Maybe. You were rather grim."

"I look irascible."

I wasn't sure if his voice held a touch of humor.

"I haven't apologized for that unfortunate evening when Chaucer frightened you. Or was it me? Forgive my bad manners," he said.

"You have had your moments, as have I, but . . ." In an effort to lighten the mood, I leaned forward, pretending to study him even though I had most of his features memorized. "But when you smile, I believe your eyes lighten a shade. From mahogany to something almost amber. It's really quite a pleasant shade."

He stared at me. And his eyes did not lighten. Instead, they darkened. I resettled back to my original position, not realizing just how close I tipped toward him.

"My lord, begging your pardon for intruding . . ."

Mr. Whittle stood in the hall, his gaze darting between the viscount and me. Flustered, I stepped back, self-conscious at how we must appear.

"Yes, Mr. Whittle, get on with it." He sounded harsher than usual.

Mr. Whittle licked his lips. "It's just that we've gotten word that Cobb has been digging holes throughout the fields near his cottage. I daresay he thinks he'll find something of value. Who knows if he has found others to join him or not? I thought you ought to know before more of the tenants take to his example and all the Hawthorn Abbey estates are pitted beyond repair."

A low curse. Lord Hawthorn snapped the sketchbook closed and handed it to me.

"Excuse me, Miss Littleton. Apparently my tenant thinks he is an antiquarian these days. Rest assured, I won't let anyone touch your artifacts, nor muddle with my land," he said as he brushed past to join Mr. Whittle. I watched him stalk out of the hallway and into the courtyard, following the groundskeeper.

I hugged the sketchbook to my chest, regretting my impulsive words and actions once again. How utterly forward. Closing my eyes tightly, I gave myself a stern scolding that would rival any lecture given by Mrs. Herriot.

On the other hand, his offer to help Daniel brought a renewed warmth, rendering me like melted butter.

I found the Ming vase perched on a pedestal in the library and did my best to sketch the piece, but my mind wandered far away. Instead of thinking of Rome and artifacts, or even the vase in front of me, I could only see the viscount who worked side by side with his men and who, without judgment, had offered a sliver of hope to reach my brother.

As I rendered the Ming vase, a gathering wind pushed against the abbey. The heavens opened up and rain splashed against the windows. Gentle at first, then a steady downpour, the roar echoing as it hit the slate roof. Mrs. Whittle brought me refreshments in the library as I detailed the trim on the vase.

"La, such weather. You won't be going anywhere for some time, Miss Littleton."

I longed to escape to the parsonage after my earlier embarrassment with the portrait of Lord Hawthorn, but with lightning striking, I stayed to finish my illustration. I didn't dare set out with lightning stabbing at the ground. I put down my pencils and approached the window overlooking the courtyard. The wind howled and groaned like a wraith, battling the windows, and the trees whipped around the courtyard.

"I do hope we won't see flooding," I said, fearing for the viscount and his men caught within the storm.

She came up beside me and pulled back the velvet drape. A hard plink bounced off the window, as if a rock had been thrown against it. Then another plink. And another.

"No," Mrs. Whittle moaned. "The orchards will be ruined."

A man could only battle so much and not be destroyed. Insects, drought, too much rain. But hail? Nothing demolished a crop or orchard with as much ruthless efficiency. I felt ill. The ice only grew in size until I saw one the size of a shilling ricochet off the stone wall of the courtyard, the impact sharp and echoing through the space. A coat of white soon filled the expanse of the road and steamed against the beaten grass.

Mrs. Whittle wept. I put my arm about her, too heartsick to offer any encouragement.

"Poor man. He will lose his investments." She wiped her eyes with the edge of her apron. "What will he do?"

"I fear for anyone caught outside," I whispered. My alarm grew until at last a door slammed. Both Mrs. Whittle and I hurried to the abbey entrance just as Lord Hawthorn stormed into the hall, his cheek bleeding. Rain plastered his white shirt to his skin, outlining hard muscles. He shook the water dripping from his hair.

My breath caught at the sight. He resembled a demigod rising from the sea, but the blood on his forehead proved him living—and in despair.

"My God," he muttered. I sensed more prayer than curse with that hissed breath.

My mouth dried as I tried to find platitudes, comfort, anything at all to offer him in such a moment of need. He had offered me comfort earlier. What could I possibly say or do for him?

He stared outside until the eerie tinkle of breaking glass echoed over the hail. Outside, the storm raged. I suspected it raged inside him as well.

"The orchard will be ruined," he finally rasped.

Before I could find words, the front door swung open again. This time, a stranger entered, his fine beaver hat dripping rain onto the floor. His coat was soaked, the collar turned up in a futile attempt to keep the downpour at bay. He removed the hat, brushing it, though his expression showed no hint of discomfort—only determination.

"Mr. Talbot," Lord Hawthorn rasped, his voice edged with either surprise or irritation. "What brings you here in this weather? I was not expecting you so soon."

Mr. Talbot gave a slow shake of his head, glancing around the hall before locking eyes with Rafe. "I wish I could say this was a social call, but it's not. I've come to assess the progress on the estate. Unfortunately the storm caught me just as I rode up the lane."

Lord Hawthorn's brows furrowed, tension rippling through his frame. He strode over to the man at the entrance of the hall while Mrs. Whittle and I remained standing just outside the drawing room.

Mr. Talbot's gaze shifted to the windows, where the hail continued to pound against the panes. He lowered his voice yet each word carried across the polished floors. "I understand the timing isn't ideal, but the Crown isn't known for its patience. I needed to see if the work you've undertaken is enough to convince them you can restore Hawthorn Abbey, but I fear this weather might change your prospects."

"I've started building the new road, expanded the orchard—this storm will set us back, but we're making headway." Lord Hawthorn also spoke softly. "Surely, you can report those changes."

"Perhaps we should retire to the drawing room," I whispered to Mrs. Whittle, who stood next to me. She shook her head, her eyes round with alarm. Instead, she gripped my arm with an unnatural strength, pinning me to her side.

Mr. Talbot stepped closer to the viscount. "I don't doubt your effort, but effort alone doesn't always sway the Crown. The estate's condition . . . it has deteriorated faster than anyone expected, especially after today."

Lord Hawthorn appeared made of stone. "What are you saying?"

Mr. Talbot sighed, clearly reluctant to continue. His eyes flickered toward me and Mrs. Whittle, silent witnesses to Rafe's impending embarrassment. His gaze softened momentarily. "The Crown is impatient. They've given you time, more than they would've given most, but . . ." He paused, as if considering how much worse this moment must feel with ladies present. "How can I return with a good report after today? The orchard's loss, an incomplete service road, the funds running dry—you're running out of options. If you can't show significant progress by the end of the month . . ."

Lord Hawthorn's shoulders stiffened, his chest rising as if preparing for a blow. "Then what, Mr. Talbot? What happens if I fail?"

Mr. Talbot hesitated. "You know the answer."

The silence that followed felt suffocating. Rafe's breath coming in harsh, shallow bursts.

"I won't let that happen," he said quietly, but there was steel in his voice. "This estate is now my life. My family's legacy."

Mr. Talbot glanced at me again, perhaps aware of how deeply private this conversation should have been. Mrs. Whittle refused to relinquish her grip even when I attempted to pull free.

Rafe turned as if remembering he had an audience, his profile grim. "Please, wait in the drawing room, Mr. Talbot, and I shall join you. I need a moment."

Mr. Talbot gave him a brief nod. His gaze lingered on me and Mrs. Whittle, who stood awkwardly beside me, before he stepped past us and into the drawing room, his wet boots leaving faint marks on the polished floor.

I stood frozen, watching the strain in Rafe's posture as he fought to maintain his composure. His body shook, and for a moment I feared he might break under the weight of the news. Without thinking, I freed myself of Mrs. Whittle and reached him quickly, my hand finding his arm.

"Lord Hawthorn, you are bleeding."

I pulled out my handkerchief and faced him. He halted when I dabbed at his forehead, wiping away the crimson trail. When I handed him my handkerchief, he snatched my hand as if it were a lifeline.

"Mrs. Whittle, perhaps you can make something bracing for our guests and the men when the storm ends. They are trapped in the brewery as we speak." He paused, still gripping my fingers. "If the storm ends."

Mrs. Whittle fled, her skirts swishing as she hurried to the kitchen.

"It will end," I said. "All storms do."

He glanced down at my hand, where he was crushing my fingers.

"I apologize that you had to witness such an exchange," he said as he released me. His gaze strayed outside, the white of his eyes bright in the dark hall as he took the handkerchief and pressed it against his cheek where the hail had grazed.

"It will all be gone, I'm afraid. The old orchard and the new. Any crops planted, both for the tenants and myself." His voice betrayed the barest tremor. "And now you've witnessed the fall of the house of Hawthorn."

"What can I do to help you?" I asked, my heart breaking for all the loss I had witnessed. Breaking for him.

He looked at me again. "Pray, Miss Littleton. Pray."

I nodded. "A friend could do nothing less."

"How we need friends during such seasons." A ragged sigh escaped him. He glanced down at his shirt and waistcoat still clinging to his form. As if aware of his dishabille, he mumbled an apology and left me within the hall.

From my position in the grand hall, I watched the clouds until they disappeared as swiftly as they had come. I did not slip into the drawing room to hear the rest of the muttered conversation between Mr. Talbot and Lord Hawthorn, no matter how badly

I wanted to stand by his side and offer companionship and support. A man could endure only so much before life crushed him altogether.

My stomach churned at all I had witnessed, even as Mr. Whittle offered a ride home in their carriage.

I wanted to pray for Lord Hawthorn. I wanted to pray for Mr. Perry and the farmers. Even Daniel. Despite my former reserve about beseeching a silent God, I whispered pleas late into the evening from the safety of my bedroom at the parsonage where no one could hear me.

23

Bridget

> For truth is always strange;
> stranger than fiction.
> **LORD BYRON**

In the days after the hailstorm, I split my time between sketching the dig site and rare items for sale within the abbey, as the initial shock gave way to efforts to salvage what we could of trampled gardens. Only the mosaics had endured nature's wrath, yet I felt no relief, my thoughts constantly lingering on the man trapped within Hawthorn Abbey.

The orchard bore the scars of the storm—twisted branches and broken limbs—but it was not entirely destroyed. Some sections remained intact, though the damage weighed our spirits.

With each passing moment, my urgency to clear the entire Bacchus floor grew, which was no small feat. So far, we had reached nearly twenty feet in length and twelve feet in width. No doubt, I stood on the grounds of an ancient palace. A very large palace, proving my initial guess correct. Vines now coiled around the god of wine as he danced, holding his goblet aloft, surrounded by drunken satyrs and maenads. Publication would bring much-needed funds, not just for me, and exposure to buyers for Mr. Perry, who faced the same urgency to rescue his small farm as Lord Hawthorn.

I also received a second letter from the Society of Antiquaries confirming that Mr. Harrington would visit within the coming week to inspect Mr. Perry's site. I replied at once, offering our hospitality at the parsonage. However, the impending visit wasn't our only concern. That same day, Father left for Chichester with hopes to settle the boundary dispute. Although the magistrate was still away in Bath, Father returned two days later with documents that left me speechless.

> Child's Remains Found at Hawthorn Abbey.

"The article mentions your name," Father said as he slapped the article from *The Times* on the table. He glanced at me, pride mingling with irritation. "It's outrageous, of course."

> Miss Bridget Littleton, a vicar's daughter, discovered a Roman-era mosaic and the remains of a child at Hawthorn Abbey, a place long associated with misfortune. More than a decade ago, Sir Randall Hawthorn was murdered, and now his son has returned after an injury in the army.

I devoured the article, dismayed by the salacious tone of the writing. "The author doesn't even acknowledge that the child might be from third-century Rome. Thank goodness for the mention of the gladiator mosaic. Perhaps that will remove any blemish on Lord Hawthorn's name."

The speed with which the papers reported the story surprised me. Had someone slipped the information to *The Times*?

Another paper proved somewhat better and noted that the grave site might be ancient. But my heart nearly stopped beating at the mention of mosaics and hidden gold. I remained hopeful we would encounter items of value, but this news would do neither Lord Hawthorn nor Mr. Perry any good. Gold would surely prove a siren's call for trouble. I could not forget Lord Hawthorn's dismay at the discovery of a child buried on his property. The more the story circulated, the less his chances of being included within polite society. The poor man was isolated enough.

> Miss Bridget Littleton, bluestocking extraordinaire, has ruffled the Society of Antiquaries into action. One must beg the question, what kind of woman indulges in grave robbery? Her father, the local vicar, is known for his radical political leanings regarding child labor, and her brother awaits trial for treason.

The paper accurately reported Daniel's predicament. But I was not a grave robber. I could not imagine a worse insult. Father hadn't underestimated the risk to our reputation at all. Somehow, someone had discovered our secrets and blazed them across London for all the world to see.

Late one afternoon, I returned to the Perry farm to join Abigail in our continued excavation work. Our cotton gowns stuck to our backs as we dug and dusted, wearing gloves to keep the dirt out of our fingernails.

Mr. Perry grunted as he stretched, keeping one hand on his shovel. "My aching back." He shielded one hand over his weathered brow and squinted into the harsh light. "Do you see that man to the west of us?"

I rose, my own back and neck throbbing. A tall man stood in the distance, too far for us to make out his features.

"I am expecting a visitor from the Society of Antiquaries," I told Mr. Perry.

He frowned. "If the gent is planning to visit you, why not amble over and say hello? Why stand there and ogle us?"

Abigail leaped to her feet and waved enthusiastically. The stranger mounted his horse before disappearing into the rolling hills.

I chewed my bottom lip. A dreadful habit, but one that came with nerves. "I don't think he is our representative, but I can't be certain."

"Maybe he's curious, especially after Lord Hawthorn's find. Do you think we'll discover more graves?" Abigail asked as she retied her bonnet strings.

I shuddered at the thought of more bodies. I did not want to throw further kindling on the rumor of me as a tomb thief.

"I certainly hope not. Should we arrange for someone to watch the field at night?" I asked.

Mr. Perry shook his head as he continued shielding his eyes from the sun. "I haven't the funds to hire anyone."

"Why not ask Mr. Barron? He said he has men aplenty and many of them know how to handle themselves," Abigail suggested.

Mr. Perry expelled a long-suffering sigh, his gaze straying to mine with a wordless caution. "No, not Barron. I refused his offer when he came by last week, sniffing around to see what he could gain. He's too much in his cups, and he's been asking too many questions about the mosaics. Maybe one of the Dixon boys can spare an evening to watch. They're young and hardy and always up for an adventure."

"Mr. Barron would prove a far more practical choice than the Dixon lads," Abigail said. "I would hate to offend him after his offer of assistance."

"You've taken a liking to him, eh?" Mr. Perry spat on the ground. "He's been sniffing around to see what you're worth, my girl. Fancies himself quite the gentleman and was in the sulks when I refused to give him answers about the mosaics. Nay, I want no business partners other than Miss Littleton. We've an agreement—she knew the value of the tiles right off and only asks that her work with the societies be recognized. She's not after our land or profits, only the scholarly credit. That's a fair deal to me."

Abigail pouted but said nothing more, her brow furrowed as she worked silently to sift through the dirt for any items of interest. She filled her basket and shook it just as I had taught her, the vibrating motion often revealing the smallest secrets hidden within the soil.

I focused on cleaning the border of the tiles, but Mr. Perry's words stung. My once-burning desire for recognition now felt hollow. Was I truly helping the Perrys and honoring Daniel, or had my ambition clouded my purpose? Unease gnawed at me as we uncovered more of the villa.

We soon finished our work for the day and pulled the canvas across the Bacchus mosaic. We had discovered a few pot shards far too shattered to reconstruct, but worth keeping and cataloging. I planned to take what I could home for inspection.

Yet I couldn't help but wonder at the strange man in the distance who seemed as preoccupied with our work as we were.

A day later, while I sat in the parlor recording the latest finds within my journal next to Daniel's worn copy of *The Ruins of Palmyra* by Robert Wood, Mrs. Herriot entered with a letter in hand.

"For you," she said with a puzzled frown. "That's the third letter to the parsonage sent by courier."

Stilling any anxiety that a cancellation of the Society of Antiquaries was enclosed, I forced my breathing to remain even.

I expected to see Mr. Archibald Harrington, the secretary of the Society of Antiquaries, arrive any day. Poor Mrs. Herriot had spent the rest of the morning fussing over the state of the parsonage, forcing Molly to polish the silverware, beat the rugs, and repeatedly dust. Father and I assumed any guest would choose the quiet of the parsonage rather than one of Mr. Barron's rowdy inns. Lord Hawthorn had the only other suitable lodgings. Considering his lack of staff, I hated to presume on him.

Our relationship, as of late, had moved into something tentative, reminding me of two fencers politely saluting each other at the end of a match.

I motioned for my housekeeper to bring the letter. She placed it on the desk with a flourish. Instead of leaving me in peace, she hovered close by, no doubt hoping to discover the contents. The heavy paper, the color of clotted cream with a muted wax seal lined with a Greek laurel, appeared different from the missives sent by the Society of Antiquaries.

"Blue," I muttered to myself as I carefully broke open the seal. "The color of loyalty, truth, and strength."

I quickly scanned the contents, my heart pounding as I read the lines.

"What on earth is in that letter?" Mrs. Herriot cried as she approached the desk again. I reached for it and showed her the elegant scrawl.

"It appears I have attracted the attention of the Society of Dilettanti after all. Mr. Beaumont's secretary demands that I send all my sketches and findings to him at my earliest convenience."

"Are we to expect more guests to the parsonage?" She squinted, holding the letter closer to read.

"I should hope not," I answered. "I'm no longer certain I want to entertain Mr. Beaumont."

Although the secretary had congratulated me on my recent success, I couldn't quite shake the condescending tone or the demand to comply with Mr. Beaumont's wishes. It was not a letter between colleagues, but an order.

It is only fitting that such a valuable discovery be placed in the hands of someone with the resources to appreciate its historical value. Please forward all of your recent research to the care of Mr. Beaumont at the soonest convenience.

She held out the letter, only to toss it onto the desk when I refused to touch it. "The same man who told you to stick to embroidery, isn't he?"

"The same," I said as I tapped my fingers against the desk, while a sense of restlessness swept through me. I had so desperately wanted them to acknowledge my find, a desire Daniel had affirmed before he left for London. Now they had done so, yet the triumph felt forced.

Mrs. Herriot's eyes narrowed as she watched me. "Interesting timing, wouldn't you say? Is it possible the Dilettanti read the London rags?"

I sighed. "I believe you are correct. They hadn't believed me when I previously described the denarii and Bacchus mosaic."

She appeared smug. "It's a shame you've tried so hard to find acceptance with the most unlikely of groups. If only you had pleased your aunt. She might have helped you with a proper debut. You might be married and blessed with children as any respectable woman ought to enjoy."

Normally, I had no trouble parrying words with Mrs. Herriot, but her admonishment felt like vinegar stinging a raw wound. She swept from the parlor, satisfied that her guidance had found the mark. I *had* traded the opinions of one group, that of the marriage mart and polite society, for another group even more disdainful, all the while thinking I was free to do as I pleased.

I was not free. Not really. Mr. Beaumont and the Dilettanti had given me enough warning through their correspondence that I would be a fool to keep engaging their interest. So bent on my quest for acknowledgment and earning the funds to help my brother escape his sentence, I had ignored the warning signs. Rejection stung. Being used for someone else's advancement stung even more.

I found a sheet of paper and prepared to draft a response. Hot words coursed through me, with all the fire and brimstone I had witnessed my father employ when defying the mine owners and their despicable use of children.

Pinching the feathered quill between my fingers, I blew out a noisy breath and curbed any inclination to unleash my emotions. Once again, I kept my answer brief, thanking Mr. Beaumont for his interest. However, I refused to part with my sketches or divulge my findings. As I addressed the envelope, I wondered about Mr. Beaumont, a man I had never met. Surely, he would give up any interest, especially now with the Society of Antiquaries involved.

24

Rafe

> Without a ruler to do it against,
> you can't make crooked straight.
> **SENECA**

Early on a Saturday morning, as the sun crested over the valley, I raced Chaucer outside the abbey, letting him stretch into a full gallop. The rosy hues of the morning sky chased away my worries. Two letters recently delivered, both equally disturbing, had driven me to seek solace in the fresh air of the countryside.

The letter from my barrister was direct:

My buyer, Mr. Beaumont, insists on meeting in two days to assess the abbey's antiques and the gladiator mosaics. All of London speaks of Hawthorn Abbey.

The attached clips from *The Times*, *Monthly Meteor*, and *The Observer* included details about the child's remains and the salacious history of my family.

I should have been grateful Mr. Beaumont even wanted to meet with me. Any entrance into polite society, regardless of my rank, was forever closed, thanks to the scandal sheets. I would continue to pay for the sins of my father and the unforgivable crime of being a gentleman reduced to a trade. Was there nothing I could do to redeem my name?

The second letter hit harder.

My military colleague wrote to me far quicker than I had expected.

Daniel Littleton is gravely ill aboard the hulk. They won't commute his sentence. A school of vice is no straightforward thing to escape. If he doesn't receive aid, he will be dead if he stays longer than a year, regardless of his trial's outcome.

A sleepless night of tossing and turning had brought a pounding to my temples not even fresh air could chase away. This was not the news I wanted to share with Miss Littleton. It seemed I would have no choice but to be the bearer of ill tidings. Daniel's plight far overshadowed my ever-tightening purse. I could ill afford to send aid to him. A groan escaped me.

I still needed to make money to cover the mounting costs. I didn't even want to think about repairing the abbey following the hailstorm. Progress seemed more elusive the harder I strained for it. I had no choice but to welcome this mysterious Mr. Beaumont and allow him access to Hawthorn Abbey's treasures. But if I granted him access to the gladiator mosaic, what might Bridget think?

Chaucer galloped past the newly planted orchard, allowing me a glimpse of the battered saplings while I tried to sort my turbulent thoughts.

My thoughts drifted to her, wondering if she thought of me. I could never forget her sketch.

Is this how you see me?

If I hadn't known better, I might have assumed, nay, hoped something more lay within her fascination. I was not an artist, yet neither could I shake the image of her from my mind's eye. How was it that in such a short period I had found myself bewitched with her? But what I wanted was irrelevant.

I returned my attention to the nature surrounding me while muttering a prayer for guidance. I had no idea how to fix the muddled mess of my life, nor that of Daniel. Nor my tenants. The more I tried to repair things, the worse the situations grew.

A horse nickered in the morning hush. Chaucer perked his ears, indicating that I had not imagined the sound. Reining him in, I studied the ruined orchard as the cool wind rustled through the saplings. Dawn crept slowly over the fields and the stone walls lining part of the southern field—stones Bridget claimed were taken from the Roman villa.

A figure rose from the Bacchus mosaic with a satchel, staring at me. Hat low, his features remained indistinct. Mr. Perry? I raised my hand in greeting just as the man whistled and sprinted across the grass. Chaucer snorted at an answering nicker. Perry wouldn't flee. Treasure hunters?

I leaned into Chaucer, and with the press of my knees, he broke into a gallop while the stranger, sensing danger, threw himself onto his own creature and darted east, in the direction of Bramnor.

Chaucer needed no encouragement to take up the chase. As a war horse, he itched for battle, and with a whinny of triumph, his hooves ate up the ground beneath us. We pursued until the stranger disappeared into a copse of trees and we lost him.

When I returned to Mr. Perry's field, the canvases normally

pinned to protect the floor beneath had been pulled back to reveal a gaping hole within the moist dirt.

I halted Chaucer and dismounted. There, within the pit, lay a scattering of stones and tile and dirt. A curse escaped me. Bacchus's impudent grin no longer greeted me.

Someone had stolen the face of the fallen god.

25

Bridget

Two are better than one; because they have a good reward for their labour. For if they fall, the one will lift up his fellow: but woe to him that is alone when he falleth; for he hath not another to help him up.

ECCLESIASTES 4:9-10

On the morning we expected the society visit, Father frowned as he reviewed the proposed menu over breakfast porridge. "A country vicar should operate within his budget," he protested. Mrs. Herriot and I had settled on consommé, roasted turkey, and custard tarts for dinner that evening.

"It is the Society of Antiquaries. King George's scholars. Surely, we can do more," Mrs. Herriot retorted.

Father stood firm, and I knew we would lose the battle. "I am a vicar, not an earl. Why shouldn't boiled potatoes be sufficient as a side?"

Mrs. Herriot groaned while I swallowed a chuckle.

Boiled potatoes, it was.

"At least dress the part instead of this . . ." Mrs. Herriot made it a point to study my puce muslin gown. She waved a dismissive hand, as if description of the blandness of my attire had rendered her speechless.

"Don't worry, I won't look like a dusty scholar," I assured her.

After she left, Father arched his eyebrows. "Really, Bridget, this entire situation is getting out of hand. I have no desire to attract the notice of the rector in Chichester, and I fear this excavation and the rumors surrounding it will prove unbearable if the Reverend Nathanial Pritchard gets wind of it."

I could only agree. I had no use for overly pious men who were only concerned with their outward appearance. Any plans I had for the morning collapsed when Molly announced a caller.

"A gentleman to see you and your father, miss—though I must say, he doesn't look the sort to be easily put off by boiled potatoes."

I had settled at my desk in the parlor and shifted through sheets of pottery shard sketches. The sound of footsteps grew closer. I stood so quickly I nearly knocked over my inkwell.

Lord Hawthorn stood in my parlor.

The news of the theft took the wind out of my sails. I paced the room while Lord Hawthorn watched me. Father had joined us and sat on the settee opposite of mine.

My pulse skittered. "Bacchus was taken?"

"Someone cut out the face and stole it. I saw a figure out in the field early this morning, just at dawn. At first, I assumed it was Mr. Perry, but the man fled on horseback. When I went to inspect the site, I spied the damage. I've sent word to our constable," Lord Hawthorn said. He stood by the fireplace, one hand resting on the mantle.

I resumed pacing. If I didn't stop, I would soon wear a hole in the carpet.

I forced myself to sink onto the settee. I wanted nothing more than to cover my face with my hands. All that hard work ruined, and right before the secretary of the Society of Antiquaries came to inspect the site. What if the thief ruined the mosaics in his haste to escape?

"And the other mosaics?" My voice cracked in the most undignified manner, and I turned to stare out the window.

"They appeared to be intact."

A rustle sounded as he sat down beside me, and the settee cushion sank beneath his weight. His presence felt solid, his leg brushing against my gown.

Forcing my clenched fingers to relax, I dared to look at him. How close we sat. I could see the flecks of amber in his eyes. No longer quite so hard. Nor so cold.

In fact . . . I averted my gaze and inhaled deeply.

"He simply rode away with Bacchus?"

His voice was steady. "I suspect he had a wagon and help overnight. I wonder if he returned this morning to seek something else. Maybe something smaller."

"Could it be one of your men?" I asked as I shifted ever so slightly to offset the warmth emanating from his presence.

As if sensing the same nearness, he edged away. "I'd hate to think so. But if that is the case, they will regret touching one tile."

"Mr. Cobb showed quite an interest in Mr. Perry's field," Father said. "The day we left the abbey, he stormed up to my chaise, sour faced, asking for compensation to dig with them. When Bridget said it wouldn't be much, he retracted. He clearly expected something more substantial, likely hoping to profit from the discovery. His disappointment was obvious."

"Mr. Cobb," Rafe repeated quietly, turning his attention from Father to me. "Has he bothered you?"

A simple question, but one laced with an undertone of threat to Mr. Cobb should he overstep his bounds. I had always suspected Rafe would be a formidable opponent if crossed. I had no other protector in my life and had discovered a measure of independence. Yet I couldn't deny a small traitorous thought circling in the back of my mind of how nice it would be to have such protection.

"No, he hasn't. Of course, there was also Mr. Barron, who insisted on supporting us a few weeks prior. But I suspect his interest leans more toward my friend."

Rafe scowled, his brows drawing down into a fearsome V.

"You will inform me if any of them trouble you again. Or anyone else, for that matter."

I clasped my fingers together before they betrayed my nervousness. "Who do you think stole the mosaic?"

"Considering the rubbish that was printed in the London papers, anyone." Again, the muscle ticked in his jaw.

"Mr. Perry wanted to hire the Dixon boys to guard the site," I said, then hastened to add when a thunderous expression crossed his face, "Oh, they couldn't be responsible for the loss. They're simply too young and—"

"Immature," he supplied dryly. "It's likely they went home after working and climbed into the comfort of their own beds. I will speak with them as soon as I can."

I shifted on the couch, all too aware of how constrained our space was and how close we sat together. "About the newspapers, I want to assure you I had nothing to do with those dreadful stories regarding the gladiator mosaic, nor the child."

"I didn't think you had," he said evenly.

A strange relief flooded me. He had once asked me if we were to be friends, and I now felt that regard keenly. In truth, I did not keep many friends. Many acquaintances, yes, but few who truly understood me.

Father's voice broke into my thoughts. "He that loveth silver shall not be satisfied with silver; nor he that loveth abundance with increase: this is also vanity."

I recognized the quote from Ecclesiastes chapter five, verse ten—likely one he now contemplated for Sunday's sermon.

"It's a temptation, no doubt," Rafe agreed. "Two things drive a man to reprehensible behavior. Temptation and desperation."

He spoke as someone who had been seared by experience.

"Don't forget pride," Father said, with a wry tilt to his lips. "I should think the original sin counts for much of our devastation."

"Pride, desperation, temptation, and all other philosophical or theological remarks aside, we must prepare because more hunters will flock to the dig, circling like a pack of crows. I can't bear the thought of Mr. Perry losing his farm," I added.

"The real question is who is responsible," Father said as he pushed his glasses up the bony bridge of his nose.

None of us had answers.

"I'll send men, not callow youths, to watch over your dig," Rafe promised. "And I'll monitor things myself as much as I can."

"But what if there is danger?"

He offered a grim smile in reply.

I had forgotten that a hardened soldier, even a wounded one, still had fight left within him.

Then a long breath escaped him. "I wish that was all I had to share with you. I wrote a colleague of mine, one with connections to the Navy. It appears your brother is gravely ill."

Rafe's words hit me with the force of a blow. *Daniel, gravely ill.* My mind raced, the room spinning as I processed the news.

"Can we not free him?" I managed to whisper, though my heart was already sinking.

Father struggled to rise from the settee, his face as pale as parchment. His movements were slow, his hand gripping the mantel for support. "My poor son. I must go to him at once and procure a physician," he murmured, his voice cracking under the weight of emotion.

I felt the pull of duty toward my brother—the desperate urge to rush to his side, to do something, anything to help him. Yet the urgency of the mosaic tugged at me, refusing to let go. Could I abandon the work that could bring much-needed funding and stability? The two burdens warred within me, twisting my emotions into knots.

Rafe's voice broke through my turmoil. "You will not be granted entrance into that hulk even if Daniel languishes," he said gently, his expression stricken. "I'm afraid all we can do is wait for further news. I'm truly sorry."

The apology hung in the air, heavy with regret. He stood to match me, rising from the low settee, and I caught the brief flicker of discomfort that crossed his face as he steadied himself. His leg must still ache from his injury, yet he never complained.

Instinctively, my hand reached out, as though I could offer him the support he had so freely promised me. But just before our fingers could touch, I hesitated, drawing back. The moment between us lingered—charged with concern and something deeper, something unspoken. His presence so close to mine, his breath warm against my forehead, stirred an unsettling sensation within me.

His height loomed over me, the stark mismatch between us all the more evident in that moment of proximity. I let my gaze drift over his features—the crooked nose, the set jaw, the dark eyes that seemed to bore into mine with tenderness I hadn't expected.

Rafe cleared his throat, and I pulled back, my knees weakening the longer I stood near him.

"Vicar, I will do everything within my power to assist you and Miss Littleton," he said, his tone measured but sincere. He glanced toward me as he spoke, and I couldn't help but feel that promise extended far beyond words.

Father thanked him, and I walked with Rafe to the door. As he paused, his hand resting on the handle, his gaze softened.

"I will do what I can for your brother," he repeated, his voice quiet.

Tears stung my eyes, but I blinked them back. Despite the destruction of the orchard and Mr. Talbot's visit, Rafe had remembered Daniel and sought to help.

"Thank you, Rafe," I whispered, catching my mistake as his dark eyes flared. "L-Lord Hawthorn, I mean. Forgive me—"

"No," he interrupted, his voice holding a note of surprise. "I much prefer the former. If you're willing . . . Bridget."

He said my name almost like a caress, and I felt the flutter of something dangerously close to yearning. But his next words rooted me in reality.

"Promise me you'll call for me if trouble arises? Please, do not take matters into your own hands, no matter how capable you are. I won't see you come to any harm."

A calm settled over me at his promise. No one, other than my mother, had ever watched over me. Not Father, who needed more care than he could give, and not Daniel, whose reckless choices had led to his imprisonment. I had always been the one watching out for others. And yet, here was Rafe, promising to look after me.

My mouth must have moved of its own accord, forming words I wasn't entirely conscious of. After Rafe bid me farewell, I resumed my pacing, feeling trapped between the weight of Daniel's fate and the looming disaster of the theft. The mosaic work needed my attention, but how could I think of that when my brother lay ill?

I halted near the window, watching as Rafe mounted his horse. How capable he seemed, how determined. He had suffered losses, yet he remained formidable—strong in ways I admired. Could I really live my life alone, facing these battles without someone by my side?

"Whatever are you staring out the window for, Bridget? You won't spy any thieves during this hour of the day," Father protested as he stepped away from the fireplace.

A thrill rippled through me when the horse and master galloped away. Never had Father and I needed an ally so much as in this moment.

Father joined me at the window to see what I was staring at. He pushed again on his spectacles. "Oh."

26

Bridget

Prosperity is a restless thing; it drives itself to distraction. It addles the brain, and not always in the same way, for it goads people in different directions—some toward power, others toward self-indulgence.
SENECA

Later that morning, Mr. Archibald Harrington arrived. His white hair was tied back, and though his coat and breeches were proper, it was his sturdy laced boots that caught my eye. I had expected an athletic man, but Mr. Harrington appeared to be an apple with a barrel chest and spindly legs and the roundest face I had ever seen.

I longingly regarded his boots, so different from a pair of polished Hessians.

Mrs. Herriot rolled her eyes when she caught my glance at his footwear.

We went to Mr. Perry's field, where I pointed out the sections, including the missing Bacchus.

"A terrible misfortune to lose such a valuable piece," Mr. Harrington said as he stroked his chin. "Your drawings at least give us some idea of what the mosaic looked like. I agree with you, wholeheartedly, Miss Littleton, that the Medusa is most unusual. Was this a portrait of the *domina*? Or someone who might have been . . . ah . . . ah . . . a *meretrix*?"

A mistress. Apparently, Mr. Harrington didn't realize the extent of my Latin. Equally apparent was that the Roman wealthy didn't differ much from the wilder ton, who aped the Prince Regent with his list of torrid affairs.

Within the hour, Mr. Harrington had marched across the field correcting my views on third-century Rome, regardless of what I showed him. Even my ideas of the owner were soundly rebuffed.

"No. Not a farmer, Miss Littleton. No farmer, no matter how wealthy, could afford such artistry as we see with the mosaics. I suggest we confine our search to the upper echelon."

He corrected how we dug, suggesting we mark the land with ropes, sectioning off squares to examine and unearth one at a time. And, of course, despite his enthusiasm for my notes and sketches, which he boldly critiqued and praised in equal turns, he recoiled when he witnessed Mr. Perry attacking the soil with a shovel.

A cracking sounded as Mr. Perry heaved the shovel full into the ground.

"Upon my word, sir! Nothing will be left!" Mr. Harrington motioned for my brush with impatient fingers. I handed it to him. He eased onto the dirt beside the mound.

"Basket!" he all but barked, and Abigail scurried to retrieve it.

After scooping up the soil, he carefully sifted it back and forth, allowing the finest particles to escape. Then, with the greatest care, as if he performed surgery, he brushed a strange piece. Pinching it between his fingers, he laughed as he held it up for us to see.

"Ah!" he cried. "Ah! By Jove!"

We had dug for weeks and found only mosaics and pottery. Mr. Perry shrugged when he met my incredulous gaze. He wiped one filthy hand across his sweating brow, leaving streaks behind.

"I see nothing to get excited about," Mr. Perry said wryly.

"Indeed, it's a clump of dirt at first glance." Mr. Harrington frowned as he removed a white handkerchief from his coat and gently polished the piece before holding it up again. "It's a gold ring, with a seal, no less. I see a man's face with a laurel wrapped around it. Could this be the portrait of the owner of the villa? Or is this the god Bacchus?"

He carefully deposited the ring into my gloved hands. I immediately spied similar features from the mosaic. The god of vice and revelry.

"Gladiators and Bacchus. I daresay this villa saw a fair amount of wine and fighting and, likely, pretty women." He flushed. "Pardon my language. In my excitement, I quite forgot about the ladies."

Mr. Perry snickered, hiding his mirth behind a grimy fist.

"There's more to discover," I added, suddenly chilled by the thought of gladiators and women and the little child hidden beneath the twisted roots of the apple grove. "I'd really like your opinion on a grave site that was discovered on Lord Hawthorn's land."

He arched a bushy eyebrow, seeming torn between excavating the mound before us and investigating yet another site.

"We found the bones of a child buried with a doll the length of my hand near the Hawthorn orchard. I'll see if we can arrange a visit with Lord Hawthorn as soon as possible."

Mr. Harrington blinked. "That is strange to discover a child buried with a toy. And most un-Roman. How soon can I meet this Lord Hawthorn?"

We returned to the parsonage, my heart beating fast with triumph since the secretary of the Society of Antiquaries said he would write his colleagues this evening. His enthusiasm seemed a near guarantee of the fifty pounds to be awarded to the best research. Even with the magnificent Bacchus mosaic stolen, plenty remained to entice Mr. Harrington. He took the gold ring to the guest room and proclaimed he would inspect it further, having brought a suitcase of his own utensils.

I went to change my dress, my spirits high. Mr. Harrington hinted that I might write a paper on the riches of Bramnor for *Archeologia*, along with my illustrations of the mosaics. But my jaw truly dropped when he casually asked if I could present my findings to the Society of Antiquaries, hinting at a permanent *position* as a researcher and illustrator to the tune of forty to sixty pounds per year.

Mind you, our current illustrator is retiring thanks to his eyesight. You will not earn his one hundred pounds per year. At least, not until you gain fame, he'd warned me.

As if he even needed to ask about my interest in such a proposition. My heart soared at the request I had pined for. Hope had never felt so real and tangible.

If only Daniel could stay safe and well within the hulk.

I slipped into a new chemise while Molly opened my armoire, removing one of the most overtly feminine gowns I owned. A pure confection of lace and froth, beribboned with a contrasting sapphire blue.

With my hair redone and ribboned, I descended the stairs with my tin box in hand, the Roman doll safely nestled inside. I ground to a halt at the sight of two strangers waiting in my drawing room.

The first man stood by the fireplace, his back to me. He wore a crimson superfine coat with a black collar high enough to brush against white-gold hair, breeches of the palest cream, and a pair of tasseled black boots with enough shine to rival my handheld mirror. The second man, dressed equally well, had brown hair teased into an enormous curl dipping over his forehead. He wore riding boots with the flat tops turned down to reveal a lighter tan leather with a delicate crest. His silken cravat brushed against his rounded chin.

I clutched the tin to my chest as I stood paralyzed at the entrance.

The first man was not as tall as Rafe, nor as big, but when he turned slowly, I stared into the iciest blue eyes I had ever seen. *Handsome* didn't even begin to describe him, but the fine hair on the back of my neck stood on end. It was like having a living Apollo within my drawing room.

"Miss Littleton, I presume," he drawled.

"Yes, but I fear you have me at a disadvantage, sir. You know my name and I do not know yours."

"Mr. Thomas Beaumont, at your service." His thin lips curved in what I could only deem a smile. "This is my friend, Lord Ainsley, the viscount of Harrowby."

Yet again, I was speechless. A troublesome occurrence as of late.

His smirk deepened as he moved toward me with a careless grace. "You wrote to the Dilettanti, didn't you? You are that same Miss Littleton who has stirred my fellow members into such a frenzy?"

"Considering the last reply I received from your secretary, I must say I'm rather surprised to see you here at all."

"Percival has the manners of a pigeon. I apologize for his unacceptable behavior on behalf of the Dilettanti." He stood close to me, regarding me intently. "I simply couldn't wait on a matter this important. My carriage traveled faster than courier."

London remained a day's travel away. Maybe even a day and a half, if one wanted to rest at an inn. I wasn't sure what to make of this man's declaration. My silence seemed to further his intensity.

The second man spoke up. "Perhaps we are too late, Beaumont." He glanced around the room, unable to hide his disdain, judging from his sneer.

Mr. Beaumont held up a hand to his friend. "Miss Littleton, I am prepared to pay handsomely for your efforts. Name the price for the artifacts and your sketches. All of it."

I had so longed for this moment, to be pursued and recognized by the best in society, to have my research praised, *to be seen*, but my spirit rebelled at the offer.

"I have made other arrangements."

He stood far too close and smelled of Bay Rum. "Who?"

"Really, it is too late for your concern, sir."

"I doubt that," he said, his eyes flashing. "I've made an offer to Mr. Perry to purchase his farm. Whether you give me your sketches is irrelevant. I can always find another artist. However, if you have anything of value, I *will* purchase it."

A sense of helplessness suffused me. If Mr. Perry sold the field, all would be lost.

Mr. Beaumont studied me as if to decode the emotions no doubt flashing across my face. "In fact, Lord Hawthorn wrote me regarding his property several weeks prior."

Surely the news was a lie, but the triumphant smile on Mr. Beaumont's face proved that I was wrong. Nausea swept through me, rending me dizzy.

Footsteps echoed heavily and Mr. Harrington burst through the doors with a small object pinched between his stout fingers.

"My dear, this stone is astounding. I must share it with you—" He paused mid-step when he saw the young man standing too close for my comfort. I inched backward.

"Mr. Beaumont, what—what a surprise." Mr. Harrington lowered his hand. He curled his finger around the ring and tucked it into a pocket. "What brings you here?"

"Is it such a surprise, Mr. Harrington? You didn't think we Dilettanti would let the society corner all the adventure, now did you? Miss Littleton has invited both of us to examine her magnificent mosaics."

Mr. Harrington's mouth rounded as if I had denied him my dance card and relegated him solely to obtaining lemonade on my behalf while I flirted with a better suitor.

I felt the weight of both men pinning me with their gazes. "It's true. I sent word to both societies, hoping to invite their interest. However, thanks to Mr. Harrington's swift and enthusiastic response, I have no need for two sponsors."

The room grew quiet with only the sound of the logs cracking in the fireplace to distract from the mounting tension. Mr. Harrington smiled triumphantly while Mr. Beaumont appeared to be cast in iron. He did not even blink.

"Mr. Beaumont, you must understand my decision. The Society of Antiquaries answered my letter first and promised to send their secretary at their nearest convenience."

Mr. Harrington exhaled, his relief palpable. I refrained from reminding the Apollo that I had sent not one but three letters to the Dilettanti.

A long pause followed before Mr. Beaumont pivoted toward his rival. "Congratulations are in order to Mr. Harrington and his society."

He tilted his head in my direction. "And congratulations to you, Miss Littleton."

"A shame you made the trip and now must return." Mr. Harrington sounded cheerful. He slid his hand into his pocket, where the ring hid.

Mr. Beaumont shrugged. "On the contrary. I intend to enjoy all that Bramnor offers before I end my stay."

"I must warn of the inns," I protested, hoping to deter him. "They are not fit for refined travelers."

He brushed past me, the visit apparently over.

"So I have heard. Not to worry, Miss Littleton, I have engaged in the hospitality of Lord Hawthorn. I understand he, too, has mosaics equally as impressive as yours."

27

Rafe

> A club, for which the nominal qualification is having been in Italy, and the real one being drunk; the two chiefs are Lord Middlesex and Sir Francis Dashwood, who were seldom sober the whole time they were in Italy.
>
> **HORACE WALPOLE ON THE DILETTANTI**

Mrs. Whittle caught me in the east wing after our guests retired to dress for dinner. Both men brought valets, easing some of the burden of my staff.

"I hope the menu will be satisfactory for our guests," she said before rattling off a list that barely registered in my racing thoughts. Lamb and apple pudding or lemon syllabub. Did I have a preference?

"Do as you must, Mrs. Whittle." I lowered my voice to calm her nerves. "Whatever you choose will suffice."

She fidgeted with her brooch. Nerves, I suspected, due to the strain of serving such esteemed guests. "I hope the rooms are to their liking. They've rung several times and Mr. Whittle is beside himself trying to serve them as best he can. Lucy served tea to the gentlemen."

I clenched my jaw. Lucy serving tea wasn't unusual, but something about these men set my teeth on edge.

"Lucy's done nothing to draw their notice, has she?" I asked.

Mrs. Whittle shook her head, her hands fidgeting with her apron. "No, my lord, she's just doing her work. But they've been . . . demanding."

I nodded, keeping my concerns to myself. "Very well, but if anything seems out of line, you'll let me know."

She dipped her head in acknowledgment, hesitating briefly before leaving the study, the sound of her skirts swishing against the stone floor echoing softly as she closed the door behind her.

The study, usually a place of solace for me, felt heavier with the weight of expectations. I needed their help—investments in the orchards, particularly after the hailstorm, were crucial. But something about their presence unsettled me.

I was about to leave the study when I noticed my uncle's diary lying on the desk, its worn cover drawing my eye. No dust remained on the surfaces, and I surmised that Lucy or Mrs. Whittle had moved it while tidying. Despite my need to join the men for dinner, it seemed to call to me.

I picked it up, a shiver of unease running through me. It had been moved while cleaning.

March 17th, 1796

I have tried repeatedly to reach Anne. She refuses my letters even now. Why won't she answer me? All I request is one letter to know where she and Rafe hide. I would collect both of them at the soonest convenience and return them to Hawthorn Abbey, where they both belong.

Surely, she must know by now that Randall is dead. The news of his death spread like wildfire in the papers, blazing his name—and mine—across the area. His drunken brawl at that inn, the fool. He could not pummel his way out of that fight. How I regret not dealing with him sooner. I have nothing left within these halls but the constant reminder of my weakness. I know what people think. They whisper that I killed him. I did not, although I often wished I had. They whisper that Rafe is my son.

I wish he was my child.

I wish I had not pressured Anne to leave with me and head to some forgotten spot on the continent.

I cannot change my past. I hardly dare hope for the future, although the good reverend assures me it is not too late to find some redemption for my soul.

Gut clenching, I flipped to the next page, only to find further sections ripped out.

Why?

A knock softly tapped on the door and Mr. Whittle called me to dinner. I closed the diary and set it on the desk, perplexed by what I had just read. Randall remained my father, even if I had no wish to claim such a monster. My uncle proved a far more complex man than I had first envisioned. Yet the past no longer dug tethers into my soul with the same strength as before.

I had asked Bridget if she believed a man could change.

Perhaps, the uncomfortable answer was yes . . . *if* God played a role in it.

The dining room, with its stone fireplace and grand table, was one of the abbey's most impressive rooms. A pair of sabers hung on the chiseled mantel. Higher, stout beams ran across the ceiling, drawing attention from a few cracks webbing across the plaster. I hoped my guests would not notice.

Normally, I ate in the solar or within my room, but tonight I would have to play host, even if I hated the idea. I met Mr. Beaumont and Lord Ainsley in the drawing room and escorted them to the grand room. A white tablecloth draped the immense table, and Mr. Whittle had squeezed into a dusty suit to serve us white soup made from chicken stock instead of veal and spiced with nutmeg.

Polite talk of the weather and the Prince Regent marked the first course. Ainsley, who eyed my coat, suggested purchasing from Beau Brummell, an up-and-coming fashion designer. I couldn't care less about cravats and other fripperies. How could I bother with such frivolity when I had a road to finish, a cider press to install, *and* a ruined orchard to recover? Too many people relied upon me to make Hawthorn Abbey a success. Regardless, I said nothing as my guests debated the latest styles with the same fervor of any young miss.

Mr. Beaumont waved his hand, the ring on his finger winking in the candlelight.

"Even the Prince Regent must abandon his jeweled waistcoats. They are no longer the thing, but you can't advise Prinny. He fancies himself the best-dressed man in the room, thanks to the flattery of *The Times*. And he positively hates, *hates* Brummell for bringing back severe fashion. I have it on good authority that Prinny and Lord Moria encountered Brummell at St. James recently. Of course, the Prince Regent ignored Brummell, a direct cut if there ever was one. Brummell, however, turned to Lord Moria and said in a voice loud enough to echo over the lawn, *Pray, who is your fat friend?*"

Mr. Beaumont snorted as he covered his mouth with a fist. "Prinny can't meet Brummell's measurements. Only a slender man can, and that fact drives the Regent nearly mad. I have it on good authority the writers at *The Times* had quite the conversation with

Brummell. A pity the Prince Regent shut down that story as fast as he could."

I smiled to cover my discomfort with the mention of one of the more prominent newspapers to blare news about my abbey across England.

Mr. Beaumont turned to me, waggling his eyebrows. "You've made it into *The Times*."

"Apparently Roman antiquities make for fascinating reading," I hedged as I picked up my fork, yet my appetite had fled.

I discovered he belonged to the Dilettanti and had taken it upon himself to bring younger men under his wing, including Lord Ainsley. While I had heard of the Dilettanti, I had never had the luxury of embarking on a grand tour of the continent, a fact Lord Ainsley soon discovered.

"You've never been to the Orient?" he asked, incredulous as he dabbed at his mouth with a linen napkin.

"My travels followed the path of Bonaparte," I replied as I fingered the stem of a crystal goblet. The claret, with the crimson hue deep enough to bring memories of the blood splattering against my uniform, made me hesitate. I chose water instead while Lord Ainsley drank freely.

Mr. Beaumont raised his goblet as if in toast. "And now you've inherited Hawthorn Abbey. Are you finding country life to your liking?"

"Refreshing," I answered readily, and surprised myself. Bridget had warned that I would not find anonymity here, no matter how much I craved it. As the days passed, I realized that I no longer wanted to seclude myself within a cloak of loneliness. I had found something precious in the valley, friendship and loyalty.

He set down his goblet with a clunk, the wine too drained to slosh over the rim. "You've met Miss Littleton and Mr. Perry. What do you think of their enterprise?"

I hesitated. "Without her tenacity and discernment, there would be no excavation."

Lord Ainsley waved his fork before stabbing at his cut of lamb dripping in butter. "But a woman? What business has she running around the countryside, ruining priceless artifacts? Those mosaics alone will collect a tidy sum from any museum."

A chill swept through me. Hadn't I thrown similar words at her, demanding to know why she wandered the countryside without an escort? To hear Ainsley dismiss her in such a cavalier manner made me bristle.

"I have found Miss Littleton to be remarkably well-spoken and informed about the history of the area."

"A bluestocking." Mr. Beaumont jeered. "Say no more."

I changed the subject as quickly as I could, desiring to safeguard her reputation. I didn't enjoy hearing her name uttered from that snide mouth. "And you, what is your interest in mosaics?"

He dabbed at his mouth with a linen napkin. "It's simple, really. I'm a second son of an earl, destined for the church while my elder brother inherits my father's holdings. Ainsley, lucky man, has already inherited his title. We met during our grand tour and found an invitation awaiting with the Dilettanti to join their ranks in hunting for rare art across the globe."

"Beaumont has had the longest tour of us all," Lord Ainsley said, chuckling as he folded his arms across his chest. "He'll do anything to avoid becoming a rector, won't you? Although time is running out, old boy. You'll need to convince your father of your alternate ambitions."

"Your father does not approve of your collecting?" I asked.

Any mirth fled from Mr. Beaumont as he drained the last of his claret. I hardly dared give him more, following a fourth glass this evening. Not if I was required to offer port later on. With his nose flushed, his eyes sparked dangerously.

"No, he thinks I am nothing more than a grave robber."

Lord Ainsley's smile also disappeared. "Beaumont's father is in the House of Commons. One must be careful not to endanger the family name. Besides, his blessed mother desires one son enter the clergy."

"I'm not a pious man by any means." Mr. Beaumont offered a rakish smile. Lucy had stepped in to deliver the creamy syllabub. His gaze wandered all over her and her golden curls as if she were the luscious treat instead of the sherry dessert she set before him.

"You live well enough in the country, I daresay," he murmured after she blushed and smiled. "I should like to explore the abbey and see this infamous apple orchard of yours. Perhaps you and I can come to an agreement that is mutually beneficial."

I remained silent, even if he offered what I most desired. If I was to rescue my investment and protect my tenants, I had no choice but to investigate all possible options of reviving my estate and recovering the loss of the apples.

But I would speak later with Mr. Whittle and advise him to keep his daughter occupied elsewhere for the duration of the visit.

My guests refused the offer of port and cigars, instead insisting upon viewing the orchard and the gladiators. Wind whistled through the twisted trees as we walked, and the remaining sun, a glorious display of fire, reached the tips of the damaged branches. We had minutes at best before twilight would envelop the countryside.

When I began sharing my plans for the abbey, Lord Ainsley stifled a yawn.

"This child you discovered, when may I review the find?" Mr. Beaumont interrupted my description of the brewery as we followed the new lane skirting the trees, a lane that needed to extend another two miles toward Bramnor and Chichester. My skin pebbled, and it had nothing to do with the brisk wind blowing across the valley.

"I have given the remains to Mr. Harrington. He believes the child to be Roman." For some reason, I felt compelled not to mention the ivory doll, nor that I had entrusted it to Bridget.

"Harrington says this?" Mr. Beaumont looked unconvinced as he pulled out a lacquered box of snuff as pretty as a confection.

"Miss Littleton, actually, and Harrington agreed." How easily I pictured her sitting on the settee within her drawing room when learning of the Bacchus theft, her eyes shimmering with wetness and her hands clasped tightly in her lap.

"Blazes, you believed her?" Mr. Beaumont rubbed a finger underneath his nose before the box disappeared into his coat pocket. "Of course, a body tucked away within an orchard wouldn't be the Christian thing. Yes, I think I would much prefer Miss Littleton's explanation if I were in your shoes. Otherwise, you'd have a calumny on your hands."

Lord Ainsley glanced around the orchard. "Wasn't there a rumor about your uncle? What was it, Beaumont? Help me remember."

Mr. Beaumont smiled again, but it did not reach his eyes. "A murder. Quite delicious and clandestine. Your father, I believe. Didn't he die?"

I dreaded the line of questioning, but I couldn't avoid it forever. "My father was murdered at an inn just outside of Aldwick. A stable hand, Ethan Hake, found himself hanged for it."

Ainsley and Beaumont gaped at me. I forced my features to appear impassive.

"Forgive our curiosity. We have no desire to offend you," Lord Ainsley admitted. "It's a curious affair."

Mr. Beaumont hurried to add, "Regardless, it is most unfortunate Miss Littleton ruined the site. Harrington ought to take it off her hands. I offered to buy her research. She refused, the gall! I hope Mr. Perry will have the sense to reconsider my offer by morning."

"You wish to buy Perry's farm?" I asked, curious now. As the second son, Mr. Beaumont might be privy to a handsome allowance, but to make offers on my property and Perry's was extraordinary. "How will you arrange the funds for such an acquisition?"

I must have probed too deeply since he halted mid-step before recovering swiftly. He glanced at me with another smirk. "I have my methods. I can be persuasive when the occasion calls for it."

"He jests," Lord Ainsley protested. "The Dilettanti are sixty brothers strong. We will all put in notes if need be. It's long been our rule to fund antiquities expeditions and publish our findings in scholarly journals."

"You do not work with the Society of Antiquaries?"

Lord Ainsley shrugged. "Partner with old men confined to their libraries? We prefer the excitement of travel and experiencing exotic locations. We are collectors, in a sense, each vetted via secret ballot votes at Brooks's. It's quite a rigorous process to be accepted."

He did not answer my question, nor did he extend an invitation to join their group. Not that I would have wanted to, even if Brooks's remained one of the most exclusive memberships for gentlemen. I understood even a few dukes attended.

Misgivings swirled within me when I showed them the gladiator mosaic. They muttered over it, walking back and forth, their boots noiseless against the fresh grass sprouting anew.

"Eh gad, but I would like to have bet on one of these fighters. Imagine them hacking at each other in the arena, hoping to cheat death!" Lord Ainsley practically glowed as he stared at the half naked forms of two men grappling with each other.

Neither man knelt on the ground like Bridget had. And their inspection took only a few moments, unlike hers.

On our walk back to the abbey, Mr. Beaumont kept pace with me. "I admire what you are doing for the abbey. I want to help any way that I can, but I can't throw money into ventures such as cider presses with no return. I need to see a guaranteed outcome. Of course, I'll take your Ming vases and the tapestries, but it's the mosaic I want. I'm prepared to pay handsomely for it. I suggest you take the funds and rebuild your land."

"I could also show you the brewery as a potential investment in the years to come—"

He raised a hand, the fingers lily white. "The mosaics, Lord Hawthorn. All of them. As much as I appreciate a stout drink, I want access to your orchard for what lies beneath. Once I purchase Perry's land, I'll be able to excavate the entire villa."

"What of Miss Littleton? She was the first to document the findings. I believe all she wants is the recognition for her scholastic achievement. Will you allow her to continue to work with you?"

As soon as the challenge left my mouth, I despised the idea of her working so closely with Beaumont. However, she had admitted that she needed the Dilettanti or the Society of Antiquaries. Was partnership with them truly what she wanted?

"No one will take her seriously. If I present her findings to the society, what then? I will be the laughingstock before all the men."

"What about the Society of Antiquaries?"

He waved aside the notion as if it were a bothersome fly. "Mr. Harrington can't do much if he doesn't purchase the farm first. The key to the dilemma is Mr. Perry. Not Miss Littleton, nor Mr. Harrington."

Lord Ainsley watched me keenly. "If need be, we could rent the field at a generous price. Perhaps even the entire estate. You could leave the countryside and set up anywhere you preferred. London. The continent."

"Or sell it," Mr. Beaumont added. "If you are last in the entitlement."

"I'll think on it," I rasped. I was not a gambling man, but I had sunk my commission into the abbey and had nothing else. The Dilettanti offered me an easy escape. But did I truly want to leave the valley, the Whittles, and my tenants who relied upon me? Or the vicar? Or . . . *her*?

Lord Ainsley clapped a hand on my shoulder. "Come, Rafe, stop looking so morose. Your Mr. Whittle shared that a country dance is to be held soon, just in time for May Day. Why don't we enjoy ourselves while you mull things over?"

He used my first name as if we were old friends. We were not. With May Day fast approaching within a week, and the investigation into my estate looming ever closer, I had little desire to celebrate. The Crown's inquiry weighed heavily on me, threatening everything I had worked for. Every step I took felt like one closer to losing the abbey, and I had yet to hear any promising news that might buy me more time.

Would either man persuade Mr. Perry to sell before the Crown's decision? My steward had tried and failed. I despised the thought of Bridget being caught between such ruthless men, especially now when so much hung in the balance.

Her eyes, shimmering with unshed tears, filled my mind. She was not someone prone to tears, as far as I could tell, and the thought of hurting her brought a bitter taste to my mouth.

28

Bridget

> Faith is a living and unshakable confidence. A belief in God so assured that a man would die a thousand deaths for its sake.
>
> **MARTIN LUTHER**

Polite society reserved visiting hours between one and three, but we Littletons hardly followed such conventions. When Mr. Harrington requested we focus on the doll and mosaics, I heaved a sigh of relief. After the unsettling visit from the two Dilettanti men, the idea of losing myself in ancient artifacts was far more appealing than engaging with any visitors.

Sensing my need for quiet, Father instructed Molly to turn away any callers.

Excitement flickered as we put on white gloves and compared our finds. The cameo of a man with a hawk-like nose reminded me of Lord Hawthorn—imperious, yet surprisingly kind. Swallowing against the lump in my throat, I pushed aside the thought of Mr. Beaumont's claim of purchasing Lord Hawthorn's land.

Mr. Perry and I had heard nothing further from the magistrate, despite Father's recent visit to Chichester, where he had hoped to speak with the magistrate directly.

All my dreams and hopes felt as though they might dissipate as readily as smoke. If I could no longer access the site in the months to come, would Mr. Harrington still find work for me with the society? Any control over the situation felt as distant and evasive as the magistrate at Chichester.

"Could this man be the owner of the house?" I asked as we observed the ring.

"Perhaps, or a god," Mr. Harrington said as he held it up to the light streaming from the window.

"An idol. Oh, Reverend, how can we allow such a hideous thing inside the parsonage?" Mrs. Herriot moaned as she bustled out of the room.

"Get a glove, Reverend, and you may hold something well over a thousand years old," Mr. Harrington said, ignoring Mrs. Herriot's protest.

Father slipped on the glove and picked up the ring. I saw a sense of wonder pass over his features as the ruby's stone glowed, further revealing the handsome profile.

"I have no idealism about the Romans," Mr. Harrington said. "When Pompeii was rediscovered, the French quickly covered the worst of the vulgar pictures."

I didn't need him to explain further. I had read plenty of Roman literature. Unfortunately, I had also seen things no respectable woman would ever admit to knowing, and they were as foul as Mr. Harrington intimated.

Father nodded at me, approval shining in his eyes at Mr. Harrington's levelheaded assessment. "Proof, my good sir, of Christianity's acclaim to change not just the individual but the course of the world. Men learned to blush again and discern good from evil."

Trust Father to find redemption. Still, his thought settled into the cracks of my soul. As much as I felt like a doubting Thomas, I could not deny the change faith brought. Pain followed it too. Pain that made me wrestle with the goodness of such a God.

"Might I see your doll, Miss Littleton?" Mr. Harrington asked, drawing me from my thoughts.

I pulled the jointed doll out of the tin, careful to keep the linen handkerchief around her. The face held no details, a blank slate waiting to be written upon.

"Somewhat of an older toy to give an infant," I admitted as he carefully reached for it. He grunted assent, and it seemed as if Father and I had faded from the room. Mr. Harrington rose and took the doll. He sank into the petite chair, its legs groaning beneath his weight.

"Ah," he crooned as he turned over the toy. Reaching into his coat pocket, he pulled out a large magnifying glass. "Ah." Then a sudden intake of breath.

He pierced me with a look. "There is a Christian symbol on her. You knew this?"

I nodded. "I wanted to be sure before I claimed such a thing. I had hoped you would confirm my finding."

"This explains why someone buried her in such a manner. Only a Christian would do such a thing. The question is, who did this child belong to? The master of the house? Or a slave or a servant?"

"I doubt we will ever know," I murmured.

Mr. Harrington didn't seem to hear my remark. "It's a cross of sorts, otherwise known as the Chi Rho, a symbol used by Constantine, the first Christian emperor. It's encircled too. At first glance, one might assume it was the letter *P* intersected with a simple *x*. The chi and the rho, both Greek letters. Using a wreath around the Chi Rho symbolizes the victory of the resurrection over death."

"Then the doll gives us a framework. We can't date the original building, but we know of such Christian symbols used around the fourth century," I said.

Mr. Harrington shot me a glance full of approval.

"Bridget, this is marvelous." Father peered over the man's shoulder to see the markings. "It's a sign from above." His voice broke. "A sign of God's mercy in troubling seasons. Of His perfect faithfulness even in the presence of evil and loss."

I suspected what he left unsaid, his fear for Daniel's well-being stealing the last bit of his strength. His eyes brimmed with unshed tears as he examined the doll with Mr. Harrington.

Yes, the doll's marking was marvelous. And disconcerting in a way. Was God trying to tell me something? That He remained in control, even as my doubt festered?

Could I trust Him with my life and that of my loved ones, as Mrs. Eacher had encouraged?

Oh, ye of little faith.

29

Bridget

> It's not that we have a short time to live, but that we waste much of it. Life is long enough, and it's been given to us in generous measure for accomplishing the greatest things, if the whole of it is well invested. But when life is squandered through soft and careless living, and when it's spent on no worthwhile pursuit, death finally presses and we realize that the life which we didn't notice passing has passed away.
>
> **SENECA**

Father didn't approve at all of May Day, which marked the beginning of the month with its pagan roots extending to the Celtic observance celebrating the beginning of spring, and if one reached further back, ancient Rome with the festival of Floralia, the goddess of flowers. The young girls wove crowns of wildflowers to wear during the parade. A flagpole draped with ribbons and set in the town square triumphantly waited for the revelers.

I didn't care about the dancing or the ale that poured freely throughout the afternoon and especially into the late evening. However, the festival had been a tradition in our village since the sixteen hundreds when Charles II reinstated it. Many a girl, including Abigail, dreamed of dancing with a handsome beau and being crowned the May Queen.

"It's Pentecost," Father reminded me when I stepped into the drawing room that afternoon. In the past, we had stayed home together, enjoying a quiet evening. The day before, he spent in prayer, interceding for blessings on the flowers, fruits, and fields.

"Abigail made me promise I would go with her," I responded, adjusting my gloves. "She needs someone responsible to ensure all the young swains don't trip over her toes. Her father will be present. I doubt you'll need to worry about either of us."

Moreover, I dreaded nursing my morbid thoughts within a stuffy drawing room while trying to guess what Lord Hawthorn and Mr. Perry might do with their land. The longer I worked on the excavation, the more Mr. Harrington and Father advised a short rest. Torn by the need to uncover more of the mosaics and chaperone my friend, I finally settled on the latter, even if I felt a prick of resentment.

Father grimaced. "Mr. Perry ought to have better control over his daughter."

I hid my smile as I touched my curls, artfully styled with ribbons, thanks to Molly's expert interventions. Of course, Father heard the same said about me.

"We won't stay late into the evening. We'll wander the grounds and sample the tarts. Maybe we'll even have a glass of lemonade. She dreams of being a queen for a night."

"Chaperone, indeed. You look as though you need a chaperone of your own," he said, taking in my newly reworked gown, sewn by Mrs. Herriot from one of my mother's dresses. The pale-green fabric, accented with lace at the sleeves and a slightly lower neckline, caught his attention.

"Do you like it?" I asked, since I had allowed Mrs. Herriot the freedom to choose what she thought best. I had never seen a woman so happy.

He grunted as he pushed up his glasses. "It's fetching enough." Then his eyes narrowed thoughtfully. "Quite fetching. Do refuse any impetuous marriage invitations while you're out. A father has to have some say in the matter."

I laughed as I draped a lace shawl over my shoulders. "You needn't worry on my account. It's Abigail who needs watching."

He arched an eyebrow. "Indeed, she does. I just heard from one of the tenants that he spied her riding with Mr. Barron yesterday."

I opened my mouth to protest and swiftly shut it. How was it that Abigail and I no longer shared our secrets with each other? I had thought Mr. Barron had abandoned her, considering Mr. Perry's refusal to bring him into our venture.

Despite my anxiety over Abigail's secrecy, there was no time to dwell on it. Before I knew it, Abigail and I found ourselves at the Hawkinses' home, exhausted from the day's events but eager for the country dance.

The large manor house, which had plenty of room for a country dance, was aglow with candlelight, and the polished floor gleamed while a fiddler struck a merry tune. A crowd of familiar faces pressed close against us, including Lord Hawthorn's tenants and the villagers. I recognized the Cordings with their son, Jonathan, at the outskirts next to a table with an enormous punch bowl. Mr. Perry had a glass of punch in hand, his nose especially red this evening.

Earlier in the afternoon, we had enjoyed the maypole, festooned with blue, pink, and yellow ribbons, as the young girls twirled with their crowns of flowers. The Green Man, one of the Devon boys bedecked in green attire and foliage, had marched through the street leading the procession of merry morris dancers. Within the ballroom, I now spied many of our dancers, including the Green Man wandering with a bit of leaf trapped in his tousled hair. He joined the other young men near the punch bowl, where a concoction of lemonade and Jamaican rum brought a steady line.

"I should have liked to have been crowned the May Queen," Abigail confided wistfully as she joined me. I smiled at her. Already the steward of the dance had arranged introductions for her to dance with a partner, so the evening wasn't a loss.

"You resemble a queen," I said.

She glowed, frocked in one of my pink gowns with flowers pinned artfully within her arranged curls. She brushed her gloved hands against the dress. "I don't think I ever want to take this gown off. I do hope I will dance holes into my slippers."

"You are only young once. Did Mr. Barron fill your card?"

She fidgeted with her gloves. "I fear he has lost interest in me unless I can change his mind."

"There are plenty of good men out there," I said more confidently than I felt. "Mr. Barron doesn't know what he is missing."

She fidgeted with her gloves, but her attention remained pinned on the youth by the punch table.

Abigail did not have to wait long to be asked to dance. A young man I recognized from church held out his arm, hardly needing to coax her to join a quadrille about to start. The music soon reached a crescendo, the violin as thrilling as could be.

I had a hard time not tapping my slippers to the rhythm. Suddenly the music ground to a discordant halt, and at the room's entrance, a disturbance caused a ripple through the dancers. Three men pushed into view, each eliciting a different reaction from me.

The peerage graced the Hawkinses' home. Dressed in severe black, Rafe towered over Mr. Beaumont and Lord Ainsley. He scanned the room, his features narrowing as if he wanted to be anywhere else. Mr. Beaumont created quite a stir, his blond hair gleaming beneath the candlelight. Again, he wore a bloodred waistcoat. His friend, with hair elaborately curled like a woman's, appeared the picture of boredom. The dance had concluded, and couples were re-forming lines to prepare for the next when Mr. Hawkins urged those near the front to make way for the peerage.

A few couples sheepishly edged out of the way to make room

for the newcomers. Mr. Beaumont's mocking smile grew wider as his host fawned over his new guests while pointing out the most eligible ladies in the room.

My gaze snapped to Rafe, who appeared stone-faced when Lord Ainsley placed a hand on his shoulder. As if sensing the weight of my stare, Rafe turned. Our eyes locked and my breath froze in my lungs. He had come with the Dilettanti. The very men I had longed to impress.

"Miss Littleton, will you not dance?" A voice purred in my ear.

Startled, I whirled around to see Mr. Barron grinning at me. "It's me or Mr. Cording by the punch bowl. Don't look now, but I believe he's coming our way. Never mind; he lost his courage. Back to the punch bowl for another drink. Poor man, so faint of heart. I'll gladly stand in his stead."

"I have no desire to dance, thank you." I dearly hoped Abigail would remain with her partner and not spy Mr. Barron by my side. I wanted no jealousy from her.

He angled closer, his spirit-laden breath igniting a spark of annoyance. "We don't need to dance, then. It's conversation I'm after. You found something else in the field, did you not? Mr. Perry has suddenly become as tight-lipped as they come. Repeatedly, he's rejected my offers to help him clear the field or post a guard. Why? I understand someone tried to steal a mosaic."

"Did Miss Perry share this news with you?" I demanded.

"She did."

"And what are your intentions with my friend?"

He opened his mouth, shocked, no doubt, by my question. "I have asked her for the honor of her hand, upon my word. Her father is quite agreeable to the notion."

I didn't know what to believe, considering Mr. Perry had expressed only disgust with the innkeeper, and my friend would likely marry any half-decent man who could provide a comfortable life.

As I inched backward, Mr. Barron placed a hand on my arm. "Please, Miss Littleton, I am worried for her. And you. I consider the vicar a dear, dear friend."

A ripple of fear chased away my former annoyance. "There is no need to worry about us, Mr. Barron. We've been careful with the excavation, and I've had help."

Mr. Barron's grasp on my arm tightened, his tone lowering. "That so-called help hasn't been enough when danger comes from unexpected places." He steered me away from the dancers, closer to the wall. The music grew louder as the fiddlers increased their tempo. With the clapping and cheering, no one would overhear our conversation.

"Miss Littleton, you are a sharp young woman, and I would expect you to notice when something feels . . . off. Don't you find it curious how our quiet village is suddenly filled with so many unfamiliar faces? You wouldn't believe the number of strangers passing through lately," Mr. Barron said, his voice tight. "Letters, messages . . . they all come through my inn since it serves for the post. You'd be surprised what kind of news ends up in my hands. Ever since the *Times* article about your excavation, men are talking."

My thoughts turned to the stranger we had seen in the field. I had never seen him before, and Rafe had verified that there was an intruder as well. Even Mr. Perry believed someone had lurked around his cottage.

Was it simply a strange coincidence of timing with Mr. Beaumont, Lord Ainsley, and Mr. Harrington? I doubted Mr. Harrington's involvement. He had been nothing but a gentleman.

"I invited Mr. Harrington and the Dilettanti," I admitted uneasily. "Each man brings a wealth of knowledge regarding antiquities and can offer the means for museums to pursue further study of my findings."

"Miss Littleton, many have offered to help the Perry family, myself included, but I find it strange that Lord Hawthorn is the one who spotted the thief, and yet the thief still got away. Doesn't that seem a little too convenient? Especially for a man with a vested interest in the land?" Mr. Barron demanded.

Rafe had rushed into my drawing room, disheveled and worried. Could someone possibly manufacture such deep understanding of my love for history and compassion regarding my brother's plight?

Mr. Barron nodded at my silence, his tight fingers finally slipping from my arm. "Please reconsider turning down my services, Miss Littleton. I know men, through and through. I would have protected your excavation. You'll need it. Thanks to the article in *The Times*, how can either you or the Perry family sleep at night?"

"That is quite enough, Mr. Barron. I thank you for your kindness, but I do not require your protection."

I was aware of a presence behind me at the same moment Mr. Barron's eyes rounded.

"The blazes, you don't," he muttered fiercely.

"Miss Littleton, forgive my intrusion, but I believe I have a dance with you."

Rafe loomed over me. He held out a hand in invitation, so unlike Mr. Barron, and waited. The music had stopped, and new dancers were taking to the floor. Several pairs of eyes pivoted in our direction. Perhaps my voice had been louder than I intended.

Rafe continued waiting. I placed my hand in his, the touch searing through my glove.

Mr. Barron brushed past us, melting into the crowd, his navy coat adorned with gilded buttons and an elaborately tied cravat—every inch of him a picture of fashion. I inhaled a deep breath when I could no longer see his well-dressed figure. His words, however, played with my emotions as Lord Hawthorn led me to the dance floor. Had I misread the viscount's intentions regarding his offer to have his men watch over the Perry farm?

Rafe had promised to send men to guard the mosaics. But where were they when Bacchus was stolen? Had they been outsmarted or simply careless? The theft weighed heavily on me, and I wondered if Lord Hawthorn had been too trusting of the men he hired—or if something more sinister was at play.

"You look . . . bewitching in that green gown, Miss Littleton." Rafe's gaze lingered on me, his hand resting at the small of my back, the pressure steady yet gentle. His thumb brushed just slightly against the fabric, almost as if he meant to memorize the texture.

"I do like green," I murmured, my heart racing faster under his touch.

"A woodland sprite could wear no other color," Rafe said with a faint smile.

I wanted to smile, but after Mr. Barron's accusations, my heart only pounded harder.

He frowned. "I hope you'll forgive my intrusion into your conversation. I saw Barron . . ." His gaze dropped to my left arm, to the skin right below the lace trim. His fingers skimmed the red mark ever so lightly. "Did he hurt you?"

Rafe's jaw tightened, and I had the distinct impression that he would unleash his anger, and it would be a fearsome sight to behold.

"No, he did not," I reassured him. My pulse skittered as he led me to the front of the dance line, as a peer would do. "Although his idea of polite conversation differs from mine."

Already, far too many women whispered behind gloved hands, drawing the attention of their partners.

"Then I assure you he will never attempt such offense again," Rafe promised evenly.

I arched an eyebrow. "He offered again to guard the dig. And he warned me about you."

"*Me?*"

At the center of the room, I took my place with him by my side as the other couples found their spots for the dance. He leaned close. "What do you mean?"

Mr. Beaumont had escorted a pretty young girl in a white gown to the center of the dance floor. Lord Ainsley had a partner too. The quadrille began, and the pairs moved with practiced elegance, their steps synchronized to the enchanting melody. With the dancers swirling and looping, conversation proved futile.

I felt Rafe's attention as we came together, broke apart, and came together, looping over and over, fingers brushing with the dance, yet I couldn't bring myself to look in his eyes. Mr. Beaumont, when his shoulder grazed mine, smiled.

"Capital idea bringing us, Lord Hawthorn. You've convinced me that your country balls are delightful with such sumptuous fare to sample."

I felt ill at the barely veiled innuendo, my stomach roiling. As soon as the music ended, I murmured a thank-you before I searched for the exit. I would not leave Abigail, but I needed fresh air. Since she kept close company to a young gentleman, her conversation animated while he handed her a punch glass, I was free to escape into a quieter room.

I ducked out into the main hall. Footsteps echoed, uneven but quick, following me. I whirled around to see Rafe.

"Bridget, please—wait." He reached me as I halted in front of a console table pushed against the wall. Above, a portrait of the Hawkinses' family peered down at us with unblinking eyes. "I don't know what Mr. Barron said to you, but I do not trust that man."

"He hinted that you may have something to do with the theft of the mosaic."

"Surely you don't believe such lies." Rafe sounded vulnerable. "I know my family has a wretched history, but I am not like my father, nor my uncle."

"No, I do not believe him."

Rafe's shoulders heaved with a breath.

"Unfortunately, that does not explain the rumor that you've decided to sell Hawthorn Abbey to the Dilettanti. Is this true? And if the mosaics on Perry's farm lie within your property, Mr. Beaumont will have access to it all."

Frowning, he didn't answer, instead leaving me to guess as to the thoughts running through his mind. But silence was an answer.

"I see," I whispered, my throat clogging with emotion. How could I have thought to trust him? Tears filled my eyes, awful, burning traitorous tears that threatened to spill down my cheeks and stain my gown with watermarks. Angrily, I dashed them away, since emotions had no place in public.

"I may have no choice but to rent my land. I don't need to tell you I have stretched myself to the limit to rebuild the Hawthorn estate, especially after the hailstorm," he began. "I have no intention of hurting you, but I cannot abandon the tenants relying on me, and I fear I am out of options, considering my last visit with Mr. Talbot."

I felt torn, my heart aching for him, yet the desperation to preserve the mosaic gnawed at me. I understood his burden, but the thought of losing this opportunity felt unbearable. "No need to explain, Lord Hawthorn. I understand. Believe me. I understand your need for capital, but must it be with them?"

Truthfully, I didn't want him to sell or rent at all. He would likely leave, and I would never see him again.

A pained look crossed his face. "Lord Hawthorn? Are we back to that again? You will not call me Rafe?"

"I believe so." My voice broke. "I thought we were friends. Allies. Now I see that I've been discarded for a better plan."

His mouth parted at my challenge.

I nodded toward the ballroom where the music soared before inching away to make my escape. "I believe those friends are waiting for you now."

30

Rafe

Indecision is the thief of opportunity. It will steal you blind.
MARCUS TULLIUS CICERO

I thought we were friends. Allies.

Bridget's words stung as I escorted a tipsy Mr. Beaumont and Lord Ainsley back to the estate. They were drunk enough to make the vein in my temple throb, especially after pulling Beaumont from a young miss in the garden.

"Capital evening." Mr. Beaumont sighed with pleasure as he sank back on the worn leather seat. "We should do this again. And you, Rafe, you seemed quite entranced with Miss Littleton. What on earth were you thinking chasing her out of the ballroom? You caused quite a scene. I didn't think a stern man like you would show so much emotion."

"I agree. Do tell us if Miss Littleton is a freethinker in the ways that matter." Lord Ainsley slurred his words as he slumped against his friend with a grin.

"I would recommend you keep her name out of your mouth," I answered heatedly. Both men stared at me, Lord Ainsley finally snickering.

"You have no plans on the chit, do you? Marriage?" Lord Ainsley pulled his cravat loose with one long finger.

Marriage? A lord didn't marry a vicar's daughter. But I didn't care what they thought. Bridget believed the worst of me, especially after our dance.

I had no intention of replaying the conversation for either gentleman. Her challenges circled enough in my mind. Handling the horses kept me occupied until Hawthorn Abbey appeared within the moonlight, its slate roof gilded with silver. I halted the barouche in the courtyard, weary of my guests.

Anticipating my needs, Mr. Whittle ran out to secure the horses. Bless that man. Had he waited at the door or window, watching for my return?

"Did you have an enjoyable time, my lord?" Mr. Whittle whispered as he unhitched the horses.

"No," I said bluntly. Somehow, I felt myself pulled in the direction of the Perry farm, searching for the minuscule lights of the cottage, even if Bridget didn't live there. I saw only darkness on the horizon. How easily I pictured Bacchus with his drink raised high, trickling down his double chin while gladiators fought to the death, their blood spilling just as carelessly as the wine of the gods.

A valley of vice with gnarled roots digging deep into the black soil. How long had evil reigned within this pastoral setting? Was there anything good that could be redeemed in this land? Was I perhaps as weak as the men in my family? Too weak to refuse the Dilettanti and their connections?

"I have offended our host, Beaumont," Lord Ainsley said cheerfully as he draped an arm around Beaumont's shoulders and descended from the barouche. They tottered up the steps to the main entrance, pitching forward as if they might fall over.

Mr. Beaumont snorted. "Never mind. He simply needs to loosen up his cravat. Those poor military men never get past their rules and regulations."

I followed them into the hall, dreading what the next day might bring. If I didn't need the money, I'd have sent them packing after eight long days. Shame whispered in my ear.

Be not deceived: evil communications corrupt good manners. The Biblical reference was long forgotten, yet my mother's admonishment lingered.

Without a backward look at me, they stumbled into their dark rooms with peals of laughter. The doors slammed, and I heard a round of curses as someone bumped into furniture. Eager to escape, I headed to my chamber, nearly colliding with a slight form holding candles in the gloomy hallway. Lucy handed me one tallow candle before eyeing the wing where our guests had sequestered themselves for the night.

"My lord, I heard noises. Is anything required?"

I shook my head. "Our company has had quite a night of carousing. I'd recommend you stay put for the evening and bolt your door. Let your father do the serving if anyone rings for it."

She gasped, but I hoped for her sake she would listen to my advice. Thankfully, she turned and fled down the hall, her flickering candlelight descending as she ran down the servants' staircase. Had the men already pestered her during their stay? Would they insist on my hospitality beyond this week?

I pulled loose my tight cravat and entered my room with the feeble candle in hand, barely illuminating the thickening gloom. What a mess I'd made of things. Both with Bridget and now the Dilettanti. The more I tried to secure my holdings, the more they seemed to slip through my fingers. I set the candle on a table, the light flickering within the cavernous room. After throwing my dress coat onto the bed, I sank in the chair beside the fireplace, and opened Bridget's tin of balm, inhaling the crisp scent. She stood by her convictions.

If only I could regain her trust.

I had fought so hard, yet I couldn't seem to ensure my future no matter what I tried. The estate would demand more money than it could earn, possibly proving to be a fruitless path in the end. I needed guidance. As the thought crossed my mind, I spied my uncle's Bible, now on my desk. Had Lucy or Mrs. Whittle put it there?

I opened it, flipping idly until I landed on the book of James, one my mother often read.

If any of you lack wisdom, let him ask of God, that giveth to all men liberally, and upbraideth not. But let him ask in faith, nothing wavering. For he that wavereth is like a wave of the sea driven with the wind and tossed. For let not that man think that he shall receive any thing of the Lord.

A note slipped free from the pages and tumbled to the hardwood floor. I reached down and picked it up.

April 5, 1798

Dear Vicar Littleton,

I did as you recommended. I wrote to Anne again and asked permission to see her and her son. For years, my plea for forgiveness has received no response. Then a fortnight ago, I received word from her sister that Anne had passed away. Did she receive my letter? Or was I too late, yet again?

It is to my detriment that I allowed my younger brother to wreak so much harm at Hawthorn Abbey. If only our father had refused permission for that sham of a marriage after Randall found out his dalliance had resulted in a child. But why would our father, who kept mistresses on the side, even care? Anne was to bring money to the struggling family coffers. My brother did not expect that her father would cut her off completely for her indiscretion. Few women, however, could refuse Randall when he wanted to charm someone. But I might have warned her, and instead I remained silent. If only I had shielded her when it mattered the most. I might have been the one to marry her and treat her son as my own.

Too often, my thoughts drift to what could have been. I am racked with regret and sorrow that I cannot escape from. I loved her. Randall mocked me for it.

There is naught for me to do other than pay for Rafe's commission. As my heir, he will, of course, inherit the estate. When I learned of his desire to enter the military, I knew it was the least I could do. Perhaps, in the service, he might find the discipline and purpose I never could. How do I forgive myself, then? How does a man break free of the deep-rooted curses that bind him?

I tucked the letter back into the Bible, my mind swirling. My mother had kept these letters from me—perhaps burned them. But was her silence meant to protect me, or to bury the truth? The more I uncovered, the more trapped I felt. I sighed, realizing I might be one step away from a grievous error in aligning with the Dilettanti. But what else could I do?

Mr. Beaumont and Lord Ainsley ate breakfast in the solar, making quick work of their eggs and sausage. I ordered extra coffee, relieved when Mrs. Whittle came to serve us instead of her daughter. While

I sipped the coffee, she delivered a note and glared at our guests before departing. I tore into it, ignoring the curious gazes of the men sitting opposite of me. The magistrate had written at long last.

Lord Hawthorn,

Forgive my tardy response. You mentioned sending several letters to my secretary. I have spoken with him and discovered we have not received a single missive until now. The records indicate the boundaries between your estate and Mr. Perry's farm are clear and have been correctly surveyed. Unfortunately, your steward, although dedicated, has labored under a false assumption for years. The map enclosed details the precise line, confirming that Mr. Perry's land extends farther than initially believed. While you may commence work on your road and orchards, you cannot legally alter or touch any part of Mr. Perry's property. Please review the map carefully.

Not received a single missive? Had the letters been intercepted? By whom? My skin prickled as I skimmed the rest of the note, including the small map which showed the property lines. A breath escaped me. Bridget would have her dig after all.

"Something of interest?" Mr. Beaumont rubbed his temples. He appeared in a fine temper this morning.

"None whatsoever," I responded evenly. "Merely business."

"Ah, the gentleman of trade. I suppose you have no other options, do you?" Lord Ainsley scoffed. I refused to feel offended by the insult. Why should a man be embarrassed by hard work?

"I find it rather invigorating. There is something about working in the soil with one's hands that is surprisingly life-giving. You might try it sometime, gentlemen."

"You think so? Then I should like to see Perry's field today." Mr. Beaumont threw his napkin onto the table.

"Agreed," Lord Ainsley said as he dabbed at his mouth, where a trace of yellow yolk clung to his chin. "I want to know how large this villa truly is. Imagine the presentation we'll make at the next meeting."

Their enthusiasm and certainty brought a prickle to my skin. Who exactly had stolen the Bacchus mosaic and hindered my letters to the magistrate? The men before me certainly knew the worth. The theft had occurred before their arrival, but were they above hiring someone to act as a scout? Hadn't they toured the continent hunting for lost relics? And for what purpose?

It was one thing to have one's research published and reviewed for the sake of educating the masses. It was a completely different thing to steal valuable pieces from other countries and flaunt such items as hunting trophies. One was an antiquarian, the other truly a grave robber.

My guests refused to be sequestered in the abbey. After breakfast, I rode alongside them toward Perry's farm, the weight of their company heavier with each passing hour. As we approached the fields, my eyes sought out the guards I'd stationed days ago. There they were, Mr. Hinsley and Mr. Dixon, posted at the edge of the excavation site.

At least this part of my promise to Bridget was fulfilled. No thief would dare approach under their watchful gaze.

One of the guards tipped his hat, and I returned a nod, the smallest reassurance settling in my chest.

The field appeared a hive of activity as Mr. Harrington barked orders like a general on the battlefield. Off to one side, Mr. Barron stood near the edge of the site, chatting amiably with one of the workers while gesturing toward the uncovered mosaic as if he were the one in charge.

I paused when I spied Bridget kneeling by a mosaic. With her bonnet lowered, she didn't see me, likely too absorbed with brushing the tiles free of debris. Then she raised her head, her eyes widening at the sight of my guests and at last lingering on me for the briefest moment. Just as quickly, she ducked her head and continued her work. Coming here might prove a mistake, but I hoped I could keep the men in hand.

Mr. Harrington raised an eyebrow. "Gentlemen, to what do we owe the pleasure?" He glanced over his shoulder. "We have had a steady of stream of guests today, including a Mr. Barron."

Jim Barron doffed his beaver hat as soon as he spied my company. With hurried steps, almost stumbling in the soft dirt, he made his way to the Dilettanti.

"We've come to inspect your progress," Mr. Beaumont declared loudly.

"Capital idea," Mr. Barron said to my guests. "A fine day for antiquities. Surely you've had the opportunity to wander Lord Hawthorn's orchards and the abbey by now. He and I have had the most delightful chats about the cider business. Not for this year, of course."

The insinuation that Mr. Barron and I had a relationship couldn't be further from the truth.

Lord Ainsley and Mr. Beaumont ignored the innkeeper and brushed past him to Mr. Harrington. They engaged the man in conversation while Mr. Barron fidgeted, his expression piqued.

"Deuced manners your guests have. I was hoping for an introduction."

"Another day," I told him.

Anger flickered within his gaze before the smile returned. "I look forward to your invitation."

My guests also ignored Bridget entirely. Eager to escape Mr. Barron's cloying presence, I headed to her, halting in front of the mosaic. She continued brushing the geometrical border stretching well beyond a trio of cupids, her head now averted. Nor did she acknowledge me when I stood in front of her.

I longed to see her expression, to offer some hope or encouragement.

When she at last raised her head, her features cooled. "Lord Hawthorn, have you brought your friends to inspect their future purchase?"

"That is not my intention. I had merely hoped to satisfy their curiosity. But I understand they have made Mr. Perry an offer for his field."

She sighed and placed her brush on her satchel. Ignoring my proffered hand, she rose. "I am on limited time, it would appear. I see Mr. Beaumont is becoming fast friends with Mr. Harrington. Next he will charm Mr. Perry."

I squinted, the sunlight far too bright. "Hardly. Mr. Perry can sense a viper near his boots."

Mr. Beaumont nodded sagely as Mr. Harrington pointed to the recently uncovered pool. The memory of Bridget standing in it and me reaching for her, ever so curt, brought a flush of regret. What a boor I had been.

She tilted her head, studying me.

"And I don't think you need to worry about Mr. Perry selling. He has refused all offers, including my steward's. In fact, I bring news that I think will please you," I hurried to add as I removed the letter and map from the magistrate and handed it to her. She took it after a brief hesitation. As she read I had an opportunity to observe her freely, and I watched an array of emotions play across her face. Her nose was slightly reddened from being in the sun, despite her hat. The smattering of freckles newly formed on her cheeks was adorable, to my way of thinking.

She folded the letter and said not a word, but her mouth trembled.

"Bri—Miss Littleton. I am truly sorry for any offense I have given you. I realize you believe me to be partnering with Mr. Beaumont. If you would allow me to explain further—"

"I am in no need of your explanations," she responded, her voice shaky.

"Please, I don't want to be enemies. When I wrote to my barrister regarding the sale of items within the abbey, I didn't know Mr. Beaumont. Nor was I aware that he held sway with the Dilettanti. He was simply a buyer, interested in the abbey's collection of art. If there is anything I can do to assist you . . ."

To prove to you . . .

"I haven't forgotten my promise to send men to guard the site," I added, trying to convey how seriously I took her work. "Mr. Hinsley and Mr. Dixon come every night, and I'll make sure they stay until you're finished. I want to see this through."

Her eyes flicked up to meet mine, and for a moment, something softened in her gaze.

"Thank you," she whispered, almost too quietly to hear.

Before I could say more, Mr. Perry approached us warily. "Lord Hawthorn."

Bridget thrust out the letter and the map. The lines about his eyes and mouth relaxed as he studied both documents.

"Thank God. You will not take my land then?"

"No," I answered. "My steward erred, and for that, I apologize. I sent several letters to the magistrate in previous weeks, but it appears he only received my most recent missive."

"Father visited Chichester, hoping to clear up the boundary dispute, but the magistrate was still away in Bath. Despite his best efforts, no clear resolution had come yet. Now the magistrate said he never received your letters. I assumed you had not sent them," Bridget said.

"I assure you I sent several," I replied. "I can't help but assume someone tampered with the mail, but I don't know whom or why."

Squinting against the bright sunlight, Mr. Perry slid the precious documents into the safe confines of his jacket pocket.

"Interesting timing to receive this document now. I've had two offers for this farm—one from you a while back, Lord Hawthorn, and now another from that fancy Mr. Beaumont over there."

I crossed my arms. "I assure you I wanted the magistrate to clear the border situation immediately."

Bridget visibly shivered. "It would appear that someone wants to meddle with you and Mr. Perry."

I smiled tightly. "One way or another, the truth will get out."

Bridget frowned. "And you, my lord, are you still interested in purchasing Mr. Perry's farm?"

I was keenly aware of her attention. "No. I, too, have received an offer of rent from Beaumont, although not for the entire estate, only the area surrounding the orchard."

Mr. Perry stroked his chin. "Farming is a brutal business, and as tricky as gambling. You pay your expenses up front and never know if you'll see a return for your sweat and blood, but it's the only life I've known. Without Miss Littleton's plan, I would have been forced to sell. Owning one's land brings a sense of freedom to a man. No one can tell him what to do or where to go. Do not be so quick to release your land, sir."

"I will do everything in my power to keep it. Miss Littleton has given you quite a gift. Perhaps you should open a tourist center," I told him.

"Aye, a fine plan and one that Mr. Harrington also suggested privately to me. He thinks I can do it in under a year. If nothing else gets taken in the meantime." Mr. Perry's expression darkened.

"Lord Hawthorn, why don't you consider a tourist center? Chances are that an enterprising gent such as yourself might open a similar attraction. A man needs all the income he can get. Bring in the shillings this way until you can offer cider when those orchards regrow."

"I agree," Bridget said with a husky voice, but it was enough to send a frisson of lightning rippling through my veins. "Why not combine what you can, gentlemen? With the mosaics stretching across both Perry's field and your orchard, it's likely the sites are connected. If someone works against us, are we not stronger united?"

The mention of a shared villa between the two locations sparked my imagination. I could almost picture Bridget wandering through the grounds with her art brushes and satchel—every bit as much a part of the estate as its ancient walls. Yes, she was the vicar's daughter, beneath my station in the eyes of some.

I had followed the rules all my life. Why couldn't I break them in this one instance?

Just as quickly, a swift rebuttal flared to life. I would act the fool and jeopardize the fragile bond between us. But I couldn't deny I wanted her respect.

The sound of arguing reached us from the far edge of the excavation site, near the boundary of Perry's field, next to the Medusa pool. Mr. Beaumont's voice cut through the air. I exchanged a glance with Bridget, her lips tightening in silent frustration. Without a word, I strode across the dirt toward the men, dust rising from my boots.

As I neared, Mr. Barron and Abigail hurried toward the group, their faces painted with surprise and curiosity, clearly drawn by the raised voices. Mr. Barron slowed, hanging back just enough to observe but not interfere, his eyes darting between Beaumont, Harrington, and me.

"You cannot be serious, Harrington." Mr. Beaumont's voice carried loudly.

Mr. Harrington folded his arms across his chest, his double chin sinking into his snowy cravat as if he were a schoolboy enduring a dressing down.

"I can present the findings, of course." Mr. Harrington chewed his lip.

Ire bubbled up. I sensed Beaumont was playing a game, partly fueled with a vindictive desire to hurt Bridget and Mr. Perry.

Beaumont, spotting my arrival, chuckled drily. "Mr. Harrington actually thinks he can give credit to a vicar's daughter for the discovery of the mosaics. She cannot speak at the society meeting." He placed a hand on Harrington's shoulder, his tone patronizing. "You'll be the laughingstock of the antiquarians. Imagine what London society will say when a bluestocking stands in front of the podium and lectures your colleagues. Do you really want to damage your reputation in such a manner?"

"I-I do not think a woman, a lady, needs to stand at the podium. She could write the articles, and I might sign off on each paper," Harrington stammered, barely able to meet my gaze.

"It's a matter of credibility," Beaumont nodded sagely.

I stepped forward, pointing toward the Medusa mosaic. "Mr. Harrington," I said, my voice low but firm, "A gentleman does not betray the lady who gave him full access to one of England's greatest finds. Do not be her Perseus."

The mortal woman was considered a monster, which struck me with irony. The Greek men feared and reviled Medusa, including the conqueror Perseus, who used her abilities to fulfill his ambitions. How dare these men speak of Bridget in such condescending tones, each intending to use her for his own gain.

Mr. Harrington flushed bright red.

"You won't let me speak to the society?" Bridget joined us, sounding incredulous as she brushed her hands free of dirt. Behind her, Barron and Abigail stood a few steps back, their expressions wary.

"Mr. Harrington, I am shocked. I wrote to you in good faith, hoping to write a paper and present my findings before the society. I even offered my research notes and illustrations for your use. Am I not eligible for the invitation your journal offered? You made assurances that I might earn a position with your society. How could you brush me away so easily?"

Mr. Harrington coughed behind a fist. "Really, Miss Littleton..."

Mr. Beaumont offered a conciliatory smile, but it felt as false as could be.

"Now, be reasonable, Miss Littleton." His tone sweetened to a patronizing level. "Surely a lady of good breeding realizes she cannot wander into any man's club at will and decide she is one of the men. Of course Mr. Harrington must take over the excavation. You did your best, but it's clear that the entire dig has been compromised. Someone dug holes all throughout the field, which is absurd. The mosaics appear damaged from a shovel or trowel, and a section went missing. You cannot protect this site, nor can you uncover it without causing further damage. Neither you nor Mr. Perry are qualified to continue."

Her gloved hands clenched at her sides. "I fear this is a plot to take over my research, Mr. Beaumont. You've dismissed me twice. Now you realize you have lost something of value, but you are too late to claim it. If you can dismiss me and Mr. Perry so easily, who is to say you won't do the same to Mr. Harrington?"

"Miss Littleton will have my protection," I spoke. "I will assist with the dig if need be, in any way I can. But, gentlemen, it would be a shame not to let Miss Littleton present her research as she has fought so hard to preserve the Roman villa. None of you would be here if it weren't for her."

The false smile faded quickly. Mr. Beaumont regarded me a moment longer than I cared for.

"Highly irregular, but I daresay it would be entertaining to see her at a meeting," Lord Ainsley said with a laugh.

I wanted nothing more than to deck that smug look off his face.

Instead, I turned to Mr. Perry and Mr. Harrington. "If you want laborers and a guard or anything else from me, you will let her name be on the documents."

The men grew silent. No one else spoke in Bridget's defense, not even her friends, Miss Perry or Mr. Perry.

But I heard Bridget's soft intake of breath beside me.

At last, Mr. Harrington mumbled an agreement.

"Thank you, Mr. Harrington. I assure you that any presentation given will meet the society's standards." Bridget lifted her chin. How proud I was of her in that moment. She would do well, no matter where she stood, whether in a field or in a salon. Her sheer tenacity alone could not be discounted.

Mr. Beaumont pulled out his snuff box, his features strained, while Lord Ainsley leaned over, muttering something into his friend's ear. Try as I might, I couldn't hear a word of what they said.

I felt a soft hand on my arm, and I caught the scent of lilacs, distracting me from all else.

I glanced down at her.

"Thank you," Bridget said. Then she added with a whisper, "Rafe."

31

Bridget

> Like the measles, love is most dangerous when it comes late in life.
> **LORD BYRON**

The next morning, Molly brought Lord Hawthorn's invitation for horseback riding. There was no mention of his other guests. Father eagerly accepted before my nerves betrayed me.

"I don't ride horseback," I had protested.

He simply smiled. "It's the perfect chance for you to face your fear of horses, and you'll get a much-needed break from the fields. At least let Mr. Harrington inspect the gladiator mosaics and tour the abbey, since you believe it was built with stones from the villa."

Would we encounter the Dilettanti? I hoped not. All my fervent wishes to have their acknowledgment had fled in light of their behavior.

I selected a dark green riding garment, slightly snug but suitable. I also found an extra tin of salve to present as a token of gratitude.

Rafe's defense of me the previous day led to Mr. Harrington's apology, and he silenced Beaumont and his companion, who left sullen and dust covered. Even Mr. Perry chuckled quietly at their retreat. I appreciated Mr. Perry's determination to retain his land more than ever.

After descending the stairs, I found Father and Mr. Harrington deep in conversation. Mr. Harrington beckoned me excitedly to the writing desk in the drawing room.

"Miss Littleton, I believe this will encourage you. Your father and I discovered a motto inserted into the ring band. *Amor vincit omnia. Love conquers all.* Eh gad, but I believe this ring must have seen quite a fight and been pulled off in a moment of life or death. No man would abandon so readily a jewel such as this. It is fit for a senator!"

"Remarkable," I agreed slowly, taking the ring in hand to examine the faint etchings. The men stared at me, as if trying to pierce through my carefully constructed expression.

But why had the ring been discarded for centuries? The inscription felt like a cruel jest. Did love truly conquer all? Once, I had believed my love for my brother would be enough to save him. Instead, it had only deepened the wound within my heart. Swallowing my emotions, I swiftly returned the ring to Mr. Harrington, who eagerly reclaimed it, his eyes gleaming with fascination.

Father straightened. "Letters can wait. We have a visit with Lord Hawthorn this morning to review his mosaic."

"Splendid idea," Mr. Harrington cried as he removed his glasses. "We are all invited?"

"Just the four of us," Father said. He cast a calculating look in my direction. "Bridget, you look especially well this morning."

If I didn't know better, I might have thought Father had an unusual sparkle in his eyes.

Rafe welcomed us in the entrance hall, fielding Mr. Harrington's questions about the twelfth-century abbey.

Mr. Harrington begged for a tour. As we walked through the main rooms, the secretary marveled at the architecture. "Hawthorn Abbey is a rare jewel and worth fighting for. I wish you success with your orchards."

Rafe glanced at me, his expression unreadable. I wondered what he might be thinking. When we stopped in the library, I had a moment alone with him as my father pointed out favorite tomes tucked away in the massive shelves.

"I brought you something," I said as I opened my reticule and pulled out the vial of salve.

He took it, bemused. "I am grateful. Despite the smell, your tincture worked wonders."

"Don't tease," I said with a grin as I ran a finger across one of the leather-bound books. "There are far worse remedies to fall prey to."

"There are. My housekeeper's daughter suggested devil's dung."

Laughter bubbled up, drawing my father's attention. He grinned when he caught my glance and directed Mr. Harrington to another bookshelf farther away from Rafe and me.

"No man wants to smell of rotten eggs. However, I am grateful for your defense yesterday. This is but a small token of my thanks."

"Think nothing of it," he said with a hint of a smile.

"But I do value it," I protested, now serious. "I was terrified my work might be all for naught. As hard as we women try to better ourselves and become more than a woman sitting at a hearth stitching samplers, Mr. Beaumont is correct. There are some areas, some societies and professions, that remain forbidden to us no matter how hard we strain for them. To have your support meant . . ." I inhaled, afraid to lay my soul bare. "It meant a great deal."

The little muscle jumped within his jaw. How grim I had originally thought him, but I no longer viewed him in the same light. Would he consider Mr. Perry's offer of a partnership? Could I persuade Rafe not to rent his land? Of course, the gladiator mosaic belonged to him, but if he rented the abbey as well, I would lose access to it.

Liar! my mind cried. *You fear you would likely not see him again if he left the valley.*

"You are not alone." His voice dropped to a gravelly note. "And while my experiences cannot compare with yours, it is a painful thing to long for so much more and find yourself excluded, while others feast at a table you cannot join."

"You lived here as a child, but the memories seem to pain you," I said, hoping he would share more of his past.

He nodded. We drifted toward a more private section of the library, an alcove with a window whose velvet curtains were drawn back to let in the brilliant afternoon light.

"The abbey held few happy recollections for me," he said. "Until now."

Under the warmth of his regard, I felt a flutter of pleasure. Had he found joy in the valley at long last, even despite the devastating hail? Could he find renewed purpose watching over his tenants?

Rafe palmed the back of his neck. "My mother left a terrible marriage and took me with her. I didn't understand it then, but she hid us from my father. My mother's family had never approved of the marriage and so we lived a quiet life, tucked away in a relative's cottage. I grew up thinking the worst of my uncle and father. My father never changed, but my uncle? Your father seems to think he did, and I've found your father to be of sound judgment."

I looked over my shoulder to see Father with Mr. Harrington, a bittersweet pride swelling within my chest. Gratefulness that the man I had idolized as a child had such a profound impact on the old viscount and the new. And sorrow that I had missed so much of his attention myself.

"He will find your regard encouraging."

"*You* have encouraged me," Rafe said after a pause. "The Miss Littleton I've encountered lets nothing stop her no matter the obstacles."

A smile broke free of me as a shiver of excitement returned, recalling my previous discussion with Mr. Harrington. I wanted to share with Rafe the tremendous discoveries.

"If you must know, we have encountered something monumental. A gold ring with a ruby." I shared the motto with him, along with the Christian symbol on the doll.

"Truly?" His eyes widened with awe. "A Christian symbol within this valley? Within a pagan home, no less?"

I nodded. "I was as surprised as you. Historians often claim Rome was one of the darkest empires despite its advancements."

"And yet, you found a spark of light in that darkness."

"It may be your land, Lord Hawthorn, but these discoveries belong to you and Mr. Perry and me. Without your men stumbling across the gladiators, I might never have encountered the grave and the doll. But this—all of this is something we're both part of now."

I had no desire to pressure him any longer, especially when he had done so much in his defense of me. But I longed to support him in some manner. Would he consider the idea of joining with Mr. Perry and me?

"Rafe," he corrected with his lips curved slightly. "And it would have been nothing but Greek to us if not for you."

"*Julius Caesar*, act one, scene two. For your information, the Romans were bilingual, speaking both Latin and Greek. It was the monks of the Middle Ages who labeled anything they couldn't understand as Greek. It amazes me that for all these centuries a message lay buried in the dirt." Not the one I was seeking, but perhaps the one I needed most.

"Shakespeare was a clever man." His smile faded and his brow furrowed deeply. "You found jewelry, after all."

I nodded. "It's not the gold ring that excites me, though. It's the story waiting to be uncovered. Mr. Harrington believes the ring fell to the ground during a tussle. Imagine if someone really pulled the ring off a man's finger?"

"You are indeed a romantic, for all your pursuit of reason and science," he murmured as he leaned against the window frame while folding his arms across his chest. "Yes, I think you would find a tale tucked away in those tiled floors."

But the warmth pooling within me dissipated when he frowned again. "Bridget, you must take care. Especially now that someone has stolen the mosaic. I don't want to see you or your father hurt, nor Mr. Perry or his daughter. I have a safe in my office. If you require it, all you need to do is ask."

"I will ask Mr. Perry if I can bring the ring tomorrow," I promised.

My father pulled out yet another tome and showed it to Mr. Harrington. Both exclaimed over it, but my attention wandered when Rafe's shoulder brushed against mine. Warmth rushed to my cheeks, fingers, and toes.

Rafe fingered my tin in his large hands. "I was surprised you wished to ride today, considering your impression of Chaucer that first night you met him."

"I'm not riding him, am I?" Alarm shot through me at the idea of mounting that enormous beast.

He set my gift on a table beside a stack of papers and an inkpot. "No, something far tamer. And smaller. Annabelle won't provide a thrilling chase. If anything, she'll be content to munch on the grass and barely break into a trot. Have you ridden before?"

"I have, but I prefer not to. My brother loved to race horses in the countryside. He simply couldn't enjoy life without pushing himself to the limit. On the last occasion we rode together, my horse bolted, and I was thrown off. I suffered a broken ankle and was so terrified of the experience, I chose never to repeat it. Daniel and Abigail had gone ahead since a storm was approaching, and I was stranded for hours."

As soon as the explanation left me, I realized how awful it sounded, and how it painted my brother in dismal hues. But it was the truth. Especially after encountering Rafe and Mrs. Eacher's care, I now viewed my other relationships beneath a clearer lens. Daniel hadn't cared what others thought of him, and I suspected, as truth dawned, he had not truly cared for me either. He was manipulative, charming, and ultimately irresponsible. He had completely let my father and me down, as much as I loved him. Not an easy admission, by any means.

"I am sorry," Rafe said quietly.

So was I. So many regrets had followed Daniel's departure and disappearance. I had accused Father of being too strict and demanding. But had I misread what my brother truly needed?

I studied the row of gilt tomes on the nearest shelf. "And now my brother languishes in a hulk, and there's nothing we can do as you noted."

"You might pray for your brother."

"Now you sound like Father." I smiled to cover my discomfort at the advice.

"Your father gives that advice often. My uncle's journals reflect it. My tenants speak of a different man than I remember. Can a man break free of his past? Can he be no longer bound by the chains of his family?"

Rafe had asked me before if a man could change. I had struggled to answer him then. But what if I was wrong?

"I have long wondered the same about Daniel," I answered.

"Truthfully, I am weary of ever hoping for him to grow up. I suppose we are the sum of the choices of those before us. But we can choose differently, yes?"

"With God's help," Rafe challenged gently.

But could a man change himself without divine intervention? As my father had pointed out to me once, Seneca's stoicism made nary a dent in Nero's depraved behavior. A man could have all the wisdom in the world and still be deceived. Even Solomon, with all his wisdom, had gone astray. It was a painful thought, slicing far too close to the bone and marrow, piercing through my esteem for the theories of enlightenment and man's achievements. If Solomon, the wisest man who ever lived, could go astray, why not me?

And I had not stayed close to God to keep within that circle of safety. I had chosen the path of science and reason, but I was no longer certain it served me.

"Lord Hawthorn, your collection of maps is astounding," Mr. Harrington called out from the other end of the library. Father shushed him, much to my surprise. But the moment between Rafe and me was lost.

With his lips curved, Rafe pushed away from the window to answer Mr. Harrington's questions, leaving me behind in a pool of sunshine. I let him go, my heart and mind replaying our conversation.

I could not deny my growing fascination with the new viscount of Hawthorn Abbey.

Annabelle was not impressed with me, nor did she impress me. Mr. Whittle held the reins while I debated how to mount.

"Oh dear, it's been so long since I've ridden a horse," I murmured as I eyed the mounting stool. Rafe offered a hand, assisting me as I eased onto the sidesaddle. I took the reins, my gloved hands hiding my damp palms.

"You are truly fine?" he asked.

I would be. Annabelle was exactly as Rafe had described: old, tame, and completely indifferent to a new rider. I exhaled and gripped the reins with my gloved hands.

Father and Mr. Harrington had similar mounts. Nothing too exciting. Nothing, of course, like Chaucer. Astride that behemoth, Rafe motioned for us to follow. Father and Mr. Harrington gleefully trotted into the orchards while Rafe waited for me. He towered over the short cob I rode, moving as one with Chaucer while I awkwardly perched on my mount, who at the moment refused to budge.

I laughed nervously, hoping she would take a step with the simple pressure of my foot. At last, she inched forward, ambling at a pace that would take all day.

Rafe regarded me with a lopsided smile. "Perfectly safe, I assure you."

"I'll never leave the courtyard at this pace."

He held Chaucer back even though the thoroughbred pawed at the ground in a bid to stretch his magnificent limbs.

"It would be far better for you to feel comfortable. She'll feel your fear if you are not careful. Of course, you can give her a little kick if needed, but there is no rush."

Except that I had already lost my chaperones, leaving Rafe and me alone. We passed the stables and took the bend around the orchard. With a few surviving flowers blooming in the older section of the orchard, the faint scent of apple blossoms was conspicuously absent. I closed my eyes and inhaled deeply, imagining the fragrance from seasons past. Beyond the older orchard were the battered rows of saplings, each one struggling to survive. How hopeful to think that in four years they would be draped in veils of white.

"When the orchards return to full health, you really ought to serve cider while Mr. Perry opens a tourist stop on his property. Imagine the visitors who would trek through for history and a cup of cider," I told him. I had not pried into his affairs regarding the Crown, but I did worry for him. I wanted him here.

"A charming idea," he said as he easily kept pace with me, but he made no promises.

"If you do rent the abbey grounds to the Dilettanti, will you leave Bramnor?" I asked before I could stop myself.

His gaze shot to mine. "I don't want to leave Bramnor. Not anymore at least."

A husky laugh escaped me. "Good. I should think the village would be very dull without its lord at the helm. I'm glad you found a reason to stay." I gestured to the rows of trees.

"Yes, I could not imagine abandoning the treasure I have found in Bramnor," he said thickly.

A taut silence ensued as we drifted beside the gladiator mosaic, which, to my delight, appeared staked and roped to mark its location. But I was distracted from it as I tried to excavate the meaning of Rafe's words. If I were a younger miss, I might cling to a helpless desire that he meant I was the treasure. Foolish, of course.

"Where are your guests?" I demanded suddenly as I pivoted in my saddle while shielding my eyes with one hand from the bright sun.

"*You* are my guest." He also shifted in his saddle, the line of his mouth hardening. "But the Dilettanti are touring the countryside, or so they said. I believe they wanted to call on Mr. Hawkins. If I remember correctly, Mr. Hawkins has a lovely daughter."

Disdain dripped from his voice, but he did not elaborate.

"Do you doubt their intentions?" I asked, my curiosity increasing. The more I encountered Mr. Beaumont, the more troubled I felt.

"I doubt any man's intentions with a woman beneath his station," he replied.

Heat crept up my cheeks at such a blatant dismissal, banishing any hopes of securing his affection. "We are not all blessed to be born into peerage."

"No," he protested. "I did not—"

A gunshot reverberated far from the trees, scattering birds in the trees to take flight. The sound cracked again. Louder, echoing across the valley.

In a single moment, I found my circumstances utterly changed.

Annabelle bolted forward as if a demon had poked her side with a white-hot pincer. The cob who had refused to do more than amble along the dirt road lunged forward, jerking the reins from my numb fingers. She galloped hard, forcing me to grasp the pommel. I managed to snatch one of the reins at last.

"Stop!" I cried. Panic blinded me as we rushed past the rows of apple trees in a blur of brown. Father and Mr. Harrington were no longer in sight, perhaps scouring the orchard or having turned back.

Any cry for help froze in my lungs as the horse ran like a frantic hare evading capture.

Someone shouted my name.

The wind rushed against my face as I pulled on the single rein, which only turned her. A foolish action, sending me careering into the trees. She did not stop, widely swerving again as I hung on for dear life.

Oh, God . . . If this was a prayer, it was all I could utter.

How I hated horses.

I could do nothing but bounce on her back, my legs desperately clinging to her. She veered left and suddenly I felt myself sliding on the sidesaddle. And then I spied the low rock wall separating

Hawthorn Abbey's holdings from another farmer, the barrier a long line between fields of grass.

"Stop!" I cried again. I shut my eyes tightly, bracing myself for the pain that would soon follow. I would be dashed to pieces on the ground if she tried to jump that obstacle.

A firm arm grabbed me and yanked, pulling me up like a rag doll, only to plunk me onto another saddle. I found myself squeezed against a firm chest, pinned against him. I opened one eye to see Rafe's blanched features.

He whirled Chaucer around, as nimble as could be, and drew the horse to a halt while I sat in his arms, quivering, with my ears ringing and my breathing shallow.

"Bridget, speak to me," he urged, his breath warm against my forehead. His chest beat with an unsteady rhythm, matching my own as we clung to each other.

I licked my dry lips. "I fear your version of a tame ride differs from mine."

He flinched despite my feeble attempt at humor. "I did promise, and I do not break promises. I don't know what happened."

I fought to control my racing pulse. "I heard a gunshot. It must have frightened her." Then, much to my embarrassment, my teeth chattered loudly.

Instead of loosening his grip on me, he tightened it. "Bridget, I am truly sorry, especially after what you told me regarding your experience with your brother. I would never willingly endanger you. If only I could prove to you my regard."

When I didn't answer, he lifted my chin with his finger, his gaze pleading as it met mine. The wind tore at his hair and his eyes darkened.

Before I could rethink my actions, I reached with one gloved hand and touched his cheek. His mouth parted. I could not imagine feeling safer than I did at that moment. He looked so concerned, I could not restrain myself.

I leaned into him and brushed my lips against his to reassure him I would be fine. Just a quick kiss. A shudder rippled through him.

"Bridget." He murmured my name against my mouth, as if to ask permission, and then he kissed me. His hand at the back of my head, his lips pressed a searing heat against mine. I was lost in the moment, inhaling his scent of leather and sandalwood. Could there be a more heavenly combination?

When he pulled back, we were both breathing hard. A low groan escaped him.

"Forgive me," he rasped.

My mouth dried as I struggled for composure. My lips were swollen. I could no longer deny my attraction to him. I pulled back, and he released his hold on me. If anyone spied us alone together, embracing no less, I would be utterly ruined.

Annabelle was nowhere to be seen. Father and Mr. Harrington were gone as well. What must Rafe think of my behavior? A hoyden, no doubt.

"I should not have . . ." I caught my bottom lip between my teeth, unwittingly drawing his attention again to my mouth. I blew out an exasperated breath. "It is completely my fault. I suppose you might blame it on my romantic fancies. A runaway horse and a near-death experience. Regardless, I am of the firm opinion that a woman ought to be kissed once in her life. And kissed well. As a vicar's daughter, I can assure you that does not happen. So, you see, the fault is entirely mine."

As much as I tried to sound unfazed, I could not keep the tiniest quaver out of my voice.

"It is not your fault. Truthfully, I have thought of nothing less than . . ." He stopped himself, his voice hoarse. Then he shook his head as if to clear his thoughts.

"Bridget, I do not take this action lightly. I have no desire to endanger your reputation."

I placed a hand on his chest. "No, Rafe. It was nothing more than impetuousness. Banish any thoughts of blame. You've done quite enough rescuing today as things stand. Let us pretend it never happened."

"How can I? At least allow me to do the honorable action," he replied tightly.

I felt the muscles in his arm strain. Dread pooled in my stomach. His heated gaze pinned me. I felt as helpless as Medusa's prey, now turned to stone and completely unable to move or think.

"Allow me to marry you," he persisted.

Numb with shock, I could only stare at him. He leaned closer, the scent of sandalwood and leather enveloping me.

"Bridget, I won't see you compromised."

My mouth dried at those hateful words. I was a burden. An obligation. I would never enter matrimony under such circumstances. I wanted what my father had with my mother. Love. Love stretching far beyond mere duty. Trust a military man to revert to obligations.

"We will speak no more of this incident," I repeated firmly, though my breath hitched, and my fingers twisted the fabric of my gown as if I could anchor myself. A wave of heat rushed to my face, betraying the calm I struggled to maintain. Was I a fool to say no? It was also a sacred commitment, binding two souls for better or worse for a lifetime.

An unreadable expression crossed Rafe's chiseled face the longer I hesitated. With his brow furrowed into lines, I struggled to decipher what he was thinking. If anything, I had endeavored to put more space between us. Riding sidesaddle would prove impossible, but so was being nestled on his lap. I could hardly swing my leg over to ride astride. As if sensing my dilemma, he secured his grip.

"No need to hold me quite so firmly. Unless you think Chaucer will bolt." When I looked at him, I caught sight of that troublesome muscle jumping within his jaw.

The return to the abbey felt abysmally long, even if Rafe held the reins lightly, his arms brushing against mine, but never confining.

As I replayed the day's events, shame washed over me. He had revealed his soul, and I had done the same. I had no desire to entrap him, even though I had initiated the kiss. A pox on that spontaneous nature of mine—it would prove to be the death of me.

When we halted at the abbey, Mr. Whittle waited in the courtyard.

"My lord, we were about to search for you and Miss Littleton. Mr. Spencer caught Annabelle's reins and brought her to the stall."

"A gunshot startled the horse and she ran away with Miss Littleton. I was fortunate enough to pull her from Annabelle before she came to harm," Rafe replied. He sounded tired. Frustrated even.

Eyebrows raised practically to his forehead, Mr. Whittle silently snatched the stool and placed it next to Chaucer. Reaching for a hand, he helped me dismount, but my legs wobbled all the same. I groaned inside at the picture of impropriety we must have presented, me riding on his lap for the staff to witness.

"There you go, miss. What a horrible fright for a lady."

A lady. I had been anything but during my ride. Cheeks flaming, I kept my gaze fixed forward, refusing to glance at Rafe to see his reaction. When I finally peeked at him, he had dismounted his horse. He kept his attention solely on Mr. Whittle. "Did you see any strangers out in the fields?"

Mr. Whittle shook his head, his features drawn as he reached for Chaucer's reins. "No, my lord. I did not. But I'm uncertain that was all the trouble. Somehow, someone had loosened the saddle girth on the mare."

32

Rafe

> Life may change, but it may fly not;
> Hope may vanish, but can die not;
> Truth be veiled, but still it burneth;
> Love repulsed—but it returneth!
> **PERCY BYSSHE SHELLEY**

Mr. Whittle apologized, mopping his brow with a worn handkerchief. "My lord, if I might have a word privately with you. Please. It cannot wait."

Dread filled me at the muttered request. Dread and irritation and, blast it, that kiss with Bridget's soft lips beneath mine would not let me go, nor would the feel of her pressed against me. I felt like I had been given a treasure, only to have it ripped away. I wanted to tell Mr. Whittle to go away so I could take her back into my arms.

But no matter what I tried to say, I only made it worse for her. And I was a fool, on the brink of losing my inheritance. Why would she want such a man?

"Mrs. Whittle will provide tea," I told Bridget. I sounded gruff, even to my ears. "If you'll excuse me for a moment."

I hated to leave her with unfinished business between us.

She halted, then changed her mind and marched toward the abbey's entrance while I followed Mr. Whittle to the stable.

He pointed to Annabelle, now secure in a stall and calmly munching hay.

"I have never had her bolt," Mr. Whittle said. "I couldn't believe it when she galloped into the courtyard with the saddle hanging sideways. I swear I secured it, but there were thorns beneath it."

"Thorns?"

"Aye. Forgive me, my lord, I would never see harm come to your guests. I can't imagine how they got there."

"Nor the straps loosened," I said. Was the shot meant to frighten the horses? Foreboding filled me, especially after Bridget's confession about the gold signet ring that would draw the greed of weak men.

You've done quite enough rescuing, she had told me in no uncertain terms.

A sick feeling pooled in my stomach. I couldn't even protect my estate or my tenants. Nor her. If only I could forget her demand that I forget the kiss and all that it entailed. Why would she not accept my proposal for marriage? I meant it.

I was nothing like my father. I would never use a woman for my own pleasure.

Truthfully, she had bewitched me. I wanted no one else.

She had stood on her own two feet for so long that she assumed she didn't need anyone. I had lived my life similarly, but it was a dangerous path to tread, relying only on oneself. I no longer wanted to stay on such a lonely road, focused on my own interests.

As I rushed up the steps to the abbey, a verse from Ecclesiastes came to mind.

And if one prevail against him, two shall withstand him; and a threefold cord is not quickly broken.

Inside the abbey, I found Bridget with her father and Mr. Harrington. Bridget folded her arms, her gaze faltering. Had the kiss affected her as much as it had me?

Both men were shocked to hear she had nearly been thrown off her horse.

"I don't think it was an accident," I told them. "Someone placed thorns under Miss Littleton's saddle girth. The horse naturally bolted with the gunfire."

Mr. Harrington gaped like a codfish when I shoved my hand into my pocket to pull out the sharp thorn to show them.

"Wretched business. That can't be an accident."

I shook my head. But why Bridget? How did they know we would ride today? The idea of betrayal was staggering.

"I can't help but think we must double the guard around Mr. Perry's field," I noted as I slipped the thorn back into my coat pocket.

Mr. Harrington narrowed his gaze as he studied me. "Are you aware we found a gold ring with a ruby?"

I hesitated to reveal Bridget's secrets, shared in confidence.

"I told Lord Hawthorn this morning." She sounded strained and averted her gaze.

"I have a safe," I offered. "You are welcome to put any valuable items inside it until matters are calm. Only I have the combination."

Bridget didn't answer, but the vicar stared at me. "We'll take you up on the offer, Lord Hawthorn."

33

Bridget

> The wise want love; and those who love want wisdom.
> **PERCY BYSSHE SHELLEY**

I tried to forget the ride, and the kiss. In the hours that followed, I repeatedly pushed the memory to the back of my mind, only to have it resurface. If I closed my eyes, I could still see Rafe's disbelief after I had discouraged his attentions.

I knew I had made the right choice to keep him free from obligation, but regret lingered.

As evening fell within the parsonage, the muted hues of purple and blue matched my dismal feelings. Mr. Harrington and Father sat in the drawing room with borrowed books spread out across the desk, courtesy of Lord Hawthorn's generous access to Roman history volumes. My own search, however, bore little fruit.

I turned a page, my finger tracing the text on Constantine's reign. In the early fourth century, the Roman Empire began its shift from paganism to Christianity, but here in Britain, the old gods held sway. Most families remained devoted to their pagan traditions, worshipping figures like Bacchus and Medusa, their symbols woven into daily life.

Regardless, Christianity had begun to take root, thanks to Constantine's edict of Milan. Some had converted, practicing their faith in secret, even while the majority clung to the familiar rites of the past.

My eyes fell on the ring we had found at the villa—the one that had been pulled off as if in a struggle.

"The villa's pagan mosaics—Bacchus, Medusa—they reflect the old ways," I murmured. "Might some members of the household have resisted the shift to Christianity, while others embraced it? The struggle could have torn families apart."

Mr. Harrington glanced up. "It's a plausible theory. We may never know the full story."

The thought saddened me—I longed to know more about the villa's inhabitants. What had they cherished? What had they feared? Had a Christian mother prayed in secret, her love for her child a flickering light amid danger?

Father sat with an ancient volume on his lap, sipping tea, unaware of my inner turmoil. I watched him, my heart a storm of conflicting emotions. Constantine's reign may have ended, but the questions left in its wake remained, echoing across time. Could love truly conquer all? The inscription on the once-lost ring had suggested so, but my own experience told a different story.

"Father, I must insist. Put down your teacup before you ruin those handwritten pages from the fifteen hundreds."

Father set down his teacup on the table next to him, his owlish eyes blinking beneath his glasses.

"What do you think, Vicar? Is the villa's story lost to the ages?" Mr. Harrington asked, looking up from his notes.

"I've often wondered about the challenges the early church faced within Britain. I cannot deny my heart is deeply encouraged by your discovery of Christian symbols. Not even the gates of hell could prevail against what God ordained. It is as if we've been given a glimpse of a miracle, tucked away until the proper hour, and dare I admit, one I needed greatly."

"Here, here! I fear we have come as far as we can for logical answers," Mr. Harrington said as he picked up the feathered quill and dipped it into the inkpot. Several papers lay on the desk, covered in notes. "Anything else will be conjecture. I am a scholar of science, not fiction. All we can note in any presentation is the suspected age of the mosaics, the jeweled ring, and . . ."

"The doll with the Christian symbol," I murmured. No matter how hard I tried, I could only uncover fragments of the villa's story. Perhaps the child belonged to a slave who kept her faith like a candle burning in the dark. Perhaps the *dominus* nurtured his fascination with gladiators and vice until his last wine-tainted breath, regardless of whether a Christian woman existed within his home.

A bittersweet end to my hungry search for answers regarding the lives of strangers who lived well over a thousand years ago.

I felt unsettled. Unfulfilled.

As Mr. Harrington and Father spoke about the items and the dig, making plans to gather and deliver the items to Lord Hawthorn in the morning, I found myself far more preoccupied with the present than the past.

What was Rafe thinking at this moment? Did he think of me? I touched my lips, remembering the kiss, but dropped my hand when Mr. Harrington gave me an odd look.

When the secretary retired for the night, I remained by the fireplace, studying the crackling flames. Father stayed with me.

"Bridget, you are not yourself this evening. Normally, you'd be putting a hole in the rug by now. What happened earlier with Lord Hawthorn?"

How perceptive he was. I flushed, having no intention of telling him anything about the ride back to the abbey, nor the marriage proposal.

"I had another accident involving horses, as you well know, and it reminded me of Daniel."

Father removed his spectacles and slid them into his coat pocket, his expression grave. "I have always regretted that day. You were in tears and stranded with a broken ankle. It was shortly after that incident when I sent him away to London to seminary, hoping he would find more honorable activities to occupy his days."

"I want to understand why Lord Hawthorn thinks his broken uncle found redemption in the end. How can a boy who had love reject it, and a man starved for love, find it?"

My father smiled at me, albeit sadly, his eyes crinkling in the corners. I knew he grieved for Daniel as much as I did. Maybe more so, like the father in the tale of the prodigal son, yearning to wrap his arms around his lost child and hold him tightly.

"Bridget, therein lies the mystery. Who can tell whom God will rescue? I pray for Daniel. I hope that within that foul, damp hulk, he will turn back to God. I have no choice but to trust His leading in the lives of my children, including providing for my son's needs."

My throat tightened as I fidgeted with my sleeve. "I fear that both your children will always prove utter disappointments. I've long struggled to believe in the goodness of God, especially after Mother passed away. You poured so much into your ministry, and I felt as though I lost you too. And Daniel . . . I tried so hard to be both a sister and a mother to him, but it proved too great a burden for me to carry. I needed you."

My voice broke and for once, I struggled to keep the tears at bay as they spilled over my cheeks.

"*We* needed you," I repeated.

His eyes also shimmered with tears, and his Adam's apple bobbed with effort. I feared I had pushed him too far with my plain speech. I never wanted to wound the one man who had represented hearth and home and all that I loved.

"Bridget . . . I am deeply sorry that my ministry caused you pain. Forgive me for being so consumed by it, especially after you lost your mother . . . and, in a way, your brother and me too. If I could fix my mistakes, I would. But I can't go back and change the past. I can, like Daniel, only live with the consequences of my choices. I was not the father you needed. I see that now.

"When you discovered the Roman doll's markings, I prayed you would see it as a sign that God loves you, just as He cared for that Roman child. That He delights in you and shows it by bringing a glimpse of His glory to shine in that murky soil of a simple farmer's field. His truth lasts far beyond Bacchus's or Medusa's influence.

"He created you to excavate. I finally understand. He led you to that precious child's grave. Is there anything that is not ordained within His sovereign will? From your brother's capture and detention to these mosaics uncovered in Mr. Perry's field, just when he desperately needed money to save his farm. I see these occurrences as signs, as miracles of His provision and sovereignty.

"None of our striving amounts to much in the end. It is only by His strength that we can accomplish anything." He heaved a great sigh and continued. "I had thought to join better men by initiating change in England and to reform the corrupt labor laws. I had such ambitious plans, but in the end, I suppose what God most desired of me was to serve one man. In these later years, after my son abandoned his faith, my ministry lay with a single man—a feebleminded, alcoholic viscount abandoned by all and deemed most unlikely to receive any grace. Too late, I learned to embrace grace and mercy. To temper the harshness of my tongue. By God, the old viscount chose that grace in those last years of his life. So, it is I who have let you down, both as a father and a vicar. It is I who failed. Please do not blame God for my shortcomings."

We, too, had been a family torn apart, divided in our beliefs, not unlike the people who lived in the villa.

Tears poured down my cheeks, and I tried in vain to mop them up with my fingers. "No, Father. You are not a failure. And I don't believe your ministry resulted in just one man. Look at the good you've done for Rafe."

"Rafe?" Father arched a brow.

"Lord Hawthorn." I corrected myself before hastening to add, "And look at the wisdom you've imparted to me and the entire village."

His smile softened, though his expression grew more thoughtful. "Yes, wisdom is a gift, but it is not always from me. What I have often preached—and tried to live by—is that what man intends for evil, God can redeem for good. I've seen it happen in the most unlikely of places and the most unexpected lives. Even in the darkest moments, God is at work."

He paused, looking into the flickering flames. "I believe He has been working in Daniel's life, even now. Mr. Harrington thinks you will receive funding and we can send further aid to Daniel in the months to come. And, Bridget, God is present in your excavation too. It's not just the discovery of ancient artifacts—it's a sign that He watches over us, even in a quiet village like ours. His hand moves in all things."

There was a brief silence as we both reflected on these words. Then Father glanced at me with a knowing smile. "Lord Hawthorn is just the kind of man I admire."

So I had not escaped Father's keen study of me from the opposite settee. My fingers tangled together as I considered how to respond, trying to buy a few moments.

Father rubbed his chin. "He knows when to take a stand, or so Mr. Harrington has informed me. He is most unconventional, rather like our own family. A free spirit. I am eager to grow our friendship and see the good he will bring to Bramnor."

I had not thought of Rafe as a free spirit, yet that moment when he had tipped his head so close to mine earlier, with the wind tearing at his hair, and his eyes darkening like a tempest, and his mouth parted as if to brush against mine, just before I kissed him . . .

A man willing to buck tradition—even the unwritten rule that said a viscount shouldn't marry a vicar's daughter like me.

Free spirit, indeed. I swallowed hard.

34

Rafe

A man afraid of death will never play the part of a live man.
SENECA

The constable had arrived early the next morning, summoned swiftly after Bridget's accident with the sabotaged saddle. His investigation, however, left much to be desired.

"A thorn you say?" Constable Wickham scowled as he wandered through my stable, his hand trailing against the stalls. A piece of straw clung to his sleeve, which he seemed completely unaware of. "Are you sure it isn't a prank of a silly boy? Perhaps I ought to interrogate the Dixon lads."

"If it was a prank, I would throttle the neck of whoever did it," I nearly growled, wanting to shake some sense into him. Too many accidents had occurred—loose animals, a stranger in the field, the stolen mosaic, and now this thorn and gunshots. Sabotage meant to frighten me. But why?

The constable had found no leads whatsoever, and I was growing tired of his incompetence.

He scratched behind his ear, eyeing both Mr. Whittle and Mr. Spencer with some suspicion. Mr. Spencer had a rolled-up blanket pinned beneath his arm, a satchel filled with supper, and matches for a fire. As soon as he was free to go, he planned to spend the night watching over Mr. Perry's field.

Mr. Whittle sweated, but he always sweated when nervous, his forehead gleaming with dots of perspiration.

"And your men had nothing to do with it, eh?"

"Of course not," I snapped.

"Nor your guests, I suppose."

A weighted stone dropped in my gut, since the same fear had crossed my mind. "I believe they called upon the Hawkins family."

"That's easy enough to find out," Constable Wickham said. He sniffed pompously. "I'll need to open a full inquiry and question *each* of your tenants."

Had I foolishly trusted the families within my care? Had one of them betrayed me?

That very evening, while I waited in the green room watching a cold slice of moonlight drag across the hardwood floors, I heard the jingle of horses, suggesting Mr. Beaumont and Lord Ainsley's return. When I approached the window and pushed aside the velvet drape just enough to peek outside, I spied Lord Ainsley's carriage, the harnessed bays glinting in the moonlight. I waited at the window, making no move to welcome them.

A door slammed after they entered the abbey, their voices echoing in the cavernous hall. Footsteps hurried, clicking against the floor, and Mr. Whittle's muted greeting.

Mr. Beaumont sounded unnaturally loud just outside the green room. "A remarkable day, eh, Ainsley? Such hospitality. I do so enjoy the countryside. We must do this again."

My breath left me in a whoosh. I let the curtain fall into place. The men had likely spent the day touring and flirting with the Hawkins girls. They couldn't have tampered with Bridget's saddle. Who, then, meddled with it? No one had seen the stranger during my last encounter. Who would dare to steal the mosaics?

In the meantime, a priceless artifact resided within the parsonage, endangering the Littletons.

A restless feeling suffused me, similar to the experience I had before the Battle of Bussaco. That quiet hour with a misty dawn, fog curling about my boots, right before all hell broke loose on the ridge in Portugal.

I resolved to call on Bridget the next day.

Morning couldn't come soon enough. I ate quickly and hurried to Chaucer, my limp less pronounced with the herbal salve, thanks to the woman who had rejected my clumsy proposal. I had spent the evening unable to sleep and wondering how I could possibly change her mind.

Once astride Chaucer, I directed him first to the Perrys' field. Dew sparkled on the grass, and Mr. Spencer greeted me with an exhausted wave.

"No trouble during the night?" I asked as I surveyed the field covered with an assortment of canvases like a motley quilt.

He tried to stifle a yawn behind a grimy fist. "No, my lord. My fire likely served as a warning to any thief. Only the Dixon boys here kept me company during the night."

Two youths lay on the damp ground, one fast asleep with an

arm pillowing his head, and the other blinking sleepily as he tossed aside a rough woolen blanket.

"Wake up, lads," I called out, with irritation. "You wouldn't survive a day within my old regiment."

They scrambled to their feet, their hair standing on end as they brushed dirt from their pants. Mr. Spencer straightened to his full height with a wry chuckle.

"Have no fear. They're good lads and stayed awake throughout the night in shifts. All they need is a stout coffee."

"Send them to Mrs. Whittle," I ordered. "She'll give them something bracing enough to put hair on their chests."

Another of Mr. Spencer's throaty chuckles followed as I whirled Chaucer around in the direction of the parsonage. With most social calls occurring in the afternoon, I knew I risked appearing a fool to knock on the vicar's door so early, but I felt it was imperative to see them. To see *her*.

The maid ushered me into the drawing room, and I waited, feeling even more foolish as each minute ticked by on the ornate clock perched on the white mantel. Like a besotted youth, pining for an elusive love. Immediately, I squashed that foolish observation, no matter how close it clung to truth.

A soft swish of a gown and footsteps, and there was Bridget. She wore a deep blue gown, a plain muslin unlike the frothy piece she wore to the Hawkinses' dance with flowers in her hair. Nor like the deep emerald riding suit that had clung to her figure the previous day.

I had rehearsed many things to say, but they evaporated like mist.

"I hope you will forgive my intrusion," I said. "Your father wished for me to place your items in my safe. I thought I would save you the trip. I also wanted to let you know the field appears safe enough. I met with Mr. Spencer and the Dixon boys on my way over. They kept watch last night and said all was well."

Her features softened. "Thank you. Mr. Harrington and I were of half a mind to guard the field ourselves, except Father would have none of it."

My mouth hitched at the idea of her guarding the dig with pistols in hand. Then I sobered. "Bridget, we must speak about what happened. I cannot let it rest."

She started when I reached for her hand and captured it with my own, her fingers cold within my grip. Her eyes widened as I curled my fingers around hers. I was certain I did not imagine how she leaned into me. Encouraged by her response, I drew closer to her.

"I have thought of nothing else."

She winced even though she made no move to withdraw her hand. "Rafe, no. There is no need to apologize again for the ride."

I winced. The military hadn't turned me into a poet, despite reading Shakespeare. I couldn't bungle things worse than I already had.

"Please, allow me to state how I truly feel—"

"I can only surmise that you will regret marrying a woman of diminished status. What will the ton say when you march to the altar with a lowly vicar's daughter?" she interrupted, studiously examining our clasped hands.

"I don't give a blaze what the ton thinks. Surely you've heard what they think of me," I answered, wishing I could make her understand how deeply I cared for her.

She pulled her hand free, her anguished eyes meeting mine. "I don't want to be a burden, Rafe. I've always felt like one. I don't want to be forgotten on a shelf. I can't marry a man who will eventually come to resent me and throw himself into his work while I wither."

I placed my hands on her shoulders, drawing her closer as understanding dawned. Her father, kind yet oblivious, had never attended to her needs. And her brother? Doubtful. No wonder she didn't trust anyone to cherish her when her experiences had been nothing but scraps tossed under the table.

"Listen to me, Bridget. I *see* you. From the moment I nearly collided with you on that awful, fateful road, you captured my attention. Then you commanded my respect and earned my friendship. I would be a fool not to—"

The door swung open, and Mr. Harrington and the vicar entered the drawing room. Mr. Harrington's smile faltered when he saw me clasping Bridget. She pulled free, her cheeks pink.

He bowed while clearing his throat. "Lord Hawthorn, how delightful to see you. I hope I interrupted nothing important."

"No," Bridget breathed.

"Yes," I answered firmly.

Our opposing answers uttered at the same time caused us both to search each other's face for some hint of emotion.

Finally, I nodded, feeling flummoxed at being interrupted so suddenly. She backtracked until she nearly hit the fireplace mantel, putting as much distance between us as she could, as if my presence pained her.

She did not want me.

Struggling to regain my bearings, I pivoted to the men. "I came to collect your items and take them to my safe with your permission. I visited Mr. Perry's field this morning and am relieved to report that I have seen no sign of tampering at the dig. There has been no word from the constable regarding our stranger, but as a precaution, Mr. Spencer will continue guarding the site overnight."

Vicar Littleton's narrowing gaze lingered on me while I heated under the collar. "How kind of you."

Bridget pulled out a desk drawer and removed a long tin, then opened it to reveal a gold ring and the ivory doll. When she handed me the box, her fingers brushed against mine.

"Mr. Harrington has agreed to purchase the ring from Mr. Perry on behalf of the Society of Antiquaries, who will donate it to the museum."

Despite being nestled within a piece of cotton, the ruby glowed with a hidden fire.

"I will guard it with my life," I promised her, even though I wanted to say so much more. But I would wait. I would prove to her that I would not disappear or forget her. I would be her friend, if that was all she chose.

Her faint smile was reward enough.

I had just mounted Chaucer and was about to return home when Reverend Littleton rushed out of the parsonage. My heart sank at his determined approach as he ate up the distance of the stone path lined with daisies and bluebells.

"My lord, a moment in privacy, if you will." He came to a halt beside Chaucer, his hands behind his back as if prepared to deliver a sermon. "I am not a blind man, and as any good father must inquire, what exactly are your intentions toward my daughter?"

I had wrestled with that burning question all night long, my twisted sheets about my limbs a testament to how agonizingly elusive sleep had proven.

"My regard is of the utmost for your daughter, sir. And for you, as well. And if I thought she would accept my suit, I would press for more. But as things stand, your daughter has rejected me." A harsh laugh rumbled through me. "To be perfectly honest, I would marry her. Gladly, with your blessing, should you care to give it."

He regarded me for a long moment. "Indeed. I have often found that patience is key, Lord Hawthorn. Patience and a bit of tender wooing. As you have well perceived since our initial visit, Bridget has a fancy or two tucked behind that practical mind of hers. A woman wants to be fought for. Cherished. If you could take that ridge at Bussaco, I believe you are more than up for the challenge of romance."

It was my turn for my cheeks to flame to life. Of all the advice to get from a vicar! Part of me feared a Song of Solomon reference would soon follow since he was so enamored with Ecclesiastes.

"Excellent wisdom, sir," I choked out as I gripped the reins within my stiff fingers.

His answering grin was all the encouragement I needed to kick Chaucer's poor sides and return to the abbey.

The iron lockbox rested in my chamber, pushed against my uncle's desk. After fumbling for the key in one of the drawers, I unlocked it. As I lifted the heavy lid, moving aside odds and ends, a yellowed paper lining the bottom grazed my fingers. My hand hovered above the document, its title blazing a scandalous accusation that I couldn't look away from. Afternoon light filtered through the window as I studied the words.

Did Lord Hawthorn Murder His Brother?

I pulled it out, skimming the contents that painted the story in both false and lurid terms. I knew the truth, but I wondered if my mother had seen a similar article. She hid within that small cottage, fearing for her life, keeping me in a safe, narrow circle with few friends or family to offer guidance or comfort. I did not resent her choices. Still, my chest tightened with emotion.

I thought of the last journal entry I had recently read.

I realize now that I am truly forgiven by God's grace. How I wish Anne would forgive our family for our wrongs, but I can only leave her in His hands and pray she finds healing one day. How could I possibly blame her for this never-ending silence? We must see to our own hearts, and the condition hidden within. He has a way of dealing with us, bringing our sorrow and sin to the surface.

My tenant had told me that the coming frost in winter forced the stones to rise within the ground, the pressure pushing them outward and upward. I recalled his words now, the meaning behind them slowly unfolding. Each year, the harsh cold and frost would force stones to the surface, just when the fields seemed cleared.

The earth never stayed silent for long, always uncovering what was buried. Perhaps life was no different—these upheavals, these moments of turmoil, were like the winter forcing rocks to the surface. But just as those obstacles had to be removed to allow the soil to thrive, maybe this was my chance to clear away what had long weighed me down. The effort, no matter how backbreaking, could yield something far greater in the end—a clear pasture, ready to be sown with new beginnings.

I could no longer hide from my past, pretending those pivotal events had no effect on my present and future. So many mistakes had been made, even by my mother as she separated from her own unforgiving kin, hiding in her poverty and the shame of a gutted marriage.

A whispered prayer broke free of me. For Bridget. For the Whittles. For each of my tenants. And I prayed that God would heal me and help me become a man others could rely upon. Nor could I assume that I alone could protect those within my care. The burden of sole responsibility, to fix and repair, that I had carried for so long—first with my mother, then with my best friend's death, and now with my tenants and Bridget—slipped from my shoulders.

I needed God's help.

After placing the article on the desk, I carefully tucked Bridget's most valuable possessions inside the safe. A sacred trust, not to be bestowed lightly. I locked the lid and deposited the key in my coat pocket. My uncle found forgiveness at the end of his life.

And me? Perhaps I, too, would find freedom from the long years of bitterness.

35

Bridget

> It is not the man who has too little,
> but the man who craves more, that is poor.
>
> **SENECA**

Sweat trickled down my back as I paused to dab at my forehead and cheeks with a handkerchief while surveying Mr. Perry's field. May proved a fickle month, hot and rainy by turns. Despite a bright beginning this morning, clouds billowed in the sky, promising a storm by late afternoon.

After giving the ring and doll to Rafe for safekeeping, we made another thrilling discovery just this morning—a mosaic featuring Ganymede flying to Mount Olympus in a blaze of glory as Mr. Harrington and I swept away the debris from the cerulean-blue chips.

Mr. Harrington, eager to secure the funds from the sale of the ring, sent another letter by courier to the society. He allowed the Bramnor men to help with the excavation, but few wanted to stay long considering how he shouted orders.

Mr. Perry, of course, and Abigail, remained by my side, eagerly combing through the dirt on the hunt for more gold. Mr. Harrington had struck a further deal with Mr. Perry, agreeing that any future items discovered might be sold, to benefit both him and the society. Father and I had helped negotiate the arrangement, and it seemed fair that I would receive a percentage for bringing in the Society of Antiquaries—much like an agent's fee.

Mr. Perry gladly agreed to his terms, including his plans for a tourist center to be built the following summer. He had also approved of Rafe keeping the items safe at Hawthorn Abbey under lock and key.

Mr. Harrington had gestured to the newest section of the floor. *The real value will occur when you grace the summer tourist guides. I imagine families will travel across the continent to see this lost palace.*

Abigail had laughed, flinging her arms around her father's neck. *We'll be rich, Papa.* She kissed him soundly on the cheek. *And we'll build a palace of our own.*

Mr. Harrington added with a grin, *I imagine you could charge a decent price for a walking tour. You might even open a teahouse and offer refreshments. The possibilities are endless.*

I had smiled at my dear friend's enthusiasm, especially when she shot me a meaningful look. At last, both of our vaporous dreams felt like a solid reality. If only Daniel was here to share in the joy.

As I stopped digging to grab my sketchbook and charcoal in order to capture Ganymede's fierce gaze, the sun broke free of the clouds, brilliant and golden. Abigail seemed in especially high spirits before she left the dig to prepare a lunch basket for us. I had spent the morning listening to her tales of the young men who had shown interest in her following May Day. Poor Mr. Perry would likely have his hands full in the days to come with marriage proposals.

Soon, the scent of fresh bread and cheese filled the air as Abigail returned with a picnic basket. We gathered beneath a large oak tree, the breeze carrying the promise of an approaching storm, and spread the blanket on the grass. While we ate, Mr. Harrington continued to discuss plans for the mosaics, his enthusiasm infectious. Abigail, flushed with excitement, could hardly sit still, dreaming aloud of what their future might hold.

Surprisingly, I'd heard not a single peep from her about Mr. Barron. Nor had I encountered him since that unfortunate conversation when he was last at the field and Rafe defended my reputation. Therefore I was surprised when a shadow fell over the pages of my sketchbook, and I glanced up, squinting despite my bonnet, to see Mr. Barron hovering over me.

I jumped to my feet, dropping my sketchbook. I had not forgotten his overbearing behavior on May Day. I clapped off what soil I could from my gloves, resisting the urge to use my apron as a hand towel.

"Good afternoon, Miss Littleton." He tipped his hat, his chaise waiting by the roadside. "Such wonderful progress, I see."

The pages of my sketchbook fluttered on the ground, whipping in the wind, but he saw enough of my drawings, including the portrait of Rafe. He laughed at the sketch before the wind tossed the pages again. I snatched it up, holding it close.

"What brings you here, Mr. Barron?" Mr. Perry and Mr. Harrington had spotted the guest and started heading our way, their long-legged strides swiftly covering the dirt. Mr. Perry appeared none too pleased.

"I wanted to make sure all is well for you, and to pass on a warning from a concerned friend." Mr. Barron pointed to the rows of mature orchard trees and the newly planted saplings. "I just paid a visit to Lord Hawthorn. I see he is thoroughly enjoying the day with his visitors. In fact, they plan to go riding later this afternoon. When I stepped into the hall, I overheard their conversation. You might be interested to know that our viscount is in league with the Dilettanti.

In fact, I believe they plan to pay him for several valuable antiques in the abbey. And they want to open a rival tourist attraction."

I didn't mind about a rival tourist attraction, and I already knew about the items to be sold, especially since I had sketched some of them. Rafe could do as he pleased with his property, but the thought of him arranging a business partnership with the men who'd tried to oust me sent a shiver of consternation across my shoulders.

"Mr. Barron, I fear I cannot spare another moment for gossip. You are mistaken regarding Lord Hawthorn. He has proved to be an ally, not a rival," I protested.

The innkeeper stepped closer to me, and I backed away, fully intending to smack him with my sketchbook. In fact, he came so close to the edge of the pool that a chunk of dirt dislodged and tumbled across the ancient floor. Something cracked just below his riding boot.

I tore my attention away from the ground and focused on him.

He grimaced and moved away from the mosaic. "Is it gentlemanly behavior to sell a gold ring he's been entrusted to protect?"

Shock rippled through me, stealing the breath from my lungs. We had all solemnly promised we would not breathe a word to anyone outside our circle regarding the signet ring. How, then, could Mr. Barron have known of its existence? Had he truly overheard Rafe offer to sell it? And I had given it to him freely. Surely Mr. Barron was wrong. Surely it was a misunderstanding. But how, then, did he know Rafe held it at the abbey?

Of course, Mr. Beaumont would want such a trophy to take back to the Dilettanti.

Worse, how could Rafe allow those men to stay with him this long? Why had he not turned them out by now, unless he planned on receiving their promised investment? Nausea clawed its way up my throat.

"Forgive me, Miss Littleton. It would appear my unfortunate

news has grieved you. But can we really be surprised that a Hawthorn backed out on his word?"

I opened my mouth to protest but not a sound came out. Mr. Barron eased away as the men approached, waving to Mr. Harrington and leaving me with a roiling stomach.

There was a simple solution to this problem. I would visit Rafe as soon as possible and demand an explanation. Hang propriety. I would not wallow in the parsonage, nursing my fears regarding his behavior or his intentions. If he had kissed me only to win my trust so he could sell the ring, he would have a piece of my mind.

But I didn't think such a thing was possible. I refused to believe that the man who'd stood within my drawing room and reached for my hand had a nefarious plan.

In my distress, I didn't look where I was headed. My foot pressed into the edge of the field lining the pool, and I heard a cracking beneath the pressure of my slipper. I knelt, fingers brushing something unusual—pot shards. I tugged, but the largest piece wouldn't budge. Resting on my knees, I pushed back my bonnet and pondered what to do. When I glanced up, Mr. Barron slanted a strange look at me before walking away, his continued attempts at influencing Mr. Perry apparently a loss. I ignored his departure, eager to be free of his accusations and his intensity.

Mr. Perry and Mr. Harrington continued discussing a covering for the mosaics, one that would allow the open air to rush through the structure so large crowds wouldn't overheat. I rummaged in my satchel for my trowel and dug. With only a few inches of dirt to scrape away, unlike the deeper pool, I suspected the object wouldn't take long to free from its earthy prison.

But Mr. Harrington, apparently in need of tea, called my name and offered a ride home in the chaise. I felt torn between staying and playing the role of a proper hostess. At last, my manners won, and I agreed to return with him to the parsonage.

The ride's balmy wind cooled my cheeks, but I could barely focus on Mr. Harrington's chatter. Who had betrayed us regarding the ring? Mr. Harrington? The Perrys? Or Rafe?

No one seemed a logical choice.

In my mind, two thoughts vied for competition as we hurried home. I had felt something in the soil, and I must return this evening to retrieve it before anyone else did. And I needed to talk to Rafe as soon as possible.

36

Rafe

> And what concord hath Christ with Belial?
> or what part hath he that believeth with an infidel?
> **2 CORINTHIANS 6:15**

The tension in the abbey since my confrontation with Beaumont and Ainsley in the field the other day had become unbearable. Each hour that passed felt heavier, their unwelcome presence a constant reminder of their scheming. As I sat at my desk paying Mr. Spencer for his work the previous evening, the weight of it all pressed down on me—every breath a struggle as the silence between us simmered with unspoken frustration.

Voices carried from the west wing, Beaumont's sharp tones echoing down the hallway. "I have repeatedly rung for tea!"

Though I'd done my best to steer clear of them, I couldn't avoid their company entirely. At dinner, their lingering conversations about purchasing the abbey's art collections left me feeling trapped, counting the days until their departure at the end of the week. Only yesterday did Mr. Beaumont finally write a note for the Ming vases. I had taken it, feeling like a veritable Judas, or as if I had signed a Faustian deal with the Dilettanti in order to satisfy the Crown's demands.

I heard Lucy's voice. "My mother brought your tea nearly fifteen minutes ago. I can see the service tray within your room. I must do other tasks for the lord at present. Ring for her and she will help you."

Mr. Spencer and I exchanged glances.

"Imagine, a maid refusing service." Ainsley's bored drawl filtered down the hall. My hackles raised, I set down my quill.

"Agreed, Ainsley. You little wench, someone ought to teach you manners." A scuffle and a startled cry sent my temper to a boil. Mr. Spencer and I dashed out the door to see Lucy on her hands and knees, picking up an assortment of linens that had tumbled to the floor. Mr. Beaumont loomed over her, his face mottled as crimson as his garish waistcoat.

I stalked down the hall, my gait uneven but heavy. Lucy ducked her head and dashed aside her tears with trembling hands. I reached for her and helped her to her feet.

"The sheets are now dusty, my lord," she said with a sniff.

"Never mind the sheets," I ground out. I spied the rumpled bed through the open door and knew exactly what Beaumont had intended for Lucy had she entered.

I turned to both men with their cravats loosened and their waistcoats open in dishabille.

"You have overstayed your welcome, Mr. Beaumont, Lord Ainsley. I want you both to pack your items immediately. Otherwise, Mr. Spencer and I will toss your clothes into the courtyard and you may have the pleasure of picking them up one by one while my staff stands by and watches. In fact, I do believe I would enjoy such a sight. You have fifteen minutes or the amusement will commence." I pulled out my pocket watch, the tick barely discernible from the roar building in my ears.

Mr. Beaumont's mouth rounded. He shut it, propping his fists on his lean hips. Then he jabbed a finger at me. "You will not get a farthing from me, Hawthorn. I won't take your books, your Ming vases, or any of your tapestries. You'll wither out here with no funds and no connections. You won't have a chance in the world to rescue your abbey and orchards without me."

A dry chuckle escaped me, infuriating him further.

"You illegitimate cur, pretending to be a viscount. London will never accept you if you cast Ainsley and me out. We will ruin you so no polite society will ever allow you to cross their thresholds."

I froze. Had he read my uncle's diary? My muscles tensed for battle. "If you are the representation of that society, I've had my fill."

Lucy gasped, and Mr. Spencer muttered an oath from behind me, but I was too irate to care. I had survived thus far without the blessing of the ton. I had no intention of changing myself to overlook Mr. Beaumont's vices or ignore the wolf lurking beneath the tarnished sheen of respectability. His veneer had worn thin within a matter of days.

"But what of the mosaics?" Lord Ainsley sputtered. "We came solely for them. I will not leave empty-handed after staying in this godforsaken place. Nor will I allow a crippled former soldier to dictate my affairs."

This godforsaken place. I had used the same words that night I entered the abbey. For so many years, I had viewed it as a specter to escape. How was it that now, when I could no longer keep the abbey, I wanted to settle deep roots in this valley and finally find a sense of home?

"The mosaics belong to Mr. Perry. As for the gladiator piece, it and anything else I discover on this property are intended for Miss Littleton and Mr. Harrington. And should you refuse to leave, I have a pair of pistols that keep me company. I assure you, my arm works well enough to pull a trigger."

Lord Ainsley dragged a palm down his face as if he couldn't quite believe what he was hearing while Mr. Beaumont glared at me.

"Don't expect me to take this insult lightly, nor will you cash my note," he snarled, but he made no move when I shouldered forward to stand directly in front of him. His nostrils flared, almost as if he expected me to deck him. The stench of port wafted from him, and likely something else. Bluish circles curved beneath his eyes from far too many late nights. It was rather gratifying to see him flinch when I moved closer.

"I shall tear up it up myself if need be." I held up my silver pocket watch, the ornate minute hand inching too slowly for my liking. "Ten minutes and counting, Beaumont."

The abbey seemed to exhale, the old walls shuddering with relief when the Dilettanti departed, taking their luggage and their cheroots and their bad manners with them. A foul wind picked up once more, pushing against the windowpanes, and a smattering of rain soon joined.

I regretted I hadn't asked them to leave after they had pushed Mr. Harrington to drop Bridget from the presentation at the next Society of Antiquaries meeting. And my threat to shred Mr. Beaumont's note had only set a fire to the situation. He had tossed his fine wool jackets, trousers, silky cravats, and pearl-white shirts into his luggage with no assistance other than his poor valet, who bore a steady stream of curses and abuse.

Mr. Spencer joined me outside in the courtyard with Mr. Whittle. We three, with our arms folded across our chests, watched the trail of dust spin on the road as the carriage rattled away. I hoped they would hit all the wretched potholes between here and London.

"Thank you, my lord," Mr. Whittle sounded entirely humble. "Few viscounts care for their staff the way you have. I am entirely grateful, and my wife and daughter too."

My mouth tilted in a wry smile. "I fear I may not be able to keep staff much longer. I don't need to tell you we are gasping for air and in our last hour. I have no hope of convincing Mr. Talbot of any future success."

Mr. Spencer shook his head. "If the ship is sinking, my lord, we shall go down with you leading at the helm."

I wanted so badly to hope, but in truth I was tired and defeated. I decided to trust these two men, who had proven far more loyal than I ever could have expected.

"Beaumont will ruin me as soon as he reaches London within a day and a half. There won't be a line of credit available to me if he plants rumors about my father. For the record, I am not illegitimate, no matter what he claims."

Mr. Whittle's gaze faltered at my frank words, but Mr. Spencer merely shoved his hands in his waistcoat. "Of course not. You have always been the rightful heir. Long have my wife and I prayed for your return."

His words, no doubt inappropriate, managed to bring a rare sheen to my eyes. I was not alone after all.

Mr. Whittle reddened too, as if embarrassed by the overt display of emotion. "If you don't mind me saying so, that gent wasn't on the up and up himself. I overheard him in the stable this morning tell Lord Ainsley he's got a heap of debts waiting to be paid in shady establishments. Both men do. Gambling and whatnot. Why, he told Lord Ainsley to be patient and see the mosaics come through for them."

Mr. Beaumont with gambling debts? The news hardly surprised me. Thank God I didn't let him edge Bridget and Mr. Harrington or Perry out of the mosaics.

I clasped Mr. Spencer on the shoulder. "I can't help but wonder if he would have honored his precious note after all."

Mr. Spencer smirked, his teeth a yellow hue against his weathered skin. "I about popped a button when you threatened to tear it up. A man doesn't forget an insult like that."

"Well, he's on his way to London. Let us hope other diversions capture him," I said as we returned to the abbey. "I believe my days of entertaining young lords are at an end."

Riding Chaucer provided the only means for clearing my head. I left Mr. Spencer and Mr. Whittle and headed for the stable. Inside, dust motes danced within the streams of sunlight. A greeting nicker came from Chaucer's stall. He nudged me with his velvet nose, eager as I to run and feel the wind in our hair.

Outside, I took him on the familiar path leading to the orchard where the hail had stripped the branches bare. A desolate expanse of thwarted dreams. The wind stirred the blighted leaves as I reined Chaucer in to a slow walk.

How strange that the abbey felt like the closest thing to home, even though it would likely revert to the Crown. Was there truly no way to save it on my own? Accepting Harrington's assistance would mean leaning on another man's resources, another reminder that I had not managed to revive the abbey by my own means. Beaumont had trampled my name, casting doubt on any chance of marrying an heiress or even securing a proper tenant to cover the upkeep.

Both ideas stung. No, I wanted to find a way to salvage the abbey on my own terms, without the debt of someone else's goodwill. I had no desire to leave the valley or abandon those in my care. And most of all, I couldn't imagine leaving Bridget—not when I'd barely begun to fight for her.

I bowed my head and breathed a prayer as a cool wind brushed past me, stirring Chaucer's mane. A thread of peace curled within me, as faint as a wisp of smoke, but it was enough. The recent events in my life pushed up what had been buried for so long. If I hadn't injured my leg, I would not have returned to the abbey. If I had not returned to claim my inheritance, I never would have known about my uncle's change of heart.

Who knew where my path would lead next? I could only trust God's whisper in my ear, telling me where to turn, even if it meant joining with Mr. Perry to open a tourist center for antiquities. I would have no choice but to rely upon Bridget and Mr. Harrington and Mr. Perry.

But if she didn't want marriage, would my presence only cause further distress?

When I opened my eyes, Chaucer had drifted a few paces forward. He whinnied, his ears perking. I patted his neck while glancing around, but when I looked over the scene, my heart stalled. A dark void replaced what had once been the gladiator mosaic, with fragments of the tiles strewn across the area.

I swung off Chaucer and inspected what remained. It would have taken several men to remove it, likely with the use of a canvas or crate to carry it away.

A man's brass button lay on the ground nearby, and I knelt to pick it up. Chaucer whinnied and I shifted on the damp ground to see what the matter was, when a thunderous blow struck the back of my head. I heard the sickening crack as stars flickered across my vision.

Reeling, I braced myself and cocked my fist, a cry ripping from my throat as several blows rained on my skull.

"Take him," a muffled voice ordered as someone yanked an itchy burlap sack over my head.

37

Bridget

> Gold tests with fire, woman with gold, man with woman.
> **SENECA**

The sun began to set after Mr. Barron's visit to the field. I slipped out of the parsonage with less than a few hours of daylight to probe the buried pot I'd uncovered earlier. Father and Mr. Harrington remained in the drawing room, deep in conversation over port—well, Mr. Harrington exclusively, as Father never touched the stuff.

I laced up my slippers and slid a pocketknife into my apron. Mrs. Herriot eyed me suspiciously as I grabbed my shawl and satchel from the hook on the wall. She hovered over a plate of gingerbread, her cheeks a bit full.

She swallowed an enormous lump and brushed sugar from her mouth. "Leaving at this hour?"

"Just a quick walk, I assure you. I'm heading to the mosaics. Not to worry, I'll be back by nightfall."

She shook her head, a few crumbs clinging to her chin. "One of these days, miss, all this gallivanting about will catch up with you."

"Think on the bright side, Mrs. Herriot," I called over my shoulder with an impish grin, "at least you can have my share of the biscuits this evening."

I closed the door, hurrying down the wildflower-strewn path, gasping for air as I passed homes and farms until I reached Mr. Perry's cottage. I would visit the Perry family after the field, should I find anything of value. And I *would* speak to Rafe soon regarding Mr. Barron's accusation.

A knot formed in my stomach as a harsh wind rushed against the floor of the valley, and the endless sky above reminded me of my insignificance.

I should be used to being mostly alone. Sadly, I had accepted morsels in my relationships and pretended they were a feast. Was solitude the safer path to protect myself from betrayal and hurt? I didn't know whom to trust anymore, especially since someone had told Mr. Barron about the ring. My heart stuttered at the idea of Rafe using it to his advantage. Or the mosaics.

Within moments, I found myself beside Ganymede, his mosaic figure soaring toward Olympus in vivid cerulean and gold—the spot where I had heard something crack. I knelt, trowel in hand. Yet, as I chiseled away the earth, my thoughts wandered to Medusa. She lay several feet away, her twisted face haunting the edges of my mind. Her story—the vengeance, the curse—seemed to reflect a deeper truth about human nature. What did her frozen fury say about the wounds we carry, unseen beneath the surface?

As I pondered these thoughts, my trowel hit something hard. A sharp clunk rang out in the quiet, pulling me from my reverie. I stared down at the dirt.

The sound of shattering brought a low groan of frustration as

I wiggled a small amphora free. The remainder of the vessel broke apart, the clay far too fragile to withstand my clumsy efforts.

A cry escaped me as a gold necklace tumbled to the dirt. My hand hovered over it, and as carefully as I could, I lifted it higher to examine it, counting eleven rounded amethyst stones, securely inset within the delicate goldwork. The heavy chain gleamed with beautiful craftsmanship, and to my amazement, a matching bracelet rested beneath it. Both pieces, remarkably preserved, revealed intricate swirls and circles, visible despite the centuries of grime.

I removed my handkerchief from my apron pocket and gently wiped the smooth surface of the gems.

Another thought circled my mind. Of course, I felt some degree of pleasure in finding such rare jewels. They would serve Mr. Perry's finances well, and my research would bring a welcomed notoriety, further securing my position with the Antiquaries society.

The longer I held the jewelry in my ungloved hand, the more my heart collapsed into emptiness.

It was simply a necklace and bracelet in the end, hidden and of no use for centuries. Had the woman who wore them chased after empty baubles, only to find that they could neither fulfill nor save her? The heavy gold taunted me, unlike the Christian symbols etched into the doll and buried with a beloved child.

I did not withhold my heart from any pleasure, and indeed all was vanity and grasping for the wind.

Father's sermon on Ecclesiastes came back in snippets. Had I, too, chased after the wrong pursuits, seeking them to fill the chasm within me when the answer I needed had been with me all along? My mother loved to share the story of the lost coin with me, of the woman hunting throughout the house until it was reclaimed. I had assumed she meant rescuing Daniel from his recklessness.

But truthfully, I was that lost coin.

"Oh, God, do you truly care for Daniel and me?" I spoke out loud as I lifted my head to the heavens, my cheeks suddenly wet. "I know the right answers, but I struggle to believe. Help me in my unbelief."

The wind brushed against me with a low moan and the clouds drifted across the sky as I awaited an answer.

"Miss Littleton!" A man's voice shouted from across the field. "Do wait for us!"

Startled, I saw Mr. Barron striding across the field with Abigail in tow. He grinned broadly at me while she struggled to match his long-legged stride.

Strange. I had not noticed him drive up to the field. Had he waited in the Perry cottage all this while? Or just emerged from behind the copse of trees to the east, where Rafe's stranger disappeared?

Quickly, I dashed at my eyes with my free hand. He had changed his foppish attire to something far more serviceable, with dirt marring his trousers at the knees and his white shirt lying open at the throat without a cravat. Before I could say anything, he reached into his shabby greatcoat and pulled out a pistol, aiming it at my chest.

I sucked in a horrified breath, my shoulders squaring as I rose. "What is the meaning of this, sir?"

He waved the pistol at me, gesturing to the jewels in my shaking grip. "You've been keeping secrets from Miss Perry. Whatever is hiding in your hand, I want you to give it to her."

"Put the gun down," I said as evenly as I could.

He cocked the hammer with a sneer. "Give the necklace to her, please. I won't ask nicely again."

Numb, I couldn't move a muscle, my shock so complete, especially when Abigail slipped up to my side and reached for my hand. She tugged it upward, prying my fingers away from the jewels. Her mouth parted at the sight of the purple gems.

"Can we distract him?" I whispered to her. "I'll throw the jewelry to the left and you run back to the cottage and nab your father." An absurd plan full of risk, but I was willing to try it if it would keep her safe.

She blinked at my proposal. "You don't understand. I haven't a choice. He—he . . ."

"The necklace, Abigail. No speaking to Miss Littleton. It won't do any good." Mr. Barron gestured again with the pistol.

She exhaled sharply. "Please, Bridget. Do it for me."

Horror dawned as my fingers clenched around the necklace. She had not been dragged against her will. She was Mr. Barron's accomplice.

"*You* were the one who informed Mr. Barron about the ring."

She didn't answer. Instead, without any further hesitation she snatched both pieces from me, scratching my palm and wrist in the process, but her bottom lip quivered.

Muttering a curse, Mr. Barron snatched my arm with his free hand, his fingers digging deep into the flesh, far more so than they had on May Day.

"What else have you found?"

"You seem to know about the ring and the doll, and now the necklace and bracelet. Did you steal Bacchus?" I demanded.

"Bacchus is safely tucked inside a crate." He dragged me away from Ganymede. If only I could turn him into a statue of stone, but he was manhandling me with an alarming speed, forcing me farther away from Mr. Perry's cottage.

"Where is Mr. Perry?" I demanded as I stumbled forward, trying to wrestle my arm free. A losing battle against his iron grip.

"He's at the Jolly Wench, celebrating a night of good fortune with his friends. I've made sure the ale flows freely. You needn't worry about him. He's perfectly happy this evening."

"Jim, where are you taking her?" Abigail's plaintive voice came from behind us as he dragged me next to a copse of trees where a horse waited. "You promised me you wouldn't hurt her. You said you would let her go once you got the treasure."

"Silence," he roared, pausing mid-step to swing the gun in her direction. Her eyes widened, and she burst into tears. I dared not jerk free only to find the gun going off and injuring her. But I had to inform Father or Mr. Harrington of where I was headed. Could I drop my handkerchief somewhere along the way? Would any of them notice my absence? A swell of panic bubbled up in my throat. I was truly abandoned, betrayed by one of my dearest friends.

"You said you cared for me. I thought we would leave for Gretna Green this evening." Abigail hiccupped loudly and wiped her nose with the edge of her sleeve. Her nose was red from crying, and her hair mussed by the wind. She hardly appeared the same woman from the Hawkinses' dance, where she kept the young gentlemen on their toes.

"I do care for you," he said through gritted teeth. "Come here. Put them in my coat pocket."

Like a meek lamb, she did as she was told, sniffling as she slid the jewels into his coat.

"Good girl," he crooned before flashing me the most impudent smile. Bacchus indeed. Here stood the perfect representation of the god of wine and drink, and I wanted nothing more than to wipe that smirk off his full lips. Could I reach for the knife in my apron? Then again, what good would a knife do against a pistol?

"I have only one question," I interrupted. "Where *is* Bacchus? He belongs in Mr. Perry's field. The gems, the ring, and all of it belong to Mr. Perry. Why ask the woman you care about to destroy her father?"

I hoped referencing Abigail's father would remind her of where her true loyalty ought to reside. She paled further, her gaze darting between Mr. Barron and me.

He waggled his eyebrows, enjoying himself far too much at my expense. "Does it really matter who ends up with everything?"

"Of course it matters. Mr. Perry will be devastated."

He pulled me close, pressing the cold tip of the barrel against my temple until it hurt. "Don't put ideas into her foolish head, Miss Littleton. Abigail's loyalties lie with me first. Keep speaking, and I'll kill you." His hot breath fanned over my ear as he lowered his voice for my hearing only. "Or maybe her."

"I beg you not to harm her or her father," I said through stiff lips.

"You lied to me, Jim. If you loved me, how could you lie so?" An anguished moan ripped from Abigail as she covered her face with her hands while he cruelly laughed.

"Aye, I loved you, lass. Loved you well enough that no other man will touch you now. Go back home and wait for my signal. Don't think for a moment that your father won't pay the price if you refuse me."

My gut roiled at the sordid implication, but Abigail pressed a fist against her mouth as if to contain her anguish. Our eyes met briefly before she spun on her heel and fled, dust whirling beneath her slippers before she disappeared from sight.

There was nothing I could do against Mr. Barron's brute strength and a pistol pressed against my head. Somehow, I would wait for the right moment and make my escape.

Pocketing his gun, he tossed me onto the saddle and clambered quickly behind with an iron arm wrapped about my middle. So unlike Rafe's, Mr. Barron's grip terrorized. I reached into my apron and tugged the handkerchief free, sneaking my hand down to let it drop to the field while the horse charged into a gallop away from the field. Would Father notice I was late? At least at twilight Mr. Spencer and the Dixon boys would arrive to camp and watch over the field. Maybe one of them would spy the handkerchief.

But by then I could be hidden far from reach, or worse... dead.

I had relied on myself in the past, but now I had only God to hear my cry.

I had never been inside Mr. Cobb's cottage, but it reeked of unwashed bodies and tobacco smoke, along with a burned cast-iron pot moldering with leftover stew. I sat on a hard chair, my hands tied behind my back while the two men stood guard outside. Although the door remained shut, I could easily hear their conversation through a broken, grime-covered window stuffed with a rag. I tried to wiggle out of my restraints, but that and reaching the knife in my apron proved impossible. To my left, wooden crates were stacked and pushed against a soot-covered wall.

"But what of the bailiff and the groundskeeper?" Mr. Barron sounded frustrated, his voice tight with barely suppressed anger.

"They went runnin' to the fields to put out the fires, just like you wanted," Mr. Cobb replied. "But I haven't seen you leave with any papers. Did you find what you were after?"

"No," Mr. Barron snarled from the other side of the door. "And I've been through that blasted abbey for weeks. There's nothing but chaos and disorder. The viscount's records are as worthless as the man himself."

"It don't matter none," Mr. Cobb replied carelessly. "I've done my part, settin' fires and causin' enough distraction. What about the money you promised me?"

Mr. Barron hesitated, his voice lowering. "I'll pay you what I owe, once I get what's mine."

"And that is?" Mr. Cobb's voice took on a dark edge. "You promised me a share if you claimed the estate. You can't pull back now."

"I told you—without those papers proving I'm Randall Hawthorn's son, I have nothing! A record in a Bible or some will or testament. Even a diary entry. It's as if I never existed. You think I want to be crawling around that cursed place every night? You think I enjoy pretending I'm less than what I was born to be?" Mr. Barron's tone was sharp with frustration. "I deserve Hawthorn Abbey after everything my mother endured. But no—he made sure it all went to the one child he actually cared about, leaving me, the bastard, with nothing!"

"What a jolly it would be to see you scrape a bow before the Prince Regent, claiming Hawthorn Abbey belongs to you. Don't rook me on the money you owe. I did as asked, releasing the sheep and horses, placing a thorn in that saddle, and beating the viscount to a pulp. You'll have nothing to worry about other than your light-o'-love."

"She'll hold true. She dares not see her father hurt." Mr. Barron snarled. "After that, we shall see if I keep her or not."

Their voices dipped too low for me to discern, but I caught snatches of it. *Viscount trapped . . . Items taken from the abbey . . . Payment owed. My runaway horse.*

"You'll have no abbey to claim, my fine lord. I set fire to it as well."

"What?" cried Mr. Baron. "You set fire to the abbey?"

"Just a wee one, mostly smoke and not much else. I needed the women gone before I put Hawthorn in the brewery. Never knew if they'd hear him hollerin'. You pay me tonight or I'll tell the constable you're Randall Hawthorn's whelp and that you've had your sights on the estate. He'll be interested to know of the accident with the horse and the vicar's daughter. Murder charges may be waiting, aye? Arson, aye?" Mr. Cobb's voice contained a razor's edge of threat. "Oh, and I'll share how you've crept around the abbey at night in search of proof of your parentage. You swore you could frighten the new viscount away. A fool's errand, if I ever saw one."

"Enough," Mr. Barron's voice came out eerily flat.

I froze on the uncomfortable stool, no longer straining to slide out of the ropes fraying the tender skin of my wrists. My muscles seemed to liquefy at what I had just overheard. Mr. Barron the half brother of Rafe? Payment owed to Mr. Cobb? For what? Killing Rafe? A jolt of fear surged through my body, strong enough to set my teeth chattering. Agony pierced me as I pictured him collapsed and bleeding in the courtyard or abbey, and poor Mrs. Whittle and her daughter, injured or worse. The palpitations in my heart increased and again I jerked on the ropes to no avail.

The two men spoke louder now, hassling over the cut of profit with Mr. Cobb demanding forty percent for keeping the mosaics within the crates. The conversation turned feral and their voices climbed in fury.

Someone yelled. A tussle against the side of the house and a body hitting the door with a violent shudder.

Grunts. Curses. A shout. And then a gunshot echoed, the sound piercing right through me.

I screamed. But Mr. Cobb's cottage lay the farthest from the other tenants, hidden within the rolling hills of the valley and nearly a mile away from the closest tenant. If only someone had heard that gunshot.

An involuntary shiver worked through me as I strained to hear if anyone had survived. My wrists ached from the rope constricting my flesh until my fingers felt thick and useless. A sound rasped against the door, as if someone dragged something away. No one entered the cottage, but the steady beat of horse hooves soon brought a cry of relief. Had rescue come at last?

My relief turned to bitter disappointment when I heard a familiar voice, rich and cultured.

"You shot him! Barron, how uncivilized of you. Why must you seed so much chaos?"

"You may blame the chaos on Cobb. I only wanted vengeance. Why should you care about one less person to divide the spoils? We have no further use for Cobb, and he has done us more harm than good. What would you have me do with Miss Littleton? I found her wandering the site. And where, pray tell, is Ainsley during all of this? Don't tell me it's just the two of us getting our hands dirty?"

"He is waiting in the carriage, out of sight. A lord has a reputation to protect, after all. You should have let Miss Littleton go. You've complicated things, Barron, and I hate complications." Mr. Beaumont's presence brought a roil of nausea clambering up my throat. "We were to steal the mosaics, as you had promised, not kill the vicar's daughter. I ought to punish you for putting me in this predicament."

A cold sweat broke out on my forehead as I listened to the men casually discuss their heist and their plans for me.

"She's in the cottage right now. It's too late to let her go." Mr. Barron sounded petulant. "I brought you the mosaics. I've ensured several distractions for the field hands. At this moment, Mr. Perry is playing cards at the Jolly Wench, gambling on what he owns. He will lose his farm, which puts you in the position of renting from me once I'm viscount. If you ask me, I deserve far more coin than you've offered so far."

The delusion of Mr. Barron to assume the Crown would ever extend him the title! But then, I was not eavesdropping on a sane man.

Mr. Beaumont laughed, the sound hoarse. "Wretch. You cannot sell those mosaics without my help. May I remind you, you approached me, not the other way around. I never agreed to murder, nor did Lord Ainsley."

"But you will get those lily-white hands dirty by the end of the night. How can you, the second son of an earl, jeopardize your family or your father's political career? What will he say when he discovers the extent of your gambling? Or the extent of your deeds in Bramnor? No, my fine jackanapes, you will do as you are told."

Mr. Beaumont cursed.

"I've killed Cobb. You take care of your end of the bargain and leave the rest to me. And when I become the next viscount, you will remember me and all I've done for you."

A long pause. And then Mr. Beaumont's low answer, "Put her with Hawthorn in the brewery. Let the fire Mr. Cobb started take care of the rest. You will leave the ring to me."

Despair filled me, tasting of ash. Would they burn Rafe and me alive together?

Before I could brace myself, the door flew open, hitting the wall and dislodging a chunk of plaster. A man filled the narrow space of the doorway. And at his feet, the dead body of Mr. Cobb.

My gaze traveled up to see Mr. Beaumont's ruthless smile.

38

Rafe

Fire tests gold and adversity tests the brave.
SENECA

"Wake up! Oh wake up, Rafe! Fire! Fire!"

So hot. I tried to lick my lips and failed. They felt strangely misshapen and swollen, refusing to move. Even my teeth ached, which was odd.

Why was I on the blasted ridge at Bussaco again? I raised my saber as the morning fog crept like a living thing through the mountains, up and over the ridge, flowing like a bridal veil. Instead of a damp mist enveloping my feet, the stench of smoke filled my nostrils, forcing me to cough.

Any moment now, I would sound the signal for the cannons to belch fire. I glanced at my soldiers, who looked to me for guidance. In vain I searched for Lewis's steady presence, but I could not find him.

"Rafe! Don't you see the flames? If you do not wake up, we'll die." The voice sounded like Bridget's. She let out a sob.

My eyes flared open. I blinked rapidly at the orange glow emanating from the southern wall with flames licking the freshly painted plaster. I winced, my head throbbing to a wicked tempo as I scanned the inside of the brewery.

I sat on a wooden chair, clad only in my shirt, trousers, and shoes. The once-white fabric of my shirt was stained with splatters of blood. My own. My wrists were tied behind my back.

And that voice that demanded I wake up . . .

Surely this was just another terrifying dream.

"Bridget?" I rasped.

"Rafe!" she exclaimed from behind me. Dread flooded through me when I tried to jerk free and couldn't.

"I was so afraid for you. Mr. Beaumont dragged me here. I yelled until I was hoarse, but I fear the Whittles and Mr. Spencer are indisposed. The Dilettanti and Mr. Barron are setting fires to distract the tenants. And Mr. Cobb . . ." Her voice broke. "He was shot dead outside his cottage by Mr. Barron. They're all in on it together, plotting to take the mosaics and the estate."

A hiss escaped me at the news. Men with their faces covered had rained down blow after blow until I couldn't remember anything. I'd known Beaumont would prove an enemy, but I had not anticipated his evil.

"Mr. Cobb is dead?" I gingerly tested the ropes.

She stopped wiggling, and the back of her head brushed against mine. I twisted as much as I could to see her, only catching a glimpse of a fiery lock mirroring the climbing flames. She tensed, suddenly silent.

"He argued with Mr. Barron regarding the profits. And . . . and . . . Mr. Cobb said Mr. Barron is your half brother. I suspect he plotted against you from the moment of your arrival."

A brother? The word hammered through me, a jagged breath catching in my throat. All Bridget had said blurred as this truth cut deeper.

"Now we will die together if we cannot break free." Bridget wiggled against me, her desperation piercing through the fog of my mind.

The weight of her words settled like lead in my chest. Cobb, dead. Beaumont, Ainsley, and Barron, traitors. They had beaten me until I couldn't remember how I ended up here. And now they were trying to take everything.

"I don't intend for us to die in this inferno," I grunted, again pulling at the ropes binding me. They bit into my wrists, tight enough to draw blood, but I didn't stop. I had to free us. I would not let her burn. "I won't let you die."

She shook against my back as if she were crying.

With her back pinned against mine and cords of rope wrapped around us, we were trapped. The flames crept ever higher, licking the lower portion of the walls. How long before it reached the ceiling and the massive beams overhead? How long before the smoke rendered us unconscious?

A surge of hopelessness threatened to steal my courage. As a boy, I had not been able to protect my mother. Then Lewis, who fell at Bussaco. And now Bridget. She would suffer in these last moments, and I would be helpless to prevent it. Why must I always lose those I cared about?

A desperate prayer came to me. To keep her safe. To escape this furnace.

Bridget twisted, her back brushing against mine. "They'll never find us in time. I dropped a handkerchief out in the fields, but Father won't know we are here."

The ancient wooden beams lining the walls groaned and a

shower of sparks scattered, a brutal reminder of what would happen if we didn't hurry.

"We have a minute before the smoke overtakes us," I told her grimly.

"I have a knife in my apron," she admitted. A sob followed. "If only I could reach it."

My fingers, nearly bloodless, grazed her lower back, and there, as I fumbled, I felt for her apron strings while gritting my teeth.

"What if I tug the string and pull the apron around?"

"Do it," she commanded.

I tugged, undoing the bow at her back.

"I see the fire now. It's spreading so quickly," she choked out.

"Would you believe your father gave me advice on courting you?" I asked to keep her distracted from the crackling fire. Smoke billowed in black clouds while the heat scorched my skin, promising further torture if we didn't hurry. A ragged cough tore at my throat.

A horrified gasp sounded behind me. "He did not!"

"Oh, he did." I could not help my smile as I pulled the string, cramping my fingers. "Lean away from me. I need more room."

At last the apron circled round. I slid my fingers into the pocket, grasped the cool edge of a handle, and lifted it out—and felt it slip from my fingers to the floor with a clatter.

"Blast!" I cried. "I've dropped it."

A pounding on the brewery door echoed loudly.

Bridget screamed. I yelled. On the other side, a man sounded frantic, and I had never been so relieved to hear Mr. Whittle's voice.

"Bang the door down, gents!" Then, "Hold on, my lord. We'll get you out!"

39

Bridget

> When thou passest through the waters, I will be with thee; and through the rivers, they shall not overflow thee: when thou walkest through the fire, thou shalt not be burned; neither shall the flame kindle upon thee.
>
> **ISAIAH 43:2**

The brewery and abbey burned, flames shooting from the upper windows, scattering ash and sparks into the night. Wood cracked and moaned, the ancient structures going up in an unholy blaze worthy of Hades's underworld.

After Mr. Whittle and Mr. Spencer rescued us and used my knife to saw at the ropes, we all fled the brewery and rushed to the courtyard, alight with the ghastly glow of the fire.

Rafe stood beside me, his broken face enough to summon more tears. I reached for his hand and clung to it. He glanced at me, his eyes blackened and swollen and his mouth bruised beyond recognition.

"Can we save the abbey?" I asked him. My heart seemed to cleave in half at the idea of him deprived of the last bit of fortune he had fought so hard to save. "I don't want you to lose it."

"Maybe," he answered as he raised my hand to his mouth, lingering long enough to brush a gentle yet searing kiss against my knuckles. "But I have not lost everything."

My tears flowed freely. I, too, felt the same, regardless of whether someone had stolen the amethyst necklace and mosaics from Mr. Perry and me. I had found something far more valuable than any gold jewelry or recognition, and I never wanted to lose Rafe.

As I glanced at the second-story windows, a form darted away and melted into the shadows. My blood chilled as I struggled to comprehend what I had just seen. I yanked on Rafe's sooty sleeve and pointed to the glass panes.

"There is a man inside. I swear I saw him in the window."

He squeezed my fingers to offer reassurance, but the jut of his jaw suggested he would not remain by my side where we would be safe.

"I'm going in, Bridget. I can't let your antiquities or the abbey burn. Wait for me here."

"Rafe, don't! No ring is worth your life," I cried, but he pulled me in for a quick embrace, pressing a kiss against the top of my head before merging into the crowd forming near the entrance to the abbey.

Mr. Spencer had brought as many tenants as he could from the surrounding farms. He and the other farmers rushed to the well with any bucket they could find. They ran into the open door of the hallway, splashing what they could.

Rafe's broad back disappeared through the crowd of tenants. Pushing past the men, I hurried after him, all the while wishing for a handkerchief to cover my nose from the smoke. My throat tickling, I coughed, betraying my presence.

"Bridget," he all but growled when he whipped around to face me. "You can't come with me." Regardless of his tone, he gently put both hands on my shoulders, pinning me in place.

"I am coming," I protested. "Two are better than one, wouldn't you agree? We seem to make a good team, and I should hate to lose you now."

A rueful smile crossed his split lips. "Quickly then. If I tell you to turn back, you'll heed me, won't you?"

I gave him a lopsided smile to reassure him, even though my pulse beat wildly thanks to the surge of strength coursing through my veins.

"And you'll do the same for me, no doubt, should I spy trouble first."

He snatched my hand, his strong fingers curling around mine as we dashed into the great hall and raced up the magnificent staircase as the abbey groaned. How many fires had someone started inside?

Meanwhile, Mr. Whittle shouted orders, and I glimpsed Lucy staggering below on the main level, her arms lugging a sloshing bucket as well.

God bless the men and women of the abbey who stood beside Rafe no matter what happened.

Rafe and I ran down the hall to his chamber, past the dusty tapestries and walnut paneling. As we entered Rafe's room, I gasped. There, amidst a growing pile of linen-clad records and ledgers, stood Mr. Barron. His candle's flame flickered wildly in the smoky gloom, casting eerie shadows on his round face. Under one arm, a stack of records threatened to topple, and in his other hand, the rusted handle of a lockbox.

With a roar, Rafe hurled himself at the form. Startled, Mr. Barron whirled just as Rafe engulfed him. The innkeeper dropped the beeswax candle on the floor, which I rushed to kick at with my slippers, stomping out the flame.

A crack of a fist against a jaw, a man's shout, the clatter of the lockbox as both men collapsed to the floor with Rafe straddling Mr. Barron while the books slid away.

"Quick, Bridget. My pistol's in the desk."

I dashed to the desk and yanked on the nearest drawer. My cry at spying the pistols was all the encouragement Rafe needed. He pressed his hands against Mr. Barron's throat.

"Yield!"

Mr. Barron gurgled a response, bucking wildly beneath Rafe, but Rafe's huge frame easily overpowered the smaller man. I aimed the pistol at Mr. Barron and cocked it.

"Stop your thrashing, Mr. Barron. You resemble a fish out of water."

With his trachea under pressure and his mouth gaping open, he most certainly gulped for air.

Rafe eyed me with some alarm, but I handed him the gun before I smelled the horrible scent of fabric burning.

"Dash it all!" I cried in the most unladylike language. Snatching a handful of the dusty bed-curtains, I yanked on them with all my might and threw them to the ground, stomping on the flames while holding my skirts up to my calves.

Only when I finished did I realize both men watched me with startled eyes.

"I could hardly let your bed burn down," I muttered as I dropped my stained gown to cover my ankles.

Rafe grabbed Mr. Barron by the cravat and pulled the man to his feet. I snatched the lockbox. How heavy it felt within my shaking grasp.

"I have a constable who will be eager to chat with you," Rafe warned Mr. Barron. "But before he does, I have questions of my own. I understand that you and I have the misfortune of being related." He grasped Mr. Barron by the cravat and shirt collar and shook him. "You tried to kill us, Barron. You've sabotaged everything from the start. Releasing my sheep and horses, digging on my land, sneaking through the halls, intercepting the letters to the magistrate, and endangering Miss Littleton with that bur under her saddle."

Mr. Barron gurgled until at last Rafe let go, allowing the man to collapse onto the floor with a thud.

"I deserve the Hawthorn name just as much as you do," Mr. Barron wheezed. "Randall Hawthorn abused my mother, a tavern maid, at an inn. When her husband caught him in the act, he killed Randall without hesitation. And he hung for it, I might add. Your family owes me, Lord Hawthorn, for each sin they committed. Your payment was to be whatever hides in this lockbox—the ring, I suspect, not to mention the farmland and your title."

Rafe's jaw slackened with the torrid admission. "Your father was . . . the stable hand who killed Randall Hawthorn? The man tried and hung for the murder?"

Mr. Barron closed his eyes as if utterly spent as he lay sprawled across the hardwood floor. "Yes."

Rafe shot me an anguished look. He lowered the gun to his side. "You have my sympathies. My mother fled for her life. A pity yours could not escape."

The tavern owner fingered his throat, his cravat mussed and ridiculous. Emotions played across his face as his lip curled back to reveal a pair of crooked teeth. His hand slid into his pocket.

No matter how awful the story, I could not forget that this man had used Abigail, murdered Mr. Cobb, and would have killed Rafe and me.

Rafe must have sensed the danger too, and he leveled the pistol once again at his half brother. "Enough games. You will leave with us before you burn to death. A fate you wished upon us. Instead, your future will be decided through the courts. Consider mercy your payment. I am nothing like my father, even if I bear his name and likeness. Let the past go instead of allowing it to poison you."

My heart swelled for the man before me who chose forgiveness and refused to be tainted by his family's past.

Mr. Barron could do nothing with Rafe's pistol pressed against his side. Even so, the whites of his eyes rolled from me to Rafe.

"You don't just want me. You'll want the Dilettanti as well. They paid Cobb and me to steal the mosaics. I won't hang for their crimes. Nor will I take the blame for Cobb setting fire to the abbey. Why, even your sweet Miss Perry had a hand in the affair."

"You have plenty of sins to answer for," I said, though my voice wavered. Abigail's betrayal cut deep, especially after all I had done for her. I dreaded facing her again, but if Rafe could choose mercy, I wanted to do the same.

We marched through the hall with Mr. Barron. At the end, in the west wing, the slender form of a man skidded to a halt near the guest bedrooms.

Mr. Beaumont.

Had he come for Rafe's lockbox as well? To my dismay another fire, one far more advanced, devoured the walls, outlining the elegant silhouette as it raised its arm.

I cried out just as the pistol went off with a puff of smoke. Rafe dragged Mr. Barron with him, lunging to the left while I stood in the center of the hallway like a deer paralyzed in the forest at the first sight of a hunter.

The bullet whistled past me, thudding into something. Or someone, considering the cry.

Mr. Beaumont missed me. Muttering a curse, he reached into his crimson waistcoat and plucked out a second pistol.

I had seen the devil in the Bacchus mosaic and had once chuckled at it. But now, the handsome Apollo at the opposite end of the corridor, the very image of Satan highlighted by flames, raised my hackles. His blue eyes, ever so lifeless, sent a shiver through me as he raised the new pistol and aimed it straight for my heart.

"You little viper," he breathed.

Oddly, my mind conjured a picture of Perseus facing Medusa in the ultimate tussle, but I had no weapon to turn him into stone. I could only duck, yet I froze, sluggishly comprehending that I would likely die within the next second.

A body hurtled on top of me, knocking me off my feet as guns simultaneously exploded. I heard a grunt and felt arms wrap around me as I tumbled to the hard floor, knocking the back of my skull in the process.

When I opened my eyes, Rafe's face hovered over me. He said something, but my ears rang too loudly to perceive it.

He slipped a hand beneath my head and drew me closer. "Bridget, are you all right? Speak to me."

"I'm fine," I gasped even if stars floated in my vision.

Rafe exhaled and gently pulled me into a sitting position, cradling me as if he would never let go. Then I spied Mr. Beaumont clutching his arm before he turned on his heel and rushed deeper into the west wing, where the flames awaited him.

Mr. Barron lay on the floor, clutching his side where crimson dripped down his waistcoat and onto the floor, his mouth moving with shock.

"He shot me! Blasted aim for such a high and mighty son of an earl."

I suspected Rafe fired first as he leaped in front of me. He released me and looped an arm around my waist before lifting me to my feet.

He cupped my cheek for the briefest moment, his intense gaze searching mine.

"I'm truly fine. Two are better than one," I reassured him.

His lips quirked, softening his stern features. Never again would I labor under the misconception that I had to face life alone.

He reached for Mr. Barron and lifted him with a grunt. "That west wing will collapse. Come, man. Unless you want to burn to death."

As if to agree, a gust of smoke billowed our way, flooding the area until we were all coughing yet again. Rafe's warning gaze met mine when I joined him. I slid my arm around Mr. Barron and together we supported him as he gnashed his teeth. We staggered forward, down the staircase, and out into the fresh air where the tenants continued fighting the flames while the abbey groaned and creaked as beams falling echoed.

My father pushed through the crowd, bringing Constable Wickham with him. I ran to Father and flung my arms about his neck, my tears flowing once again.

"Bridget," Father said, clasping me as though he would never let go. "I found your handkerchief, and Mr. Harrington sent for the constable after Miss Perry came to us. She was beside herself, weeping over what she had done."

I jerked back. "She betrayed us, Father!"

"She arrived not long after you were taken. She hasn't stopped crying since, and it seems remorse has taken hold of her."

I wanted nothing more to do with her.

A sigh escaped him. "She trusted Jim Barron regarding the dig, and now she is deeply grieved over how he played her for a fool. She'll pay a heavy enough price in the days to come for her choices, but she insisted on joining Mr. Harrington and me."

Sure enough, Abigail waited with the other tenants, her tearstained face highlighted by the fire's light as she stood near the secretary of the Society of Antiquaries. My stomach twisted as acid flooded into my mouth.

First Daniel, now Abigail. I released them both in that moment and felt a peace I had never known before. I had Rafe and my father, who both loved me dearly. My heavenly Father had not abandoned me either. I did not worship a treacherous myth like the fickle Minerva who abandoned Medusa.

No, God had placed Rafe and me within His tender grip, drawing us both to a place of safety where no enemy could touch us. Goose pimples rose on my skin as I recalled my desperate prayer just before Mr. Barron kidnapped me. Did God value me?

The certain answer threaded through me, stitching what was once torn. I would never have to earn such immense love and grace. I couldn't, even if I tried. I held these priceless thoughts close as a rumble occurred within the west wing and the section collapsed. Several in the crowd cried out as the heat scorched us.

Rafe spoke with the constable, pointing to the damaged wing. Had Mr. Beaumont escaped, or had he succumbed to the floor caving in, only to find himself trapped by the flames he tried to condemn us to?

Meanwhile, the people of Bramnor did what they did best. They served, following my father's example. Mr. Whittle found a blanket and pressed it against Mr. Barron's side. The Dixon boys remained close to Lord Ainsley, who sat on the ground, his face pulled into a grimace. With his hair sticking straight up, he resembled a rooster. One of the boys offered a cup of water to the disgraced lord, much to my amazement. My father's legacy of ministry had not been in vain.

Rafe's military tone emerged as he shouted orders in all directions, gesturing at the east wing, where the men continued to fight the flames like a row of knights battling a monstrous dragon. I bit back a smile as I watched him. Despite his gruffness and his rigidity, a kind man with a tender heart needed only the right nurturing to come alive again. My chest fluttered as I considered the future before us. How could I be so blessed? He sought to rescue the gold ring, putting my needs above his own. He had defended my honor when other men sought to use or undermine me. And he had refused to let Jim Barron get what he deserved.

Mrs. Whittle found me and draped a shawl around my shivering shoulders. "We will rebuild again," she told me. "Already the tenants are discussing how they can take turns to repair the damage."

I agreed. What started out as a gloomy night with nary a cloud in the sky now burst with silver light as the moon broke free from her tether in the clouds. I breathed a prayer of thankfulness to God for seeing me and rescuing me in ways I couldn't have imagined.

Father heard my prayer and took off his glasses, wiping his eyes with his fingers.

"Amen," he whispered. He placed a hand on my shoulder, and tears swam within his eyes as he cleared his throat. "Bridget, I feared I had lost you forever."

I tried to soothe him, but he pulled me into a tight embrace, stilling my speech. "You've shouldered far too much in our family, but for what it is worth . . . I'm proud of you. Very proud of you, my precious daughter."

Wetness lined my lashes and I blinked it away in surprise, yet my heart all but melted at his loving words. Too overcome to speak, a rarity indeed for one such as myself, I reached for his hand and clung to him as we waited for Rafe.

40

Rafe

> To have joy, one must share it.
> **LORD BYRON**

At dawn, the tenants combed the ruins, but there was no sign of Beaumont. The building still smoldered, too hot for any search. Had he died in the fire? I dreaded what we might find later, but I knew my bullet had found its mark when I dove for Bridget and shot my pistol simultaneously.

Never had I been so afraid of losing her. She was standing with the women, wearing a shawl with her red hair loose on her shoulders. A more beautiful sight, I couldn't remember.

Two are better than one, she had told me.

I agreed. I never wanted to leave her—if she would have me.

As I strode toward her, I overheard Mr. Barron promise a statement implicating Mr. Beaumont and Lord Ainsley in the attack. Bridget approached Abigail, who wept openly. I suspected the girl would weep much in the days to come.

To my surprise, Bridget took hold of Abigail's hand and clung to it. I stopped to give them a moment.

"I forgive you, Abigail. Father and I will visit, but only if you wish it."

"Don't waste it on me. I don't deserve it . . . I would never forgive if it was me." Abigail's voice cracked, each word brittle with shame. "I had no choice, you realize. None at all." Her hand drifted to her belly, the unspoken truth hanging in the air between the two women.

Abigail pulled free, and her face crumpled as the constable led her away to a waiting carriage. He also took Lord Ainsley and Mr. Barron. All three would face further questioning with the magistrate.

I reached Bridget's side, noting the silver tear tracking down her cheek. Inwardly, I cheered her generosity toward her former friend.

"You've lost so much, Rafe," Bridget said as she drew her shawl closer. "First the hail, now the fire. It is overwhelming."

Such a loss of funds and property would have overwhelmed me a year ago. "I think I can at last trust God, even amid this loss. And it is never too late to start again."

I longed to take her in my arms, but with so many of the tenants watching, not to mention her father, I dared not embarrass her.

Her answering smile took my breath away. "No. It's never too late. And I want to rebuild with you, Rafe. Together."

Unable to restrain myself, I reached for her hand and pulled her toward the stable, away from the crowd, into the quiet shadows where Chaucer waited. My heart was racing from the fire, the fight, and, more than anything, from the woman standing before me. Her hair reminded me of the night I brought her home in the rain, when I should have kept my distance but couldn't. Even then, I had wanted her near.

"Bridget," I murmured, taking her hands in mine, "I don't have wealth or a grand estate to offer. Everything I have is falling apart, and I'm half a man without you." I cupped her cheek, my thumb brushing across her skin as I met her eyes. "But when I look at you, I see the woman who braved storms in nothing but slippers and found beauty in broken, lost things. You've been my courage when I had none. Bridget, you are my home."

Her lips twitched, a glimmer of mischief lighting her eyes. "Ah yes, those impractical slippers. I never knew footwear could make such an impression on a man."

I chuckled, but her expression turned tender as her hands settled on my chest. "But, Rafe, your estate, come what may, matters not. I only need *you*."

She rose onto her toes as she whispered, "I love you, you stubborn, impossible man."

"Will you marry me?"

"Will you do me the honor—"

We spoke at the same time, her words echoing mine. The sound of her laughter sent warmth flooding through me.

"Are you asking me to marry you?" I teased, though my voice was rougher than I intended, shivering with a need I could barely suppress as my hands slipped to her waist. "Bridget, it is the man who ought to ask."

She flashed a sheepish smile, as if realizing her impatience. It was one of the many things I adored about her. But before I could continue, her words, laden with emotion, broke the air between us.

"Then show me. Tell me I matter to you. Tell me you'll always cher—"

I cut her off with a fierce kiss, unable to stop myself any longer. One hand wrapped around her waist, pulling her closer, while the other cradled the back of her head, my fingers tangling in her loose hair.

When I finally pulled away lest I lose control, her lips were still parted, her breath mingling with mine. I gazed down at the woman who had become my everything. "Woodland sprite," I murmured, the words filled with reverence. "You've utterly bewitched me and stolen my entire heart. Will you promise never to leave my side?"

"I will never abandon you. Never," she whispered.

I felt a flicker of fear despite her declaration. "I will not be a rich man, Bridget. Rent from tenants and sheep shearing will be my only income until the orchards grow again. I will likely lose everything if the Crown has its way. You'll live in a cottage next to a burnt abbey, and people will reject you because of the Hawthorn name."

She smiled. "You do have a remarkable library in your favor—if it survives. And a marvelous land full of hidden history, and truthfully, I don't care a whit what others think. As long as we have each other, what else do we need?"

I rested my forehead against hers. "Then I am yours, always, and you will be mine. I want to spend a lifetime pursuing you." A surge of excitement filled me as I added, "Besides, I have a sudden interest in opening a joint tourist site with Mr. Perry, if you'll both allow it. Imagine the museum we could build together, protecting this place for the world to see."

She hugged me tightly, and I buried my face in her hair.

"Cider presses and palaces with you and me together," she murmured, her voice soft against my chest. "I can't think of a pairing more lovely."

EPILOGUE

Bridget

> Love in its essence is spiritual fire.
> **SENECA**

Three days later, I received a formal invitation to present my findings to the Society of Antiquaries. I hardly dared break the beautiful seal—a testament that my research would finally find an audience. My joy nearly overflowed as Father and I read the letter in the drawing room.

"You did it, Bridget. At long last, the entire world will learn of the Roman villa discovered in Bramnor. And I imagine this will not be your only excavation," he said with a tremulous smile.

"They've offered to pay me for the presentation and some of my sketches in advance, and by the end of the month! We can at last hire a lawyer for Daniel," I replied. Strange how my eyes watered so often as of late. I dashed aside a tear with my knuckle as I scanned the invitation again, allowing the pristine script and perfect penmanship to sink into my memory.

"Yes," Father murmured beside me. "Although, Bridget, God may yet have a purpose for your brother in that hulk. A refining, if you will. I will go to him at the soonest convenience with the good news. I must make amends with him as I have done with you. I can only hope our relationship will be restored."

"It can, Father," I reminded him. "After all, if the old viscount could find redemption, surely we can hold on to hope for Daniel."

My heart pounded with joy. I planned to run all the way to the abbey to find Rafe and share the letter with him, but when I went to retrieve my poke bonnet from a hook on the wall, the door opened in our entranceway and there he stood.

Father cleared his throat and started to leave the room with his paper folded beneath his arm. In fact, he barely offered a greeting to Rafe, although I thought I saw a sparkle in Father's eyes. Hard to say with his spectacles reflecting the morning light.

"You're leaving?" I asked Father.

"I'm certain I left a book in my study," he said as he slipped through the drawing room door and into the hall.

Rafe removed his beaver hat. At once my mouth dried.

"Have I told you how beautiful you are in that dress?"

I glanced down at the green gown. A favorite color, but nothing spectacular, at least according to Mrs. Herriot.

"No, but I appreciate a compliment as well as any woman," I teased. I showed him the letter, and at once his features relaxed as he scanned the contents.

"Bridget, how tremendous." He smiled, his eyes crinkling at the corners.

"Yes. They have invited me as an informal member and wish to include me in other excavations. Bramnor is just the start. We could travel together after the wedding!"

"Capital idea." He captured my hand. "I have news of my own. I reached out to Mr. Talbot the day after the fire. After hearing of my brother's schemes, he has allowed an extension to prove myself in the joint venture with Mr. Harrington and Mr. Perry. Bridget, we have another year to keep the estate. Mr. Talbot is most intrigued with the idea of tourism."

"You shall be an antiquarian at long last."

"I'm only concerned with the future." He winked as he reached for me and took full advantage of my father's absence.

"And after your presentation, where should we go for our honeymoon?" he asked, when he finally pulled back enough so I could breathe again.

"Honeymoon!" I cried. "Surely you jest. We should save our coins."

He shook his head, a small grin tugging at his lips.

The money from the publication in *Archeologia*, along with my presentation and sketches offered a tiny boon, with just enough to escape to a single destination. Moreover, Constable Wickham returned the stolen mosaics to Mr. Perry.

Following the fire, Mr. Perry tearfully offered the recovered amethysts to Rafe instead of the society to help cover the costs of the abbey as restitution for his daughter's treachery. Rafe sold the gems for five thousand pounds to a secretive buyer. We wondered if it might be the Prince Regent, who had expressed his interest in the ongoing research. Using the funds to pay the debts Rafe had incurred, he still hoped to return industry to the valley come fall with a new harvest of apples from the trees in the old orchard. There was just enough coin leftover to invest in a joint tourist center.

Rafe, Mr. Perry, and I committed to offer an educational experience that would showcase not only the villa and its exquisite floors, with ongoing excavations, but also bring new life to the abbey grounds. Visitors, eager to explore the rich history of the estate, would be welcome to tour the ruins of the abbey, the Roman villa, and the surrounding orchards.

Rafe dreamed of one day turning the abbey into an inn, making it a place of hospitality.

I could finally breathe a sigh of relief at such a change in fortune.

But time would be needed to heal our wounds fully.

Mr. Perry's grief over his daughter had gutted him, even though the magistrate found Abigail guilty of no more than lying and foolish behavior. Somewhere in the English countryside, she now hid with another family member until the babe was born. I held hope that Rafe and Mr. Perry would grow to be good friends now that he had no family to lean on.

Mr. Barron and Lord Ainsley were not so fortunate as Abigail. The magistrate sentenced Mr. Barron to transportation to the penal colonies, his crimes of conspiracy and attempted murder unforgivable. As for Lord Ainsley, his title could not save him. Stripped of his lands and wealth, he, too, faced a harsh sentence—ten years in a London prison for his role in the conspiracy and his attempt to ruin the estate.

The day after the fire, Mr. Spencer had found Mr. Beaumont crumpled beneath a beam, his sightless gaze pointed to the sky and a pistol gripped in his hand. *The Times* ran with the story, claiming *Hawthorn Abbey Cursed Yet Again*.

Rafe and I knew the truth, of course. Curses no longer held sway over my future husband. He had broken free from his past and was ready for a new beginning.

And now, with my intended in my arms, I couldn't help but agree with him regarding that future.

"Bridget, what better opportunity to have a proper adventure and meet these academics in person," Rafe murmured against my ear.

"I never could travel on Father's purse," I answered wistfully. "You know women do not have a grand tour."

"Nor did I. I spent too many years fighting. Scraping by. One day, we shall have a grand tour together," Rafe promised. "You won't feel cheated with only a small trip this year?"

"No," I said as I caught his fingers and pressed a kiss against his knuckles. "Not with you."

"Surely, you have one destination in mind," Rafe pressed with a hint of a smile as he drew closer.

"Greece, if you insist on traveling," I answered dreamily. "Greece and the Parthenon. I'm of half a mind to pursue the city of Troy and its gold. Do you recall the story of Helen of Troy, the most beautiful woman in the world?"

He tightened his embrace. "I doubt she compares to you."

I laughed as Rafe pressed kisses against my jaw, inching ever closer to my mouth.

And there was no more talk. Not for a long while. At least until Father coughed from the doorway, conveniently timed with his book in hand.

Six months after the fire at Hawthorn Abbey, Rafe and I married in a quiet ceremony, much to the delight of my father, who couldn't quit beaming during the sermon. Mr. Harrington attended and Mr. Perry, who clung to the back pew in the darkened recess despite Father's protests. I felt Abigail's absence keenly. And Daniel's. I prayed for them whenever they crossed my mind.

We had learned that my brother recovered from his illness, and with good behavior Rafe thought Daniel might earn a reprieve in his sentence. We waited breathlessly for when we would be allowed to see him, sending him as many letters and tins of gingerbread and biscuits as we could.

Life settled into a quiet rhythm around the abbey as winter approached, a light frost gradually covering the scorched stones and charred remains. The crisp air brought a kind of stillness, as if the abbey itself was pausing, waiting to heal. While the trees in the orchard stood bare, I held on to the hope that come spring, new life would return once more.

A fortnight after the wedding, during my honeymoon, no less, I traveled to London with Rafe to visit Mr. Harrington and present our findings to the Society of Antiquaries. To my surprise, some members of the Dilettanti came to the session, offering red-faced apologies for Mr. Beaumont's and Lord Ainsley's atrocious behavior.

After I presented my research on the case of the ivory doll, the bones now dated to the fourth century, and the early church presence within Roman Britain, several society men clapped while passing around my research paper with illustrations. Mr. Harrington promised to publish a book with my findings within a year. But what brought my heart to brimming occurred when Rafe turned to me.

"Bridget, I have never been so proud of anyone as I am of you in this moment."

"And I you," I whispered back. "As much as I've enjoyed London, all I can think of is spending my days alone with you in Greece."

What followed would forever be branded in my mind as the sweetest joy of marriage, as we enjoyed each other's company in all the ways that mattered as we toured Greece.

On a particularly memorable night, the Temple of Apollo at Delphi loomed against the night sky, its ancient stones casting long shadows in the silver moonlight. We sighed over countless marble statues and ornate carvings. Yet I halted mid-step when I saw a sculpture of a woman trapped in marble, her beautiful face contorted with writhing asps crowning her head. Medusa, cursed to be alone for all eternity.

Rafe stood beside me, one hand reaching for mine, his warm hand curling around my icy fingers. He brought continual warmth to me, as I did for him.

And I thought of the buried child and the owners of the villa, their hidden stories. And I thought of Rafe's mother, of Mrs. Eacher, and the circle of women in my life who knew both love and loss, triumph and defeat.

How easy it was to have a heart of stone in this life. To bury oneself in noble pursuits and yet risk losing connection with those we loved. How easy it was to avoid what I needed most. To avoid love because of the fear of pain.

But I was finally free, no longer imprisoned in my repressed anger or my desperate need for recognition. I finally understood the value God had assigned me. Stepping away from the marble sculpture, I studied the man by my side, who had been broken over and over again and still retained a sense of softness deep inside.

We were never meant to live life alone in our own strength.

I squeezed his fingers, relishing the feel of them curling about my own. Torches lit the path as they had in ancient days, and the museum was soon to close its doors.

"Come, Lady Hawthorn." Rafe grinned when I indicated I was ready to leave the museum. "What adventure shall we choose next?"

A Note from the Author

Dear Reader,

Where do the lines between fiction and fact blur, particularly with the history of archeology, or antiquities?

In 1738, Charles of Bourbon, King of the Two Sicilies and founder of the House of Bourbon, hired antiquarian Marcello Venuti to further investigate the rumored Herculaneum shafts. Venuti supervised the excavations and translated the inscriptions. His 1750 work, "A Description of the First Discoveries of the Ancient City of Heraclea," remains in print. The early efforts of such men labeled them as "pothunters" or, perhaps more appropriately, "looters." Without sophisticated technology, several sites endured damage, including the famed city of Troy. However, their exploits also flamed the imagination of the public and encouraged the growth of archeology as a scientific discipline.

Do palaces appear within the sleepiest of pastoral settings?

To satisfy your cravings for the truth, in 1811, a Regency-era farmer dug up a mosaic in the beautiful valley of Bignor, England. Surrounded by hills, orchards, fields, and sheep, he stumbled across the discovery of a lifetime. Other notable men soon assisted. Mr. Hawkins from the Bignor Park, noted antiquary Samuel

Lysons, and George Tupper excavated the entire villa and built a museum to cover the stunning floors preserved in near-perfect condition. Tupper's descendants continue to run the museum today. The museum opened in 1814 to the public and collected thousands of entries in the visitor's book in the first nine months.

Some of the discovered artifacts border on the fantastical, including a little girl's skeleton and a magnificent golden ring.

Samuel Lysons, in his work *An Account of the Remains of a Roman Villa Discovered at Bignor, in the County of Sussex*, stated:

"The artifacts unearthed at Bignor should tell us something. There have been some intriguing finds, including a beautiful gold ring with a red gemstone . . . It may have belonged to the owner of Bignor—or it may not. It was found near a wall; was it lost accidentally, or did it come off the wearer's finger in a struggle? There are some fascinating objects included in the nice little museum at Bignor, such as an iron stylus—so someone could write—and, disturbingly, the sad skeleton of an infant girl. What was her short story? Probably, it was a natural, albeit tragic, death—but it felt a little uncomfortable gazing down on her pitiful remains inside a glass case."

Samuel Lysons presented his paper to the elite Society of Antiquaries. He published the engravings of the mosaic art. After the initial excavations in the early 19th century, Bignor Roman Villa saw limited activity until renewed interest led to more comprehensive archaeological work in the 1980s. The villa today includes three wings, with a bathhouse in the southeast. The northern corridor extends over seventy-nine feet, making it the longest mosaic corridor in Britain. Not far away, archaeologists uncovered an even more magnificent palace. You can also tour the Fishbourne palace, which is rumored to compete with Nero's Golden House. Not one, but several children were buried away from the villa and discovered. Why? The Romans believed that infants were not fully-fledged people. They often buried them wherever convenient, hence close to the villa. The infants were discovered during the excavation of the mosaics.

Did a vicar's daughter help excavate the ruins? No, sadly, Bridget is nothing more than a figment of my overactive imagination.

The Bignor Manor house, which inspired Hawthorn Abbey, also holds dark secrets. Charlotte Turner Smith, who might be one of England's earliest Gothic authors, found herself trapped within a brutal marriage to the violent Richard Smith, a West Indian merchant and the director of the East India Company. His wasteful spending forced him to flee creditors and spend a stint within the King's Bench Prison, a prison for debtors. Despite Charlotte's success as an author, she struggled financially. After two decades of abuse, she took her children and left him permanently. Her novels demanded more legal reforms for women to have increased property rights. She sold Bignor Manor to John Hawkins, who worked closely with George Tupper. Charlotte provided a loose inspiration for Rafe's mother. Escaping abuse proved all but impossible for Georgian women.

And who were the Romans who lived in the valley? Some archeologists date them back to the second century or as late as the fourth. With access to London, known as Londinium, and several coastal cities, the area grew with tremendous wealth. As Rome fell into decay, those in the furthermost regions of the empire were kidnapped by Saxons or escaped back to Rome. When Rome fell, trade took a turn for the worse. Many of the villas lay abandoned, with the stones and building supplies repurposed or left forgotten. To see such grandeur lost brings to mind the poem "Ozymandias" by Percy Shelly from 1817, or Solomon's declaration in Ecclesiastes chapter one, that all essentially is vanity. Percy writes:

My name is Ozymandias, King of Kings;
Look on my Works, ye Mighty, and despair!"

*Nothing beside remains. Round the decay
Of that colossal Wreck, boundless and bare
The lone and level sands stretch far away.*

The perfect answer lies with Matthew 6:19–21: "Do not store up for yourselves treasures on earth, where moths and vermin destroy, and where thieves break in and steal. But store up for yourselves treasures in heaven, where moths and vermin do not destroy, and where thieves do not break in and steal. For where your treasure is, there your heart will be also."

In the end, it's the relationships we have that matter the most, their impact reaching far beyond accolades or wealth, or anything else fleeting within this passing world.

Blessings,
Jenelle Hovde

Acknowledgments

No author truly writes alone. To readers who have sent so many encouraging notes and cheered each book, thank you! I am very grateful to you!

To the team at Tyndale and my wonderful editors, Stephanie Broene and Jodi Hughes, thank you for believing in the idea of a bluestocking vicar's daughter. What a joy to write for you!

In a sense, this book has a bittersweetness to it. I often sat at a kitchen table with my mother, discussing literature over coffee. We sighed over Mr. Rochester in Jane Eyre and giggled over a dashing Jace Buckley found in Linda Chaikin's Silk series. My mother dreamed of writing a novel but poured countless hours into my life. I would not be the author I am today without her sweet guidance during those early years. Sadly, cancer took her before she ever saw my first novel in print.

A special thank-you to Regency author Jessica Nelson, agent and friend Tamela Hancock Murray, English teacher extraordinaire Adrianna Gaitlin, and author Maddie Morrow, who brainstormed with me at breakfast before homeschooling.

I also could not have written this book without the support of my wonderful family, who have waited patiently through deadlines. I love you! My thanks to my husband, who inspires each hero I write.

Finally, all thanks go to Jesus, who gives beautiful dreams and good gifts. What in this life can compare to Your immense love?

Discussion Questions

1. Bridget comments about the Bacchus mosaic: "Isn't it fascinating that vice often carries a pleasant facade?" How do we see this displayed in different characters throughout the story?

2. Bridget found a Roman coin as a child. Do you have a possession that is precious to you, even though it lacks any monetary value?

3. People have different expectations for how Bridget should act as a vicar's daughter. Have you experienced the weight of others' expectations? How did you cope?

4. Bridget believes we should study the past so we can avoid repeating the same errors, but Lord Hawthorn says the past is better left buried because some things are not meant to be known. Which one of them do you agree with?

5. Mrs. Eacher reminds Bridget, "We all grieve in different ways. Your father chose to do it alone, distracting that pain with duty." How have you experienced people grieving in different ways?

6. Mrs. Eacher suggests that Bridget is chasing after things that may never bring her the peace she longs for. In what ways do we do the same thing?

7. Lord Hawthorn asks Bridget, "Do you believe that God can change a man?" Give some examples of God changing people, either from the Bible or from your own life.

8. Bridget wrestles with the idea of God being good when there is so much pain in the world. In what ways do you resonate with this struggle? What advice could you share with someone in Bridget's situation?

9. Bridget's father says, "Is there anything that is not ordained within His sovereign will? From your brother's capture and detention to these mosaics uncovered in Mr. Perry's field, just when he desperately needed money to save his farm. I see these occurrences as signs, as miracles of His provision and sovereignty." How have you seen signs of God's sovereignty in your own life?

10. How does the title *No Stone Unturned* reflect the ways in which both Bridget and Rafe grow as individuals and in their relationships with God?

11. Bridget cries, "Oh, God, do you truly care for Daniel and me? I know the right answers, but I struggle to believe. Help me in my unbelief." Can you relate to Bridget's struggle to believe in her heart what she knows in her head? Why is this sometimes so difficult?

12. Bridget realizes, "We were never meant to live life alone in our own strength." What are some of your experiences of living life with others, supporting each other, and relying on God?

About the Author

JENELLE HOVDE, an accomplished illustrator, author, pastor's wife, and homeschooling mother, ventured off the beaten path when she transitioned from her career as a doctor of audiology to pursue her passion for writing. While her eight novels span different eras—from the ancient worlds to World War II—her favorite genre is sweet Regency romance that enchants readers with tales of love and intrigue set against the backdrop of nineteenth-century England.

Drawing inspiration from timeless treasures found in antique stores, Jenelle pens historical romance novels that captivate readers with vivid storytelling and gentle messages of faith. Her stories have garnered impressive showings in multiple writing contests. Often found writing at the Florida beach, she navigates life with her family and manages two saucy cats who insist on interrupting her creative endeavors.

To stay updated with her latest works or subscribe to her newsletter, visit her online at jenellehovdeauthor.com.

CONNECT WITH JENELLE ONLINE AT

jenellehovdeauthor.com

OR FOLLOW HER ON

- Jenelle-Hovde-Author
- jenellehovdeauthor
- JenelleHovde
- Jenelle_Hovde
- jenelle-hovde
- Fairytaleblue20

TYNDALE HOUSE PUBLISHERS IS CRAZY4FICTION!

Become part of the Crazy4Fiction community and find fiction that entertains and inspires. Get exclusive content, free resources, and more!

JOIN IN ON THE FUN!

- crazy4fiction.com
- Crazy4Fiction
- crazy4fiction
- tyndale_crazy4fiction
- Sign up for our newsletter

FOR GREAT DEALS ON TYNDALE PRODUCTS, GO TO TYNDALE.COM/FICTION